Anna Burns

was born in Belfast in 1962. She moved to London in 1987. This is her first book.

From the reviews for *No Bones*:

'Strong and convincing . . . shot through with energy and drama right from the start. Burns goes headlong into a world of rubber bullets, kneecappings, shootings and Saracen tanks. Gradually we follow Amelia through the years, the child replaced by a teenager and then a woman, but her character essentially still childlike, unquestioning and naïve. *No Bones* is suffused with the sadness that comes of violence, self-destruction and lost opportunities over the years as Amelia, her family and her city all do their best to pull themselves apart. Crucially, there is a good, strong vein of black comedy to Burns's prose, which has a fresh, original quality to it, not afraid to experiment.'

The Times

'Anna Burns's uncompromising first novel depicts a world in which grievances are proclaimed from the rooftops and retaliation is a way of life. It is a hard place to grow up in, when your best friend may get blown to pieces on her way to a disco, and teenage delinquents are given their orders to turn up to be kneecapped in Logue's old bar-room at seven o'clock sharp . . . Darkly comic . . . with its episodic structure and colloquial expressiveness, *No Bones* is geared to make an impact.' *TLS*

'Anna Burns proves herself a skilful writer with a keen wit . . . *No Bones* is a novel about the blackness to be found in love and loyalty. I'm looking forward to her next outing.'

Bassline & Blank

Further reviews overleaf

'Like a painting which, instead of graphically depicting the horror, conveys its message through distorted shapes and muted colours . . . [*No Bones* is] an accomplished first novel. Some of the expressions Anna Burns uses are beautifully simple – such as her description of a pregnant woman sitting down, "arranging her pregnancy before her" . . . In Amelia, Burns has created an ordinary, sensitive soul, who responds, self-destructively, to the violence around her. Only at the end does Burns allow a glimpse of hope or optimism to peek through the clouds, looking hopefully at a brighter future for all both within and outside of her novel.'
Sunday Tribune

ANNA BURNS

No Bones

Flamingo
An Imprint of HarperCollins*Publishers*

Flamingo
An imprint of HarperCollins*Publishers*
77–85 Fulham Palace Road,
Hammersmith, London W6 8JB

Flamingo is a registered trademark of
HarperCollins*Publishers* Limited

www.**fire**and**water**.com

Published by Flamingo 2002
9 8 7 6 5 4 3 2 1

First published in Great Britain by Flamingo 2001

'Babies, 1974' first appeared in *QWF* magazine in 1998.

Photograph of Anna Burns copyright © Jyl Fountain

ISBN 0 00 655238 2

Set in Bembo

Printed and bound in Great Britain by
Clays Ltd, St Ives plc

For Georgia, for Margaret,
and for Mitzi

Contents

No Bones

Thursday, 1969

The Troubles started on a Thursday. At six o'clock at night. At least that's how Amelia remembered it. On the sunny morning of that day, just after half past ten, she was standing at the top of Herbert Street, which was her street, at the junction of the Crumlin Road facing the Protestant chip shop, and she was stroking her caterpillars and talking with her friends. Her friends were Roberta and Fergal and Bernadette and Vincent and Mario and Sebastian and as they were talking, another friend, Bossy, came up wheeling her go-cart and said,

'Do youse not feel sad? I feel sad.' And then she didn't say anything else.

Bossy was like that. She'd throw out a bit of information to get them all interested and then she'd clam up, as if accidentally, and they'd be left there, wondering and puzzled and begging for more. Amelia did find herself wondering and being puzzled, but she refused to beg for more. Vincent, on the other hand, fell into the trap every time.

'What d'ye mean? What d'ye mean? What d'ye mean?' he cried.

'There's goin' to be trouble,' said Bossy, talking quick now, for her head was busting with the new knowledge she had to get out of her. 'It's startin' tonight. It's already started in Derry. It's goin' to be dangerous and it means something awful. It means we won't be able to play up here anymore.'

The others stared. How could something be so dangerous that they couldn't go on as usual? Be so bad as to stop them playing at the top of their street anymore? They waited to see if Bossy would give more information. She wouldn't. She had given the second bit and was now waiting to be prompted by all their excited gasps. Amelia got annoyed.

'We don't need you to tell us this Bossy,' she said. 'We know already, we already know' – even though they didn't.

'Oh,' said Bossy. She was dejected. She thought they did need her to tell them. She took Amelia at her word though, for on the whole, she wasn't as watchful and distrustful and as pertinaciously suspicious as Amelia, and she picked up a caterpillar belonging to her friend which had fallen out of Amelia's hair onto the ground. She handed it back and Amelia took it, feeling a bit ashamed now at having been so snappy. She just wished Bossy wouldn't try to be in charge every time.

'Well,' said Amelia, settling the caterpillar in her pocket, on top of five others which were already in there. She tried to be more generous. 'We don't know all of it Bossy. Maybe you can tell us the bits that we don't know.'

So Bossy did. She cheered up and according to her, and she may, of course, have been adding on imagery, her ma told her da, after listening to the news and talking to the neighbours, that riots were going to happen and that, if there was any stored-away hardware – that meant guns, Bossy explained – then this was the time most certainly to get it out. There would be shootings and bombings and hand-to-hand fightings and that if they didn't find somewhere else to go, to get out of Ardoyne

2

and away from it, there was nothing else for it but to be burned in their beds.

This sounded too much. It must be a made-up thing, for how come none of the others had heard anything about it? Of course they'd heard rumblings. Everybody'd heard rumblings. But the rumblings had been about Derry, which was another country, another planet. What had Derry got to do with Belfast and with them?

So they dismissed Bossy's news and played that day at the top of the street as usual, on one side of the narrow Crumlin, which separated them from the Protestant Shankill across the way. It was obvious Bossy had only been trying to be important, to know everything about everything. It was obvious too, she'd got it all wrong.

The Troubles started on a Thursday. At six o'clock at night. And seven whole days later, for Amelia was counting, she could hardly believe it, for here they were, still going on. Every evening since that first day, she had been brought in early, thick boards had been put on the insides and the outsides of their windows, and the front and back doors had been securely barred and locked. Amelia lived with her ma, and her brother Mick, and her sister Lizzie, and her Aunt Dolours, and her da when he was there, though often he was not. He was in the Merchant Navy and so this time he was in South America. Amelia's ma kept sending telegrams. She didn't know whether he was getting them or not. As well as these people living with Amelia, there was also her beloved horde of caterpillars, her dolls made of paper, the pregnant family dog, and her brother's friend Jat. Amelia's mother was also pregnant, and although Amelia could understand the dog and the puppies, for some reason she couldn't understand her mother and the baby. Her mind

3

couldn't hold onto such a strange piece of information and so, time and again, she simply forgot.

By the Wednesday, after the first Thursday, when Bossy had given the news to them, Amelia had counted thirteen houses from the top of one side of her street and nine houses from the top of the other that had been burnt in these Troubles so far. Amelia's house was eighth up from the bottom so, according to her sums and the laws of rationality, that meant there were still six houses to go before the burners got to hers. That night, before the rioting, she tried to tell her mother this. She thought it might calm and reassure her mother but strangely, it did not.

'Amelia!' Her ma was looking an awful lot distracted. 'For the love of God, child, I don't know what you're running on about. Give me peace now. This is really, really serious. Go and be quiet and be good for your ma.'

Amelia stopped trying to explain. Some people just did things different. The women in the household apparently had their own ideas about these house-burnings and about this war. The boards were up, the women themselves had their sticks and their bricks and their knives and their pokers ready, water was in everything and the long hose was on the tap. Lizzie and Amelia, in their outdoor clothes, their Dexters and their shoes on, were put under the table with cushions and blankets and told to sleep there. Mick and Jat, who were twelve, were allowed to help the women. Lizzie, who was eight, was very annoyed, for she was not.

The dog was under the table with them. It was on a lead and it, too, was very annoyed. It knew something was wrong and that shortly, the yelling and the men's footsteps and all the noise outside would be starting again. It pulled on its lead, which was tied to the tableleg. 'Don't let her go. She'll only get in our way,' said the women. Amelia talked to her. Lizzie held her by the scruff.

4

Lizzie was growling and snarling at having to mind this wee yap of a younger sister. Amelia knew she was angry and tried to cheer her up. She tickled the back of her sister's neck and offered to tell her a story, but Lizzie wasn't interested in the Famous Five, or Mary Poppins, or Mr Macbeth, a king-killer, and was overwhelmingly disgusted with a Princess Petrushka, from a fairy tale, who cried just because she fell down in Russian snow. Her mother switched off the lights so nobody outside could peek in through cracks at them. There was only the glow from the fire, and that had burnt low. Amelia got another idea, but because she'd made her Holy Communion, she knew it was a sin and a bad idea. Her mammy wouldn't approve of it. She wondered if she'd have to tell it in confession. She decided she wouldn't tell it in confession. That settled, she leaned over to whisper in Lizzie's ear.

The bombs had started but nobody had come down to try to get into their house yet. Amelia's mother and Mick were in the kitchen by the back door. Her Aunt Dolours and Jat were positioned at the front. The dog growled and Lizzie scowled. Amelia touched her on the arm.

'Why don't we guess what's been blown up, Lizzie?' she whispered. Lizzie was interested and stopped being angry at once. Her imagination for this though, was much greater than Amelia's. Try as she might, she herself couldn't think beyond the chapel and the school. She hated the chapel, but it was nothing compared to what she felt for the school premises. There were no other buildings anywhere, inside of which she felt she couldn't function. There was no doubt about it. They both deserved to be blown up. So every bomb that went off, Amelia tried to place it where she thought it should be. Lizzie, meanwhile, decimated every structure in Belfast, then suggested they start to guess, next, who had been shot. This didn't work so well. After each shooting, try as they might, apart from a few teachers, they found they couldn't name a single person.

For some reason, that part of the game wasn't as easy as the first.

Amelia felt for her caterpillars. They had stopped hanging onto her fingers with their funny little teeth and feet-things and were now crawling over the blankets. She spread out her hands to try to find them in the dark.

'Shush!' whispered Aunt Dolours for the dog was now whining and Lizzie was starting to complain again. They all heard a noise. A soft noise. It was coming from outside.

It was at the door. It was trying to push open the letterbox. The letterbox had been sealed by Amelia's ma four days before. Whoever was there, they gave up, and left the letterbox, and crept to the window. They were directly on the other side, with only the wooden boards, a sheet of glass and a few inches between them and Jat.

Amelia's ma and her brother tiptoed out of the kitchen and along with her Aunt Dolours, felt their way to this window. They didn't stand right in front of it though in case they got shot. There were whisperings on the outside. Those inside could hear them. Whoever was out there, it seemed they had a plan. There were scratchings, and then squeakings, followed by some twistings and soon it became clear they were doing something to the outside board. Mick listened, then leaned over to his mother. 'They've got tools with them, Ma,' he said. 'They're taking the board off.'

Amelia's ma felt for the poker, then she set it down and picked up the breadknife, then she set that down and rushed, her big belly out in front of her, to make sure the second board, which was inside, was definitely, securely, up. Those outside got the first off. It fell and it crashed and they let big yells out of them. Then they were back at the window and right away they broke the glass.

Thumps landed on the wood. Heavy. They were heavy. They were hitting the outside of the inside board with objects, and louder bangs started to come from the back yard too. In confusion, the two boys ran in there, leaving the two women. The noise continued. And then it all stopped. A sly rap sounded at Amelia's family's front door.

'Hello?' wheedled a voice. 'Is there anybody in there?' It could have been a man's voice. It could have been a woman's. It was a man's. It was distorted. It was stagy. 'It's only us,' it said. 'Be a sport. Why don't you open up?'

'Stop the messin',' hissed another voice. 'Ye're always friggin' messin'. Come back over here, will ye, and help me get this thing off.'

Amelia's ma and her aunt and the boys tried to put second inside boards over the first inside boards. Lizzie rolled out from under the table and jumped over to help in the dark. The dog half-broke away, barking and shrieking, her belly swinging, her puppies sloshing. She was dragging the table after her and when Amelia tried to pull her back, she spun round with red hate for Amelia and snapped.

Then Amelia forgot. She fell back under the table and set to worrying, terribly worrying. She was worrying about her caterpillars, which were all becoming lost. Her paper-dolls also. She cut them out every week, along with their paper clothes, from the latest issue of the *Bunty*, and she kept then in a pile on the windowledge near her bed. She'd meant to bring them down before the rioting, and have them here beside her, but in all the big mad rush, it had gone out of her head and she had not. She had left them up there, and they were still there, all alone, with no clothes on. She was down here, with only two caterpillars. The rest of them had gone.

She fell asleep. She dreamt she bought an apple from an applecart that was sitting at the bottom of her street, which was Herbert Street. 'Herbert Street, Herbert Street.' She wondered, in her dream, if she was saying that out loud. The man selling her the apple said he was the Devil and that, as she was the age for Holy Communion, he had a long list of her sins if she wanted to have a look at them. But instead of showing them, he turned into a red stripy spider and he let out a big laugh. There was no applecart there in reality. She knew that – even in this dream of hers she knew that. When she awoke, she was still in her outdoor clothes, stretched out on the settee, with Lizzie, grunting, asleep, lying half on top. The overhead light was on and Amelia was licking her palm. She had been thinking it was the juice from the apple she'd bought off the Devil. But it tasted of warm sweaty skin. Amelia stopped licking and wiped her palm on her arm. It was morning. Even though the board was still up, she knew it was morning. The rioting was over. Everybody had gone. She went to get a drink of water and she still had to pull the stool over to the sink in order to reach across to do so. It was dark. In the kitchen the light wasn't on and the board was still up. She didn't turn on the water immediately. First she had to pull hard, then pull harder, to get the long hose off the tap.

She fell asleep again, then awoke again, then fell asleep, then awoke proper. Her ma and her aunt and the others were already up. It was quiet. Amelia's ma had gone to see if it was still possible to send another telegram. Mick and Jat had gone out to discover what had happened in the night. Amelia, plus two caterpillars, plus her paperdolls with their detachable clothes now sellotaped on, went with her friend Roberta to count how many more houses had been burnt. Her Aunt Dolours told her not to wander off, and not to be hanging about at the top of the street anymore. Aunt Dolours herself retrieved the outside board from the road then took out the brush and swept up the broken glass. Lizzie, who was about to wander off and hang about all the places she knew she wasn't allowed to, was sent out the back instead to get rid of those burnt-out sticks in the yard. It was a Thursday, the second Thursday since Bossy had first given Amelia the warning. In Amelia's mind, according to her calculations, that meant it was now the beginning of the second week of these Troubles so far.

An Apparently Motiveless Crime, 1969–1971

James Tone was conceived in a half-house in Old Ardoyne in Belfast 1953. His parents had the two rooms up and his mother's relatives, the Lovetts, the two rooms down. The Tones moved to England before their child was born and when they did, they cut all ties with Ireland on the way.

Jamesey grew up in London with his parents rarely speaking to him, barely speaking to each other and never inviting anybody. The small quiet mother spent her evenings on the edge of the settee, practising harmless smiles, while the small quiet father sat twisted in his armchair, casting focused malevolent looks across the room at both the woman and the boy. Periodically he would have to get up to hit them. One day when Jamesey was twelve, something stirred inside and he leaned over to his father and said,

'Dad, what is it?'

This was so unprecedented that the tiny man gasped, and when he recovered, he leapt from his chair, darted over the room and punched his son in the head. Getting him down, he dragged and kicked the boy into the kitchen and there, outraged, reached for something with which to kill him. He couldn't get his hand on anything from where he was, so instead, and still holding his boy down, he pulled on the gas stove and pulled on the gas stove until it fell over. When it did, and he was able to get a better grip, Mr Tone used all of his strength and all of his weight on top of the cooker until underneath, on the white and black shiny tiles, his son stopped struggling and lost consciousness.

The child was brought to Intensive Care. He was in hospital for nine weeks. Reports were filed about the dreadful accident, the adults didn't refer to it again and James just couldn't remember. When he got out of hospital though, he seldom stayed at home anymore, preferring to go to friends or acquaintances instead. Four years later, on his sixteenth birthday, he joined the British Army.

In November 1969 he was sent to Belfast. As soon as he docked and was billeted, he went straight out, in his helmet, with his rifle and his backpack, to patrol the streets of the Falls. Everyone came out to greet him. He was given tea and bread, tea and cake, tea and biscuits, tea and crisps, tea and lemonade, tea and cigarettes. Tea.

He was excited, very excited, but by nothing more than something in particular he'd discovered from his mother days before he'd left. In one of her rare, give-away-for-nothing moments, he'd found out there were people in Belfast to whom he was related. Family. He already knew there were Tones in the Republic but of them, apparently, it was best to say nothing. These new relations though, were called Lovetts and were living in this place he was going to be. Of course that meant he would visit them.

So that night, still in uniform, and like some other soldiers who had relatives in the country, Jamesey set off with three friends from his unit to visit the Lovett family in Ardoyne. Instead of his rifle, he carried gifts and he worried the whole way there that they might not be suitable or, no matter how many presents he had brought, somehow there might never be enough. His mother had no idea how many Lovetts there were now, but told everything of what she did know and of what she could remember. So he bought hooks and eyes and buttons and bows for an Aunt Mariah, the great seamstress, then worried he should have gotten perfume instead; he got milk chocolates for an Aunt Dolours who might prefer dark; cigarettes for an Aunt Sadie who might no longer smoke; nothing for an Uncle Tommy who was just about never there; a bead necklace for a cousin Lizzie who would be nine or ten and a silver belt buckle he'd traded from a Russian soldier in Dover for another cousin, Mick, who his mother had heard was about three years younger than himself. As standby, he had extra sweets for extra people he might discover he was related to, and he set off worrying that none of these people would like him and then worrying that they might start off liking him but might not continue to like him if he did something wrong without in the least meaning to.

Soon the four soldiers reached the dark kitchen house in Herbert Street in the tiny, old, Catholic district called Ardoyne. Only Private Paton was carrying a weapon, his own personal, unauthorised handgun. He carried it everywhere because it felt great to do so and most of the other soldiers, who didn't already have one, were looking into the possibility of getting unapproved handguns too. The four reached the street just after eight in the evening, the chill in the air making their breath visible by the dim yellow sitting-room lights. These lights came from the few windows that hadn't yet been boarded up and from the last street lamp that hadn't yet been broken. It turned out that the half-houses near the top of the street where the Lovetts had lived in the Fifties had been burnt in the riots just before the British Army had arrived. But, after asking some locals, who were coming out to greet them, Jamesey discovered this Lovett family had moved a lot of houses further down. They went to the door the neighbours pointed out to them, knocked and a howling dog and a child's voice immediately started up.

'Mammy! The door Mammy! There's somebody at the door. Mammy, listen! There's somebody at the door.'

'Who's that?' said a woman's voice. She was some distance within, not directly behind the wood itself. Jamesey said,

'It's James Tone. Bridey Tone's son. Is that you, Aunt Mariah?'

There was a silence, followed by an intense bout of whispering, before bolts were drawn back and the door opened almost wide. A heavily pregnant woman in her mid-thirties, with a thick plait hanging down the side of her head, peeked round the doorframe at the four soldiers standing in front of her. She looked amazed and, after a second, the door widened further and full light spilled out onto the four of them. They were dragged into the kitchen house and squealed at, by the three sisters, all in their mid- to late-thirties, all with plaits hanging from their heads. On their faces was pure astonishment and something else that made Jamesey Tone happy. They were delighted to see him and, feeling warm, less apprehensive, Jamesey was soon feeling delighted himself. He noticed one girl, pretty, interested, not a bit shy, looking on, very curious. This was Lizzie, he discovered, and a smaller girl, seven or eight, had run behind the dog to hide. The dog was a middle-sized, heavy-teated, growling, edgy mongrel, which continued to snarl, its velvety face completely wrinkled up. It bared its teeth and darted its eyes from one stranger to the next stranger, but wouldn't move from the frayed blanket it was coveting on the floor.

The dog was shouted at by the women, then the other English boys were introduced by Jamesey, then the four boys were pushed onto chairs and the women just stood and stared. After a bit they came to their senses and laughed and the teapot was put on and Lizzie was sent to Dallisons. She was told to get cake and biscuits and anything else nice that the shop might have. Jamesey, face flushed and happy, everything going the way his fantasy would have it, opened his bag and handed out his gifts.

'So where are ye stationed?' said the aunts. 'How's your ma?' they said. 'Never writes you know.' And, after a pause – 'Is he still alive, yer man, you know, him, yer da . . . ?'

Jamesey answered about his family, while smiling at the youngest. She stayed down in the corner, peeping out between the ears of the dog. She especially peeped, he noticed, at that long scar his da had once given him. It ran the length of his temple right down to his jaw. Seeing him looking at her, the girl swivelled her stare to look at another soldier, then another – their short hair, their green clothes, their pink faces, their shiny boots. She ducked her head every time Greg Paton caught her looking at him and ducked again whenever she looked back and he'd still be winking and pulling faces over at her.

'Where's Uncle Tommy?' said Jamesey, turning back to his Aunt Mariah. He took some Battenburg she was forcing onto him from a giant plate.

'Ach, he's in hospital, that Tommy. Does it deliberate. Does it to get attention. He likes those wee foreign nurses. South America this time.'

'Is he very sick?'

'Ach, don't know. Ach, don't think so. He can have fierce amounts of energy when he wants to. Having a rest, having a flirt. Pretendin', that's all he's doin'. Nothin' wrong with him really. He'll outlive us all.'

She sat herself carefully on the stool, smiled, breathed deep and arranged her pregnancy before her. She said nothing more about her husband and Jamesey could see that, as a long-lost nephew, never mind a saviour soldier, it was he himself who was astonishing to her. What none of the Lovetts seemed to realise, he noticed, was that they were just as astonishing, or more so, for they were his family, newly discovered, very much alive. He jumped up, along with his friends, to offer their seats to the women. The women shooed them back down. They did as they were told.

'Look,' said the youngest. Her name was Amelia. She had drawn herself forward to be standing by the knee of Jamesey at last. She was holding a box of bright colours. She opened it up, leaning it over so as to let him see into it. It contained buttons, a ton of buttons, hundreds it seemed, and these were her toys.

'My Treasure Trove,' she said. 'It's called my Treasure Trove. It's private but I'll let you look if you want.'

'Look,' she said again, showing four other things – a tiny tractor, a one-inch pitchfork, a white plastic sheep and a Black Queen chess piece. Jamesey looked. She put them all in his hands and disappeared upstairs for her paperdolls and farm set.

'Bridey's done well having a boy like him,' said Aunt Dolours. The others nodded. Again they had started to stare. Jamesey's colour rose. His friends turned and grinned at him. Flustered, he leaned over to pat the dog. It would have bitten him but a key sounded in the lock and the bitch, instead of snapping, ran whining to the door. She jumped up as Mick Lovett came in. Thirteen, small, a rubbery double-jointed boy. He was carrying a duffelbag over one shoulder, and absently making fists, then relaxing his hands. The dog jumped at the bag when she saw it and the youth, stiffening, looked at the soldiers sitting there.

'It's your cousin, Mick, James Tone. He's in the army. He's over from England!'

Jamesey stood up and immediately, clumsily, handed over a small box containing the buckle. He felt awkward, for what he'd meant to do first was just hold out his hand. The buckle was bordered with unfamiliar lettering and Mick gasped as he was opening it and snatched it out of the box into his hand. Everyone was startled. They looked at Mick. They waited for him to explain himself. Why had he pounced, why had he behaved like that?

'From the Soviet Union,' explained Jamesey. 'Military. I thought you might want it.'

'Oh.' His cousin seemed disappointed. He stopped staring at it. He dropped it into his pocket and slapped his dog away.

'Down, Dachau!'

'Dakcow, it's all right,' soothed Amelia. She tried to control the dog's leaps for the duffelbag. 'They've gone to nice warm houses. They're happy. They're all gonna be okay.'

Lizzie snorted.

'Lookin' for her pups,' she said to the soldiers, but she said it in a tone that conveyed more than her words. She was smiling. They looked at her. She gestured towards her brother.

'Our Mick's been taking care of it. The puppies are okay.'

Amelia looked up, her expression alert to something nasty, and their mother threw a warning glance to Lizzie, who seemed older than her years. The aunts clicked their tongues but also said nothing. Jamesey, meanwhile, this time did extend his hand. Mick, busy taking a lemonade bottle out of the duffel-bag, didn't notice or wouldn't notice. He didn't shake the hand.

'Oho!' cried Private Paton. 'What's this? Is this the famous – what's it called – pa-cheen?'

'It's holy water,' said Mick, handing the bottle over to his mother. Aunt Sadie said, 'To bless the house with at night times.' Paton looked amused. He glanced at Jamesey but the teenager was happy and didn't want to take part in jokes about people who talked funny, about holy water in lemonade bottles and about dead dogs with an anxious mother her surly owner had called Dachau.

Three more youths came in. The women introduced them. The kettle was refilled. Mick's friends were as fascinated with the army as everybody else in Northern Ireland had been of late.

'So what regiment are youse in?' asked Liam.

'Are youse really fit like and all?' asked Terry.

'Can I see that gun?' asked Jat. He had spied it, with X-ray vision, down Greg Paton's waistband.

Paton let him see it and he didn't take the bullets out. Why would he? Jat, no doubt, would want to see the bullets as well. Although unable to demonstrate with their own rifles, Privates Rose and Hansford instead drew diagrams. They explained the rundown of a weapon, including stripping and reassemblage and checkings of the breach. The male audience was enraptured, the female indulgent and smily, with the youngest moving around the soldiers, butting in now and then, no longer shy, to show everything she had. Mick, silent, sat on the edge of a chair, and looked over at his cousin and at the others. He rebuffed Jamesey's attempts at contact and annoyed his mother with his envy and unfriendliness. The other boys made up for it, for they were warm and inclusive and full of admiration, Jat McDaide being the nicest, the warmest, the most welcoming of the lot.

At the end of the night two of the soldiers got up to do the dishes. The aunts gasped and wouldn't hear of it. Lizzie would do them, they said. Instead, the boys got ready to leave, suffered hugs from the aunts, shook hands or nodded to the others. Out on the street Jamesey watched Mick shuffling, kicking at his feet and at the ground. He realised his cousin was working up to saying something.

'That watch, that pocketwatch thing,' Mick got out at last.

His voice was quiet, he hardly looked at Jamesey. 'Is it still in your family? Do youse still have it, or what?'

Jamesey was at a loss. 'What watch Mick?' He leaned towards his cousin. He wanted to be helpful. Mick's voice got lower. He didn't want to be heard by anybody else.

'You know,' he squeezed the words out. '*His* watch. Wolfe Tone's watch.' Jamesey continued to look perplexed. Then he remembered another of his mother's effusive give-away moments a long time, years ago.

'Upstairs in your da's drawer,' she'd moaned, after another of his father's violent fits. She was holding a wet rag to her newly-split lip. Young Jamesey was holding a similar one to his. 'I've tried my best since we came to live in England,' she said, 'and I'd throw the likes of that away only I don't know if he remembers it's there or not.'

'Wolfe Tone's watch!' cried Jamesey, attracting the others' attention. Mick didn't like that. Jamesey's face had cleared. He was glad to help out in something that seemed important to Mick, his cousin. 'I know what you mean, Mick.' He had got the point at last.

Jat McDaide looked over.

'Oh, so you're related to Wolfe Tone too then?'

'Who's Wolfe Tone?' said Paton, raising his eyebrows.

Jamesey looked at Mick. He knew his mother's family were no relation of Theobald Wolfe Tone, but his cousin had gone red so he said yes, they were related, both Mick and himself. Jat was not listening. He was excited and off again, as he was on the least excuse always, explaining heroes and martyrs of Irish politics, this time to bored British Army Private Greg Paton, who yawned and didn't give a damn.

'He was a Protestant though like, wasn't he?' interrupted Terry. Liam nodded. 'And he was a bit fond of doing the "Poor Pat" number.' It seemed they weren't impressed. Jat was annoyed. As a leading member of the United Irishmen . . ., he said. As the Father of Irish Republicanism . . ., he said. Having died for his country and for his beliefs . . ., he said. The three boys began to argue amongst themselves. Greg Paton grinned. He jerked his head towards them. Jamesey was puzzled but then jumped as Mick turned to him and said,

'Do me something, will ye?' His voice was urgent. 'Trade me for it. Give me the watch. I want the watch. What will ye take instead?'

Jamesey looked at his cousin, surprised at the animation in a voice that had been self-excluding all evening. He wished for Mick's sake that he could be related to his own distant ancestor, for it seemed to be the only thing that made him come alive. He touched him on the shoulder.

'That's all right, Mick,' he said. 'You can have it. I'll ask my mum to send it over.' Mick looked surprised. And then distrustful. When had anybody, just like that, given anything away for nothing? Rubbing his misshapen jaw, he grunted something that might have been thanks. Jamesey realised he was staring at his cousin's disfigured face. Immediately he looked away. Mick saw this and left his jaw alone.

'Accident,' Mick explained. His voice was gruff. He was embarrassed. 'With m'da. Years ago. Don't remember how it happened.' He looked at Jamesey. He grinned. 'What happened to yours then? Accident as well?'

On Jamesey's next tour all was changed. The British Army was no longer welcome in Ardoyne but still it came into it. Stones were thrown, binlids banged, whistles blown, bare hands were used, 'm-u-u-r-dher' yelled most especially at night and Teasie Braniff was hated for she still brought them tea. 'Somebodies' sons,' she said. But when they kicked in her door, pulled up her floors, threw her holy statue down the toilet and cut her

Bullet's throat at night for barking at them during the day, she changed her mind. 'Beings from Hell,' she said. 'So Hell roast them!' Jamesey meanwhile sent a letter to each of his aunts. Not one of them answered. He also wrote to Mick. He wrote after his mother had written to him. Watch! Pocketwatch! Her words had looked startled. What watch? She could find no watch. Jamesey was dreaming. Anyway, she went on, what did he want to be raking up that auld connection for? Didn't his poor auld father have a hard enough time in England without that sort of stuff gettin' out all over again? Jamesey wrote back and told her to look further. He had promised his cousin, he said. She forgot to write back. Then, when his father was murdered in England, Jamesey forgot too, and only remembered when he went back for the funeral. He found the watch easily, in his da's tallboy bottom drawer, wrapped up in a hankie, plain silver, broken, dirty, and it was fat. He shined it up. Antique now maybe, he thought. Maybe cost a fortune. So what? It didn't matter to him and she'd have thrown it away in the end. It mattered to Mick though and he'd promised it to his cousin. He packed it with his things and returned with it to Belfast.

It was 1971 and a mighty number of apparently motiveless crimes were happening, particularly in the shape of dead bodies that some newspapers, in their back pages, diligently reported upon. Jamesey, like his comrades, had become aware of all the things he was told to become aware of, and they patrolled, memorising faces, watching hands, scouring rooftops, windows and doors. He used walls as protection, or children, and took constant aim at everything, knowing that if he saw a gunman, a man with a weapon, then he was allowed to fire, he was allowed to shoot him. 'Although you moan about Ireland,' said some of the soldiers, 'you know at least you're going to get a chance to shoot somebody.' 'Better than skiing or mountainclimbing,' some other soldiers said.

So Jamesey was doing the inevitable foot patrol with nineteen others down Butler Street in Ardoyne one day when, turning and turning about in some macabre waltz with his rifle, he saw his Aunt Dolours and his cousin Amelia coming his way. His aunt had her face averted and showed no sign of recognition, and the girl was trotting alongside, a small duffelbag at her back. As they drew close, he rashly slung his rifle to his shoulder and said with all his breath,

'Aunt Dolours?' The woman said nothing back.

She walked on but Amelia, in the green furry hat and the waterboots, looked up at him and after a moment, her face opened and cleared. She remembered him. She tugged at her aunt and raised a mittened hand towards his scar.

'Aunt Dolours – the soldier! The cousin! It's him!'

'C'mon you,' said the woman. She pulled roughly and the child stumbled against a tar-spattered lamppost. She tried to steady herself. Jamesey reacted and stretched out a hand. The woman swiped it away without acknowledging it had been there.

'Oh wee girl, stupid wee girl,' she said through her teeth, 'watch where you're going, will ye?' She took Amelia by the scruff. 'In God's name pick up yer feet!'

The two civilians passed, the girl continuing to look back until she got a clip round the earhole. Jamesey had stopped moving. He was standing right out in the open, looking directly at their backs. Another soldier came up and prodded him.

'Keep moving. What's up? Old trout say something? Keep moving. Don't let it get to you. Keep moving. Don't stop.'

Aunt Dolours must have been afraid, thought Jamesey. He walked on. He looked at the gable wall. She must be afraid. The wall said NO FRATERNISING. Big white letters. NO FRATERNISING. He looked at the tarred lamppost. Afraid, he decided. She was afraid for them all.

21

He was oblivious now to where he was going, just followed the soldier's boots in front. He no longer scanned faces or took mental notes or watched corners with his mind's eye. His mind was elsewhere. It was beginning to form an idea that might make things a lot better for everyone. He decided that next day, while he was off duty, he'd rush in his civvies and go and visit them. It would be a lot easier. Aunt Dolours would be able to explain her nervousness and he would say 'That's all right Aunt, I knew it was that'. And he made further plans of how it was all going to turn out, and by the time he returned to base, his heart was very light.

Not for long. The deadness came back as he sat in the mess. His aunt's taut face, her granite skin, and that ever-present sensitivity to snubs he'd always been aware of, rose again, to torment him, from within. His eyes grew dull and in the end he couldn't swallow. Without knowing why, he got up and went to ring his mother before going back out on late patrol. He slid the coins in.

'Mum . . .'

'Oh Jamesey, I don't have time. Susan Wilson is hosting another dinner party. I'm invited! Twelve people this time. Judge Summers is going to be there. *I'm* sitting next to him!' His mother's English-Belfast grew more Belfast-English. Her excitement at being with important people just grew and grew and grew. 'Imagine like!' she cried. 'A widower, Susan says . . .' She carried on, but her voice was now annoyed at something else. '. . . At the hairdresser's it was . . .' and before long, she'd slipped into pure Belfast. 'I told the wee skit, I gave her what-for . . . No more than she should be, the wee milly . . . and I said how dare ye, wee girl, ye wee fish and chip, I'll skelp yer arse for ye, if ye speak to me like that! Can ye imagine! All the age too! Jamesey son, I need to go. Taxi's here.'

It was pouring down as they patrolled the Short Strand. A few five-year-olds came out in the cold and rain and shouted

'Ya ya – Brit fuckers' and fired a few stones. Then other five-year-olds came out and shouted and threw stones as well. 'Brits out! Brits out!' yelled even more five-year-olds and all this went on, right up to their bedtimes. Most older people ignored the patrol. They weren't there. They didn't exist. Don't give the time of day to a British soldier. It's one way to deal with them. They can't stand to be ignored. By 4 a.m. the soldiers were finishing and climbing into their vehicles. They were going to head back to barracks, along empty Donegall Street.

They noticed him at once. A small man, like a boy, and he was stumbling out of Library Street. He was drunk. He fell into Royal Avenue. The Saracen and jeep stopped.

'Probably was taking a leak.'

'Let's do a P-Check.'

They got out, reinvigorated, and surrounded him at once. The man was bleary-eyed and he looked up at them as he pulled a tobacco-stained coatsleeve across his wet mouth.

'Identify yourself,' said an English voice.

'What were you doing up there?' said another English voice.

The older man blinked and looked at the blackened faces above and around him.

'Who *are* you?' said another English voice. It shoved him from behind. It shoved him between the shoulder blades and made him fall forwards. He fell against Jamesey. Jamesey shoved him back.

'I . . .' began the man but stopped when he was whacked round the head by somebody. They began to talk over him, slapping him every time he looked up.

'. . . refusing to answer questions.'

The man put up his arms. 'Now lads, ach lads . . .'

He was pushed to the ground and someone brought a boot under to bring him back up again. Jamesey realised with a mild surprise that this person was himself. He had watched himself do it and he watched the others do it after him.

23

'M'name's McAdor—' the man was trying to say something. 'Glencairn . . . I live . . .'

'What's he saying?' 'What's he saying?' 'Oh, who gives a damn!'

After he died on them, two broke away to drag the body back up Library Street, which was little more than a dark poky cobbled entry at the very best of times. They left it face down in the shadows, then started to clean the bowie and the sheath knives but in the end, they changed their minds and couldn't be bothered with any of that. They went back to their vehicles, climbed in, and returned to barracks.

'. . . now lads, ach lads . . .'

Jamesey woke in his bunk.

He was dizzy and he was sure he'd spoken out loud. The others were still asleep, there were stains on his hands. He could see them. He looked again. There were no stains on his hands. He breathed deeply, in and out. It was all right, it would be all right. He remembered his plan. He was visiting his family tomorrow. His family in Ardoyne. He closed his eyes and returned to sleep. Before doing so, he recalled that as he'd helped drag that tiny dead Glencairn person back up into the alley, he'd seen a 'Death and Dishonour' tattoo, a 'Union Jack' tattoo and a 'God and Ulster' tattoo on the scrawny old arms. A Protestant. The little man had been a Protestant. Jamesey's own father had been a Protestant. Jamesey felt a feeling and that feeling was relief.

Late the following afternoon he was in his good jeans and light shirt. He put Wolfe Tone's plain watch, still wrapped in his da's hankie, still for his cousin, into a pocket near his waistband. He shivered. His skin was pale.

'James Tone! You're not going out?' said someone. Jamesey could barely pay attention. 'Don't you know . . . ?' came another question. 'Haven't you heard . . . Those three Scottish boys, killed the other night?' Jamesey forgot to answer. 'Stay

24

in town mate,' said the voice. Jamesey looked back. Who had said that? And what had happened to Greg Paton? Oh. He remembered. Legs blown off, that was right.

He left the barracks for the town centre to buy things for his aunts and his relatives. He bought cigarettes and left them on the counter, bought chocolates and a bottle of spirits a few doors on. When he left both shops he was carrying nothing. He went to a bar first to get himself a drink.

It was crowded. There was a lot of noise and there was this woman in particular. She was near him when he walked in and she was still near him even after he'd walked over to the bar. She was looking at him. She was waiting. He knew this but he didn't know what to do with women. One day, perhaps he would. Not that day though, not now.

'Hiya,' she said, fed up waiting for him to start it. She sidled her backside onto the stool just beside him. People around them were talking. Nobody was paying attention. Apparently, as far as Jamesey could see, this woman was on her own. But he was wrong. At that moment she was thinking of getting involved in his murder. Jamesey didn't understand the significance of being English in Ireland at all. Outside the sky was thundery and inside, nobody in the world whom he knew was at that moment about him. The woman touched his hand. His hand was holding a glass.

'What's that you're drinkin'?' she smiled. He didn't know. He didn't remember ordering anything. She flung her hair away from her face and it swung back and forth behind her like a black shiny pendulum. He thought it would be nice hanging down in a thick plait. She was nice too, he could see. She seemed friendly but still . . . He moved her hand away.

'Please,' he said. 'I've got something to do. I want you to go.' The woman started and was so surprised that she suffered a lapse in her whole intention in being there, got off the barstool and watched as he set down his glass. She raised her eyebrows to her male comrades, who were sitting watching from the far corner and, for some perverse reason, nobody followed this obvious soldier out the door to have him killed.

Instead he reached the timbers at the top of Herbert Street himself. He went through the tight militarily-installed turnstile and walked straight into the area to the Lovetts' front door. A group of women queueing for fish and chips outside the supper salon and some others, on their doorsteps, looked at this stranger who had come into Ardoyne. He was sick-looking, he had cropped hair, he was English, he was a soldier. They called quietly to their menfolk and their menfolk appeared beside them at their doors.

Jamesey rapped on his Aunt Mariah's. Some of the people watching disappeared, satisfied. He knew the Lovetts, fair enough, he mustn't be a soldier. Others though, remembered soldiers coming to the Lovetts' during the honeymoon, during the tea period, and those people with the longer memories came out to get a better look. Jamesey didn't notice this, for he was wondering where the things were that he'd meant to give as presents and why he'd nothing in his hands to offer his family when they came to the door.

'Who's that?' said a woman's voice from far behind the wood again. 'Who's that? What d'ye want? What're ye knocking on this door for?'

'It's James Tone. Is that you Aunt Mariah?' There was no sound from within. The dog wasn't barking. Maybe Dachau wasn't there, didn't exist anymore.

'Will you let me in Aunt?' Nobody answered. 'Aunt Mariah?' he tried again.

'We're saying the rosary,' she said.

'Can I say it too?'

Another silence, then his aunt said, from deep in her gut,

'No you can't. Go away. Ye're an English bum. We don't want ye here no more.'

He heard the inner door slam and then the murmurings of rote prayers. He looked at the brown wood, bubbled in paintpatches here and there. He leaned his forearm against it. He leaned his head on his forearm. Inside, a baby started crying. Eventually he pushed himself off.

He walked unsteadily down the street, towards the heart of the district. Some of the men and some of the women looked at each other and began to walk that way too. Excited children tried to come after, but were threatened with backhanders to stay put, to get inside again. Jamesey turned the corner into The Pad, which took him even further into Ardoyne. With a bit of intention, he could have gone up The Pad, up the way, towards Ardoyne chapel and then out of the area. There were no militarily-installed turnstiles as yet in place up there. Jamesey Tone though, had no intentions left.

As his silent pursuers turned the corner after him, someone flashed by and got in first. Seeing who it was, the others stopped and stepped back, to let him get on with it. Jamesey himself heard the fast soft footsteps and turned to look too. He had stopped at Herbert Street entry and this could be Aunt, he told himself. Maybe she was sorry for what she'd said, and was coming to say she didn't know what had come over her, and to take a hold of him, to take the whole of him, and to bring him home again.

It wasn't his aunt. It was Jat McDaide and he was on him like a monkey. The arm came up, the knife went in and Jamesey went down like water. Lying on The Pad, with the blood bubbling out, he stared at the rolling clouds in the fifteen seconds left to him of life. Jat rolled him over, searched him for the Great Man's watch, found it, and ran away, with it safely in his hands. The others were already gone. They were returning to their houses. Picking up their pace, they moved faster and faster. They got inside. They closed their big doors and locked and barred them tight. Nobody would speak about what had happened. Nothing really had happened. It was just another of those motiveless crimes that were going on all over the place.

In the Crossfire, 1971

The child Amelia was engrossed in a poem. She came across it in a book in class. Using her finger, with the book wide open on her lap, under the table, she focused on every word as she went along. She was delighted with the way it went. It went like this:

> Young Ethelred was only three
> Or somewhere thereabouts when he
> Began to show in divers ways
> The early stages of the craze.
> For learning the particulars
> Of motorbikes and motorcars,
> He started with a little book,
> To enter numbers which he took.
> And though his mother often said
> 'Now do be careful Ethelre—'

Amelia was shoved sideways, fast and hard and with intent. She grabbed hold of the desk to stop herself from falling and at that moment realised there was utter silence in the room. She looked up and saw that the attention of everyone, but everyone, was fixed upon her. This was truly awful in one of those truly awful ways, for getting the attention in that class was never, ever, pleasant. Everyone went on staring and instead of just the one, massively violent, insane teacher there usually was, there were now three, all fit to bustin' and tickin' away like bombs. The other schoolchildren were quiet but also happy in their own anxious relieved little ways. This time it was to be Amelia Lovett being shouted at and not one of themselves being picked on that particular day.

'Are you deaf or just stupid?' said the shover, Miss Jean Hanratty, who once was to have become Mrs Noel Keenan only Mr Keenan caught himself on and ran away. 'I was talking to you!' Miss Hanratty's scary face shot close. She had ginger hair, black freckles, brown lips and always wore rough tartan skirts and tweedy clothes that had no petticoats and no knickers underneath them. This made it very hard for her not to scratch.

'I said,' she cried, she scratched, she nipped herself deep. 'I said, I said, I said, I said—' But it was no good. Miss Jean Hanratty could never remember what she'd said, her bad temper and long-established alcoholic state always so high as to blot out any idea of a short-term memory. Instead she snatched the book out of Amelia's hands and fired it across the room. *First Aid In English* it was called, or seemed to be called but, as a matter of fact, it wasn't. Only the cover was called that. A naughty child had interchanged all the covers of the books in the class library one day for a laugh and, after laughing on the other side of her face when Miss Jean Hanratty got a hold of her, missed out on a few when she was crying and interchanging them all back. Also, this book really belonged to P7 but had managed somehow to slip down to P6 by mistake. Anyway, after Miss Hanratty threw it, it landed with a great crack and a broken spine in the corner and that, sadly, very sadly, was the end of that. It was dead.

The other two teachers, Miss White and Miss Ghess – yes, that's right, G-H-E-S-S – both just as ugly and pathologically off their heads as Miss Hanratty though in slightly different ways for God makes everybody different, shook their heads at the terrible waste of time that had just taken place. Here was their poor colleague, Jean Hanratty, who had just spent three whole minutes explaining the procedure for the competition to the class, and what happened? – that wretched girl in the corner hadn't been listening! It would serve the wee eejit right, they thought, if Jeannie here chose not to explain again. What would the wee miss do then?

'I'm not explaining again!' screamed Miss Hanratty. She moved closer, raking the front of her thighs through the thick yellow, black and brown plaid. 'I've explained once already! I'm not explaining again! Do you think I'm here for the benefit of you! Do you think I've got nothing else to do! Do you think –'

She stopped, not because she'd caught a grip on her mad self and thought perhaps she ought to change her behaviour to something a bit more normal. No, she stopped because there wasn't much time before the competition would be over, and look, her class hadn't even yet begun. Children, on the other hand, could be hit anytime. So she settled for a good glare at Amelia for the time being, gave her own legs another good rake, moved her short but pointy fingernails up around her ample behind, then stopped all of that so as to get a move on.

'As I was saying,' she said, attempting to explain again – already having forgotten she'd just said she wouldn't. But not even a second after remembering what it was that was in her mind, she forgot once more and had to be prompted by Miss Ghess. 'Yes, yes, all right,' she scowled after Miss Ghess had whispered it all back to her. 'You don't have to be so detailed. I'm not demented you know.' She turned back to the class. 'Today's a Special Day of Hope as well as being unfortunately Spy Wednesday. Every single nine-year-old in every single school in the whole of Northern Ireland is going to be doing exactly the same thing as you. In fact, they are already doing it. We're a bit late in getting started but you're not going to disappoint me for all that. You're going to do exactly as I say which is sit down, be very good, very clever and very quick. I want you all to write a poem about peace.'

The children were dismayed. None of them wanted to do this. It was the very last thing any of them wanted to do. They had other plans mapped out for themselves that day. The two Marys, for example, wanted to work out what age they'd be in the year Twenty Hundred. Mary thought she'd be thirty-nine but Mary said no, that was wrong, she'd be forty. Mary said no, *she* was wrong, and that she'd add it up and subtract herself and find out. Mary said well, all right, go ahead if you wanna be like that, if you think I'm wrong but I'm right, you'll see. Mary said okay, she would, and Mary said okay, do. But then, before Mary could get a chance to do any of this, this here happened and they were being catapulted into writing poems about peace. Apart from the Marys, who were now not talking to each other, there were also all the others who didn't want to write poems about peace too. Roberta was one of them. Roberta wanted to write about stairs and staircases.

'I love stairs,' she confided to Amelia on the way in that day. 'We've got nineteen stairs in our house Amelia, and four steps out the back, but I don't count those.' Amelia listened, for Roberta was her friend but really, she herself wasn't passionate about stairs anymore. She used to be. Of course she did. But that was when she was a baby. That was when she was eight. Now she was nine and she had grown out of stairs a long while back. She had moved on, as one did, to buttons. Roberta must be a bit slow in developing, she thought.

'I went upstairs Amelia,' Roberta went into the details. They were hanging up their coats and taking off their waterboots in the cloakroom. 'Then I came downstairs. Then I went upstairs again. Then later on I came downstairs. Then I went upstairs backwards, then I came downstairs sideways, then . . .' She told it to Amelia because she couldn't contain herself but really, she had been planning to write this exciting little narrative ever since it had occurred to her over the weekend. She had been saving it up and saving it up, so as to be able to write it in class the following week, and show it, and let everybody see it, and get praise and smiles and attention – nice attention that is – from all of them. And that wasn't all. No. After she'd finished actually writing the piece, her next plan had been to add in some pictures, hand-drawn, by herself, of herself, going up and down their house's stairs, front, back and sideways, with her long hair – which by the way she didn't have – swinging out joyously to the right, joyously to the left, and joyously all about her back and shoulders. She had it worked out in her head exactly how she was going to do it, for she'd been thinking about it non-stop for four whole days. But now here she was, thwarted and upset, as the others were thwarted and upset also, all because of these poems that had to be written about peace.

Amelia, of course, thought *she* had the bigger problem. Who cared about stairs when there were poems, already written, in books to be learnt? And not peace poems either, of course. Who wanted to bother with them? She wanted to learn poor Ethelred's story, all thirty-three verse lines of it. She'd keep it in her head and walk about, saying it to herself over and over. Amelia liked learning poems and saying them to herself, but only if she was fond of them. If she wasn't fond of them, she'd frown, put the book down, and turn away. But now, having learnt the beginning of Ethel, *First Aid* was dead, violently battered, its tiny spine broken-up and lying bleedy by the wall. Amelia was shaken by Miss Hanratty's barbarity but as Miss Hanratty was the adult, Amelia thought it must be she, herself, who had got it all wrong. Bernie interrupted Amelia's mind while it was having its think to whisper, 'You think that dead book's a problem? You think not being allowed to learn a poem off by heart's a problem? You'd really know what a problem was Amelia, if you wanted to cut up potatoes and stick them in paint, like me.' That was what Bernie wanted to do. She desperately wanted to do this and so to her, peace poems were a terrible curse and a scourge upon them all. They were interfering, had an awful lot to answer for, and how did one set about writing a competitive poem about peace anyhow? What was there to say? What did the teachers mean by it? Would they be given a clue? Did it have to be vague and include everybody, meaning Protestants, or had it to be detailed and be only about themselves? All in all, they thought, the poems were a bad omen. Why bother writing what nobody was interested in? Of course none of the children voiced this, which was very, very sensible, the teachers in their school not being of the most democratic, peaceful, loving kind.

Miss Hanratty was now explaining the ground rules for peace poems, for apparently there were some, made up by somebody, somewhere. Clutching her long cane, she slapped the desk between each major point and sometimes just after some phrases. The poem – slap! – had to be the original work of the child – slap! It had to be done there and then – slap! – in the school – slap! – not to be taken home and finished by some adult on the sly. It had to be called 'Peace' – slap! – start with the line 'I wish for Peace in my country' – slap! – and end with 'But Peace will come oh sometime soon/Yes, Peace will come sometime' – slap slap! Every time the word 'Peace' was used – Miss Hanratty here stressed the importance of this next bit by doing a series of fast choreographed slaps on the tabletop

34

– it had to be spelt with a capital letter. As her class had done all their letters, small, capital, cursive and all the rest, Miss Hanratty would multiple-slap anybody who didn't get it right. She wouldn't stand for unreadable writing, anything neurotic, exotic, experimental or new. This would include 'm's and 'w's that had bits missing, 's's that went on too long, 'g's that looked like 'j's or 'j's that looked like 'g's but most especial of all – pay attention here slap slap! – she didn't want writing that slanted to the right and then fell off the edge of the page. Anybody with slanty lines would be slapped. Anybody who messed up more than two pages would be slapped. Anybody who broke nibs or got pen marks on their tongue would be slapped and, concluded Miss Hanratty, 'I want nice little borders drawn all the way round.'

Having said this, the formteacher sat down and took snorty breaths and huffed and puffed and scratched herself while her class sat down too and waited for the essentials to be handed out. Miss White and Miss Ghess, in matching sittie-out dresses, pearls and twinsets, were already in the process of doing this. When everyone was as ready as everyone was ever going to be, Miss Hanratty hurled 'Go!' and the children lifted their pens – and held them. They glanced at the teachers, they glanced at each other and nobody would start first because of the horror that would be in store if they wrote a poem about peace that was wrong.

Like the others, Amelia too was in confusion. It wasn't that she'd anything against peace. It was just that she didn't have anything for it. What did she know? Who could she ask? Nobody. Nobody she knew knew anything about peace. On the other hand, she brightened up, she did know about Eth-le-red, the boy with the engines, who gets killed at the end of that *First Aid* poem. He was deep in her mind and making her sad, so why not write a poem about him instead?

'Good Lord! God Almighty! What is this?' Miss Hanratty

had a heart attack and thwacked Amelia twice across the shoulder blades. When she saw that the mad child was writing a scrawl about a boy on a bike who grows into a man driving a train who gets killed by a tractor at a garage, she had to clutch the desk to keep herself from falling. She gasped, scrunched up the page in fury, hauled Amelia out of her seat and dragged her about by the ears. When she'd finished, she dumped the child at a desk at the other side of the room, stomped off, stomped back and threw more writing materials down on her head.

'You have ten minutes,' she said, checking the big purple clock on her wrist. 'If you know what's good for you, you'll use them wisely.'

Tears – of rage – fell out of Amelia. Two of them, heavy, plopped and plashed and left wet marks all over the page. 'I wish for place in my country' she wrote, without paying attention, putting a small letter pee then remembering she wasn't supposed to after it was far too late. She changed it to a splurgy capital Pee but then it looked like a Bee with a tail so she scribbled at the tail until it looked like a Bee in a muckfield. Realising there was nothing further she could do, she left it as it was, hoping Miss Hanratty wouldn't notice. She carried on the hateful poem at the next bit. She slanted the second line, curious to see if it would cover up her teardrops. The words left black smudges entirely in their wake. She frowned. She licked the nib and wiped it dry on her schoolblouse. A child was hurled across the room. Amelia didn't notice. She was starting to get interested in the mechanics of this exercise. She began her third line and soon was well into the swing of it. Forgetting all the instructions, she made the biggest mistake of all, and wrote what turned out to be her own little war poem about peace.

This poem had a river, a very angry, tetchy, touchy, paranoid, on-the-defensive river, that killed people, by pulling them apart

36

and then floating them about. Legs featured prominently in this poem, particularly upside-down ones, in upside-down sittie-out tartan dresses, as well as female torsos wearing twinsets with scrawny necks that had strings of pearls wrapped around. The river swole up and then it swole down and at the end of each swelling was a dead person. Amelia was starting to feel happy about her peace poem and was just starting to wonder what rhymed with 'shark' when Miss White, far away, lifted a chair and banged it.

'Time's running out!' she shrieked. 'Time's nearly up now. Round those poems off now, children! Listen to me! Round! Round! Why aren't you children rounding?'

Miss Ghess also shrieked to tell them to get on to their borders, to colour in their borders and Jesus, Mary and Joseph – were they deaf? – to leave those poems about peace now well alone. Miss Hanratty yelled that she'd go round and slap anybody who wasn't doing what Misses White and Ghess were wanting. She'd also slap anybody taking her time and not hurrying up.

It seemed the children though, spent more emotional time on their borders than they'd done on their poems about peace. Roberta's border, for example, was intricate but hardly varied, consisting of staircases, with little stick figures, all with long swishy hair, constantly going up and down them. Amelia's border consisted of fangs and teethmarks, pointing inwards, especially around that title word 'Peace'. The two Marys had put a lot of sums and mathematical calculations, with Mary putting a total of '39' in big bold colourful numbers at the bottom of her border and Mary, on hers, equally bold, and in gold, and undaunted, putting '40'. Bernie had drawn potatoes with orange and yellow and red spicy lines coming off them, Bossy had Cowboys and Indians, Marionetta, scalps and bonfires, Debbie, whistles and binlids and Pauline, rows and rows of little tiny soldiers, lining up and searching rows and rows of little tiny men. These borders didn't go down well with Miss H, Miss G and Miss W, but they'd have to do, they reckoned, for there was no time to slap everybody and have them do them all over again.

Amelia swang and swung her legs under the table, added in the finishing touches, and was even seriously starting to think about another poem about peace when a Miss Sittie Outtie Prettie Dressie approached and snatched it off her.

'Time's up!' she shrieked. 'Gimme that peace poem! Look at the state of you! You're so scruffy! What sort of home is it that you come from?' She went on to the next. 'Gimme that!' She snatched the poem out of the child's hand. 'Look at you! You're so scruffy! What sort of home . . .' Amelia drew a doodle on the desk. Although she didn't know it, it was of Miss Sittie Outtie Twinsettie Deadie, spreadeagled, in the junior play-ground. The other children, with no more writing pages either, snivelled and snuffled and doodled violence on their desks as well. Soon, all peace efforts were collected and solemnly put under lock and key. It was time, said the teachers, to go and have lunch.

'So go and eat and give our heads peace!' cried the teachers. 'And for the love of God, stop that whingeing! What are they whingeing for anyway?' They rolled their eyes and shrugged their shoulders and scratched tartan skirts and flattened pastel dresses. The little ones, subdued, not hungry, trudged into the dinners, and ate, unhappily, on their feelings. The day though, was not over yet.

After lunch, the children were still shaken and shook with snuffles and snarts but nothing was contagiously outright. 'We're going to play a game,' said some people coming through the door and closing it. 'Nothing to worry about,' they said, which meant that there was. What followed was one of those dream sequences that are rapid, different-angled, and over in no time. Did it really happen? Were the children hallucinating? It had been a trying morning session for them after all. These new people, on the whole, seemed friendly and nice but the children knew instinctively there was something wrong with them. They smiled too much. They touched too much. They had stuff in one bag that they weren't showing, and chocolate and sweets in another, that they were. Amelia noticed – and how could she not – that Misses Hanratty, White and Ghess were no longer with them. Were these new people doctors then, come to give needles?

'We're going to have great fun,' said a woman with a gurgle who had a stack of cards with the children's names on. No, thought Amelia. No, said Bernie and the two Marys shook their heads and held hands. 'Nothing to be frightened of,' said another gurgle, putting a pair of very thin white gloves on. She picked up a box of smudge and some papers. A few children leaned forward to get a better look. Most leaned back and wanted home.

> The children were lined up,
> Amelia there too,
> Not one of them able to get out of it.
> When it came to her turn,
> The policewoman took hold,
> And forced Amelia's fingers into the thick of it.

> When she'd left all her marks,
> She was given a card
> And passed along to another to be dealt with.
> This one smiled a thin smile,
> Wiped Amelia's hands dry
> And patted her backside and said 'Move it'.

So Amelia moved on,
Was given a book
And told to be quiet until hometime.
It was *First Aid In English*
And was broken in bits
And had lost the best parts with poor Ethelred.

So she sat and she worried
And tried to remember
What had happened just after line twenty-three.
Had he died, had he lived,
Had he given himself up,
Or was he gone forever in a lost memory?

When it was time to go home they all got a sweet.

Treasure Trove, 1972

Every single night and every single day Amelia went upstairs to look at her treasure. She classified the precious belongings in it as Minor, Medium and Main. Although every piece of it was a very exciting treasure in itself, best of all by far were the thirty-seven black rubber bullets she'd collected ever since the British Army started firing them. She'd run for them, dived for them, traded other children for them and saved them up to the point where she was sure she had the biggest collection in the whole of Ardoyne, maybe in the whole of north Belfast. She kept these thirty-seven, six-inch long, one-and-a-half-inch thick rubber bullets, along with all the other classes of the treasure, in a big battered suitcase under the bed. It was marked:

> AMELIA BOYD LOVETT OWNS THIS
> PRIVATE PROPERTY
> KEEP OUT

One day, after admiring her treasure for as long as it took, she locked it back up, put it away and went out into the street to see what was going on generally. Fergal McLaverty was on a pair of skates.

'Hiya,' he said.

'Hiya,' she said.

'Want a go?'

They played about a bit.

'Guess what Amelia?' said Fergal. 'I forgot to tell ye. The Brits are buying back their rubber bullets. They're giving fifty pee to every kid who brings one to the barracks!'

'So?' said Amelia.

'So! What do you mean, "so"? So why don't you sell yours? You got about ten, haven't you?'

'Thirty-seven!' said Amelia, annoyed. Fergal was staggered.

'Amelia! You'll be rich! Just think – thirty-seven times fifty pee . . .' He tried to do sums in his head.

'They're not for sale!' snapped Amelia. And she meant it. The other children could sell their rubber bullets for all she cared – but they'd be sorry when it came to the end of their sweets and they'd nothing left to show for it. She, on the other hand, would still have her collection, by then maybe even bigger than the whole world.

'Well I think you're mad,' said Fergal. 'What if they do a housesearch? They'll just take them anyway and then you'll get nothin'.'

Amelia looked at him. She was shocked. She hadn't thought of that. So far, their house had only been searched once and at that time, she'd been collecting buttons. She remembered having two hundred and sixty-three of them, all shapes, all colours, all sizes, and all divided by circles of threads into little families that she kept in a big old tin of Marvel under the stairs. When the soldiers came, they emptied them out, poked among them, walked on them even, but when they left, they hadn't stole a single one. Somehow though, she had a feeling it would be different this time. If they searched again and found this, her latest treasure, she had a feeling they'd be sure to take that one away. There was a good chance too, they would search again, for as her brother Mick was getting closer and closer to internment age – she'd heard her ma say this more than once – there was bound to be trouble any day now.

So things were serious. She rushed away from Fergal, forgetting even to say goodbye. A new hiding place had to be found at once. She banged into the house and ran up the steep stairs to the front bedroom. It was crowded out with bunk beds, a single bed, a table, a massive wardrobe, a chest of drawers and a cot with her sleeping baby sister in it. Kneeling down by the single bed she shared with her Aunt Dolours, she stretched in among the balls of fluff and dragged out the suitcase.

Unlocking it with the key she always kept on her, she first took out the Minors and Mediums which were sitting on top. These were: a miniature plastic sheep, a Black Queen chess piece, a tiny box with a flick-down-shut lid, a small musical keyring, shrapnel she'd dug out of the front door, a penny prayer for serenity, a grown-up lace handkerchief, a dried starfish, bits of coloured glass, the browny-pink corner of an old ten-shilling note, sixty-four lollipop sticks, a pot of glue, a tube of glitter and a sheet of sticky gold stars. Placing these quickly but carefully to the side, she turned back to the four rows of long hard giants lying at the bottom of the case. They lay, solid, prominent, like kingly sleeping rockets and they were fat, fatter than her father, fatter than a stick of fat rock, as fat as a fat fat candle, she had decided. Scattered about here and there between them were various normal bullets, spent cartridges and a funny switch thing, all of which she'd found, picked or dug up here and there along the way.

The less important treasures could all go back in of course but the rubber bullets would have to be hid somewhere else. She began to take them out two at a time.

'What's them you got Amelia?'

She jumped, quickly threw the bullets back, slammed down the lid and threw herself over it.

'Nothin'!' she cried.

'Them's rubber bullets!' cried her older brother. He reached over.

'It's not. Go away!' She pushed the case under the bed out of his grasp and now laid herself in front of it.

'How'd you get them?' said Mick. 'How'd you get so many? How many you got? Let me see!'

She felt sick. No one in her family had ever asked about her Treasure Trove before. No one had ever been interested. Least of all Mick. She knew he'd been leaving her suitcase alone all this time because he thought it was full of stupid pictures of Donny Osmond and David Cassidy. She did, in fact, have pictures of Donny Osmond and David Cassidy but they were in her Janet and John book downstairs.

Mick's eyes had gotten glittery and big, his fingers stretched out to their limit. In his excitement, he trod on a Medium Treasure: she heard the keyring crunch. She pushed the case in even further with her big toe until it touched the far wall. This meant she was mostly under the bed now herself.

'If you let me see them, I'll let you play all my records for a day.'

'No!'

'I'll let you play them two days.'

'No!'

'I'll let you look at the sun through my binoculars.'

'No!'

His voice changed.

'I won't take you prisoner anymore.'

Amelia realised her mistake.

'Yes,' he said, nodding and smiling, in that old familiar way, the way she didn't like. 'You walked right into it this time

Amelia. It would be really easy for me to trap you in there right now. I could pull over the wardrobe and the drawers and the table and then you'd be captured and stuck – for as long as I want. Maybe I'd give you food. Maybe I wouldn't.'

He rubbed his hands down his cords and, in his excitement, seemed even to forget her for a while. She suspected, for she was heightened to every click and turn her brother's brain gave, that he was now thinking about his Forgotten Prisoners, those model kits he spent a long time lovingly putting together at the kitchen table down the stairs. These Forgotten Prisoners were one-foot high displays of half-rotting skeletal figures chained to walls, surrounded by rats and skulls and tiny jail doors that nobody ever opened. Amelia had nightmares about those doors. Most of these 'ornaments', as her mother called them, sat about the house, upsetting nobody, it seemed, but Amelia herself. To say so though, would have been madness. To say so, would have been asking for it. To say so, would have been handing over the ammunition to be turned against her, her very own self. So she said nothing about these scary Forgotten Prisoners and tried not to look at them whenever Mick set them in front of her or when he sat painting them in his favourite dark paint colours, his mouth slightly open, the tip of his tongue protruding, his breath going heavy and just that wee bit too fast.

He began to rearrange the furniture, starting with the chest of drawers. Amelia opened her mouth and let out a big scream. The kitchen door was yanked open and her mother shouted up from the bottom of the stairs.

'Amelia Lovett! If you wake that child . . .'

'Mammy!' cried Amelia. 'Mick's taking me prisoner. Mick said—'

'Ye've been warned wee girl!' Her mother went back in and closed the door.

'I didn't say I was taking you prisoner,' said Mick. He rolled his eyes. 'See how you jump to conclusions! I said I could if I wanted.' He looked at her. 'Y'know Amelia, seems to me like you want to be taked prisoner.'

She lay on the oilcloth under the bed, her body rigid, her eyes squinting up at him. The naked lightbulb, that always had to be turned on because the house was so dark, was behind his head. It seemed to be on his side, glaring down at her, she noticed, all the time supporting him. Her heart raced and her senses quickened as she tried to work out where he would be coming from this time. As usual, she was too late. Mick had already arrived.

'I know!' he said, softening his voice. There was a smile and a caring expression on his face that would have suggested to someone who hadn't a clue about the Lovett family, that Amelia perhaps was his best sister. This was not the case. Amelia recognised the expression as a preliminary for something nasty and she took a big breath and braced herself for harm. 'How about a nice game of chess?' he said. 'You like chess don't you Amelia? And you know, we haven't played in ages.'

This was true. They hadn't. And that was because last time they'd played, three years ago, she had come so close to winning that Mick had tried to throw her out the upstairs window. They had been playing in this very room and she had rescued his Black Queen from his confining cruel clutches and was refusing to trade it back – not for all her captured pawns, not for her horse, not for her castle, not even for the promise that she could be Black next time. She'd shaken her head and foolishly looked happy and Mick had flown into a rage and kicked the chessboard to the side. He'd dragged her to the window-ledge and tried to lift her up and over it and she struggled and kicked and was only saved when their father, disturbed while listening to his football yells down below, came bounding up the stairs, to pull them apart and hit them. All this Mick had forgotten.

'We'll have a great time,' he said, rubbing his hands and reaching for the box on the shelf.

'I'm not playin'!' she shouted.

'I'll be Black,' he said, 'and oh! – how about a wee bet to make things interesting? You bet whatever you have in your case there and I'll bet that I won't take you prisoner anymore.'

'Leave me alone, ye twisty pig!'

His features hardened. Mick, like most in the Lovett family, was not very steady in his emotions. The chessboard he'd just set up again went flying, the top of a whiskey bottle, standing in for the long-missing Black Queen, fell between them on the floor. He kicked it in her face.

'Come out and play or you'll be sorry!'

Expecting him to dive in after her, she grabbed up a piece of coloured glass. Again though, a different notion seemed to come over him and he dropped to his hunkers and picked up the Black Queen instead. Her heart jumped.

'Gimme that!' she cried.

He took out his penknife.

'Gimme that Black Queen!'

'Gimme them bullets.'

She hesitated. He started to cut off the Black Queen's head.

Propelling herself out from under the bed, she jumped and stuck the glass in his cheek. He flicked her to the side, kicked her for the cut then reached in smooth and slick for the suitcase. She was up within a second and flung herself again, only this time, she fell onto nothing. He was gone. Swaying with the rape of it, a few moments passed before her mind could function remotely, and when it did, she ducked under the bed and let out a big wail.

'My tr-ea-sss-urre!'

There was a thundering on the stairs and her mother banged into the room and dragged her from under the bed and up onto the oilcloth.

'I told you! Didn't I bloody tell you!'

Babby Jo was awake and crying, standing and reaching through the bars of her cot. Amelia's mother shrieked 'Jeeesss-us!' into the ceiling, smacked Amelia then dropped her like a dirty duster and picked up the screaming Josephine. 'There-there-there-there-there,' she said. 'There-there-there-there-there.' She threw the baby up and down in a way that she would call soothing, which prevented her from throwing it against the wall, in a way that she would call Just about had enough and my God, why doesn't something good ever happen? Amelia, meanwhile, was out of the room and on the small landing, kicking and banging and throwing herself, anyway she'd go, against the locked, back bedroom door.

'Rubber! Robber! Mammy Daddy Aunt Dolours!'

Her mother was shouting and cracking up, Babby Jo was screaming and cracking up and Amelia was still flinging and crying, in deep shock at her sudden loss. It was a terrible injustice that had been done to her, but she couldn't get it straight in her head, never mind convey it with any coherence to another person. 'Ma!' she cried. 'Ma!' she tried. 'Mick – trick . . . prisoner . . . thirty-seven . . . mine, fat, black, bits of shrapnel, gone!' She got it out in her own way, and her mother, hearing something of it, tried to deal with it in hers. Holding Babby Jo on her hip, she banged on the back bedroom door.

'Hey boy!' she shouted. 'Open up! Give her back her toys. D'ye hear me? Now, Mick!'

From behind the wood came the secret finishing touches of concealment, the comings and goings and clickings and closings that had Amelia beside herself with worry. Where oh where was he hiding them? Mick took his time and, of course, as far as Amelia was concerned, that was exactly what he'd always done and exactly what he'd always gotten away with. Finally, an isolated lock locked shut and, with her bullets, now his, in some invisible place he now wanted them to be, Mick could afford to dander to the door and open it. He had a grim, pained expression on his face.

'It's a trick, Ma!' Amelia shouted before he'd even said anything. 'Whatever it is, it doesn't count and he knows it!'

'Ma,' he said, solemn and sad. 'I hate to tell you this but I heard her saying out in the street that she wants to join the Provies when she's sixteen and that nobody's goin' to stop her.'

Amelia's mouth fell open. She couldn't believe the barefacedness of it all. To come out with something like that at a time like this, when the only plans she had for when she was sixteen – which was another five years, six months and three weeks away anyway – was to get out of school as fast as she could and never, oh never, to go back to it. Apart from that, she hadn't yet decided what she was doing with her life. Oh he was clever, she thought. He was sneaky. She herself was speechless, unable to say anything. So was her mother. Even Babby Jo had grown quiet and was staring at them all. Mick went on.

'And look what I found in her case Ma, which proves it.' He held up the funny switch thing she'd found in the middle of nowhere, on the wasteground, lying by itself, all lonely, one day. She was puzzled. It was just a bit of a spring contraption, a wire contraption, a sort of tube with corks at each end. It didn't mean anything. It wasn't even a real treasure. She'd only taken it home and added it to her collection because she'd felt sorry for it, looking depressed, rusty and sad, as it did that day.

'I'll get rid of it Ma,' went on Mick, acting the Big Good Son. 'Don't you worry. I'll take care of everything.'

'What the hell is it?' said Mrs Lovett.

'It's a primer charge Ma.'

This meant nothing to Mrs Lovett, or to Amelia, or to Babby Jo. He had to explain further.

'It sets off bombs Ma.'

Mrs Lovett gasped. Amelia gasped too.

'Jesus blessus!' cried her ma. 'Is this true Amelia?'

'No!' cried Amelia. 'No, I don't know!'

She was stunned at the cheek of Mick. There he was, cool as anything, stopping at nothing, sneaking the subject away from his own greedy thieving, by pretending to be grown-up about something they both knew didn't count at all. So what if it was a primer charge! So what if it set off bombs! At that very moment it was just a bit of nothing with no bomb attached. It wasn't eye-catching. It wasn't glorious. It wasn't thirty-seven, rich, dark, fat, rubber bullets – rubber bullets she'd fought for, and rushed for, and gathered up under competition and stress. They can kill you know, she'd been told, and so often she'd never forget it, and she knew also that Rosemary Rafferty had had one of her eyes put out by one of them. So she'd taken some chances so she had, she'd run some dangers, she'd worked hard for those there rubber bullets. She knew that. Mick knew that as well. Their ma though, would never understand anything. Grown-ups never understood. They were stupid, distracted, mindless sorts of beings. They never had a clue. They always got it wrong.

Just as her despair was about to envelop her completely, a great and inspirational idea started to take shape. It was similar to the clever move she'd made to the black square on the third line of that chessboard three years ago, when she'd rescued the Black Queen from ever having to belong to the likes of him again.

'Ma!' she jumped up and down. She felt she was a genius. 'How does he know then, what sets off bombs?'

Now this was serious and their ma would get the point of it. She'd have a fit, for people *were* being killed and it was obvious – for she was only ten and a girl – that it couldn't be her doing it. Mick on the other hand, wasn't a girl, and he was nearly sixteen, so he'd no defence as far as most people would see. Amelia's ma, for all her stupid adultness, saw the sense in what her daughter was saying and turned to Mick with a really big frown.

'How *do* you know Mick? How *do* you know, what sets off bombs?'

Amelia was gratified and mollified and happy for a moment, but only for a moment, for at the back of everything, she knew she still hadn't gotten her beloved Treasure Trove back. Mick seemed not a bit put out.

'Ach ma,' he said, playing the good little altarboy. 'Everybody knows them things from the TV. Comics even, books even. Go down yourself and have a look in the library. They're common as petrol bombs, or rubber bullets, or riots, or tea.'

He smirked at Amelia from behind their mother's back, for Mrs Lovett had turned away, fed up, especially as Babby Jo was starting to cry again. She descended the twisting stairs with a 'Throw that thing away' followed by 'And not in our bin' followed by 'And if I hear you talking, wee girl, of joining the IRA . . .' and then she disappeared into the kitchen and closed the door. Amelia and Mick were left on the landing alone.

Luckily for her, Mick wasn't in the mood for physically tormenting her. He had other plans and so didn't take her by the throat and choke her, on and off, for half an hour. He laughed as she stepped away and he threw the primer charge after her.

'Here stupid,' he said. 'You can have that. It's just a bit of rubbish, a mercury tilt switch, not a detonator or a primer charge or anything worth having at all.' And with that, he opened the bedroom door, went inside, closed and locked it. Amelia was alone on the landing. Everybody and everything had gone.

So the contraption, which turned out to be nothing, bounced off her chest and fell to the floor. It landed on the oilcloth, amidst all the other treasures, but only the Minors and the Mediums, for the rubber bullets were no more. She dropped down in the corner of the front bedroom, her chest heaving, her leg cut, her arms, head and cheek sore, and she rocked back and forth, and began to grieve her loss. She kept up this rocking until, catching sight of the Black Queen, lying smug and triumphant on a white square of oilcloth, Amelia went still and felt angry, for two things occurred to her at once. One was that she had abandoned her beloved treasure to come out from under the bed to save the Black Queen when, two, the Black Queen hadn't needed saving for she'd been Mick's Queen after all. She frowned and picked this Queen up and reached for the box with the flick-down-shut lid and put this Mick thing into it. Then she snapped it closed and felt avenged, but only for a little while. Her anger then came back and so she pushed this box far underneath the chest of drawers and laid herself on her own bed and turned her face to the wall.

The Pragmatic Use of Arms, 1973

Someone banged on the big door. Silence. A pause. Mr Lovett strode over and opened it. Two IRA boys were standing on the stoop. They were in their late teens and they were pissed off, but pissed off with that air of authority, with that air of those confident in having the upper hand, the last say, the power to do something, whatever they liked, about it.

It was all on account of that woman Mariah Lovett. She was the sister of Sadie Lavery and the two of them had been fighting on and off for years. Apparently Mrs Lavery had just had her scalp pulled off in an argument and had taken herself round to the Boys with the blood still dripping, to complain about her sibling, to show them her wounds and demand they do something about it. Mariah Lovett was mad, she said. Sister or no sister, she was a savage and something should be done to deter her, to restrain her, to teach her a lesson – to help, for the love of God, Mrs Lavery get some revenge. The eight IRA men in the small back room in 79, Havana Street went on sipping their tea and looking at the distraught and distressing older woman with her shrieking voice and bloody bits of proof. When she'd finished rampaging through the English language and had stopped waving her scratched and ripped arms about, they sighed, set down their cups, said they'd look into it, that they'd see what they could do, that they'd send somebody round to investigate.

'But understand do, Mrs Lavery,' said one of them. 'We act solely in a mediating capacity, to try and effect a reconciliation. We don't get involved personally – unless someone tries to shit us. So as it stands, we won't be helping you get revenge.'

Mrs Lavery was massively disappointed but decided to settle for what she could get. Of course she didn't want a reconciliation – she wanted mayhem and war and blood and dead bodies – but having the IRA go round was at least something in the way of getting her own back, and that was better, far better, than nothing, or in letting that bitch, her sister, get away with it. So grudgingly she said thanks very much, that she appreciated it, that they were a nice bunch of lads and then she left.

When the door closed after her the IRA men looked at each other and decided between them that yes, once and for all, it was time to do something about that annoying family. For although it was trivial, domestic, risible and not as real or as grown-up as killing soldiers, this here long-running notorious feud had to be put a stop to, for it was getting on their nerves, causing mounting disturbance and attracting the wrong sort of attention just when they, the IRA, did not want any sort of attention attracted at all. The British Army, barracked round the corner in Flax Street in what used to be the old mills, had taken it into their heads to pop round in their Saracens in the hope of catching gunmen every time this here family started up. The drop of a pin, never mind the crunch of a sibling's bone or familial crack of a head, was enough to saturate the area with troops and cause the budding Irish organisation great, but great, inconvenience. If they had more arms, it was true, these would be perfect occasions for the use of natural bait, but as it were, they didn't have more arms so it was just a big meddlesome chore or maddening bore, or both.

That was why two of them were now on the Lovetts' doorstep as instructed by their elders and betters. They were looking at Mr Lovett and Mr Lovett, who had been making the dinner when his flustered wife had run in, a bit dishevelled, a lot triumphant, and with a mass of sisterly hair in her fingers, was standing with one hand on the wood and looking back at them. Inside the dark house, Mrs Lovett was already moving again to the door to meet this, the next trouble, and three of their children, twelve-year-old Lizzie, eleven-year-old Amelia and four-year-old Josie, were eating chips, beans, sausages, beans, eggs, beans, tea, bread and butter in the far corner. They too paused with their forks in mid-air, to see what was going to happen next.

What happened next was that one of these fellas said to Mr Lovett and in not a very nice voice, 'Get you in. Send out your wife. If we want you, we'll call you.'

The children looked at each other. They were shocked. It was the first time they'd heard anyone speak to their parents, and especially their da, in that particular way. Did that boy not know any better? Did that boy have something wrong with him? Did that boy not come from around here?

Mr Lovett punched the boy out onto the road. Then he pulled him up off it and punched him again and again until the boy fell over the bonnet of the one and only car in the street, a white one, parked neatly by the edge of the opposite cribbie. Mr Lovett then leapt over the bonnet of this car and, pausing in a moment of indecision, the other IRA boy then leapt nervously over it too. Mrs Lovett pushed her children, who were now in the way, out of the way, grabbed up the poker from the hearth and ran back out and over to the car also. She cracked the poker over the second IRA boy's head but after that she couldn't really get involved for Mr Lovett was a tornado and it was necessary to keep back in order to stop herself from being swooped up and dropped, broken-boned, right in the middle of the Shankill, on the other side of the barricades, a stone's throw away. The neighbours all rushed out to watch, from a distance of course. The Lovett children went back to their dinners.

Eventually, and very quickly, all that remained of these two young fellas was one of them. The blood streaming down his face and going in his eyes, he tried to drag the other, who was unconscious, or dead, along the road, away from Mr Lovett, who was still kicking and wiping the street with him, unaccepting of the fact that this was a fight all over. After a few more steps of this dragging and staggering and hauling on a dead weight with a madman taking pot shots without stop-ping, the second boy lost his nerve, let go of his comrade, gave up the mission and ran away. Mr Lovett, like a crazed animal seeing a flicker of life it can rush over and annihilate someplace else, instinctively went to go after, but Mrs Lovett dropped the poker, grabbed her husband's arm, shouted 'Tommy! Tommy!' and managed to get her man to click out of wherever he was in his head, and turn it, and look down, and see her.

'Come on!' she hissed. 'Get in! Come on! Get in! Hurry up!' She pushed and pulled the thwarted, dazed, still raging giant back into their small kitchen house and slammed the door. The neighbours disappeared, just as quick and just in time, for as all doors banged, the British Army rushed round and up from the corner of Flax Street. They looked up and down the quiet dead road. The prone IRA boy was gone, all was deserted, all was silent. The soldiers looked at the closed doors, at the couple of piles of freshly spilt blood, at the smashed, dented white car with red splats all over it and at a further trail of blood suggesting a body had been dragged – or had dragged itself – as far as the burnt-out old house a few yards away. A poker, three whole feet long and a bit stained also, was lying on the edge of the cribbie.

Some of the patrol went to investigate the burnt-out house, others went to the front door of the car owner who, according to their records, was a Mr Duffy, who lived alone. The rest stood guard, looking right and left and left and right and up and down and taking aim, for practice, at anything. The soldier in charge banged on the door of the white car's house and Mr Duffy, looking very surprised, opened it.

'Oh!' he said. 'Has something happened to my car? I didn't hear. Thank you very much for letting me know. Goodbye.'

'Just a minute,' said the soldier, putting his boot in the way of the wood. Mr Duffy raised his eyebrows but looked helpfully obliging as he did so.

'Well, sure, these things happen,' he said, after nothing was said on either side for a moment or two.

'What things?' said the soldier.

'Oh,' Mr Duffy shrugged. 'Don't know.' He sighed. He looked around, first at his feet, then at the soldier's feet, then at all the soldiers' feet, then at bits of their rifles, then at his utterly destroyed windscreen, then at the dented bonnet, the reddish-black bits of blood and lastly at the Lovetts' long thin poker angled outwards and very much implicated on the ground beside him.

'So are you saying,' said the soldier, who had been watching him all this time, 'that you didn't notice anything happening out here while you were in there?'

'No ... no ...' lied Mr Duffy. 'But you see,' he started another lie. 'I just come in this minute.'

'You've just come in this minute,' said the soldier. 'And you didn't happen to notice the state of your car and all this blood and this thing,' he kicked the poker, it clanged onto the road, 'on your way in just this minute?'

'No no, you know it's like this, I didn't, but as I say, thanks very much for pointing it out.'

He was acting suspicious, of course he was, the soldiers knew that, even he must have known that, but as everybody here acted suspicious, it wasn't really very much to go on. So they let him go back in, the other soldiers found nothing in the deserted house – not a dead or an unconscious IRA person for example – and they left the poker where it was for they couldn't be bothered doing anything with it. Throwing a last glance around the quiet dead street, they went back to their barracks, perhaps for a cup of tea and, who knows, maybe a rest and a putting of their feet up.

Across at the Lovetts' there was a great commotion going on. Mr Lovett was punching the wall, one-two, one-two-three, taking aim at a garish red and gold fleur-de-lys on a wallpaper that had been hung lopsided twenty years ago on lopsided walls in an even then falling down forever damp house. The plaster, what was left of it, on the old slatted walls, trinkled and rippled down behind the paper and fell out at the bottom of the skirting board. Mrs Lovett was trying to talk to him.

'Why d'ye have to go and do that for Tommy?' she shouted. 'For the love of God, why d'ye have to be so impulsive all the time?' This was a bit rich, it must be said, coming from someone who still had clumps of her sister's blonde woolly hair in her hands and the face of her second cousin's wife in her nails from a fight two days and a half before that. But Mrs Lovett was a woman who, with hindsight, tended to have sensitivity to the implications of actions just done. She could see that beating the crap out of her sister was one thing; kicking an IRA man to death or nearly was another. People had disappeared for much less. Mr Lovett, on the other hand, paid no attention whatsoever to consequences. In fact, he didn't really believe they existed. In his world, everything boiled down to tones of voice, looks on faces and whether someone was trying to shit you or not.

That was why he wasn't interested in a word his wife was saying and that was why he was starting to annoy her. Two red dots appeared in the middle of her cheeks and they usually only came out when she'd really had enough and was about to start laying in. In this she felt justified. After all, did he think she was helpless? Did he think she couldn't fight her own battles? And why did he always have to make everything be about him? And now, just when they were in the middle of this new mess, if he thought that, because he'd butted in and taken over her violence for her, that she was going to drop everything and take on his worrying for him, then he could take himself off and jump in the Lagan.

So Mr Lovett stayed angry and kept up the punching and Mrs Lovett stayed angry and kept up the haranguing and this went on until they sensed something was the matter with their children. They turned to see what it was for the three girls had stopped eating their beans and were looking instead at the closed front door. The adults, on the alert immediately, stopped making noise and looked over also. There was no sound from without but all the same Mr Lovett, taking his fist out of the wall and behaving just like himself, strode over and pulled on the handle and opened it.

This time there were six of them and this time they were older, the same age as Mr Lovett himself. Also this time, they had three handguns between them. They had come round to guard the front and back doors so Mr Lovett couldn't escape although why they thought Mr Lovett would think he should be escaping shows a marked lack of understanding of this man's psychology. They were waiting for Billy McDaide to come round, for it was to be the top man himself who would decide what was to be done about the problem this time.

'Oh no!' cried Mrs Lovett as Mr Lovett rushed out to fight the six of them. This was exactly what the children, and Mrs Lovett, if she was being honest with herself, would have known he was going to do. With Mr Lovett, strategy counted for nothing. It was all improvisation, based on long experience of past similar encounters, where you found out what you needed simply as you went along.

It was really only because they all wanted a go at him and kept releasing their grip in order to get one, that Mr Lovett was able to get in any digs at all. Of course they still over-whelmed him, three holding while two got stuck in. The last took out his gun, but it was really just a ruse to threaten and frighten, for he wasn't going to use it. He couldn't use it, because of the proximity of the soldiers round the corner in Flax Street. This gunman jumped and danced and waved his weapon in Mr Lovett's face in order for Mr Lovett to look up and be afraid and surrender, but Mr Lovett was too intent in trying to win his own war that the poor embarrassed gunman, realising he was dealing with someone who didn't know there were rules to be followed, and feeling a bit silly as all the neighbours were watching, gave up, put his gun away and simply joined the others in the hammering.

It all had to be done in silence though, because of those soldiers, and it was being remarkably so managed until Mrs Lovett, swinging the poker on behalf of her husband, missed her target, which was another IRA head, and smashed the rear window of Mr Duffy's poor car instead. The noise travelled deliberately towards Flax Street.

The place cleared in seconds. The IRA grabbed up the now unconscious or maybe dead Mr Lovett and threw him and the woman back into their dark little house. They squashed in behind them, taking lookout posts by the windows. With three guns between them, they weren't exactly ready, but they were as ready as they were ever going to be for the shootout.

The British Army rushed up and round the corner of Crumlin Street. They looked up and down the, once again, quiet dead road. All was deserted, all was silent, all front doors were closed. This time though, there were more, even fresher piles of blood and the white car was further damaged, ruined, with that long poker now lying the length of its back seat.

'Just come in again have you?' said the soldier in charge to Mr Duffy after banging on Mr Duffy's front door. Mr Duffy, standing on the threshold, looked around, first at his feet then at the soldier's feet and then at all their feet and so on and so forth. Of course he was acting suspicious. The soldiers knew that. He knew that. And so on and so forth too. They sighed. This was getting annoying. The trail of blood this time led straight over to the Lovetts' and according to their radioed records, this family wasn't involved but was troublesome and bothersome as a group for all that.

Ordering Mr Duffy to stay on his doorstep, they went over and banged on the Lovetts' front door. Mrs Lovett opened it, even as they were still banging, and she startled them with the sight of blood all over her. She had blood coming out her mouth, out her nose and more out the side of her head. There was a long, congealing wound running the length of her fore-arm, given to her as a present by her sister with a knitting needle earlier that day. Her face was damp, her mouth was open, her teeth were perfect, her chest heaving and her faded little bottle-green dress ripped as far as her breasts. The soldier in charge and all the other soldiers stared and for a moment didn't get round to asking anything. Mrs Lovett looked back, but only into the eyes of the man who would matter, for it would be he, and he alone, who would decide whether they'd come in or not. She held the door loosely as if it didn't matter whether or not they entered, but not so loosely as to let them see her battered husband lying on the carpet or the gunmen making shadows on the walls around her.

'What happened?' said the soldier in charge.

'Fight,' she replied, swallowing before speaking and wiping the blood away from her mouth after that. The blood was bright and raw and running down and as she kept wiping at it, the soldier thought her distracted, not particularly unfriendly, just someone who was past caring whether he came in or not.

'Yours?' he asked, stretching out his arm and handing her back the poker. She stretched out her own and took it.

'Thanks very much,' she said. Her voice was hoarse and her hand was shaking. Both she and the soldier maintained eye contact until he let go and looked away first.

Seeing this, the other soldiers, starting to crowd round the door, moved back also. They were leaving. Mystery solved. Not anything serious. Just that mad Lovett family at it again. Throwing a last, and as far as was possible for them, relaxed glance around the quiet dead road, they went back to their barracks, perhaps for another cup of tea and who knows, maybe another bit of feets-up.

Mrs Lovett closed the door and heaved a big sigh. One hurdle over. She turned then jumped, for Billy McDaide had entered her house through the back way. He was now standing silent in the living room. He was looking over at her. His gun was out. It was hanging loosely. The safety catch was off and the muzzle was pointing at the face of her husband. Her husband was still lying out cold on the floor. He was on his back, on the carpet, his whole body running the length of the settee and his children were crouched on top, looking over and down at him. Their da was a mess, their da was looking terrible and each daughter tried, staring very intently, to find out whether he was breathing or not.

'Still got that hot black temper Riah, hasn't he?' said Mr McDaide, keeping his gaze, for he couldn't help it, on Mrs Lovett. She came closer, closer to him, into the living room. He indicated to his men to wait outside or in the kitchen or wherever they wanted, but to get the hell out and close the door after them. They were reluctant to do this for they knew he wasn't going to be as severe as he should be, and as he most certainly would be, if it wasn't on account of that woman. But they did as they were told for he was Billy McDaide and he was in charge.

Billy McDaide looked at Mariah Lovett over Tommy Lovett's still body. He put out his hand and touched the blood on her cheek. He touched her cheek. He touched her. She took his hand away. He sighed. They both sat down in opposite armchairs, he with his gun, she with her poker from the hearth.

'I can't have him going around beating up my men Riah,' he said. Mrs Lovett refrained from saying 'They started it'. This was not the time. She had her husband's life to save.

'He'll be away again soon Billy,' she began, her voice getting hoarser, her lip already swelling. 'Back to England, to London, to work . . .'

'This here business with your family Riah,' the IRA man went on. 'Can you not just patch up your differences?' Mariah Lovett looked shocked. 'Bury the hatchet?' Mariah Lovett looked amused. 'Come to some compromise between youse?' Mariah Lovett just looked. Billy McDaide went blithely on, preaching and talking at her and completely missing the point. 'Try to keep principles in mind rather than personalities, for you know Riah,' he added, 'that's what we do.' Mrs Lovett was scornful but careful, oh very careful, not to show it. Billy McDaide then got up, thinking he was understanding the woman he just never had understood – the English soldier had managed better in a second. He put his gun away, made for the door, then looked back, his hand on the doorsnib.

'I'm not always gonna be in the position I'm in Riah,' he said. She stood up too. 'What I'm sayin' is,' he paused, 'maybe you should tell him to stay in London. This decision-making, you know, won't always be down to me.'

When he'd left, shaking hands with her in the tiny square hallway, Mrs Lovett closed the big door and now was distracted for real. Oblivious to her children, she dropped the poker and went into the kitchen to fill a big basin at the watertap. Her children, equally unaware of her, continued to stare at their father. Their mouths were open, their chests were heaving, their minds were filled to the brim with a question. If their da was lying there, and he was, unbreakable and yet broken, what chance was there going to be for any of them in the world?

Mrs Lovett came back with the water, cloths and Dettol. Setting everything down on the carpet, she told her children to go away. She then pushed back her hair, sank to the carpet and leaned over her husband. She kissed the face of her husband, her one, her only lover, and cradled his head in her arms.

Babies, 1974

Mary Dolan had her baby someone said. There'd been problems with it coming out, maybe because of all the age she was. Her da was still pretending he'd nothing to do with it and her ma was still not noticing. Nobody got in the doctor.

She started to wheel it about in an old toy pram, pushing it up Brompton Park, round the corner, down Highbury, round the corner, up Holmedene, round the corner, down Strathroy. They said she worked her way along that whole row of streets until she reached the barricades. Then she turned and came back. Again and again and again.

I met her doing this on my way home from mitching school. It was hometime and I'd just climbed out the back of Logue's old firebombed pub and was wiping the dust off my uniform when I looked up and there she was in front of me. I started to cross the road because I didn't want to say hello but the pram veered round and squeaked over after me. When I reached the other side, I turned quick. Mary stopped dead, in the middle of the road, one foot in front of the other.

'Mary, what are ye doin'?' I snapped. 'Why are ye followin' me?'

She didn't answer. She just stayed still, like she thought I couldn't see her. Her head was down and I saw pus on the scabs where she'd been picking at herself. I tutted.

'Well aren't you gonna get that pram off the road?'

She wheeled it over on to the cribbie and left it – in front of me. Then she moved to a hedge nearby and picked a leaf. I watched her fold it and fold it and fold it until it broke and her fingers got damp. She picked some more.

'Mary, will ye move yer pram,' I said. 'I can't get by. I have to go.' She nodded and carried on nodding but still she stood there, on her stick legs, with bits of leaves all over her.

'Oh for God's sake!' I started to push by when I stopped. The baby smelt like cabbage, like someone had said it did.

I looked at Mary. She was nodding more noticeably now, like she was agreeing with me. I looked back at the pram. A cord of rattles in the shape of ducks was stretched across it. Some of the ducks were hanging over the side. The pram cover was on and the hood was up. I glanced behind me.

It was teatime and the front doors were all closed. No one was on the street except me and Mary – and the baby. Then, in the silence, a Saracen came round the corner from Flax Street, moving slowly towards Brompton Park. The foot patrol came next, sneaking along the front of the houses. They looked up at us.

'Baby,' said Mary behind me. She made me jump.

'I gotta go,' I said.

'Baby,' she said again and looked up at me. I stepped back onto the road.

'No. Go away,' I whispered. 'Go away from me Mary Dolan.'

But instead of taking herself and her dead baby off, and before I could stop her, she stretched over to the pram and pulled down the plastic hood. Under it was a pile of yellow dusters wrapped around a tiny bump. I moved closer and stared. It wasn't a baby. It was a strange-looking parcel, grey and plumped up with bits of dark wire and putty at the top.

I was trying to work it out in my head when I saw the barrel of the first soldier's rifle. I looked up at him. And as I was noticing he was too young and was wearing a beret I didn't know, it dawned on me what it was Mary Dolan was wheeling about.

The soldier looked at the pram. Then he turned to me. Not to Mary. To me. The pram was beside me. It's her, I was thinking. I didn't know. I'm not with her. She came over to me. And within three seconds I saw myself dragged to the Saracen, in the court, in the jail, forever.

He looked away and passed on, along with the other soldier on the other side of the street. The next two came up, then the next and soon we were in the middle of their patrol.

'Baby,' said Mary more loudly. This time I got a hold of myself and pulled the plastic cover up.

'She wants a baby,' said the English voice. Another soldier said something else and they laughed.

'Well, she's too old for that doll,' said the first one. He looked at her, grinning, the way soldiers do. She lifted her head and noticed them for the first time.

'How many guns do you think I have?' He looked back at his mate who was listening. Mary stared, then opened her mouth but her tongue lay dead on her lip.

'God, you're an ugly little bird.' His friend behind him laughed. He laughed too. Keeping their hands on their rifles, they both laughed – and thought it was a doll. I turned to Mary.

'We'd better get going.' My voice was cracked and far away. 'Time to get home. It's din-dinner-dinnertime.' Mary went on looking at the soldiers.

'Take the pram Mary.'

She didn't move. So God help me, I leaned over, put

my hands on the pushbar and tried to wheel it away myself. The hanging ducks began to slap and rattle against the back wheel and my schoolbag kept falling off my shoulder as I tried to wheel a doll's pram the way tiny Mary Dolan wheels one.

Then Eddie Breen's icecream lorry, which sometimes was a lemonade lorry, a milk lorry, a whatever-was-wanted-at-the-time lorry, came screeching round the corner. It saw the soldiers and screeched even faster round another. 'The Donkey Serenade' blared out like Pinky and Perky as it went. The soldiers fired on it just before it turned into Highbury Gardens. Then they ran to their Saracen. As usual, everything was fast-motion and slow-motion at the same time. I picked the pram up in my arms and started walking.

'C'mon Mary,' I called behind. 'Take m'arm. Are you coming out with us tonight?' I sounded as if I was always asking her to take my arm and come out with us.

She didn't answer and I didn't care, just so long as she didn't say 'Bomb' in that voice of hers.

'Bang,' said the last soldier, lowering his rifle from where he'd been practising aiming it at my head. He got up from his crouching position behind a garden wall.

'You're dead,' he said. Then he ignored me and jumped into the moving Saracen before it rushed off after Mr Breen and his icecream, if it was icecream he was stocking. We strolled on, in the opposite direction, back to the old derelict bar. As we did so, people started coming out their doors with their knives and forks. They looked up the street to the commotion.

Once in Logue's crumbling backyard, I put the pram down and took Mary Dolan by the shoulderbones. I shaked her hard until her rat's tails were flying about her dopey face.

'Don't!' she squeaked. 'Let me go.'

'God you're stupid!' I said. 'You're so stupid!'

I pushed her away. She fell against the old wall and her eyes began to water. She groped for a stone to put in her mouth. I reached over and slapped it out of her hand.

'Will ye stop that!'

We stayed still for a minute in the quiet, then I said,

'Listen Mary – why's that bomb in your pram?'

Mary pulled at a strand of hair.

'Where did you get it?'

She put the hair in her mouth. I looked at her and just wanted to shove her under a tank.

'Mary! Will ye answer me? Where's your baby?' She looked up, surprised, then pointed to the pram.

'No,' I said. 'That's a bomb.'

'No,' she said. 'A baby.'

She looked around for something else to eat. I looked back at the pram. Then I went over and lowered the hood. I pulled off the cover and lifted all the cloths. The cabbage smell was thick. It was sickening.

I peered at the grey package. There was definitely strings or thin wires, you know, just under the surface. Was it a bomb? What did a bomb look like? Not like a soldier anyway. I touched it. It felt leathery and dry and a bit soft. I pulled at the thick putty at the top to open it.

And that's when I realised the material was see-through. Most of the putty was on the inside only it wasn't putty. It was a bit of a baby's head. Then among the mash I saw a curled-up foot, webby, like a duck's. In the centre was a black cord. I jumped away.

'God Mary God! What have you done? What have you put your baby in?'

'Nafin,' said Mary. She stood apart from the pram, her shoulders up.

'What's it in? Tell me!'

'Don't know.'

'How can you not know? It's a bag! You put your baby in a bag!'

'Didn't.'

'Did.'

'Didn't.'

'Did.'

'Didn't.'

'Well who did then?'

'God.'

A cat with a busted face jumped onto the yardwall, whiskers up, tail up, saw us and jumped off again. Mary left off fiddling with things and took a step closer towards me. I stepped away.

'It come in that,' she said. 'When it come – out – that's the way it come. It was white and red then it went that colour.'

I stared at her. How could she be telling the truth?

'You're a liar Mary,' I said. 'How can it come in a bag?'

'It did. It come in a bag.'

She was watching me and starting to shake. I couldn't stand it. I was too warm in my uniform. It was making me itchy. I lifted the corner of my jumper and wiped my face with it. Then I reached for my schoolbag and moved back to the hole in the wall. Mary didn't move an inch but as I was going through the hole I heard her call, just once, and not at all loud.

'Amelia,' she said.

I got out the hole and went on home.

The Least Inattention, 1975

Discos were great. The Powder Keg was Mondays and Fridays, Reconnaissance was Wednesdays and Saturdays, the Artillery was Tuesdays, the Rearguard Thursdays and the Holy Blessed Child, Sundays. Last night was Tuesday and that meant the Artillery as usual. I went with our Lizzie.

We split up when we got there of course and she went over to be with Grainne (her friend, and not the Grainne who was shot the next day) and those other mad girls she hangs around with. I met up with Bernie, Roberta, Bossy and the others and we began to dance and drink our Carlsbergs as usual. It turned out after a bit that this boy asked Mario to ask Fergal to ask Roberta to ask Bossy to ask me if I wanted to go with him. I thought for a minute and said yes and eventually they got the word back to him. I remember thinking to myself that I didn't recognise this boy. His name was Seamus and we walked and talked and kissed and parted and he only tried to slip a hand once. I can't remember where he said he was from, or if he even did say, or come to think of it, if I even asked. Anyway he asked to see me again and I said no because that's what I always did. One walk out from a disco was enough.

Next day was Wednesday which of course was Reconnais-sance night. It was sunny that morning and for some reason I decided to go to school after all. I got to the Brickfield and could see from where I was standing that Bronagh McCabe and Grainne Bates were facing each other in tempers by the side gate. I could tell from the looks on their faces and by the way they were holding themselves that there was going to be a fight that day.

'Hiya Bronagh,' I said and walked on through. I didn't say anything to what's-her-name because I couldn't stand her. She was one of those beings that did everything for badness, liked to put the boot in and understood the subtleties of nothing. Take humour for example. Once auld Delaney, the English teacher, who spent a lot of time in the men's toilet being depressed, made the remark 'This is war, 3A!' because some of the girls kept making kissing sounds at him every time he turned his back to the blackboard. When Bronagh piped up, 'But Sir, it's not us. We're all ho-mo-sex-u-al', everybody in the class laughed, including him. All except Grainne. 'I'm not queer!' she shouted, her face all ugly and red. So you see, she just couldn't get a joke unless it was diggin' somebody in the head or else spillin' their blood over a pavement. Boasted once of her IQ too. Apparently they had to give her a test at the hospital one year because she was so thick. They were making sure it was thickness in case it was really intelligence so intelligent it only appeared like stupidity to normal people. But no, it was thickness all right. 'So what's IQ stand for then?' I asked when she came back from the hospital. She didn't know and didn't forgive me either for asking and making all the others laugh all over again. But I really didn't know and that's why I was asking but you see what I mean – it was just like her not to see subtleties where there were some or else to see them exactly where there weren't.

Anyway, to move on, to get back to where I was, which was her and Bronagh. I found out a bit later that the sharpness between them had to do with Grainne, the big dope, going out with Bronagh's boyfriend the night before from the Artillery. Bronagh hadn't been there. I thought it surprising Bronagh had a boy – that one would be mad enough to take up with her, never mind go as far as do the dirty and cheat on her into the bargain. But it seemed that one had, and because of it, those two, Bronagh and Grainne, kept having wee digs at each other all morning. Bronagh got more and more wound up and Grainne kept her goin' by basically refusing to deny having seen this boy. That to me was madness. Who in their right mind would go out with Bronagh McCabe's boy in the first place, never mind not deny it afterwards? But as I say, Grainne's IQ . . .

At lunchtime I met our Lizzie in the cloakroom and happened to mention that if she was interested, there might be a fight on the Bone Hills after school. All the girl fights took place on the Bone Hills and Lizzie generally attended, given as how she was in most of them. It would be between Bronagh McCabe and Grainne Bates, I said. I gave her the gist. Lizzie liked gists. She knew where she was with them, they settled her down and they saved on time and explanations. She laughed and said I'd better watch out. I said why's that? – and she told me. At first she didn't believe me when I said this was shocking news to me, for how could I have known, and then she said she thought I must have known, that everybody knew, so how could I seriously have not? When I finally convinced her I really hadn't known and how could she seriously think I'd go out with Bronagh's boy, knowing he was Bronagh's boy, she started to see the sense in what I was sayin'. She shook her head then and murmured 'Ohhhhh dddearrrr' in a very long, drawn-out, concerned sort of voice, but I knew, because I knew my sister, that really, she wasn't a bit concerned at all, that if anything, it was all just a big laugh to her. Some people are terrible. Lizzie and I were different in our approach to how we lived our lives. It amazed me constantly the things that never worried her. Violence in her world seemed some sort of vitamin-taking experience. It tended to be the opposite in mine.

'Keep your voice down!' I hissed, even though she hadn't said anything. I had become aware of all the coats hanging upon pegs in the cloakroom and of how easy it would be for some ears to be earwiggin' among them. She just laughed outright like I'd told a great joke and then dandered off, just like that, to have her dinner.

I was left standing with my gymskirt for the afternoon in my hand. I was in a state of shock for Bronagh was one big beef of a girl, bigger than most big beefs of girls I knew. My only hope was that Grainne Bates would continue to refuse to deny involvement no matter what happened to her. I couldn't eat a bite at lunchtime or get a bit of sympathy from anyone. All my mates, it turned out, thought I'd known all the time too.

By the afternoon classes, I was very jumpy and couldn't stop biting my nails. Everybody knew the fight was booked and it was on for after school. The last two classes were PE.

'We're going outside today,' said yer woman, the teacher, 'to play rounders. So everybody, get changed and make it snappy, hurry up before I lose my temper.'

Bronagh was put in the opposite team, Grainne was in mine. The game started. Bronagh was run out. People shouted 'Out! You're out!' then their voices died away with the dark look of temper on her face. Maybe she wasn't out after all, we decided. Grainne Bates went on shouting, 'Out! Out! You're ugly and you're out!'

Bronagh turned on her. 'Not out,' she said and in a voice that suggested Grainne had better not push it too far. Grainne pushed it too far. She jumped up and down. 'Ye're fat, ye're ugly, yer boy doesn't want ye, ye're a big waste of space and ye're out!'

Bronagh went to her schoolbasket with its little flowery cover and reached her hand in between the slit.

We all agreed afterwards that the basket was suspicious in itself. Nobody ever took their schoolbaskets that held their books and calorie counters into the yard for PE. As for the something that was shouted, some people said it was, 'We'll see who's out!', others said it was the name of her boyfriend – and we all know by now what that was. Everyone agreed though, that it was nothing at all to do with the Provies, the Ra, the Inla or the Troubles generally, but whatever it was, I didn't hear for, at the moment Bronagh was pulling the trigger, a flash of a memory went flying through my mind.

It was of a day at primary school when something different was going on and I didn't like it and I didn't know why. 'We're going to play a game,' said one of these people, mostly women, who came in through the school door one sunny afternoon. They had with them covered-up bags full of what turned out to be black messy stuff and they also had big see-through bags full of chocolate and sweets. They told us about this game that we were gonna play and they lined us up in a row to play it. A man stood at the door and I knew it was so nobody could leave. Then, with everything in place, everything ready, we were called up one by one to have our fingerprints taken. We had our names checked, our hands taken hold of, our fingers stretched over and our prints, in little boxes, spread across. We were talked to all friendly and asked happy gurgly questions by the happy gurgly women, who took and held our fingers and wouldn't let them go. They pressed them down hard in the muck and I remembered my hand being yanked over to a nice clean surface where a female smiling monster pressed it down and made me leave my mark. Then she gave me a chocolate and patted my backside and now, years later, as Bronagh McCabe shot Grainne Bates in the secondary school playyard, all I could do was stand there and think, how strange it was, the way things came back.

After the shooting, the teachers wouldn't stop talking. They became chatty and twittery and wouldn't settle down. Some of them even forgot their positions as teachers and acted as if they were our very best friends. 'She must have been planning to shoot all the time!' whispered Miss Tennyson, digging me hard in the ribs. Why, she had the gun planted, didn't you see it Amelia? In her basket! Why, she this! Why, she that! She can't be in the Provisionals. Isn't she too young to be in the Provisionals? Don't you have to be sixteen to be in the Provisionals?

I couldn't stand it. It was doin' my head in.

I had to get away. I wanted to think about that fingerprinting business and I wanted to know if there was any more of it to come. It was a very slippery memory and the least inattention and it might slide away forever. I didn't want to lose it, not for the second time. I didn't get a chance though, to think about it, for the Peelers turned up and nobody was allowed to leave. I made a note in my jotter, to remind me to remember it. Three Peelers stood at the door and all the questions began to be asked of us. And as well as the RUC, the Brits, a helicopter and an ambulance, the shooting also brought out those other, invisible, sometimes not invisible people, all wanting to know what it had all been about.

As for Grainne, she was taken away to recover from what turned out to be a minor gunshot wound. Bronagh was taken away to be charged as an underage gunman and I forgot her for quite a lot of years. In fact, I can't remember the order of things much after that day. The two things that stick out are one, it had been a sunny, no, a hot day, and two, on a different sunny hot day, I'd been given a chocolate for letting RUC Special Branch get my fingers dirty for their own purposes for a minute sometime in 1971.

Somethin' Political, 1977

Somethin' happened political. Now what was it? Was it the hunger-strikers? No, not yet. Was it a Butcher killing? No, not this time. Was it someone shot in the area? Oh, that's right. It was someone shot in the area. She was a past pupil and she was shot in the area and that's what started it.

Her name's gone now but it happened when she was sitting by the fire in her house in Gracehill Street, just round the corner from the school. It was late morning and the Loyalist gunmen got in to do it, did it and got away. It turned out pretty quick she'd been IRA so Sister Mary Fatima, who wasn't having any of it, announced she wasn't having any of it. She was not going to acknowledge the shooting or say prayers for that soul in assembly. This didn't go down well. The schoolgirls weren't pleased. The schoolgirls weren't satisfied. The schoolgirls decided to riot.

Now, not everybody was that way inclined. That goes without saying anywhere. And some people didn't want to riot but felt they had to, for a political reason that was somethin' to do with their own beliefs and somethin' affecting their own souls. But with other people – and you know the ones I mean – the inbetweeners, those special sort of sympathisers, who weren't Ra themselves but who always turned up at times like these – well, saying no to the likes of them when you were surrounded was never, ever, easy. Yer woman, that teacher, Ms Bannon, or whatever her name was, for all her toughness and hanging out the fifth form window shouting 'Ignoramuses! You know nothing about Ireland! You couldn't point Ireland out on a map!', missed out on something completely. She didn't have to pass them in the areas when she went home in the night because she didn't go home in the night to those areas. So what does not knowing anything about Ireland matter? There's ignoramuses and there's ignoramuses, it seems.

So while Ms Thingy was screeching out the window and the schoolgirls were screeching in the window in a mini-riot, with the main riot taking place on the fringes of the Bone, I was going into the second sitting of the dinners a lot quicker than I initially expected to. It seemed the first rebellion was to refuse food.

Well, I was already doing that, had been for over three years and all for a reason that was inner, top secret and to do with my own soul. Unfortunately for me though, that particular day had been an eating one. I had three a week. The strict rule – and I knew it well, for I had set it myself – was that if I chose not to eat on an eating day, I couldn't then just carry it over to a non-eating day, oh no. Non-eating days were for non-eating. Eating days could be either. That was the rule and it was implacable.

It turned out the tables at the first sitting had all been refusing their food, had crucially been seen by Sister Mary Fatima to be refusing it and, point made, they then had gone on out, on the rampage, joining the general riot which was creepin' ever closer to the streets of the Bone. Now it was our turn. We trundled into the dinners. I was starvin'. We headed for the tables. I could see the stainless steel dishes of potatoes sittin' waitin'.

There was eight, so there was, to a table, and you had to sit wherever you ended up. That was one of Sister Mary Fatima's rules, and it too was implacable. She couldn't bear the sight of a girl for example, going over to one chair, only to change her mind and go to another, especially if she'd already pulled the first one out. It sent that nun into a terrible state. I ended up beside Mary Galt who was hopeless but who used to be okay. Try to say hello to her these days though, and she'd snap the face off you or not even bother answering at all. If ever we ended up together now, take it from me, it was always by accident.

There was also Debra Lawlor, who was sitting opposite. She was jealous of me and I could never understand why. 'Why are you jealous of me?' I wanted to ask but you don't really ask that sort of thing like, do you? So I had to put up with her always looking me over sleakit and making those wee remarks that were never exactly solid enough to lose face or get into a fight over. Then there was Majella Magee who used to be okay but a bit dopey, but who then became not okay and even dopier. She changed her personality, either when she took her first periods or else when she got in on the Provie Scene. She said the Provie Scene was where it was all at. Maybe it was, I didn't know. Vivienne Dwyer of course *was* IRA, and very much an unknown quantity. She always came to school, always looked neat, always did her homework and always came first in class. That's about all you could say of her. Oh yes, and that her brother'd been shot, and then her da'd been shot, and then her other brother'd been shot. She wasn't unfriendly like, but also, she wasn't the sort to go looking for chums or make them known to others if she had any. Put it like this, I never seen her in a disco. The two servers at each end of the table were republicans in name only – Grainne Bates who I hated and Sinead Toal, that slithery girl with the dull eyes who I was scared of. The last person I can't remember. She must have been somebody who didn't feature. Sister Mary Fatima had everyone say grace and then told us to sit down and start eating.

'We're gonna refuse to eat on protest,' said Debra Lawlor. If *anybody* ever tells you to do something, said my ma, don't you be bloody doin' it.

'Yeah, we're gonna stand up to her,' said Bates. 'Tell that nun where she can stick her food. Then we're gonna go out and join them'ins in the fightin', then we're gonna march and sign the petition, then we're gonna . . . then we're gonna . . .' Judge by their tone of voice, said my ma. You'll know it when you hear it. I was hearing it now. They had it all worked out between them and they were looking, first at me, then at Mary, then finally at that other person I can't remember. Then they turned to me again. As I say, feelings were high and scapegoats were always welcome.

I glanced at Mary. She wasn't even listening. I couldn't see her standing up to them though, because she didn't seem to be aware that they were there. On the other hand, I knew she wasn't goin' to eat because she never did. She just turned up to look at the food and there she was now, looking at it, as if, if she'd let it, it could fill her up just by its very appearance. As far as I could remember, her system seemed to be something like: seven days off, followed by seven days off, followed by seven days off, followed by a plate of rhubarb. Something like that. Of course it had been a while since I'd been in her company, and it goes without saying, it was not the sort of thing you'd insult somebody with by asking them about. Just bear in mind she may have refined a few details since.

The others pushed back their chairs and started to stand up, still looking at us, and especially at me. Grainne Bates and Debra Lawlor had these wee smirks on their faces and of course my ma was still in my head. Although I'd always been a bit confused by some of my ma's ideas – it's your disgrace for example, for being bullied, rather than their disgrace for example, for bullying

– I was never able to think of anything better myself. I knew I wasn't goin' to stick it out on me own and who cares for the approval of Sister Mary Fatima or that mad history teacher when it comes to matters in the real world? So in the end, which was very soon, I pushed my chair back too. I couldn't look them in the eye when we left.

I didn't go round to riot though, because that was never my buzz. I knew they were watching from the opposite side of the crowd and I was glad they were seeing me leave. I wasn't going to do everything they said, but all the same, I felt shame about what had happened at the table and about not being able, ever, to do fights. I turned the corner to get home.

The riot had been very loud but already going down The Slant it seemed less. The school wall muffled one side of me and the Bone Hills the other. As I got to the corner by the Fieldy Dam and was already starting to think of something nicer, I lifted my head and there they were, looking at me and this time they were standin' waitin'. They must have hurried round the other side and there was just four of them now. Vivienne was gone. They came up close.

'Why aren't you riotin'?' they said. My ma's fighting rules started up in my head. There are two of them. Here they are:

Rule Number One: (a) Don't start fights. (b) If someone else starts them, get stuck in, for you've got to save face no matter what. (c) If you're not in safe territory, fight in unsafe territory, for you've got to save face no matter what. (d) If one person alone starts the fight, use bare hands and feet unless the other person has a weapon in which case – (e) – use as many weapons as you like. (f) If there's more than one person and even if they don't have weapons, use as many weapons as you can, in order to make up for your lack of numbers. (g)(1) If there's more than one person and the odds are bad – they've all got weapons, you haven't, it's their territory etc. etc., then go for only one of them. Make a quick decision – you'll know by their cut –

and stick to it. (g)(2) Pick the most dangerous for the second most dangerous doesn't count. (h) Think 'I'm going to kill this person' and pretend that that's all you've got to do that's unpleasant for the rest of your life. (i) If really limited – no weapons, load of people comin' at you, not much time, go for the most dangerous and go for one thing – go for the eyes. Yes, ma nodded, it may not be much but when you've been murdered, and you will be, you'll at least have done your best and you won't have run away. Rule Number Two: Never run away.

Of course our Mick, our Lizzie, and even our Josie who's only eight, were able to act on these rules well and quickly, with Mick and Lizzie maybe twistin' them a bit so as to start the fights first. Somehow though, they just didn't work for me. Rule Number One, for example, was hard to get off on the spur of the moment and for some reason, I just couldn't come to grips with that Rule Number Two at all. It seemed to me there was something terribly wrong with it. I never raised this, it goes without saying, for I don't think ma would've liked that. 'I'm givin' it to you straight in black and white,' she told me once. 'Listen to me Amelia. I said listen to me. Calm down and listen. That's better – now listen. Why're ye complicatin' things with questions? Don't you understand? Can't you get it into your head yet? In moments like this – there's just – never – the time.'

There was no time now. Of course it would've been obvious to a bit of dead wood lying drunk in the Bone swamp beside us that Sinead Toal was the most dangerous of the four of them. By the very cut of her, the giving orders side of her, the way she scared the life out of me, I knew my only chance was to bring something down on that head, get her down, keep her down and get those eyes out quick – and to do it now – while they weren't expectin' – while they weren't thinking *I'd* do it, that someone like *me'd* do it, I mean. But I couldn't. I couldn't lay a hand, I couldn't touch that skin, that cold skin, a snake she was – with spiders on. I glanced then at the second most dangerous – but ma'd been right. With the first most dangerous still up and running, the second most dangerous really didn't count. Of course they hadn't yet surrounded me and I could always have run back but you see, there was always the problem of that Rule Number Two.

They surrounded me. Sinead Toal was at the side, small, quiet, standin' as if her mind was somewhere else and as if she just couldn't be bothered. At least that's what it looked like, but when I turned to check the others, she brought somethin' down on my head that I didn't even know she'd been holding.

I lost my balance and they got me down proper and got on top and got stuck in. Thoughts flew about my head in a terrible mixed-up scramble as I pulled and twisted and grabbed and missed in a very all over the place way. Fights were never my thing, had never been my thing, even though I lived my life constantly expecting to be in them.

They got me on my back and Grainne jumped on my front. She was wild with excitement.

'Hurry up,' she squealed.

'You hurry up,' said Sinead Toal. 'Do it like I told ye. Do it now!' Sinead was cradling my head real tight, almost choking me with her forearm across it. Still she sounded fed up, like it was all just not worth the bother. That, of course, meant nothing, as the last time she seemed like that, she'd hit me over the head with something. The other two were scrabbling about, lying over my arms, my legs, my whole body. Majella, I'd given up on. She'd stopped being a friend a long time ago and Debra was just dying to get revenge for something she thought I had that she couldn't get too. It was Bates though, who brought her hands to my face and I screamed when I realised what Sinead was putting her up to.

Straddling me on the dried-up muck and the brown grass of

the Bone Hills, her ugly mouth open, the very saliva drippin' out of her, there was a look on Grainne Bates' face that had lost all sense of itself. Her body jerk-jerked against mine and as those fingers grappled my strugglin' face and Sinead pulled on my head and my hair to steady me, Oh Ma Oh Ma, ran through my head for I knew what it was they were up to. It was my eyes they wanted. My eyes. I closed them tight. I squeezed them hard. It was my last chance, so it was, to hold onto them.

'Grainne Bates!' I heard a voice say. 'I see what you're doin'. I see you, Grainne Bates. I said I see you.'

There was a sound in the air close to us – a strange clickin' whirrin' noise – that at first I thought was part of the riot going on behind us. It was only when it stopped, that I realised it had been coming out of Grainne Bates' throat and that she herself hadn't known she was doing it. She looked up, gave a sort of strangled sound, then immediately let go and got off me. The others did the same. I sat up and spat dust out of my mouth and looked around. Vivienne Dwyer was standing a few yards away and Sinead Toal, in a split second, had disappeared.

Vivienne was standing in her shiny Oxford brogues, her clean beige tights, her long polyester skirt with the front pleats that had gone way out of fashion at the end of Second Year. Her black blazer with the gold buttons that nobody ever buttoned, was buttoned all neat to her chest and her school basket, with its green and yellow flowery cover, was hanging all neat and tidy from her elbow. Her hair was in two plaits, as usual, with no stray bits coming out, and they were fixed at the ends with old-fashioned bows. These ones were gold and purple. From where I was sitting and because of the state of my mind, the sun that was going down behind her made a light come from around her edges. She moved closer and I saw she was looking at Grainne Bates as if Grainne Bates wasn't right in the head, as if she was somebody who'd been caught doing something, the same thing they were always being caught doing, that might have been funny once but now was not in the least bit funny at all. Grainne stepped back from Vivienne and of course, so did the others.

'You'd better dust yourself down Amelia,' Vivienne said. She helped me up and did my back. Then she did my front also. I don't know what I did. I remember seeing her basket sitting on the ground, the little elasticated bits of the cover around the sides and the wooden ruler sticking up through the slit. I remember seeing a lot of things – the marshy pink reeds that grew in the middle of the swampy ground, long and thin and swaying in the air, UP THE PROVIES, UP THE RA, UP THE IRA in white paint on the Fieldy Dam wall, the chalk that ran down the side of one hill, the railings at the top of all the others, the sky, a puffed-up white cloud – I saw a lot of things. The others, meanwhile, had snuck off.

Vivienne took a Twix out of her basket, broke it open, pushed one up and offered it to me. My hand was shaking when I took it. I said thanks and any shame that'd been starting about me getting myself beat up and about the terror for my eyes, seemed to just die then and go away. She crooked her arm out and I linked it and we started walking down the rest of The Slant, away from the riot that was going on in the distance, past the Shamrock that would be packed for drinkin' that night and on down, into Ardoyne, together.

Miscellany and Drift, 1978

A few things happened at the same time. First there was that film starring Robert De Niro, the one that had the Russian roulette in. Then there was that treasurer fella from Sinn Fein, the one who was supposed to be minding all the money but who was secretly spending it instead. Finally there were the fed-up and easily-bored delinquents, who took it upon themselves to dress up and muck around and pretend to be vigilantes for a day. These three things came together the way three things generally do and produced a fourth, unexpected thing. Some in the know though, said that was a load of rubbish, that the fourth had nothing to do with the other three, that it was a long time coming, but that in the end, it would have happened anyway.

The ones who decided to play the Russian roulette were the usual type of people who would decide to play Russian roulette. They didn't see anything wrong in what they were doing because, as far as they could see, they were just a normal bunch of lads who, on a different occasion, might have decided to go out and wreck and tear and be disruptive and have a laugh for a day. It just so happened though, they'd seen that

87

Robert film the night before in the Shamrock and had been very taken with it. It had been dark and daring and very, very exciting and had left them all thinking that it would be a great idea to go out and get a gun to see if they could miss shooting themselves too. So the next day, in the late afternoon, they went and got a gun, and they didn't bother with the bit about the betting or with the bit about the money because what, they'd all wondered, had been the point about that? None of them realised they weren't supposed to be eager and 'What Vietnam War soldiers?' a puzzled few had even said. They 'borrowed' their weapon, a proper sort of gun with a proper sort of spin, and a single bullet, from an arms dump they weren't supposed to know about or were supposed to leave alone if they did. Wrapping the gun in a Co-op plastic bag, they headed down to Logue's, the old derelict bar at the bottom of Brompton, where, by convention, all bizarre, subliminal, dark behaviours of the inhabitants of the area were always and forever carried out.

So while the Russian rouletters were on their way down Etna Drive, all in happy fantasies of being Hollywood moviestars or else of having people weeping copiously at their funerals, Aloysius Fallon, one of the Sinn Fein H-Block Sub-Committee Stand-Ins for the Stand-In Deputy Treasurers, watched them pass from his upstairs window and was jealous. He was jealous of their youth, jealous of their lack of worry, jealous of their carefree natures and jealous of the way they never had to give a damn about anything. Look at them, he thought, jaunting around, smiles on their faces. Oh, how easy life was for young people! He sighed, dropped the curtain and turned back to his own dire predicament.

He had gone up to his room to count what was left of the generous H-Block donation and to say that he was horrendously terrified at what he had found, would be a bit of a gigantic massive understatement. This man was supposed to have handed over six thousand, three hundred and twenty-seven pounds and fifty-six pence to Dessie Agnew, the temporary Stand-In Treasurer of the H-Block Committee. But when Agnew got himself arrested under Section 11 of the Prevention of Terrorism Act, Fallon was then instructed to hold onto all this money himself. This he had been doing or rather, he hadn't. Little by little, and then big by big, he had been losing it on the horses and losing it on the dogs and was wondering what, for the life of him – for the very, very life of him – he was going to do about that now.

He looked again at the open coffers on the bed. He'd spent three thousand on the mangy mutts, two thousand on the big fat horses, a fair whack on all types of drink and five pounds a time on those mean bitches of prostitutes down the town. Other bits and pieces went here and there on God knows what, and what was left was two pee. Even deluded and suffering, as Aloysius Fallon was, from crazed addictions to gambling, alcohol, sex and everything else, he knew he couldn't possibly hand over two pee to Sinn Fein and expect he'd be able to get away with it. He thought of the IRA and of all the people he had known who were dead and he slumped against the war chest and quietly panicked.

Meanwhile, somewhere else in the area, five teenage boys were being warned by a man from the Ra about their juvenile delinquency and their disruptions of the peace. When this man went away, giving last-ditch warnings about kneecappings and beatings which the five did their very best to pay attention to, they kicked and shuffled their feet in the dust and finally decided that one way to pass the time and have a bit of a laugh would be yes, to juvenile delinque all over again. So they dressed up in that dark, menacing colour, the one lots of legal and non-legal organisations are very fond of, accessorised their outfits with gloves, monkey hats and sunglasses 'borrowed' from the chemist and tied their mammies' multi-coloured, hairspray-smelling headscarves round their faces. When they were ready, they admired each other with cries of 'Ha!', 'Get a load of Spud!' and 'Right on Fergal!' and got down to business, which was to stop everyone and everything coming into the area and question and bully and check all ID. They exempted a few grannies from this interrogation, and that meant, of course, their own.

It had all been meant as a geg really, for they didn't believe for a second they'd be taken at all seriously, but what they discovered was that, in spite of the fact they hadn't set up a roadblock, and weren't even pretending to have any weapon of any kind, every single person screeched to a halt, wound down their window and tripped over themselves to be nice. They handed over whatever information they were asked for and the teenagers, delighted at so easily getting their own way, assumed the power they were given and abused it. They carried on being tough and uncompromising and basking in glory until half past five, when they felt a bit peckish and decided it was time to go and get a little tasty something or other to eat.

Just as they were about to go and hold up old Tom's for Dark Chocolate Homewheat, some nice Mr Kiplings, milk, bread, cooked ham, lemonade and whatever else that took their fancy, a three-ton brewer's lorry rounded the corner from Chatham Street. They heard it and saw it and simultaneously whooped 'Drink!' and ran with happy hands out to seize it. Their hunger pangs forgotten, they together and as one, had the great, predictable, gut reflex idea of robbing the lorry of all its lovely vodka and rushing down to Logue's and getting drunk.

Unfortunately for the delinquents, although certainly a liquor lorry, it belonged to none other than that notorious hothead of the area, Eddie Breen. That meant it was full of something else. It was full of IRA dynamite, being lovingly transported from one IRA arms dump to where it was being likewise awaited at another. Needless to say, Mr Breen was not happy at this interruption. He was a man who considered himself easygoing and of gentle good nature, but it was not the sort of gentle good nature that had stood up well, even once, to being tested. On being waved down by the youths before they realised their folly, he slammed on the brakes, made a fist out the window and hollered, 'Pull down them scarves, yiz impostors!'

The vigilantes did no such thing. They ran away down the street and although Mr Breen would have liked to have given chase and run them over, he was a punctual man with a great sense of his priorities. Instead, he satisfied himself by shouting that, when he was finished, he was going to come back, and discover all their identities, and hunt them down one by one, and kill them.

The vigilantes tore down Butler Street towards the Brompton Park corner, collapsed against railings and wet themselves. They staggered about laughing, howling, whooping, punching the air, shoving each other until they fell over in the narrow entry and couldn't get up again. Rolling about, they clutched at whatever there was and wept and gasped, for it seemed playing vigilantes was definitely the Bee's Knees, funnier even than sex jokes. When at last they calmed down, they exclaimed how lucky they were, what a laugh everything was, wouldn't they live to be a hundred and did any of them have any ideas as to what they could do next?

It was six in the evening when the eight Russian rouletters stepped over the threshold of old Logue's Bar. The first thing they saw when their eyes adjusted to the darkness was Vincent Lyttle talking to himself in the far corner. As soon as the youth saw them, or more to the point, as soon as he caught sight of the gun being taken from the plastic bag, he rushed over to Rab McCormick who just so happened to be the one holding it.

'Rab!' he cried. 'You are Rab, aren't ye? From Oakfield Street? Well listen Rab,' he got in close. 'I don't know if you'd be interested or not, but I could arrange a standard or a relief-cut scroll engraved with a monogram on that there forty-five. What do you say? Take time now and think about it. Don't rush into these things. You would be getting distinctive decorative markings unique only to yourself. It's all the rage in America. So what d'ye think? Do you want a scroll Rab, do ye, do ye? Or how about,' he changed over to Rab's other ear and almost, but didn't, put his arm around him, 'an underground gun storage container? Holds sixteen guns all at once. And if you're interested in trigger hammer, ambidextrous thumb safety magazines that are well-bended but not blued – although you'd have to prise the rounds out singly with a knife to fit them into that there gun – oh well never mind, generally speaking though,' he went back to the first ear, 'do ye know much about saving time and ammo and long-life lithium batteries that can be purchased easily at any camera shop?'

'Guy's fucked,' said the others, watching him and whispering behind their hands.

Poor Rab McCormick swallowed and being quiet, shy and a bit nervous of mad people, looked to the others for guidance. Vincent Lyttle, as anyone in Northern Ireland could tell you, was quite definitely known as a person who was mad. This was common knowledge to everyone, even the Royal Ulster Constabulary and the British Army, who normally didn't pay attention to the little things like that. He was always in and out of Purdysburn, took tablets designed for mad people, had to go and talk to psychiatrists, and cut himself with forks, knives, glasses, papers, pencils and whatever, wherever and whenever he could. Worst of all, he was known as someone who went about trying to sell guns and ammunition to normal sorts of people when it was obvious to everybody he didn't even have any. What more proof did one need?

So as this boy now tried to persuade all the others to have fancy little designs put on all their weapons, they ignored him, turned away and got busy. They pulled over the old tea-chests, empty beer kegs, planks and whatever came to hand easily, and arranged all in a circle for their game. One teenager then steered the mad boy towards the door in order to get rid of him but wasn't able to because, at the critical moment of shoving Vincent out, a whole bunch of other young people busted right in. They had seen the rouletters striding purposefully down the street and naturally wanted to know what they were up to. They looked around the bar at the industrious rearranging and the first thing they said was, 'What's that there gun doin' on that there crate?'

The treasurer went quickly down to Logue's with a determination to end his life before his terror of death could stop him. If he moved fast and kept focused, he told himself, then the mistakes and the messiness attached to an existence that had never worked in the first place would be over with. He didn't consider whether he was hanging himself because of his sexing, his drinking, his moneying, his robbing, his deceiving or whatever those things he was addicted to were standing in for. What he did know was (a) he couldn't face an IRA reprisal and (b) he couldn't do it at home for he didn't want his young son dandering in and finding him. So, ignoring, as he'd always done, the ordinary things – his neighbours, the sky, the pink early-evening sunlight, the breeze from the end of summer upon his arm – he went straight down the street, not looking at anything. This made sense in Aloysius Fallon's world. What was the point in looking at ordinary things? No ordinary thing could ever save him now.

Inside Logue's was a racket. He peered over the threshold at a pile of squawking teenagers, squabbling and fighting and, as he saw it, having a great time. His eyes roamed in the semi-darkness to the only sturdy beam in the place and then back to inconsiderate youth who had gotten in before him. Little shites, he thought, and with this he turned and left. He clasped tighter than ever the plastic Co-op bag with his suicide note and his wife's red nylon washing line within it. Apart from somewhere to hang it, he had everything he needed for the rest of his life.

Eddie Breen, the explosives deliverer, who also worked as a milkman, lemonade man and hobby horses operator, had just come from an impromptu meeting of the local IRA. He was sick sore and tired, he said, in fact he shouted, of juvenile delinquents, holding everybody to ransom as if they owned the bloody place. As a deterrent, and to stop them reoffending, why didn't he nip out now, he suggested, and shoot them? He was soothed and dissuaded from this by members of his unit who told him he was a top man, of great talents and abilities, not someone to go wasting on miscellany and drift. They told him to go on home and have his dinner and cool down and put his feet up, for they'd be needing him for an important job later on. After he left, appeased but not as yet back to his self-styled kittenish good humour, the Provisionals sent Joe Columba Hale to seek out the offenders, which he now did for the second time that day.

He found them this time staggering down Butler Street with a big pile of stolen drink in their arms. They had a keg of Smithwicks, a keg of Bass, a crate of spirits and whatever else alcoholic they could get their hands on. They were taking it all to Logue's to get drunk and were surprised when Joe Columba stepped out in front of them. In spite of, or maybe because of, the reality all around them, the young people in the area didn't really accept that they could die. Their neighbours or brothers, or mothers or sweethearts perhaps, but they'd go on forever and they'd have great crack. Besides, they thought, with so many bigger disruptions going on all over, was there really any point in bothering with the likes of them? Apparently there was. Joe Columba, now all stern and military, and without the least preliminary or a 'How're youse all doin'?', gave them short shrifting orders to turn up to be kneecapped in Logue's old bar-room at seven o'clock that night.

'I did warn youse, youse pack of eejits,' he said and then he went away to get on with his own personal kind of normality. The boys watched him go and they were upset and some said 'I'm not going!' and others said fuck, fuck and fuck, but this was all just swashbuckle for they knew what would happen if it turned seven o'clock and they didn't do as they were told and show up. That meant there was no time to lose. They had to get drunk immediately. They synchronised their watches and as they couldn't hold on till they got down to Logue's bar-room, they sat down where they were on The Pad and started drinking. They had fifty-three minutes to get blocked. Doctors on the TV warned about getting blocked. 'If you're going to be kneecapped,' they complained, 'please please please – don't get drunk! It's hard to deal with the injuries when you're drunk, it makes our job that much more difficult.' 'Tough!' said the boys with complete total selfishness. They had every intention of getting drunk and as drunk as they possibly could.

Most of the new arrivals in Logue's considered the Russian rouletters off their heads and crazy, but all the same, they wanted to watch and be a part of it all. They went to the sides of the bar-room, as far away from the gun as they could manage, and they waited for the shooting, the ritual, to begin. There were fifteen players, the original eight now joined by six others, plus Vincent Lyttle, who hadn't a clue why he was sitting there. The participants were in a haphazard circle, sitting on old planks placed across tea-chests, with an upturned crate in the middle that was holding the bullet and the gun. The players had more or less reconciled themselves to having an audience and some were even beginning to like the idea. The few who didn't, and who expressed their objections through grumpiness, sulkiness and cries of 'Them or me!', didn't really mean their ultimatum. Everybody wanted to be part of this innovation, to be important, to matter, to be remembered always, to play the first Russian roulette (or so they thought) ever to go down in Ardoyne.

This obsession with making an impact had started in earnest to grip audience and players alike. Every one of the young people, except Vincent, speculated as to how often a game of Russian roulette could be carried on. Could they turn it into some sort of institution, move it towards the weekend, keep it private and exclusive, have it as some Friday night cachet? Would its reputation spread and make them all famous? Would enthusiasts make films? Would learned people come from all over the world to do documentaries and features about them? The fantasists carried on, making plans, building castles, altering and re-altering details, until Rab McCormick, the sixteen-year-old, who both hated and craved attention, put the bullet into the chamber, spun the cylinder, pulled the trigger and fell dead off the plank at their feet.

The vigilantes heard the shot but of course they weren't interested. They were busy rendering themselves as near unconscious as they could get, without actually passing out and becoming so. They knew they had to leave enough awareness to get themselves to Logue's in order to be kneecapped, but they didn't want to leave that much awareness that they'd feel the pain of the bullets going in. Just as they thought they'd judged a nice distinction and were staggering to their feet to get going, a whole bunch of other boys came belting round the corner and knocked them back over with cries of 'Guess who's dead!'.

On hearing Rab McCormick had shot himself, and in a game – of all things – of Russian roulette, the vigilantes were first of all peeved and a bit sulky as to why no one had thought to invite them. They had no time though, to start laying accusations because, amazing and unbelievable as this piece of news was, the fact that poor Rabbie had done it in the old bar-room meant that the Peelers and the Brits would be along there at any time. The vigilantes' predicament was that, if they didn't turn up to be kneecapped as ordered, the presence of the security forces would be seen as a feeble excuse. But if they did turn up, the Peelers and the Brits would lift them without question, for it was natural after a shooting to arrest any young man. They'd be taken to Castlereagh to be unfairly treated about something intriguing they knew nothing yet about. It was a frustrating, disillusioning position to be placed in and they couldn't think of solutions or get any of their thoughts straight because of the clamour around them and because they were drunk.

In the end, they supposed they'd have to go along and hang about the sidelines because the Provies, who would be spying on the Crown Forces, would see, if nothing else, that at least they'd turned up. The five were in agreement and were about to set off to do this, when a twelve-year-old boy rushed round the corner to give up-to-date news. In his role as a Fianna scout, this boy had been sent to tell the vigilantes they were not now to go to Logue's to get themselves kneecapped, but instead to go to an empty safe house that was nearby. They were to go round the back, Junior said, where they'd be let in by a responsible sympathiser or, in other words, he puffed his chest out, his very own self. They were to wait in the house until the security forces had gone away, the coast was clear and everything was again peaceful, for then the proper people would come along and take them out and shoot them as arranged. The boy then left to pick up the keys of the safe house and the vigilantes made their way to this new rendezvous. They took extra drink with them for they had no idea how long they might be made to wait. They needed enough alcohol, ideally, to last them forever, but to see them through the night would be something if nothing else.

At the junction of Brompton Park and Etna Drive a crowd had now gathered. Older adults, running to dark Logue's on hearing the shot, found a body they couldn't recognise lying in a pool of what looked like black oil. Some of the young people who had been involved in the shooting had run away to the Bone, not to return until everything was over with. Others only ran as far as the Brickfield, for they wanted to sneak back in just a little while. The latter, more addicted to detail and onrunning excitement, stopped when they got to the Brickfield. They got their bearings, their breath, and then headed back again. Not one of them said a word about the shooting to any of their elders, who anyway weren't asking, but instead were trying to shield their offspring from something unsightly lying in Logue's nearby.

The Royal Ulster Constabulary arrived and took over, accompanied by Saracens, foot patrols, a clattering helicopter and an ambulance or two. The crowd alternated between watching the scene, listening for information and whispering the usual 'What's going on? What's happened this time?' They themselves rapidly cleared up the mystery of the dead young person by taking stock of the number and identity of those who were left. Of course there were no witnesses and when the police got round to questioning, they had to make do with no information, which was the most, usually, that they could ever get. They circled flesh and blood on the floor, flesh and blood on the walls and on the ceiling of the old bar-room, and the media composed notes on scraps of paper in their hands. The people of the area watched this, in the open, or else spied from safe distances. Others again practised taking aim at uniforms from behind windows and partly-closed doors.

While all this was going on, a plainclothes detective got out of an armoured car and peered across the road towards the commotion. He was looking at Vincent in particular, for the poor mad boy, unlike the others after the shooting, hadn't had the sense to follow their example and run away. He was standing by the white tape thrown up around Logue's old bar-room and was now, as he usually was, in a fantasy of his own. The detective was peering, not because the boy was sick and peculiar, which he was, but because he had a spray of dots all down his right side. The dots were red and they were minuscule and the policeman went on squinting until a uniform, seeing this, went over to put him right.

'No need to bother with him Sir,' he whispered. 'He's a headcase, a spacer, a one hundred per cent nutter, a boy with built-in speakers, a total balloon.'

The detective looked annoyed. 'Well, correct me if I'm wrong Constable,' he said. 'But is the spacer covered in thousands upon millions of red dots or is he not?' The constable had a look. 'Oh yes,' he said. He peered. 'He's covered in dots all right. D'ye want me to go over and arrest him then?'

The police, soldiers and ambulances went away, taking Rabbie McCormick, Vincent Lyttle and the rest of what they could glean from an uncooperative population with them. As they did so, they passed the little Fianna boy, who was on his way to hunt out the keys of the safe house. It turned out though, much to the boy's frustration, that somebody else had already taken them, which meant he had to go all the way to Rosapenna to pick up the spares. He'd hurry, he thought, for his plan was to pick them up, get back, get that door open, get those boys in, return the keys, then rush away and discover more of what that exciting Russian roulette had all been about.

So he got the keys, which in reality didn't take a second, but children being the impatient, can't-wait, hasty wee things that they are, he considered it something like a lifetime. He rushed round to the supposedly empty house at No. 79, Havana

Street, fitted the key in the lock, turned it and went inside. He shut the door after him and took a step into the darkness. Something was wrong, and that's what made him stop. Peering across the room, his eyes started to adjust to this darkness, and when they had adjusted, he looked, and saw his da, hanging dead down the wall.

The four operators assigned the kneecappings went round to No. 79, Havana Street but there didn't seem to be anybody there to let them in. Very amateurish, they thought. Very, very unprofessional and, frowning, they went round to the back to see if they could get in that way. In the entry, they found the five vigilantes, twitchy, biting their nails, worrying, one second, that they might not be drunk enough, then worrying the next, about their state of sanity for ever having turned up in the first place. It transpired the back door of the house was locked also but, given the gunmen now had everything they needed, it no longer mattered whether they got in or not.

Jat McDaide, the leader of the team, took his gun out and ordered the five to line up in front of him. He told them to spread out, to be still, not to squirm and then said he was going to do them in both legs. It was no longer to be just in one, and he explained that this was because of an updated instruction. This updated instruction didn't exist in reality for Jat McDaide had just made it up on the spot. Jat was like that. He added extras to every job he'd ever been sent on and the other recruits, raw, unquestioning, sixteen years old, said nothing. They stood to attention and waited to be told what to do.

Now Mickey Lovett, not one of those operatives and, in fact, someone people weren't sure was a Provisional, a member of the Inla or just another leader of something with his own murder squad, got to hear of this imminent punishment and was not a bit happy when he did so. Apparently his one-time friend Jat had kindly offered to do the kneecappings but Mick suspected this was all part of a big ruse. He believed that Jat had requested the job so that, after splurgily going to town on four of the vigilantes, he would do as little damage as possible to the fifth. The fifth just so happened to be Jat's own cousin, Brendy, who, if Mick read the situation right, would end up with something like a tiny wee cut. This was not at all fair in the circumstances, thought Mick. It was something that sullied the very name of punishment and it was something Mick was determined Jat wouldn't get away with.

Now, it wasn't that Mick Lovett was of a particularly high moral character or even that he had anything personal against Brendy McDaide. It was just that (a) Brendy McDaide was Jat McDaide's cousin, (b) Jat had a habit of killing other people's cousins whilst leaving his own alone, (c) Mick had a cousin once mysteriously killed and (d) Mick knew there'd been no mystery about it. And it wasn't either that Mick had minded Jat killing his British soldier relative. It was just that, fifteen years old at the time, he still would have liked to have been consulted first.

Of course Mick didn't admit this openly, to others or more importantly, to himself. Instead, he first made up his mind to kill Brendy and then he worked backwards to find a good reason for doing so. This didn't take long. He used the logical, linear, grown-up side of his brain, weighed pros and cons for thirty whole seconds, was rational to the point of insanity and came to the conclusion that the killing wouldn't arouse conflict, altercations or any sort of controversy, just so long as it was essential and in the interests of The Cause. He decided it was in the interests of The Cause and so, that settled, all he had to do was to sit back and wait and find out how Jat had proceeded and discover whether his own suspicions were really true or not.

This didn't take long. Jat and the team reported back to their unit at forty-six minutes past nine. They said that, on the whole, everything had gone satisfactorily. Jat himself had put sixteen bullets into the legs of four of the anti-socialers but somehow, he smiled sheepishly at this point, he'd gone off target with the very last one. He managed only to nick him, he said, although he didn't say the nick had been with a Swiss Army Knife, and a toy, plastic, indeed imaginary Swiss Army Knife at that. In summing up, he announced that four out of five wasn't bad for a single punishment outing, and that it would deter other delinquents and so, overall, was good work for The Cause.

Now one has come to expect in any kneecapping situation, that someone will always end up being dead. This kneecapping was no exception. On hearing Jat's version reported back to him, Mick immediately left the building and headed round to Havana Street. He found the vigilantes, as the recruits had abandoned them, squealing and crying, in a bath of their own blood. They were bobbing up and down, trying to get up, grabbing at bystanders' ankles, then moaning and shrieking and falling back down again. They kept begging anyone who would listen to go quickly and get them ambulances. It hadn't occurred to them to call ambulances themselves before being kneecapped.

Mick found, just as he had expected, that Brendy McDaide was not among them, so after asking round the area, he discovered which tin shack, sawdust-on-the-floor drinking club his quarry was now in. It turned out to be the Saunders and, picking up his pace, he checked his gun in his waistband, and then he headed up Butler Street to get to the Saunders too.

Brendy indeed was there, and he was sipping, for he was now tired, on an orange-apple lemonade. If it seemed he had no time for his recently shot buddies, that was exactly because he had not. Brendy, like everybody else in the area, had to forget and move on to the next thing. The next thing was to be in the Saunders talking to some other boys. He was giving a little lecture on how to be a vigilante, how to be a daredevil, how to dare death. He was relieved and quietly exhilarated that he hadn't been shot by his cousin and he boasted about this also because he couldn't stop. 'Gosh, is that right?' said an awestruck rouletter. 'That's absolutely incredible! How d'ye have the nerve for it? So what happened next?' What happened next was that Mickey Lovett came into the Saunders. Brendy stopped declaiming. Everybody looked up.

Minutes later, the police, soldiers and emergency crews came back again, some of them to the Saunders, to pick up dead Brendy, the rest to surround No. 79, Havana Street. First the wounded were brought out on stretchers from the entry, crying for ambulances even though three ambulances had already arrived for them. The vigilantes gave off a mighty stench of alcohol and 'I do wish they wouldn't' was all the ambulancemen said. While this was going on, the police in their flak jackets, their guns at the ready, waved down traffic, searched all vehicles and checked everybody's ID. At the back of Havana Street, they gave up circling single bits of blood and single bits of bone and single bits of undeniable other evidence and chalked around the whole blood-soaked entry instead.

Inside the safe house a routine was in progress, involving the Fianna Fallon boy, the security forces, the sniffer dogs and the dead. The Fallon child was frozen with his hair sticking out the back of him, and a soldier was wrapping him up in a blanket and carrying him out stiff. The treasurer they left hanging, for the CID, the forensic pathologist and the police photographers. The man's hands still seemed alive, clinging to his throat. Perhaps he'd changed his mind at the last minute and that would have been typical of Ally Fallon. Aloysius Fallon had always been a vacillating, fluctuating, erratic sort of guy.

And then there were the neighbours. Neighbours varied greatly. These ones had come out to speculate as to what was now going on.

'Yes, but why hang yourself?' said a man after the suicide

note had been passed round among them. Another Fianna boy had managed to sneak it out just in time. He'd been unable to budge Ally Fallon Junior though, for the boy had just gone on staring, stubbornly refusing to look away from his da.

'Aloysius could have explained his predicament to the Provisionals,' said a deluded woman.

'The Provisionals would have understood him,' said a deluded man.

'They would have been sensitive to his problems,' said a deluded woman.

'He could have paid them back in instalments,' said a completely insane man.

'What I want to know,' said another of the neighbours, harking way back to poor Rab McCormick's death earlier on, 'is why that poor boy shot himself when he had his whole life in front of him – his whole life, you know, another sixty or seventy years?' None of the others had any answer to that and they shook their heads in puzzlement. They grew silent and heavy and lowered their heads and got depressed. All in all, they had no idea, couldn't figure out, why one person would choose to kill himself to stop someone else from doing it for him, or why a sixteen-year-old might not want to live another sixty or seventy years.

As for poor Brendy, most people, of course, said nothing. He'd been a cousin of Jat's, who'd once been a friend of Mickey Lovett's, who'd once had a cousin killed in a so-called mysterious murder affair. All the neighbours knew therefore without asking any questions, that when it came to feuds and personal grievances, some things were best left forever unsaid.

There were no funeral masses on the Sunday but on the Monday, Aloysius Fallon, Robert John McCormick and Brendan McDaide shared a service. They were buried in Milltown Cemetery later that day. Everyone said wasn't it terrible, wasn't it awful, wasn't it a waste, wouldn't it always be remembered? But it wouldn't. And it wasn't. Everything got eclipsed, always got eclipsed, by the next, most recent, violent death.

Echoes, 1978

The DHSS said I had to go on this new Youth Training Programme instead of signing on the dole. It was being opened in the old mill on the Crumlin Road, just up from the jail, a new idea, they said, to bring the school-leavers of both communities together. The boys could do Painting and Decorating, Carpentry, Car Mechanics, stuff like that, and of course, us girls could learn to type. When I got there on the Monday, the place was still being fixed up. There was plastic sheets over most of the concrete floor, with partitions here and portakabins there and drills going and wires hanging and people wandering about everywhere. The big old flax machines were gone and the place was cold and full of echoes.

I went into the makeshift office and was glad to see Bernie. Bernie was from Ardoyne too. The others were from the Shankill. There weren't many Catholics on the factory floor either. I was told they had two supervisors in every workshop to stop sectarian fights among the boys but only one in the office because there was just us girls.

Bronagh was two hours late. I was trying to get the hang of a typewriter when I heard her big voice saying,

'I'm not goin' into no office Mister!'

I looked up and there she was, laughing at Clement Strain, the poor manager, who didn't know what to do. Then, when she looked through the window and saw me, she jumped up, ran over and banged on the plastic.

'Amelia! Were you made to come too? The bastards! Aren't the dole just bastards!'

'Do you know her?' said Mabel, turning to me and looking disgusted.

'She lives over our way,' said Bernie, waving back to Bronagh. Bronagh saw her too and banged harder. The plastic broke.

'Bronagh Immaculata!' cried Clement, who was one of those soft-spoken forgettable people who always went on BBC2 late at night to talk about peace. Bronagh laughed again.

'She's not coming in here,' said Mabel in a low voice. Kay just grinned.

Clement got up and walked round the desk to tell Bronagh off. He examined the broken plastic, took measurements, then told Bronagh that she had to pay attention, to be careful, to be cautious, to pay attention and above all, to pay attention. Wasting his breath there, I thought.

I turned to reassure Mabel that Bronagh would be going out to join the boys in the muck and that she'd nothing to worry about.

'Who's worried? I'm not worried! Who said I was worried? I'm not afraid of her!' I shrugged and turned to my Agatha Christie, which was a clever way of having a read and learning to type at the same time.

Bronagh went into Painting and Decorating. That lasted two hours until Dennis from the Shankill had a go at her about padded bras. He laughed real loud. Bronagh laughed real louder, and reached over to him.

'Got your dick yet?' she said. 'Let's see.' She took hold through his overalls. A fight broke out and paint was spilt off a ladder, along with two boys. Bronagh was given a verbal warning and put into Car Mechanics and Dennis was sent home to rest his balls.

Next, Bronagh wanted a go on Mario Morelli's new motorbike.

'Lettus have a spin! Lettus have a spin!' she'd cry, thumping him hard in the top, bottom and middle of his back.

'Haven't got it Bronagh,' he'd answer. 'It's in Ardoyne, I swear to God. Leave me alone.'

'You're a liar Morelli,' she said. 'I'll find it.'

And she did. On Wednesday I was typing an article about insanity from a magazine to get some speed and practice and Mabel was timing me with the stopwatch. 'Go Amelia! Go!' she yelled and I took off. We'd just come to this bit about people who saw maggots in their food that weren't really there, when a racing of the precious bike was heard. Bronagh speeded by the office window and straight into the tea-hut. We rushed to the door.

'She's outta here,' said Eddie, one of the supervisors in Car Mechanics. He was rolling out from under a car at the noise over the way. 'God knows what she'd do to our stuff. Plumbin' can have her.'

Plumbin' didn't want her. The boys gathered in a corner, muttering and slapping basin wrenches and foot-long spanners into their palms. When Mike, one of their supervisors, appeared, they rushed over to him.

'Mike! Why us? She'll ruin everything. Send her into the office with the other girls.'

'Yeah – into the office, into the office,' they all bleated.

'Oh no you don't!' cried Mabel, barring the way with her beefy little body. 'That's *sex* discrimination!'

At the mention of sex discrimination, Alicia Flo, our office supervisor, threw open her door and glided out like a big sailing ship on the move. She was about forty and spent a lot of time reading someone called Mary Daly, crying out 'Gender bias! Gender bias!' every time a man said anything at all. She also kept talking about some spiritual trip she made to south Queensland when she was only nineteen.

'I lived in a treehouse,' she told us on our first day. We just looked at her. She nodded. 'Yes, that's right,' she said. 'No Radio One, no "I Lost My Heart To A Starship Trooper", no ABBA, no Miss Selfridge, no powderpuffs, no . . .' She was off, amazed and taken aback by everything there wasn't. We went on looking, amazed and taken aback by her.

Now here she was, coming out of her office which was a kind of grocer's shop. A basket of newlaid eggs sat on her desk and a ham shank hung, strung on the wall beside her year-planner. She glanced at all the males in a sulky huddle with beautiful Bronagh picking herself up in the middle of them.

'God that was great,' laughed Bronagh, glowing with happiness and wiping a load of dust off her. ''Cept I was a bit slow in stoppin' I think.'

'My bike!' wailed Mario.

'My dear!' cried Alicia Flo, shoving Mario out of the way and going straight over to Bronagh. 'You're covered in blood!' Then she frowned and leaned in close. 'Tell me Bronagh Immaculata. Don't be afraid. Did one of those boys strike you?'

Bronagh laughed even louder.

Digory, nicknamed Dock, took a step forward. He was a plumbing supervisor and he looked an old man with all the worrying he did about all the terrible things in the world that were bound to happen sooner or later.

'We think, Alicia Florence,' he said, 'that Bronagh Immaculata here would be better off going into the office with the other girls – I mean young women.'

'Gender bias!' cried Alicia Flo.

'Religious discrimination!' cried Bronagh, enjoying herself.

'They're all Snouts in Plumbin' so they don't want me!'

'Oh hush my dear, hush,' whispered Alicia Flo. 'Of course it's discrimination, but rather . . . *sexual* discrimination.'

A roar of protest went up from all the boys and it was then they noticed that, as Protestants and Catholics, they were standing a bit too close together. They didn't like that and right away began to fix it. They pushed and shoved and cursed with little words like 'Watch it Fenian bastard' and 'Fuck off Orange dirtbird' being thrown in.

'What's going on?' said Clement Strain, arriving back happy from his BBC2 interview on how well all the young people were integrating. The scuffles were broke up and everybody ran over to speak first.

'Quiet!' he shouted, his hand a big Stop Sign. Bit by bit, he pieced together what had happened and surveyed the damage. He turned to Bronagh.

'Now young lady, this is your second verbal warning. Next time it'll be a written one. Get yourself cleaned up and go with Mike.'

All the plumbing boys groaned and a few said fuck's sake but nobody said cunt because they knew Alicia Flo was specifically listening with pursed lips and folded arms for one of them to do so. When they'd all shuffled off, she said 'Very good, carry on' to us and turned and went back to her larder. We watched her go, shaking our heads. She sure was peculiar, that one.

For a while things went well in Plumbin'. Bronagh really showed an interest. Apparently she bent half-inch pipes with her hands and really liked it, bent three-quarter-inch pipes with bending rods and liked that even more, sorted out her fittings, was very fond of flux and soon Mike and the baby plumbers stopped being so jumpy. This lasted till the third week when she went and fell for Lester.

Now Lester was from the Shankill. He worked in Carpentry but the main things about him were his eyes and his smile and his long-legged look. Us in the office noticed those legs right away on Day One.

'Funny kind of name though,' said Bernie, pulling a face. 'A Protestant English sort of name. I'd be cut off like, to go with someone called Lester.'

'Well Bernie,' I said, 'not everybody can be called Ignatius St Stephen Findbarr,' which was her boy's name.

Of course Bronagh didn't notice him at all until one morning we watched as she got herself twisted round a cistern, up some ladders, round a corner and very near to Carpentry. Lester was watching too. He went over, looked up at her and 'Want a hand?' he said.

She came into the office.

'That blond boy with the funny name,' she said, 'what's the crack with him?'

'Lester doesn't go with Taigs,' said Mabel in a firm voice, keeping her back to Bronagh. 'It would be unthinkable. An unnatural bestial act.' She leaned over to me and Bernie. 'No offence or anything youse two.'

'What about Roisin though?' I said. Roisin was the new girl who had started having wee chats with Lester during break-times. Our complaint of course, was not that she might get him, but that, being from Turf Lodge, she shouldn't really be on a training programme over our way in the first place.

'They're trying to balance it out,' said Kay. 'Get more of youse Catholics in.'

'But they still shouldn't have her,' said Mabel. 'I know youse are Catholics like, but at least youse live just over the road. She should be going to her own YTP up the Falls or something.'

Bronagh, meanwhile, was frowning during all this. Then her brain cleared and she said,

'Well, I'd better go and ask him out before she does.'

We all squealed.

'No, Bronagh, no! Girls don't do that!'

'And I already told ye,' said Mabel, giving a big huffy sigh. 'Lester doesn't go with Taigs.'

'Besides,' she went on, swivelling round to look Bronagh up and down, 'you're not exactly feminine are ye?'

Bronagh stopped on her way out. For once in her life she was flustered.

'What d'ye mean?' she said.

'I mean,' said Mabel, 'look at *you* compared to Roisin!'

'What d'ye mean?' said Bronagh, looking down at herself.

'I mean,' Mabel rolled her eyes, 'look at *you* compared to Roisin!'

'What d'ye mean?'

Roisin walked in and we all went quiet. I saw Bronagh looking her over and thought she was sizing her for a fight. But she just stood quiet with her head on one side and then, instead of going back to Plumbin', she went in to see Alicia Flo about something. At lunchtime she disappeared.

In the afternoon she came back into the office with a brown chemist bag.

'Listen Amelia,' she said, fiddling with it. 'I'm leaving Plumbin' to learn office sort of stuff startin' tomorrow.' I couldn't believe it.

'D'ye see this here eyeshadow . . .' she said quickly, opening the bag.

'That's rouge Bronagh.'

'Oh! Well, d'ye see this here eyepencil . . .'

'That's lipliner Bronagh.'

'Oh! Well, d'ye see . . .'

Me and Bernie and Kay all looked at each other. I'd never seen Bronagh all dolled up and was sure it could only be a disaster. I was right.

Next morning I was typing a Dr Very Important article on The Only Way To Cure Anorexia Is To Forcefeed. Mabel was giving herself a spelling test – and cheating. Bernie was playing

Monopoly with Kay, and Roisin was outside, very relaxed, talking to Lester, also very relaxed, by the hardboard. The door opened and Bronagh walked in.

My God, I thought.

'Oh Bronagh!' cried Bernie.

'Well I ask ye like!' said Mabel, her finger at her next unmarked spelling. 'Is it the whole face or just the bits that are coloured in?'

'I'll deal with this,' said Kay, picking up her own make-up bag and steering Bronagh down to the toilets.

When they came back, Bronagh looked nearly normal except for her cheeks which were scratched red where Kay had had a scrub at her. While they were gone, Bernie decided it was time to have a wee talk with Bronagh about that blouse she was squashed into, that skirt that was too small for her arse, those shoulder pads that were lost on top of her – those sorts of things – and I said I'd have a wee word too. I'd talk to her about that chisel, hammer, screwdriver, wheelbrace and all those nails and things she had, that were stuffed like mad into her new clutchbag. But before we could do any of this Tom, the supervisor from Carpentry, shouted down from the office roof,

'Lester, get up here please. It's not breaktime yet.'

'My God!' cried Bronagh, jumping off the desk, kicking off her wobbly high heels and yanking open the office door. 'Twinkle's out there – chattin' him up!'

We saw Lester's lovely, gorgeous legs leaping up the ladder and Bronagh's not so gorgeous ones going after.

'Wait for me Lester,' we heard her cry. 'I'll help ye.' A boy yelped and jumped off the roof, probably before he got pushed.

'Bronagh Immaculata McCabe!' came Tom's voice. 'What are you doing? You must go down. This is dangerous! Watch that beam, watch that . . .' There was a ripping sound.

'Her skirt,' said Bernie, nodding. We all looked at the ceiling.

113

'Keep away from that plank . . ' don't put yer . . .' There was a crack.

Bronagh's big calf came through the ceiling, followed by the rest of her, then Tom, and then all the other boys.

'Ach!' said Mabel, jumping up with the rest of us out of the way. 'That wee girl's no shame.'

Gentle Tom lost his patience. He gathered Bronagh up and dumped her, covered in dust, into the first swivelchair he came to. Then, holding her there with one shaky hand, he grabbed up typing paper with the other and shoved it anyhow into the machine. He tried to put her fingers on the keys while she carried on smiling over at Lester, who was getting pushed out the door by Mabel, along with all the other dusty shaky boys.

'Type! Type!' Tom cried, pushing her fingers down. He was desperate and the hammer in his toolbelt kept banging against the edge of the desk. He looked over at us.

'Look yous'ins, help me!'

Roisin dandered over and leaned over the typewriter.

'Bronagh,' she said, 'these here are called keys. You hit them hard and they leave a mark.' She paused. 'But more important than any of that rubbish, Lester and me're goin' to the pictures tonight.'

'Ach sure, he's an auld cunt anyhow,' said Kay at the end of the day.

'And come the Twelfth, they'll be fell out,' I added.

Nothing. Bronagh wouldn't be cheered up.

'I just hope Lester knows what he's doin',' said Mabel. 'Practically puttin' his foot on the wrong leg there, so he is.'

Clement busted into the dust-filled office, coughed, slapped Bronagh's first written warning down on her desk, glared at her, coughed again, then turned and left. Bronagh hadn't noticed.

'Well, if ye get the sack,' said Mabel, 'the likes of *you* could always get a job down at Dew Barry's.'

Bronagh lifted her head. 'What d'you say?'

Mabel sniffed.

'It's a well-known fact,' she pronounced. 'Only hoors wear anklechains.'

Bronagh looked down at the dainty silver string wisped around her heavy industrial foot. Frowning, she sat up and shoved a chunk of masonry off her desk.

'What d'you say?' she said again.

'You heard me,' said Mabel. 'Only hoors wear anklechains.'

Two doors opened. Alicia Flo came out of her office and Clement Strain out of his.

'What d'you say?' said Bronagh.

'What's going on?' said Clement.

'Only hoors wear anklechains.'

'Mabel!' cried Alicia Flo. 'What did you just say?'

'What d'you say?' said Bronagh.

'Only hoors wear anklechains.'

'What did you say?' said Clement.

'What d'you say?' said Bronagh.

'Stop that!' said Clement.

'Only hoors wear anklechains.'

Clement banged the desk.

'What d'you say?' said Bronagh.

'Bronagh Immaculata! You will receive your second written—'

'Only hoors—'

'Mabel Dempster! Consider this your first—'

'What d'you say?'

'. . . wear anklechains! Wear anklechains! Wear anklechains!'

'What d'you say? What d'you say? What d'you say?'

Clement Strain spun back and forth, dizzy and dizzy-making to look at. Bronagh, standing, legs apart, hands on hips, her red 36B Wonderbra bustin' through her dusty ripped blouse, was at one end of the room. Mabel, back straight, head up, in a navy pinstripe suit, now also dusty, at the other. The office had started to fill up again, for this time the whole crowd of boys from the factory, and there were a lot of them, were all trying to squash in too. Every one of them had some sort of tool or other in his hands.

'Only hoors wear anklechains,' said Mabel, blushing now because of the boys, but carrying on all the same.

'That's it – you're fired!' shouted Clement.

'Girls! Women!' cried Alicia Flo.

Bronagh opened her mouth.

'You're both fired!' Clement went on, jumping in before her.

Still facing Mabel, Bronagh's gaze then moved across the room to Roisin, standing beside her own typewriter in the corner.

'Hey!' cried Clement, seeing all the boys for the first time. 'Get back to work!' he yelled at them. 'Get back to work!' he yelled at us. Neither the Protestants nor us Catholics moved.

'Go on Bronagh,' said a boy, nudging her from behind.

Still talking to Mabel but now looking at Roisin, Bronagh opened her mouth.

'What did you say?' she said.

The Peelers interviewed everyone in Casualty. I was getting the last of my stitches when finally they came round to me. I told them there had been cries of Fenian, Taig, Billy Boys, Remember, general effin' and blindin' and No Pope Here. No, I didn't hear what became of . . . No, I most certainly wasn't involved in the . . . No! I didn't witness what happened with the Black & Decker, I didn't touch any of them breezeblocks and – were they stupid? – of course it was about the Border.

Except for Roisin that was. She was in Intensive Care. Bronagh was in the barracks. The typewriter was in the barracks also. The machine and her were being checked for fingerprints and I had a feeling I wouldn't be seeing Bronagh again, for another lot of years.

The BBC decided not to do the documentary on the mixed community pilot scheme in Northern Ireland after all. What was left of the factory was closed that day and the next day, I went down to the dole and signed on.

Troubles, 1979

Mick and Mena came in early from the Star. Giggling, they squeezed onto the old, fake-leather, L-shaped settee between Mick's ma, Mick's da, one sibling, four cousins, five friends, three neighbours, their own four-year-old daughter and began to slabber and paw each other as usual. Pretty soon they were having sex. Everyone else kept their eyes on *Starsky and Hutch*. After a while, Mena whispered loudly that she'd soon be needing the toilet roll, a remark so witty that both she and Mick giggled all over again. At this, Mick's ma spat up a huge lump of catarrh, Mick's da twisted the poker in the fire and a neighbour turned up the TV. Not enough. Mr Lovett then asked his child, or one of his nieces, or one of their friends or maybe his granddaughter – he could never be sure – to be a good girl and switch to Ulster TV. There, something bloody and gruesome was just about to happen so everyone tried to settle to that. Except for the lovers. Nobody, it goes without saying, noticed them.

Eventually Mick's ma remembered she had to go upstairs and scream her head off and got up and left the room to do so. Mick's da remembered he had to go and stand at the gate and thrust his daughter-in-law's shuddering leg off his lap to get out there. The three neighbours said ach sure, given it's a fine night, why not stroll about and see what the crack is? Ten-year-old Josie said she was going to get drunk and her cousins and friends said they'd help her. Finally, when little Orla went off to tie up her dollies and give them damn good hammerings for being bossy, there was nobody left in the room but the couple themselves. They tore off their clothes, jumped onto each other and had big, spread-out sex everywhere. Every so often they moaned and whined on top of an old bit of furniture and Bullet, the mongrel, paws in ears, moaned and whined underneath it.

At half-time, Mick said 'Let's go eat' and they went into the kitchen holding hands. This needs some explaining. They weren't actually holding each other's hands, for that would've been embarrassing. No. After a bit of preliminaries, they ended up sort of holding their own. The preliminaries were these: keeping Mena naked as usual, Mick tied her hands in front, using cord, wound round and round, and round and round, and round and round and round, and then the other way, between her wrists, and round and round and round. When he'd finished, was satisfied it was tight and that she'd never break free on her own, he then tied her ankles similar. Mena prepared, he then slipped back into his shiny purple trunks, the ones he was so very, very proud of, held his wrists together and pretended – for Mick had a great vivid imagination – that his hands were tied tightly together too. Of course they weren't, and indeed, certainly never would be, for Mick was of the opinion that only pervert men had things done to them like that.

So when everything was snug and tight, absolutely right, exact and precise as Mick needed it, the couple ended up in the kitchen holding hands. Of course the first thing they noticed was what was on the stove. As usual Mick's da had made a big pot of curry and a big pot of rice for the next day's dinner the night before. Mr Lovett always left the dinner sitting on the stove to cool down, nice and slow and at its own little pace, growing all sorts of bacteria on the way. Mr Lovett suffered depression and this 'Will the dinner, won't the dinner poison us?' routine was his latest way of coping with his circumstances. So that's where the pots were, on the stove, cooling down and gathering tiny invisible microsomethings. The biggest pot, full of chicken curry with mango chutney from a jar sauce, was at the front, and the second biggest pot, full of white sticky rice, was sitting piled high behind it on the back.

Mick released his pretend tightly tied-up hands and felt the outside of the currypot with his fingers. It was cool. He lifted the lid and stuck his hand in. Mena awkwardly stuck her hands in too. They both ate and stuck their hands in. With greased curried fingers, that wouldn't go numb awhile yet, Mena then lifted the slanted lid off the rice. They both stuck their hands in and then licked the clingy sweet grains off their palms, their fingers, their knuckles, their arms, and prised them off their teeth with their tongues or else just flicked them away with their fingertips. It's important to note here that Mick and Mena licked their own palms and flicked their own rice off their own teeth, for if there was one thing they strictly weren't into, and in fact were very much against, it was mixing any kind of sex stuff with food. 'There's something wrong with that,' said Mick once in a terrible scowly mood and of course Mena was not going to gainsay him. 'There's something wrong with that,' she said too. 'People who mix sex and food are sick bastards,' said Mick. 'I think people who mix sex and food should see psychiatrists,' said Mena. 'Those sorts of people should have their heads kicked in,' said Mick. 'I love you Mick,' said Mena. Mick and Mena were definitely not peculiar. They believed in keeping sex and food close, very close – but when it came down to it, they still had to be separate.

So there they were, stuffing away in the tiny kitchen, Mick, small, slim, very strong, taking pride in his tiny firm butt and Mena, large, a big explosive pear, taking pride in the amount of room she took up. Mick tore open a loaf and they pulled off clumpy bits of that and slabbered and gobbled and laughed as they chewed their way along. Because they couldn't eat like normal people, because, word was, they weren't normal people, they spat tiny bits of food all over the place. These bits landed in the sink, on the window, by the dishrack, on top of each other or simply just back in the pot.

'I suppose we shouldn't be doing this,' said Mena just when they were coming to the end of doing it. On the whole Mena never ventured an opinion unless Mick had given it before her. The reason she was doing so now was because she'd just had her first half of glorious, wonderful sex and knew that if things were to go well and she was to have her much craved-for seconds, she'd have to, during the interval, throw some reckless piece of effrontery into her talk. Indeed it was expected of her. Sometimes Mick responded by allowing her to get away with it, sometimes he didn't and would gag her.

A few bare bones: if there was one thing Mick Lovett couldn't stand, besides perverts and people who put curtains up in cars, it was the sorts of girls who walked and talked and swung their arms and said whatever they liked when they felt like it. Those sorts of girls drove Mick to distraction, sent his brain into whirls of desire and his groin into spasms of hatred. From no matter what angle he looked at it – and he did try to be fair – it just kept seeming to him that the more those sorts of girls opened their mouths and threw their weight about, the more they were asking to be incapacitated. Usually the way he dealt with these sorts of girls was for Mena to pretend to be one. Sometimes she would be an annoying person they both actually knew and sometimes she'd be a made-up one. Today she was a made-up one and, although they were carrying on

121

as usual, including all the Had To Says, Had To Dos, Had To Looks, Had To Bes and Had To Seems that Mena had to take care of, the fact was that, ever since they'd borrowed that real girl from down the town that time, their pretend stuff had never been the same. There had been something so fantastic, forbidden, unrestrained and essential in that wholly satisfying encounter that, for the sake of their very sex lives, they knew they needed to get their hands on another such real girl quick. In the meantime, until she came along, they supposed they'd have to make do with the imaginaries.

'. . . suppose we shouldn't be doin' what?' said Mick picking up from Mena's very cheeky, outspoken, opinionated remark. He hated bossy girls. There was no way, no way, a bossy girl was gonna snap the trap on him. 'I hope you're not givin' me cheek Mena. Are you givin' me cheek?' He licked his fingers and shoved them in.

'No, Mick,' said Mena. 'Although I can be a vain, man-hating bitch and deserve every good lesson that's comin' to me, in this case I just mean maybe we should leave some for the others. Yer da made it for everybody after all.'

Mick scowled and they both looked in the pot. There was nothing left to leave or, more accurately, there was so little left, there may as well not have been.

'We'll leave that,' he said. 'Just a wee bit more. Eat Mena, I said eat.'

'Okay.' Mena pawed in some more curry and pawed in some more rice and Mick watched her closely from the side-lines.

'That's enough,' he said. 'I said that's enough. Make the tea Mena, I said make the tea.'

'Okay.' Mena hobbled over to the kettle and lifted it with her clunched-up bunch of greasy fingers, hobbled over to the sink and set it in. She then turned on the tap with her clunched-up bunch and stuck the kettle's spout up underneath

it. All this took some time and she was still panting and struggling and reaching up and stretching over and leaning down
and searching and searching for the Marvel and the tea when
one of Mick's sisters, the middle one, the anorexic one, opened
the door and walked in.

A few bare bones: this sister was called Amelia, she was
seventeen, she never ate any food, suffered constant tummy
aches, didn't understand why and was outrageously, sexually
thin. She came in the door with that arm-swinging vigour all
six-stone hunger-strikers are very keen on – or at least while
on one of their extraordinary highs. So it could be said she was
happy till that moment. Catching sight of her relatives however,
she stopped being happy, stopped swinging her arms and her
high dissipated in an instant. Apart from the obvious signs of a
brother watching the spectacle of his struggling wife with his
penis peeping more and more from his purple, and his gasping
wife in her tied-up, bare-fleshed, amply confident nakedness,
reaching here and there and everywhere to encourage it, most
sisters could have told anyway from the familiar state of the
pulled-apart house what it was their brother and his wife had
again been up to. I say most sisters because, although the settee
had been overturned and devastated in all its segments,
the sideboard destroyed with all its drawers splayed out, the
china cabinet in shock, the dog's tail between its legs and the
entire upholstery a bit scary to sit on, Amelia Lovett still tried,
by a massive effort of will, not to see anything and not to
respond.

This, of course, was part of the deal. For yes, there had long
existed between Amelia, on one side of the coin, and Mick
and Mena, on the other, an unacknowledged equilibrium
whereby she spent a lot of time determined not to notice what
they were up to, and they spent a lot of time determined to
shove what they were up to in her face. This unspoken arrangement had worked well down the years, until recently, when

Amelia began to find she couldn't do it anymore. To her shock and dismay, and Mick and Mena's surprise and delight, the starver's fortress was at last beginning to crumble. Chinks were appearing in her armour, her precious lack of food was saving her no more and their greedy sexing was becoming apparent from every nook and cranny of the house. For Mick and Mena, this was marvellous news. For Amelia, their sister, it was the opposite.

Still holding the doorhandle, the anorexic took in the big fat stuffed-up scene and reeling for the first time from the up-close inescapable reality of it, began, 'Youse are two . . .' But instead of finishing with 'manky shitty dirtbirds' or 'mingin' piggin' gorbs', she turned and shouted the unprecedented upstairs.

'Ma!' she yelled. 'Da!' she shrieked. 'I know youse are up there! Come down and do somethin' about this!'

This was unfortunate. First of all, it was a bad time to walk in on Mick and Mena and second, it was always a bad time to turn and shout for help. Of course Mr and Mrs Lovett Senior were never going to come, and of course little Orla was far too busy on the bannisters, masturbating her dollies before hanging them by the neck until they were dead, to go and tell Granny and Grandda they were wanted. So when Amelia, alone, turned back to deal with the lovers, the lovers, together, came forward to deal with her. Unbeknown to Amelia, while she had had her back turned, they'd exchanged a look very significant, a look full of excitement, a look that presaged a pulsating little agenda, top secret, all of their own.

For yes, using that quaint little process called telepathy, they consulted and agreed to jump their sister, get her down, stop her from moving, partially restrict her air passage and stick as many things as they could up inside her. They didn't consider this rape or anything nasty like that because in the way certain minds work, they managed to convince themselves that it was just one of those playful sorts of behaviours that stop a bit short of unsociable. She'll be all right, they told themselves. It wasn't as if she was intelligent. It wasn't as if she'd remember and anyway, weren't they going to leave her alive at the end of it?

Exchanging further glances and telepathic communications therefore, and trying to look harmless, which was difficult for them, they slowly, very slowly, edged their way out of the kitchen towards her. Mick was rapturous at this incredible spontaneous adventure and was amazed, above anything, at not having thought of it before. He forgot, of course, that he had. Mena, more indulgent than ecstatic, was always happy to do whatever her beloved wanted, just so long as she got her whack at the close of it. Besides, she thought, if skinny arse here was to get a shock at being fiddled with, that would be entertainment now, wouldn't it? She might put on a bit of weight, Mena speculated. She might become a compulsive eater. She might surpass Mena herself in the things she could consume. That was a really fun thought for Mena. It amused her immensely. If there was one thing that consoled her in her great loathing of anorexics, it was the joke life constantly played against them. No matter how gluttonously they starved themselves, no matter how indulgently they self-deprived, if they didn't die eventually of their complete utter silliness, then they always got fat in the end.

So, panting with genuine effort, Mena readjusted her features, tried not to lick her lips, tried her best to hide her anticipation, tried to look helpless and supplicating, and lifted her bound hands to her sister.

'Oh Amelia,' she pleaded. 'Help me.'

Amelia didn't want to help her. Preferably, she wanted Mena to fall over a cliff and bust open with a big bang at the bottom of it. She considered her sister-in-law a gross, repulsive, big fat monster, who doubled her bodyweight daily deliberately. She began to back away from this outrageously constructed, disorganised piece of tissue and before long, was out again in the hallway. Mena, followed by Mick, hobbled and hopped after, their daughter watching while doing what she called her 'ticks' on the bannisters. The child's dolls hung from these bannisters also, and they, too, were bobbing up and down. The others hardly noticed as these tied-up naked dolls kept hitting them. Absently, they kept brushing them aside. Mick and Mena continued to advance, smiling all the while at their sister, but it was hard work, this smiling, this trying to be patient, and soon their patience ran out and their fingers twitched and clutched as they prepared themselves to grab.

On the whole though, things were going splendidly for the young couple. They were now just a few feet away, and if only Mick had left well alone and allowed Mena to get on with it, they might well have achieved all they were after. But no. Just as Mena was about to clamp Amelia, trap her easy, get her nice and good, Mick made the error of mixing foreplay of fighting with foreplay of sex and broke his own strict food rule into the bargain. In one rash moment, he let his lack of control run away with him and flung a lumpful of curry at his sister. It should have landed slash-splat exact on her cheekbone but Amelia saw it coming and ducked and instead it slash-splatted Lizzie, another Lovett sister, who was not at all anorexic and who was just that minute coming in the door.

A few bare bones: Lizzie Lovett was nineteen, had boundless destructive energy and always and everywhere, solved everything with fights. Most people took time off, at least sort of, to have, say, sex, but not her. Lizzie's mindset was such that she forwent lovemaking at every opportunity for anything properly confrontational that might lead to a brawl. This could be a fleeting brush of words, a so-called teasing banter, a heavy non-stop hammer, a locked and bloody embrace. In this violent behaviour, she very much resembled her parents, at least as they

used to be, before they'd become useless and afraid. Lizzie of
course didn't notice their new condition and why on earth
should she? She was young and fit and ruthless and free and
had forever and ferocity on her side. She never joined the
Provisionals because the Provisionals wouldn't have her, and
she never joined the Inla because the Inla never took time
off from their vicious, murderous, internal feuds to consider
anybody else but themselves. Initially disappointed in not
being allowed into any illegal, proscribed, paramilitary organisation, in the end she came to be glad of it. Just think. Being a
Volunteer would have hampered her enormously.

So here she was now, coming through the door, minding
her own business, humming a little tune even, and what happened was a handful of slish-slat got thrown at her face. She
frowned and so did her best friends, always to be found in the
vicinity of each other. There were seven of them – Sharon-
Mary, Bea-Mary, Theresa-Mary, Grainne-Mary, Ann-Mary,
Mary-Mary and Mary-Ann-Kate. The eight of them had
known each other since childhood, had started school together,
ran away together, took Catholic sacraments together, been
teenage vigilantes together, practised first kisses and slipping
things in vaginas together, all showing a high regard for each
other and a pathological antagonism for everybody else. So,
having just come from a fight, which they judged so-so to
satisfactory, the Girls, excited and bloody and coming through
the doorway, witnessed Mick Lovett's provocation together. It
was clear he had started it, but equally clear he wasn't going
to get away with it, for as he and Mena jumped upon Amelia,
Lizzie and the Mary-Marys jumped upon him. The Lovetts
Senior, of course, stayed away in their bedroom, and Orla
Lovett and dollies, busy at the bannisters, paused in their sexlife,
to look and learn on. Only Bullet, suffering multiple, severe
nervous breakdowns since puppyhood, got his chance to run
away, and did so, yelling and crying, far down the road.

Now this thing of motivation has to be gone into. As far as Mick was concerned, it was not a bit about rape, of course it wasn't. He had merely been going to borrow Amelia, stun her, get her down, get Mena on top, while he became exploratory, taking it a bit further, then a bit further after that. The curry splat had been an accident, Lizzie should not be so hot-headed and her friends should completely mind their own business, he thought. It was like they'd no separate lives, he'd noticed. As if they couldn't operate independently. Bizarre like, he'd call it, if anyone were ever to ask.

As far as Amelia was concerned, it was absolutely about rape, of course it was, but there was no way she was ever going to admit this. And how could she? She was counting calories, swallowing laxatives, shoving up suppositories, turning round mirrors, being friends with food, not being friends with food, nightmaring about clothes, being at war with her body, indeed, with any body, so it was inevitable, now wasn't it, that bodies would be the very things that would hit her. Ten bodies to be exact – or eleven, if you counted, as she would, her own.

As far as Mena was concerned, this was simply about persecution and about how she and her dear husband were forever intruded upon. Here they were, minding their own business, about to incapacitate Amelia, but prepared, as always, to leave Lizzie and those head-the-ball friends of hers alone. She knew, given their sudden appearance, it wouldn't be long now before she and Mick were lying dead together and this terrible, yet at the same time romantic thought, made her hope that afterwards, when it was all over, Mick would untie her and hold her, and croon and butterfly-light kiss her, while she fell asleep, crying happily in his arms. In the meantime, she thought she might as well hack away at Amelia and do her damnedest to inflict whatever harm that she could.

Last of all came Lizzie and her intimates and, as far as they were concerned, it was all about Mick Lovett, so they kicked fat Mena out of the fight early on. Amelia, superfluous to everything any of them had ever stood for, naturally they never got round to noticing at all.

The fight went on, of course it did, and then it was over, not because Mr and Mrs Lovett Senior came rushing downstairs crying 'Oh no! What have we done to help create this situation, and is there anything we can now do to help change it?' No. That was what didn't happen. The fight ended because, after a lot of punching and pulling and crashing and banging, Lizzie drew out the poker, the long, hot poker, that trusty old treasure from so long ago, and whacked it with a 'Take that ye whore!' a whole lot of times off her older brother's head. She burnt his hair, burnt his head, burnt his back, burnt her hands, burnt everybody else and burnt giant holes all over the carpet. Eventually Mick fell over and she and the Marys flung themselves on top. They ripped him apart, tore his flesh from his body and left him to die in the hallway. The whole thing took a matter of seconds and when it was over, the Girls went into the kitchen, refreshed and reinvigorated. 'Cheer up,' they said to Mena, slapping her bare bum on passing. 'Givvus a smile. It'll never happen. Take it from us, you'll see.'

Mena, pins 'n' needles in her fingers, fierce biting sensations in her stomach, and a blunt wee butterknife in her bound hands, left off attacking Twig Amelia, dropped the weapon and crawled her way, widowed, to her husband. Amelia, holding her head, which was ripped down the middle, also crawled, in the opposite direction, down the hallway. In the kitchen, which was at the end of this hallway, the Girls were already again in a tight circle. They were laughing at the weirdos that existed in the world and in proof of this, and of perverted people everywhere, they tossed Mick's lurid trunks back and forth between them. They were eating salt and pepper, which is entirely within their characters for, not knowing food like Mick,

Mena and Amelia, they hadn't yet grasped there were other things they could have. They were feeding themselves, feeding each other, stroking, fondling, raucous in their lovemaking, and only broke off into silence when Amelia, whom they vaguely felt was related to one or other of them, pushed the door open and fell in onto the floor. They stopped what they were doing, looked at her, looked at each other and, from their expressions, it was clear not one of them was liking what she saw.

It wasn't that Amelia's blouse was ripped open and she was naked to the waist, for their blouses were ripped open and they were naked to the waist too. That was fine. Nothing wrong with that. It wasn't, either, the blood, or the way her cut nipples were protruding, for they had their blood spilt from their nipples and they were excited about all that too. No. It was none of that. It was her face, or rather, it was a nerve in her face, up near her cheekbone, which was twitching and jerking repeatedly up and down. The Girls knew immediately that jumping nerves were mental things and that mental things were scary things so they looked at each other and were very very afraid. Sick-in-the-head people were frightening, sick-in-the-head people were infectious, sick-in-the-head people, they knew instinctively, were people you had to stay away from. They decided to cheer Amelia out of it.

'Hiya,' said Bea-Mary, trying to pretend nothing was the matter, that Amelia, whom they didn't dislike after all, wasn't having a breakdown right here in front of them.

'Where've you been?' said Mary-Mary, warmy, smily, friendly and inclusive. 'What happened to your face? Get up and sit down Amelia, and spill the beans and tell us all.'

'You missed a great fight,' said Mary-Ann-Kate and Theresa-Mary together. 'We got Pervy Mick. He's dead. Did you not see him then, on your way in, lying out in the hall?'

'Here,' said Lizzie, offering Amelia a tray of laxatives. 'Have some of these. We know you like them wee things.'

130

As Amelia didn't respond and didn't even seem to hear her, Lizzie left the tray on the floor by her foot. It was true they themselves didn't care for those things called Senacot, and this was not sacrilegious. The likes of them would never understand the magic power that existed in one of those round pills. So, having cheered Amelia up, at least as they saw it, the Girls closed ranks and turned away from her again. They forget about everybody, divided a twelve-year-old nutmeg out between them, chewed a few icecubes, then washed everything down with an ancient packet of dried mustard and a rusty tin of peas.

Amelia, still on the floor, put a hand out in front of her but jumped and pulled it back when her leg, spasmodically, kicked the tray away. It rattled against the washing machine and banged into the corner and she couldn't get herself up and out, for between her legs had gotten wet. This had never happened before. She'd made damn sure it had never happened before – and, although it had been an accident, nobody would believe her, they'd point and get angry and say it must have been her fault. They'd say arousal and wetness was proof she'd been asking for it, proof she'd been deserving of it and proof that whatever then happened to her could only serve her right. She must stay where she was therefore, and not move a muscle, and when she was dry again, the evidence against her would be gone. So she stayed where she was, lying in the kitchen, and didn't do anything except have two thoughts over and over. How could anyone, went one of these thoughts, ever engage in that stuff willingly? How could anyone, went the other, choose to do that thing, sex?

Out in the hallway, the lovers were not destroyed. It was true, bits of Mick were strewn all over but Mena, loving him in sickness and loving him in health, and loving him in ripped-up pieces, gathered up these pieces in her now greyish-blue hands and tried her best to stick them back together. A martyr she was, uncomplaining, submissive, full of devotion for her husband. Mick knew this and opened his eyes and was touched to see her administering to him. She was bending over him, attending to him, nursing him, just like any loyal, loving wife would do in such a situation. He was outraged, of course, as any loyal, loving husband equally would be. This was in seeing his woman tied up and treated so sadistically and one of these days, he thought, his sister Lizzie would go far too far. His patience would run out, he knew, and he'd lose his temper and take a long stick to her, but not today, he thought. Today, he was much too in love with his wife to hurt anyone at all.

'Darling,' he murmured, stretching up and kissing her. 'Here, let me help you. Let me untie those awful bonds.'

'Dearest sweetheart,' he cooed, going on, as Mena started to cry softly. 'Oh wee one, oh honey, it's all right, it's all over, I'm here now, oh don't cry my pigeon, oh don't cry my love.'

So he helped her with her bonds and she helped him with his pieces and it was all so moving that, had there been anybody in the audience bar their own daughter, their four-year-old Orla, the whole place would have broken down at the sheer romance of it all.

On the landing, Orla finished watching her parents, finished doing her 'ticks', got off the bannisters, kicked her knickers off one ankle and hauled in her dolls. She untied them and kissed them and murmured 'Darling dears, oh honeys' and put them in a shoebox, and put the lid on. She fell asleep by their side on the landing and near her, the door of the bedroom of Mr and Mrs Lovett Senior never opened. It wouldn't open until their children had gone out of the house again for the rest of the night. In the kitchen, the bad peas the Girls had eaten exploded one by one inside them, and they found this so comical, it made them all laugh. Delighted, they placed their hands on each other's tummies, to share this new phenomenon, and feel and squeal at each other's bangs and pops. The hunger-striker to the side of them went on sitting doing nothing and in the hall, the loving couple cuddled and fell asleep. After the lull, this quiet time together, the household would reassert itself, stretch and yawn, and become activated once more.

Mr Hunch in the Ascendant, 1980

'Listen to me, all of you,' said Mr Parker, who had his legs casually crossed and was wearing one of his famous twenty-four changes of costume. Vincent's two favourites were the Star-Spangled costume and the Glitter and Tinsel costume and his least favourite was the Hacked With 153 Stabwounds costume. It used to belong to his father that one, but now it was the property of Mr Parker, no longer a baker's fresh, bread-smelling uniform but just a dull ripped-up cloth turned the nastiest shade of red. Today's costume was the Plain White Coat and Clipboard.

'Psychosis is one of the worst experiences there is,' the doctor went on. 'It is isolation deadland, it is a world of absolute horror, but worse than that everybody, it is a place full of hate. I think it's time we talked.'

Patients woke immediately from their deliberate angry slumbers and peeked out in sullen astonishment from that very sphere of hate. All the ashamed, passively depressed, drugged male patients and all the hyper, furiously aggressive, drugged female patients stopped in whatever inner tracks they were on and waited to hear what this damned psychiatrist was going to say next. Flickers of light appeared in empty eyes, creaks sounded in granite-tight jaws, icicle bodies gave, if anything, hostile, non-committal twitches and this was a lot, considering all that had been said. Mr Parker had never spoken three such direct sentences in a row before and all at the outset of therapy too. It was shocking and tingly and spellbinding and uncalled-for and even Vincent gave his full attention, which was the first time for him.

'Between you and me,' went on Parker, 'my job is to assess, monitor medication, section when necessary and not bother much with anything else. That, folks, is not on. Today, I'm going to propose something different. Ready?'

As far as Vincent was concerned, although the doctor started off audibly, even if bizarre and outlandish and off-the-rails wrong, everything he said after this sounded as it usually did, indistinct, blursome and 'bla bla bla'. The reason the young man could no longer follow what the older one was saying, was because Mr Hunch had come between them and was him-self now starting to speak. Mr Hunch always came between at the least sign of anyone else usurping and although Vincent could never see him, there was never any mistaking when Mr Hunch was in the room.

'What did I say Vincent?' he rasped at the teenager. 'Don't you know by now when you're being made a fool of? Don't you know by now when a big liar's telling a lie? Of course Parker seems caring, of course he seems insightful, but if you listen proper, you'll hear what it is he really says.'

Vincent obligingly listened proper and sure enough, Mr Hunch, as usual, was right. Before Vincent's eyes, and before the teenager could do anything to stop it, the psychiatrist had changed costumes and was wearing that baker's uniform Vincent never – anymore – liked the look of.

'As for you Vincent,' he said, turning full frontal. Vincent could see a ton of red knifemarks all at once. 'You were in freefall, Acuting, in Concentrated Panic Stage, in possession of toy guns, imaginary explosives, with voices giving commentaries on events that never took place. Is it any wonder,' Mr Parker smiled at him, 'you ended up back in here?'

Vincent was appalled at the blunt-handed way this new therapy was being done. He was sure it wouldn't have been allowed in the old days of the hospital and who knows, maybe it wasn't even being allowed now. Mr Parker was a strange doctor and between themselves, the patients often wondered if he really even was a doctor or whether, in reality, he was just another person like themselves. The man himself, meanwhile, had turned to Billy Battles. Battles, always physically restrained except when he accidentally wasn't, was being told he was nothing but a murderer and a bigoted bore. Ena was told she had shingles when she wanted to be told she had a psychopathic inferiority complex, and this set her off screaming and having a fit. Parker ignored her and turned to 'A'. 'A' had aphagia, he said. He turned to 'B'. 'B' had hypomania and, he turned to 'C', 'C' had a case of everything but all of it so mild as to be hardly mentionable at all. He pointed out the defects and shortcomings of everybody and of course he got away with it, because he was a doctor with a captive audience.

Now, it wasn't that Vincent disliked Mr Parker for, to give him his due, he wasn't a sceptic about mental illness. He never sneered at depressives. He didn't snap 'Oh how very convenient!' every time a patient remembered any type of bad thing. He encouraged a lot of talking, which aroused a lot of controversy, and frequently sent shivers down the other psychiatrists' backs. But what was he on and should he be allowed it and what about themselves and all their human rights? As usual, Vincent said none of this, preferring the rubbery playground sort of floor as a thing to sit and stare at, rather than at what might be exchanged if he looked into someone else's eyes. This floor was made of big plumpy tiles of white inlaid on white, not quite hard, not quite soft, the sort of floor that sufficed if things got thrown about a lot. Things got thrown about a lot in this place, Vincent vividly could recall.

'It doesn't have to be like this,' he heard Parker say, but now from a very long distance. 'Listen to me everybody – there doesn't have to be this inner war.'

'Of course there does,' said Mr Hunch. 'What the fuck is he talking about? Come on Vincent, get up. It's time for us to go.'

'Where are you going Vincent?' said Mr Parker. 'The session's not over yet. You know the rules. Sit down again please.'

Vincent had scraped back his chair, and in spite of the medi- cation, walked himself by everybody and got himself to the door. Mr Hunch told him to hurry up, for they had contacts to meet up with, deals to get sorted, hardware to check, mer- chandise to shift. They had to get down the town and at once attend to business. He knew the door would be locked so he didn't try to open it. He went through it the usual way and in no time at all he was gone.

Outside it was night, and it was very, very satisfactory. The wind was blowing nice and there was a dull, buffeted-about light. It came from a gold–orange gigantic moon, hanging low on the horizon and there was a pale thin misty green all the way around. Vincent liked pale misty greens for they were the opposite of murky greens and he liked moons too, generally speaking. He found them remarkably intensive but tonight, he hadn't time to be remarkably intensified, so he said goodbye to the moon and turned completely away. He could never comprehend that the moon would go on hanging, that it would continue to have its existence whether he remembered it or not. That lack of understanding, Mr Parker often said to him, was a part of his pathology. 'You need to understand my boy,' he said, 'lots of things – and people – don't disintegrate just because you stop thinking about them. They don't stop existing because you think they're no longer there. Life goes on whether or not you're in contact with it, whether or not you even like it and in fact, it's you, yourself, Vincent, often, who chooses to go away.' Vincent hadn't known what the poor new doctor from England was talking about and he surmised that this Parker fella had a few defects and shortcomings himself.

He looked around. It was very noisy. Stalls and promotions were crawling with activity and only the attraction opposite was in trouble, that was for sure. It looked forlorn and extremely painful and was called How To Sit With Your Depression and it was not, it goes without saying, popular with any of the punters nearby. They were more interested in the dazzling spectaculars, like Death And Half-Death! and Falling Off The Roller Coaster! and especially the Identify The Body display. That one had a queue a mile long waiting to go into it and the gang, Vincent noticed, was in this queue, each member jangling his pinmoney up and down. Vincent turned away, even though he would have liked to have greeted them, but there was something too previous, too raw on the shinbone, too Concentrated Panic Stage about the Identify display.

So he did a turnaway and bumped immediately into Mick Lovett who shoved him and punched him and called him a cunt. Vincent fell over and Mick Lovett made to kick him but he was distracted and in a hurry and swung his leg out far wide. He rushed on by then, without taking a second go at Vincent, and Vincent noticed he was heading towards the Identify display. Lovett kept ducking and diving and looking constantly behind him, exactly as one might if one's life was on the line. Vincent lost sight of him and got up and dusted some of the dust off him, but then stopped and took a red pen out and drew lines up and down himself. He did these lines exactly on the places Mick Lovett had touched him, five long red lines up and down his forearm. Then he put his pen away and put his coat back on again and buttoned it up and dusted the dust, then looked around and saw Mary Dolan. She was standing over the way.

She was looking at him and she was looking worried and he could see that, as usual, Mary Dolan was in a mess. Mary was a long-time friend from childhood whom Vincent still saw occasionally, for she seemed to turn up at these events now and then. Although she couldn't help it, she was also Jat McDaide's cousin, or else his sister or his half-sister or his daughter or semi-wife. Vincent was very nervous of any Dolan-McDaide connection, and Jat McDaide in particular was Concentrated Panic Stage. He had his own private army, his own freelance murder squad and for that reason, Vincent did his best to keep out of his way. But Mary was looking worried and Vincent knew he couldn't leave her, so he went over to see if there was anything he could do.

Mary was happy to see him. She looked glad and said something immediately. She kept repeating it quickly over and over again. After piecing it together, because Mary wasn't good at words, Vincent worked out that she was pregnant and that this was for the second time. The first time was six years earlier but for all that, she still didn't know what to do, and of course, neither did Vincent. He only knew about bombs and about guns. He'd heard little bits and pieces though, about this female phenomenon and he told Mary what he could of them but Mary didn't look like she really wanted to know. She said she had no memory of how it had gone last time except that she hadn't liked it when the baby was coming out.

'Take it out now then,' said Vincent, 'and have it done and over with.' Mary hesitated then opened her legs wide with a sick look on her face. All the same, she bent over and took it out and they both came close to have a look at it. It was sitting on her thumb and it *was* a baby, there was no bones about that. There was no bones either, about who the father of this baby was. Clear as day, sitting on Mary Dolan's thumb, was a girl-ba with Mickey Lovett's face.

Mary was most shaken by the fact it really and truly existed and almost uttered coherent words, which would have been amazing coming out of her. Vincent though, became frightened, for he felt somebody approaching and he looked up and became more frightened when he saw it was her da. Oh don't do that, he wanted to say for Mary looked as if she was going to show it, but Dolan was already close and having a good look for himself. He got angry when he saw that it was a baby belonging to Mick Lovett for Mary was only allowed to have babies by himself. So he hit her and he knocked her over and he hurt her until her mouth was bleeding but he couldn't get the baby off her, because it was sewn on with a rope.

When Mary had been hit three, four, five times altogether, by her da, then her uncles, then her cousins and brothers too, they went away to find Jat McDaide to tell him what had happened and to get him to tell them what he thought they should all do. When their big plumpy footsteps disappeared into the distance, Vincent came back over, for once again it was safe. He told Mary that he was sorry but now he'd come to think about it, she shouldn't take the baby out unless she was intending for it to die. If she wasn't intending it to die, she would have to widen herself quickly and get it back in again, first using something a lot bigger, for then the baby, being smaller, would slip, very easy, in. Mary lifted a Nambarrie tea-caddy and positioned it under her body, with neither of them really believing she'd really and truly get it in. A few moments later though, she had.

'That's enough,' said Vincent, judging carefully from a distance. 'You can take the tea-tin out now Mary and quick as a flash, slip the baby in.' Mary took the tin out and Vincent, who had been holding the Lovett on his thumb, slid it over onto her thumb, and she positioned it on her finger, then popped it, very easy, in. Vincent didn't touch Mary to say well done Mary or anything, because Mary wouldn't have liked that and, of course, Vincent being Vincent, neither would he. Instead, with the sweat running off him, he left Mary with the sweat running off her, and drew a red dot on his thumb where the Lovett babby had been. Then he put his pen away and went towards the Big Top for he was anxious to find the rendezvous the Inner Circle had instructed him to attend.

Mr Hunch and the Inner Circle had gotten the message to Vincent earlier, via the usual link in his body, that started in his brain. The evening before, while in a one-to-one with Mr Parker, the gang had tuned in to tell him about their newly-hatched plan. Mr Hunch, Dexter Green, Snatch McGovern and a few of the others had agreed to meet Vincent at Identify The Body at zero two hundred hours. He was to stand inconspicuously by Greedy McDermott's Pie Parlour but he was not to eat any of the food for it was bugged by MI5. He was to go nowhere near the rifle stands for they too were under surveillance, and he was to keep his eye out for men in crombies flouting fake accents and holding boxes with wires coming out both ends. When he saw these boxes he would know they were army cameras and that they were transmitting pictures trained on GetOutOfTheWay's Dodgems. This would mean, decoded, that Vincent was in the wrong spot. When he got to the right spot, he was to check he hadn't been followed and under no circumstances was he to bring any hardware along. 'Got that?' 'Got that?' they said, all of them, one after the other, and Vincent nodded and said that yes, of course he had. Mr

Parker, who had been talking to him all this while, leaned over and said, 'Vincent, who is it you're talking to this time?'

'Shush,' they whispered. 'Don't tell that Nosey Parker.' Then they dispersed and switched off the link, which was always at their end. 'Don't forget,' they switched back, tuning in to remind him, 'you must come absolutely, entirely, anti-dependently on your own.' They disappeared again. In a snap.

At this point, as usual, Vincent felt abandoned and, also as usual, his blood began to shake. He couldn't cope with being alone although he told himself it wouldn't last long. The Hum would start up which was a sign the Inner Circle hadn't really gone away. Mr Parker, whom Vincent suspected was really just a figment, stared closely at Vincent as if waiting to be informed. After a while, during which Vincent informed about nothing, the doctor resumed his own blabbing – about dead babies, dead bakers, hallucinations and delusions and all the other things doctors generally felt qualified to blab on about. Vincent ignored him.

So now, at the right time but in the wrong place Vincent, due to the disorienting drugs given to him by the Bad Parker, mistakenly rapped to get in by the trapdoor. He was surprised when it was opened yet again by Mr Parker, wearing a crombie and faking an accent and holding a box with wires coming out both ends. Vincent went on guard, for the psychiatrist was obviously following him, insatiable for information and tagging him from braincell to braincell. It was on account of the pen-marks, that he was sure of. Parker's personality wouldn't let the subject drop. It was avid to know what Vincent felt when he drew his red lines. When he thought of it later, Vincent suspected also, that Parker might be an undercover double agent, for it was rarely clear who was who in this particular game. If he was Inner Circle, this of course would explain the randomness, but as Vincent wasn't sure, he thought it best to play along.

'Come in, Vincent, my dear boy, come in,' bellowed the Parker, a large man, a big man, for that's what he was, a big powerful man with giant joints, a bit loose and floppy, which was all part of the camouflage of the harmless shaggy dog. He had the cheek to be wearing Vincent's father's blood-soaked apron and he waved Vincent to a spotlit chair he had placed in the interrogation room nearby. Vincent sidled over, refusing to sit on the chair in case it was boobytrapped. Instead he sat on the floor, made of big plumpy tiles of white inlaid on white, displaying brown dried bloodstains from the people who had been interrogated before. Vincent pretended not to notice these stains, or the flesh, or the tissue, or the teeth, long and sticky, and he noticed the doctor pretending not to notice these things as well. Two can play at that game, thought Vincent and, as agreed earlier with the gang, he kept quiet about everything. Transmissions were flying thick and fast about the place.

'. . . doesn't respond to treatment, Parker. Face facts you maverick! Why rock the boat? . . . wasting your time . . . filthy wrecks . . . little you can do with these people.'

'. . . don't agree . . . couldn't be classed in any other category . . . couldn't quite be classed as schizophrenic . . . – and as for that label, Dennis . . .'

'Oh for God's sake! Borderline then. Psychotic incidents, call them what you will! Listen, you're mad yourself, gonna lose your job. Never mind, what time you off? Fancy a drink in the . . .'

The psychiatrist closed the trapdoor and the Voices and the Noises and the People went away.

'Well now,' Parker said. He sat down, though not, Vincent noticed gladly, beside him. He held his hands together like a steeple and his eyes looked at Vincent as if they cared. He then began to play with the floury ties tied around his middle and Vincent remembered he used to play with those same ties as they hung, years ago, from his mother's washing line.

'And how are you feeling now Vincent?' he said. 'Have you given any thought to what we discussed yesterday?'

Vincent didn't answer. He didn't remember what they had discussed yesterday. He didn't remember yesterday. Mr Hunch, anyway, had instructed him that the only way to deal with these filthy sorts of people was to say nothing and not to get involved.

'Who's your main man?' said Parker. 'Do you trust me Vincent? Can you help me? Is it a man? Is it a woman? An object? Visible? Invisible? Audible, I bet. Come on Vincent. Spill the beans. It's been a while now since you talked. You told me about Snatch and Greedy and McDaide and Lovett but I know you never want to tell me about your main man. Is it in the room with us now?'

Vincent still didn't answer. He hoped the Inner Circle would come soon and rescue him, for with these Parker drugs, he didn't know how long he'd be able to hold out.

'I heard the Voices out there, telling you I'm schizophrenic,' said Vincent. 'I'm not schizophrenic.'

'Vincent,' said Mr Parker, 'I agree.'

'Schizophrenia,' went on the big man, or somebody, dressed now in his RUC uniform with a black balaclava pulled down over his head. His eyes were dark inside it. 'It's just a term you know Vincent, used by us psychiatrists. It applies to people who tend to see and hear things that aren't really there. Strange ideas Vincent, would come into this category also – strange ideas, that's to say, like the type you tend to have. But there's also such a thing – do you know this Vincent? – apart from schizophrenia, of becoming psychotic, of actually starting out sane and then being driven mad? Let's take this feud for example, the one you keep referring to, the one you were talking about yesterday, between your characters – Mickey Lovett and Jat McDaide.'

Vincent still said nothing although his tongue was definitely twitching. He realised it was trying to betray him and give him away. This was a mortifying problem and his mind wondered what would be the best thing to do in the circumstances. After all, if you can't trust your own tongue, whose tongue can you trust? He took a bite out of it and it bled. He swallowed the blood and it tasted salty. He knew he was fooling Parker and that was something, anyway.

'. . . and Mary,' went on Parker, looking at Vincent closely and Vincent got a shock when he heard Mary's name and spat out some unswallowed salty blood.

'I'll be back in a minute,' said Hunch. 'Remember Vincent – say nothing about me.'

'I'm sayin' nothin'!' cried Vincent as Parker jumped up and pretended to help him. 'You can't get me to talk,' he said and then 'No!' he heard himself cry. He was shaking and when he realised he was shaking, he became scared for he didn't like it when his body took over operations. It sometimes would push itself forward, and breathe him in and out. This breathing business was dangerous, especially from below the head area. Vincent whispered 'Shallow, shallow' to his breath, to keep himself from Concentrated Panic Stage. He could hardly pay attention as Parker told him breathing was good for him, especially deep breathing. He covered his ears but Parker went further and slipped in enquiries about the Inner Circle murder gang. 'Part of you,' said Parker quietly, 'doesn't want to let go of them. They're you, a part of you.'

'Wrong!' shouted Vincent. 'They're not me. They're a life apart from me every time!'

'So far,' said Parker, recrossing his legs the other way and again making a steeple with his hands. Vincent peeped through squeezed eyes and after a bit, he breathed himself up again, shallower, far from his torso, once more at the top end.

'Well Mr Parker,' he said. He opened wide his eyes. 'You're

wrong. They're not a part of me. So what are you gonna say, now you know where I stand on that score?'

'The same,' said Parker, who seemed much calmer than Vincent. Vincent noticed the psychiatrist's abdomen was breathing him in and out. 'I'll say the same as I've been saying a long time now son.' He leaned over. He smelt a bit like baked bread himself. 'They are yours Vincent. You don't, for the most part, really want to let them go. So,' he leaned back. 'What are *you* gonna say, now you know where *I* stand on that score?'

'A life apart,' persisted Vincent although his voice was much weaker and good Lord, he thought, this Parker guy was good. He must have got trained at some top goods Special Agent camp. 'A life apart!' he tried again, but his attempt fell on the floor.

'It's hopeful,' said Parker, his steeple fingers opening and closing. 'Things happen Vincent. It doesn't have to be this way. You must let yourself know how much you can depend on me, or at least be aware when you're determined you will not.' Parker here shifted his weight and Vincent noticed its sneaked-up proximity. He grew wary of this human body just inches from his own. He edged away.

'You talk about projection all the time in your exciting stories,' went on Parker, with a smile and an eagerness that was rashly out of joint. It was the type of jolly smile that would have annoyed any mental patient but perhaps it was forgivable for Vincent was revealing more than he ever had. 'What stories?' he said, politely, though coldly would have been nearer the mark.

'Why!' beamed Parker, still not realising his error, 'your stories of gun-toting, dangerous deals, the Lovett and the McDaide characters—' He stopped. Vincent could see the man must be kicking himself and tongue-biting himself for falling into such an elementary trap.

'I don't make up stories,' said Vincent. 'I don't know what

you're talking about.' He turned his back as far as it would go and stared at the largest of the plumped-up tiles. They were white inlaid on white, neither hard nor soft, bloodstains on all of them. The tiles and the bloodstains led nowhere at all.

'Okay,' said the psychiatrist. He threw up his hands. 'You win Vincent,' and he laughed. Vincent laughed too, just to show he wasn't afraid or anything and thought, he's mad that Parker. I'd better watch myself around him.

'Let's talk about Mary,' said Parker suddenly. He was no longer laughing. Vincent realised he himself had now fallen into the trap. He felt sick.

'Mary's nothing to do with it!' he cried. 'I don't know any Mary. Why don't we not talk about her? Why don't we talk about something else instead?'

'Her da and her brothers . . .' he went on. 'Her da and her uncles . . . Her da and her cousins . . . Her da and Jat McDaide . . .' Now why had he said that? he wondered. Mr Hunch wouldn't approve of that. Mr Parker raised his eyebrows.

'But why did she appear Vincent?' he said. The big man was speaking gently. 'Tell me the rest of what you both did with the tea-tin Vincent. This could be hopeful. Perhaps we can explore that.'

Vincent was dismayed. He hadn't known he'd blabbed about the tea-caddy. He began to stammer but luckily for him, the gang arrived at that moment and stopped him giving further details away.

'Come outside,' ordered Hunch. 'Ignore that man,' he said. 'That man's gonna be dead soon.'

'Excuse me Mr Parker,' said Vincent. 'I have to go now.'

'Certainly,' said Mr Parker. He got up to let the young man past. 'A plot in your own story Vincent,' he said, and he said it as a parting shot. 'A plot in your own story Vincent, a plot in your own head.'

'I told you not to trust him,' said Hunch when they were safely again on the outside. They were in the moon's murky green and the tent they'd just left was all lamplit aglow. Hunch was annoyed, and he was in a hurry and he was freezing with the hatred he felt for everybody. Vincent knew this hatred because, like the gang, he'd learnt it was best to be aware of Mr Hunch's feelings too. He shivered. 'Don't you remember Vincent?' said Hunch, 'or would you like to be reminded, of how awful it is to be abandoned and alone?'

Vincent couldn't remember in any sort of detail ever having had to cope without his friend, his adviser, without any of the gang. He suspected there was a blot somewhere in his memory and he looked to the others to see if they would help him. The gang stood well back. This was between Vincent and his maker. Vincent could sort it out on his own. Vincent said,

'I'm sorry Mr Hunch, but it's Mr Parker. He gets them to inject me and then it's hard to get away.'

Mr Hunch grunted. After a moment though, he seemed to thaw. He spoke to Vincent in a lighter tone. He said,

'I notice you haven't set up your attraction Vincent. You need to set up your attraction. Get out your rifles. Show the world what you can do.' With this, he went away and the others naturally went with him. Vincent was left standing, again, on his own. The Hum did not hum this time.

It transpired he was not really on his own for a crowd had gathered around Billy Battles opposite. Battles had also escaped from the asylum that day. He was setting up a stall that was really just a soapbox and this suited Battles for preaching at people was all, it seemed, he'd been manufactured for. He was over-righteous and implacable and stuffed with disowned unhappy guilty feelings which he transformed into anger and projected onto everybody not like himself. This was according to Mr Parker and also according to Mr Parker, Battles' severe psychological violent pathology stemmed from his thwarted need for exclusivity and absolute control. He had a fierce allegiance to his land and to his clan which was absolutely extraordinary, given these were the very things, Parker said, he kept ending up in mental hospitals for. He had a habit of stabbing anyone who looked like his mother or his father, or his granny or his grandfather, or his other granny or other grandfather or his uncles or his aunts. For some reason, this turned out to be anybody of the opposite religion and there were thirty-three names on the list of charges against him in court so far. When he was sad, the doctor said that was a bit hopeful, and when he was cheerful the doctor said that was pretty bad. He went from being pretty bad to fantastically awful whenever his mission reasserted itself, which it did whenever the drugs he was on, wore off. Then, he would become disruptive and grab Vincent's secret biro and stick it with vitriol into any papist-looking eye. He would be taken away and given a talking-to about this thing called attempted murder and Vincent would be told off and have a patch put over his eye.

So Billy had escaped and was preaching his three effs – Faith, Family and Fatherland – and playing his holy tapes – 'Hello. This is God speaking' they always began. God had a Belfast accent. God said, 'I want you to listen carefully to what I have to say.' Billy played these tapes in between his great eff speeches and it transpired, which was fine by his followers, that Billy, in fact, was taping these God tapes himself. There were also books with the title *Politeness and Courtesy in the Face of Difficulty and Disquiet*, but inside these false covers were other books, called *Get Them!* which were the real books Billy Battles believed he had a mission to sell. And they did sell, for Billy's premise was clear. 'It's all very well,' God said, 'calling sectarianism an evil, but look at it this way: no matter how tolerant, no matter how peaceful, no matter how fair-minded, we always get pushed too far. It only takes one of them to get up and start bigoting, and we want to get up too, with a hatchet, and lop them all to bits. There's nothing wrong with hatred. There's nothing wrong with blaming. There's nothing wrong with finding a target for what's been done to you so far.' Still in his white hospital gown, Billy gave off a sharp boldness, a boldness which only came across as insanity from within his hospital bed. He preached about the need for more guns, more ammunition, more jails, more doorstep killings and threw slogans by the handful to a crowd who lapped it up.

It was a small crowd though, compared to those for the Big Dipper, for the Roller Coaster, the Identify, the Come And Get Your Dead. But it was growing and it was substantial and a group of killers was amongst it, 'a nice bunch of lads', someone who didn't know them, or did know them, casually might have said. Across from the killers was their intended victim in his forties, a small, squat baker with a distracted look upon his face. He had orange hair, a red face, a solid body, massive shoulders, and he was dressed in colours that would certainly get him killed. He had on gold shoes, orange socks, white baker's trousers, a white waistcoat, a green check shirt with sleeves completely rolled up. He had thick golden-tanned forearms with floury ginger hairs on them and around his middle was a white apron tied at the front. It gave off boiled fruit smells. At his feet was a murky green holdall, also smelling of boiled sultanas, mixed with sweet cinnamon, yeast, mace, cloves and nutmeg. The man was fidgeting and flinching and scanning an old newspaper, a *Belfast Telegraph*, dated Nineteen Sixty-Something, lying at his feet. It had a tiny backpage headline, announcing that something unpleasant had again happened, and had then been discovered by a man, walking his dog, at first light.

'The truth of the matter is,' cried Billy, 'you should always

love your family. Never blame your relatives, no matter what
it is they once did.' The fidgeting baker picked up the paper
as Battles preached on. The family was good, he shrieked, the
extended family was even better but best of all was the holy
community – provided it was only of one specific kind. The
crowd looked at each other and then they looked at that baker.
It was clear the man in the tricolour was the odd one out.
The baker slapped round the pages, not noticing he was being
scrutinised, not reading either, for who gave a damn about
apparently motiveless crimes? So he flicked and he rustled and
finally he threw the thing away from him, and as the others
made their way towards him, Vincent stopped looking and
turned away. Thank goodness, he thought, I don't know that
person. Thank goodness, he thought, that baker's not my da.

He went back to his rifles. For yes, while Billy had been preaching, selling his God tapes and his hidden books within books,
Vincent, given his pathology, couldn't help setting up his own
rifle stand. There were fifty-seven rifle stands at the fairground
already, mostly of Armalites but naturally, of other types as well.
Vincent had Armalites too and some of them had MERCHANT
NAVY. PROPERTY OF THE US GOVT stamped upon them. He
looked up and saw Jat McDaide approaching. Jat had brought
his own private gun along. It was dangling from his right hand
as he stepped over to Vincent. He held it against the side of
Vincent's head and took the safety catch off.

'Madboy,' he whispered, for Jat never bothered with niceties.
'Did you see Mickey Lovett? You better've seen him or I'll
blow your head off.'

It was times like these Vincent wished the Inner Circle would
come and save him but strangely enough, it was times like
these, the Inner Circle seemed most to stay away. The Hum

sometimes hung about doing a bit of humming, but it never advised on anything and, at the best of times, consisted of very little emotional content anyway.

'Down at the Identify,' said Vincent but Jat couldn't understand him. 'What's the Identify, stupid?' he said and he fired some live rounds by the side of Vincent's head. Vincent pointed with a shaky finger to the Identify The Body, and Jat let go of him and signalled to the others, his very own Inner Circle murder gang. They sneaked down to the Identify with their weapons at the ready and Mr Hunch gave a snigger which Vincent thought in bad taste.

He thought the snigger was on account of the killing about to happen, of Mickey Lovett who'd went and got his face put on Mary's ba. But it wasn't. Mr Hunch was amused by Vincent's prizes at the rifle range for he was offering, in descending order, Special Treats, Mere Flesh Wounds, Two Dogs Stuck Together Backwards and A Dead Moth Squashed By A Boy's Bare Foot. There was also mustard-coloured sand, flowers moving on wallpaper, a million rounds of ammunition, complete funerals, and so much more. There was nothing on abortions, difficult labours, early breakings of waters or knitting needles to get rid of things. Vincent didn't like this turn to women's dark places and wondered if he was going into Concentrated Panic Stage.

He paused to take out his red pen and once again, went over himself. He did a dot here, a line there, a coloured-in section on the cheekbone – everywhere where Jat's hand or his automatic weapon had been. He was still doing this when Mr Parker turned the corner of the rifle stand. He had a big sheaf of papers clutched tightly in his hand. He seemed surprised to see Vincent, but delighted also, and said Vincent was just the chap he was looking for. Hunch tutted for he had just about had enough of that nosey Englishman. He pointed out to Vincent the shapeless tweeds and twills this Parker fellow was very fond of, and did Vincent know their main purpose was the concealment of surveillance bugs? Vincent shook his head.

'My dear boy,' said Mr Parker, who had been talking about something, 'I wish you wouldn't deny it.' Vincent wished Mr Parker wouldn't keep calling him his son or his dear boy.

'I want to read you your signed confession,' said Parker. Vincent was startled. He couldn't remember any confession, signed or otherwise. 'It wasn't me!' he shouted. 'I didn't do it. It was Jat McDaide and the Inner Circle murder gang.' Mr Parker shook his head and looked sad for a moment, but then he held the sheets up again in an ever so friendly hand. He perched himself on a high stool, took a sip from his strawberry milkshake and began to read from the top of the very first page.

'"Know great,"' he read. '"'Snappy story right?' To what, don't know. 'It, and together!' about the beating that what. About know Hunch also, Snappy great come. Snappy. Hunch. Snappy. Write about Snappy. It's a disguise. 'Would that great about murder,' don't and would Hunch come? It and together. Make it great. Know about Hunch. Make Snappy to it. Make. It. All. Stop. And the great right? Snappy would, 'Don't! Don't do it!' That make to what. Yes and don't, and together. Snappy it that great. Know Jat. Must know Hunch."'

Parker looked up as he turned to the next page. 'Getting somewhere at last, eh Vincent? I like Snappy. Who's Snappy? Tell me more about Snappy. Oh, and by the way, I know it's not important, but tell me while you're about it – about that other one – you know, the one called Hunch.'

'No!' cried Vincent. 'I cancel my signature. You can't pin that confession on me. I didn't mean any of that.'

'"The latest trouble started on 23rd July 1980,"' read Mr Parker, ignoring Vincent and reading from the top of the second page. '"About two o'clock in the morning. I started to hear a carnival outside the kitchen window. Couldn't be a carnival, I thought, not on the Lisburn Road. I got up to see. It was somebody else's flat. Can't remember whose. I was staying in it on my own. The noise stopped. The road was empty. I lay down again on the floor by the sink unit. I pulled the blanket over my head. Immediately it started again. There was that organ music, that grinding music, that humming music – you know? – wrung out of a mangle, strange music. The notes were jangled, squashed together, rolled into one. Pronouncing voices. They started, they shouted. Pronouncing voices. They were chattering. 'Roll up!' they said. 'Win your sweetheart a toy!' 'Penny a throw!' they said, and then they turned up the volume. 'Who killed my da?' I got up to see. Silence and golden. I lay down again. They started. I sat up. They stopped. I lay down. They started once more. I tried my fingers in my ears. Inside my head got itchy, my ears and fingers ached, my jaw and cheeks got sore. I tried sleeping by the window, standing up, pretending I was looking. It didn't work. They wouldn't let me, I couldn't go back to sleep. They went on till I gave up. I went out to be with them. It was the middle of the night. They were at the carnival and they had shovels and they were looking for Mickey Lovett. Mary Dolan, you see, was the cousin of Jat McDaide." '

Mr Hunch interrupted to remind Vincent that he, Hunch, was in the ascendant and that Vincent therefore didn't have to say anything to this Mr Parker guy. He instructed Vincent not to listen, said Parker was British Intelligence and that the confession was a ruse to get him into jail fast. 'Do you want to end up charged and imprisoned for murders you'd nothing to do with? Do you want to be taken away, tortured and then killed as a tout?' Mr Parker was Special Branch, said Hunch. Mr Parker was a murder gang. Mr Parker was in cahoots with Billy Battles and Jat McDaide.

' " . . . and bla bla, bla bla, bla," ' concluded Parker reading the last line of the last page. He looked at Vincent. 'Vincent, you stopped taking your medication when you were on the outside. Do you remember I said you'd have to come back in if you didn't take it as you were told?'

Vincent didn't answer. He hung his head. He was in confusion. Just for a moment he didn't know what on earth was going on. But just for a moment. Then he got his reality back.

'I think Vincent,' Parker waved the papers, he gave a sigh, 'we're back to the same old stuff again. This is the Sectarian Murder Gang Fantasy we've been through many times before. You didn't witness any murder. No murder ever happened – except for that of your poor father all those years and years ago. Jat and Mickey are your characters, and you do them in great detail, but you do do them, Vincent. They have no reality of their own. Oh, I agree they're fabulous,' he went on. 'They're fantastic, and who knows, maybe one day you'll write a nice little story about them. But my dear boy, don't let them rule you. They don't at all exist. That goes for Mary too,' he went on further. 'Little Mary. Displacement theory, we call it son. Don't worry. Lie back for now Vincent. We're trying this new drug. Let's see how it pans out.'

'Just so long,' says Hunch, 'as he never knows about me.'

'By the way Vincent,' said Parker. 'Do me a big favour. Let me have a look at what you've done to your left arm.'

'Vincent,' said Hunch. 'It's time for your attraction. Dump those rifles and go and do what you've come here for.'

'Cuts again?' said Parker. He looked closely. 'Oh that's good. Just some more penmarks. Better than cuts but Vincent,' he went on, 'this too, will have to stop. How many are there this time? A hundred and fifty-three again I reckon.' He sighed. 'I wish I knew who was sneaking you those pens.'

'Mr Parker,' said Vincent, feeling the pillow soft behind him. 'I'd like to tell you something about the leader of the murder gang.'

'Vincent,' said Hunch. 'Do you hear me talking?'

'Yes Vincent,' said Parker. 'I'm listening. You said you'd like

155

to tell me something about the leader of the murder gang.'

I'm warning you Vincent, Hunch's voice was much much closer. Just for a moment Vincent believed it was inside his own head.

'Mr Parker . . .' said Vincent.

If you don't start cutting and making red stripes immediately, said Hunch, I'll make you identify that body down the hall.

There is a scream. It happens three times with a minute between each. It is the boy and he is screaming because of the silence in the house. He does one long scream and then another long scream, three times, and he is trembling. Nobody comes. His naked foot is out of the blankets and he can't pull it back and he can't push it out. He can't move. On the third scream he hears, for the first time, the Hum. It is deep and it starts low down in the skirting board. He listens to it and then he asks, 'Can you tell me if you know my mammy?' and 'Hello?' He doesn't say 'I'm afraid' in case the Hum, like the silence, is bad. He is in disarray. Half his pyjamas are still on his body and halves of his body are in and out of the bed. His shaking is violent. He wants to tell the Hum about the problem, about how he wants to take his pyjamas off and put his trunks on but is afraid because he doesn't want anything out there to see his private bare bum.

'Poor little boy,' it says. It is in the pattern of the wallpaper. It is called Mr Hunch. It says, 'Shall we help?' The boy sniffs and nods and says yes and Mr Hunch is very indispensably helpful. He tells Vincent that it's easy, that all he has to do is to slip his pyjamas off and after that, slip his trunks on. He can do all this while still under the blankets. Nothing and no one who might just be watching will get a chance then to see his private bare bum. He talks the boy through it and the boy is very grateful. 'Thank you,' the boy says, his eyes red-rimmed and sad. He is perpetually sleepy but can't fall asleep for he is one of those children who have to stay awake. Mr Hunch tells the boy he has coped well with his predicament and after this friendly exchange, the boy yawns and does sleep.

She climbs the stairs and puts the plastic bucket on the landing. It is entirely all for him, she says, to do his weewees and poppies in. The boy doesn't like her going but knows that she will because she hums 'It's me oh Lord, it's me' and 'Something shining bright – My Soul,' even though she isn't happy. She always hums when she's going away and her hum, too, is never happy. She washes at the sink and does her hair and rolls on her stockings. Her Mum deodorant is already put on. In her pink vanity case are her rosary beads, her penny prayers, her scapulas, her holy medals, her black mantilla that she'll be wearing going up Mount Derg on her knees. Her vanity case is by the door. She buys him Special Treats so he'll not miss her. His anxiety rockets. He cries even more.

She takes him up to the bedroom with her coat and scarf already on her and she puts him on the bed.

'Listen love,' she says. 'Don't be going downstairs. The Devil's downstairs whenever I'm away.'

'The Devil?' says the boy. 'Is Dracula there too?'

'Yes. Dracula too but the Devil—'

'Frankenstein? Is Frank—'

'Yes but Vincent—'

'The Werewolf?'

'Be quiet darling and listen.'

She tells him that all the monsters he's ever dreamt of or thought of are downstairs waiting to get him and she says this to protect him so he won't, while she's not there, go down.

She doesn't want him to touch anything electric or the matches or go at all near the fireplace, to keep away from all doors and go nowhere near the stove. She tries to stress the Devil because with her, it's the Devil who counts most. With the boy though, it's the Joker, Mr Freeze, the Nun's Head, the Hairy Tongue, the Little People, the Banshee, the Baker with the Crisscrost Face. The woman blesses the house, blesses the boy, kisses the boy, takes up her vanity case. She goes away, closing the big door, and locks it in the night. He hears it slam and he looks at the clock. She'll be back, she says, when the hands are like so-so. But not on the first day nor on the second but on the third day she will come. He pulls his knees up to his chin and he leans on them and waits for her. The hands on the clock are nowhere near where they have to be.

It is dark. He munches on a Treat. He fingers a comic that features a carnival. There is a seesaw, a merry-go-round, a carousel and a compère. The compère could be good or bad, in his glittering costumes, his sparkly shiny clothes. The boy begins to pray to God in the sky to help with the bad things. 'Dear God and Angels . . .' He looks around the room. He is afraid. 'Good Angels,' he adds and looks around again. 'Not Bad Angels.' This time, he's afraid to look.

'Don't let the ghosts,' he prays. 'Don't let my daddy.' He hides under the bedclothes. He doesn't breathe from far down. He begs Batman for help and then Peter Cushing. 'Amen,' he finishes and blesses himself three times. He's afraid to go to the bucket for the bad things might be on the landing. They might be in the room. They might be on the bed.

'Look what I have for my boy!' cries the widow. She is going away to do her self-imposed penance and he sees the Treats in the black shopping bag. There are Tayto Crisps, Jammy Dodgers, Dairy Milk chocolate, sarsaparilla, milk, potatobread, applebread, triangular cheeses and dulse in a brown bag. There is black sugar also which she thinks he'll like but he doesn't. He turns away and holds onto her but she disentangles him from her legs.

'Mammy!'

'Darling. Do you want God to cry?'

She lifts him in one arm, the bag of Treats in the other and takes everything up the stairs and dumps it on the bed.

She pulls off his jumper, his arms get caught in the sleeves of it. She puts him under the blankets and goes out, leaving on the light.

'They all belong to me,' says a voice.

The boy listens. He is astonished.

'They *all* belong to me,' says the Voice again.

'Mr Freeze belongs to you?'

'Yes.'

'The Joker belongs to you?'

'Yes.'

'Frankenstein?'

'Yes.'

'Dracula? The Nun's Head? The Cloven Hoof? Johnny The Bomb? The Banshee? The Wet Baby That Fell Out Of Her—'

'Be quiet Vincent and listen!'

The boy looks out from under the blankets.

'I can stop the baker downstairs from coming upstairs to get you,' says Mr Hunch, 'the one you're most afraid of, the one with the sewn-up face.' The boy is happy and likes Mr Hunch more than ever. 'Don't leave me Mr Hunch,' he says. 'Stay forever. Stay till the end.'

She takes his hands. She is now in her outdoor coat and her vanity case is ready. More beads and prayers are stuffed in her pockets. She is ready, only the boy to be explained to and left.

'Now my love,' she says. She pulls the blanket to his chin. 'Be good for mammy and be good for God. Look at the clock!' Vincent looks. 'See this big hand . . . ?' Vincent nods. He knows what is coming. He has heard it before.

The house is dark. Downstairs is murky green. He hears a Noise, a Voice, and a Person Outside. 'Is that you?' he says half-aloud. Was it her or the baker or the baby that fell out of her or a piece of furniture just stretching and settling itself back down?

'I have some friends with me,' says Mr Hunch, moving the tendrils in the pattern of the wallpaper. 'Would you like to meet them?' The boy is happy to do whatever Mr Hunch wants. He's totally unalone now with Mr Hunch here beside him. He nods and Dexter Green comes out of the wall by the wardrobe. The child laughs and he likes, he thinks, this unsmiling man Dexter Green. Next Greedy McDermott comes up out of the floorboards and Snatch McGovern is already, somehow, on the bed. The boy laughs again although none of these men will laugh with him. They won't look at him either. Vincent doesn't notice. Vincent doesn't care. Mr Hunch included, they all make up the Inner Circle and Hunch says they are his friends and that if he's good, they'll stay forever and never go away.

A voice wakes him. It is sunlight and it is the third day. Somebody outside is knocking. He gets up and pulls a stool over to the window. The person knocks three times and when he doesn't answer, because Mr Hunch won't let him, they stop knocking and he hears them go away. From his window, he sees it's his friend Mary Dolan and she has her skipping rope entwined about her hands. He watches her skip down the street to where two dogs are stuck together backwards. Another runs round the corner and throws itself on Mary's leg. Mary squeals and pushes it off. It throws itself again and Mary's afraid because it's stronger than she is. A stranger dog, Vincent thinks, that is bald and unfed. Barky too, he adds and drops the curtain and treads on a big moth which has its wings spread on the oilcloth. It cracks and he jumps onto the bed with it stuck, tight and broke-open, on his foot.

March Nineteen Sixty-Something. The woman is getting ready. She washes at the kitchen sink. The boy is by the door. The dead baby is gone, unbaptised, forever. Better out of it, she says, and some neighbours say so as well. Savagely, the woman, his mother, drags Mum deodorant up and down her armpits, splashes sick eau de Cologne on her wasted milk breasts. She reaches for her clothes and puts them on religiously. Her best clothes for God. On a pilgrimage she must go. She's going to say she's sorry and three days is her penance. After that she'll be forgiven, for she killed it under duress. All the boy sees are shoes and the vanity case, the Treats and all the holy things, and then that bucket and knows, again, he's to be left.

She takes care of his provisions for she is not a monster. Biscuits and sandwiches and crisps and lemonade. Batmans are piled high in the bedroom by the window and she leaves his light on plus a bucket for him, outside his door. He is not to go downstairs, not to touch the cooker, to keep away from the fireplace, to keep away from the front door. She lifts him. He is crying.

Mr Hunch is angry and says he's going away. He is going to leave the boy and he is not coming back. The boy is unnerved and doesn't know what he's done. The fault of everything he is – the dead baby, the dead da. He looks around. He wants to see Mr Hunch but Mr Hunch won't show himself. Greedy, Snatch and Dexter are silent. They stay in the wallpaper. If Hunch goes, then they go too.

'You're right,' says Mr Hunch. 'The Devil is downstairs and so is Dracula and the Werewolf and the Banshee and the Hairy Tongue.'

'And the Baker,' he adds. The boy wails. He discovers how to bite himself. He bleeds himself and bites himself and bleeds himself once more.

Mr Hunch says he'll stay. But Vincent has to leave the girl alone. She's not a nice person says Hunch and his own mammy, she's not a nice person too. Mr Hunch ends by stressing all the dangers that exist in the world and in the afterworld and convinces the boy that only he, Hunch, can protect him from all of them, and the boy is happy to believe this for Mr Hunch is going to stay.

Mrs Lyttle comes back. She is ecstatic. She is forgiven. She may not be at one again with humanity but at least she is at one again with her God. She doesn't notice her boy and her boy doesn't notice her. He doesn't run over, fling himself or cry upon her. This is the first time of how it'll be from now on.

She can go on her pilgrimages. She can disappear forever. Vincent's not afraid.

Vincent's found a new friend.

It was a vignette perhaps. It cost fifteen pee to view it. Vincent paid his money but it was incomprehensible and kept repeating itself. Worse than anything, he'd also watched it alone, for there had been no one else in the whole cinema. Coming out, he shook his head and wished he'd picked an action-packed thriller instead.

The next thing that happened was that he walked into murder. They were dragging Mickey Lovett onto the carnival spareland. They had him and couldn't wait to beat him, so they stopped dragging him and they did beat him. Using their shovels, they got the flesh from his feet and when he couldn't get up, they took a gun out and shot him in the head. Still he was alive, and crawling around, as they set to, digging a hole for him. When they'd dug it, they rolled him over towards it, and toed him, very easy, in. They filled it up, patted it down, wiped their brows and felt pleased with the way things had panned out for them. Then they left the scene, taking their shovels, ignoring the red scrabblings, the footprints, the disturbed earth all around. Vincent edged away and ended up backing into the Identify The Body display.

He hadn't realised it was there and he looked down and saw Mary Dolan beside him. She looked again, more than ever, in need of somebody's, anybody's, help. She was now near her term, her body big and ready to open. 'As it's a girl,' she said, 'I'm gonna call her Dawn.' She took his arm and he felt pleased and this was a shock. Mostly to be touched brought deep dark discomforts, of the type that could only be gotten rid of by cuts or red lines.

'What are you gonna do about that murder?' she asked, looking straight in front of her. Vincent looked too and saw an open coffin up ahead.

This wasn't a good sign and he wasn't expecting Mary to draw his attention to it. He wasn't expecting Mary, in fact, really to be there.

'What murder?' he said, feeling for his pen.

'Mickey Lovett's,' she answered.

'There was no murder, Mary. Mickey Lovett doesn't exist as a person. None of them exist.' He left out 'you as well'. He didn't want to hurt Mary by making sweeping remarks unnecessarily. So what if she didn't exist? Did she really need to know about that? 'Mr Parker told me,' he said, referring again to his other figments. '"There's nothing to worry about, Vincent," Mr Parker had said.'

'Who's Mr Parker?' Mary asked. Vincent was thrown by the unexpectedness of the question. Who Mr Parker was, he simply didn't know.

'I think it's time you examined that body,' said Hunch. 'A case of spaghetti-fication. Know what I mean?'

Vincent felt himself going forwards. Mary had disappeared from beside him. A booming man up ahead said, 'Come over here my dear boy.' It was audience participation and Vincent, as always, did exactly what he was told. He went over to the man by the coffin and he was picked up. He was five years old and he was with a crowd of strangers. His mother was sick and couldn't come down because of the dead baby that had come out of her, bloody, up the stairs.

'Cutting and flesh wounds might seem necessary for you to be able to identify with your father,' said the man. 'To identify with how your father must have felt at that time.'

Vincent was surprised. He looked at the man holding him and it was none other than Mr Parker. He was by the coffin and holding Vincent tight in his arms. Vincent didn't answer or say 'But I was too young Mr Parker. All I remember is that he was a ginger person, a ginger person in a floury apron with a very strong baker, crushed cardamom smell'.

'Shall we look in together?' said the psychiatrist. 'I think we should look in together. I really don't think you make enough use of me, my poor boy.'

They looked in together.

It was hardly like a father, more as if a five-year-old had tried to put a father together, alone, untutored, but creatively, by himself. There were rags and rubbish and graveclothes and clay clumps, all sewn together with lengths of thick black thread. There was a bruised puffy skin, striped and black and blue through the make-up, smatterings of stains from a hundred and fifty-three knifewounds. There were stripes along his face, stripes along his throat, about his back and front and everywhere. Could this have been a person? thought Vincent. He sniffed. No baker smell there.

He struggled to get out of Mr Parker's arms for Mr Hunch didn't like it. Parker sighed and set him down and hummed 'Something shining bright – My Soul', which told Vincent he must be going away. He told himself it didn't matter for he was at home, in his way of living, without this Doctor Parker. He hummed as well, to show he didn't care. The friendly nurse called Kayo came over. She smiled down at him, in his hospital bed.

She took his empty hands in hers and said that he mustn't fret and worry. A new doctor was coming tomorrow and that Parker, although the Powers That Be were very much against him, was doing his damnedest to get back to the hospital anyhow. In the meantime, if Vincent wanted anything, anything at all, she stressed this, all he had to do was ask her for it, and

Hunch laughed and said, 'Oh very touching Vincent, but we've no time to play the romantic persona now. We've business to attend to. Come on, draw your hand away.'

Vincent drew his hand away, but asked Nurse Kayo if there was another pen he could borrow. She laughed and rolled her eyes and said she'd see what she could do.

She let him hold it till the drugs took effect and then she took it easy back again. As far as Vincent was concerned though, he thanked her for it, forgot about her promptly and rushed out of the hospital with it tight in his hand. Mr Hunch and the Inner Circle were waiting for him at the carnival and they were happy for, with Parker now gone, they could stay hidden, forever, amongst all the murder gangs.

No Sign of Panic, 1981

It's Sunday night. My da says there's an American murder film on TV. My ma goes to bed, saying she isn't in the mood for it and anyway, she wants him to talk to me.

'She's thinking of going to London again Tommy,' she says. 'Tell her she can't go.'

'Who says so?' I say. She turns on me.

'Listen wee girl, you're not so big you can't be put over my knee.' I turn on her.

'No you listen ma. You're not so big you can't be put over mine.'

We stare at each other, not moving. Then, 'You've turned into one cheeky wee bitch,' she says, and leans over to pick up her book and glasses. 'Go to bloody England then. Get yourself killed. I'm away to bed.'

When we're alone my da says, 'Maybe you'd better wait till you're sixteen Amelia.'

'I'm nineteen da.'

'Oh – well, what about yer schooling then?'

'I left three years ago.'

'Oh – well, what about yer job then?'

'What about it?'

My da shrugs and we settle down to watch the film only he doesn't watch it and instead starts telling me about him living in London which I never knew. From there he goes on to mentioning all the countries he's been in and especially their hospitals. He smiles, his voice rises and he comes alive on remembering how often he nearly was dead.

'Name a country Amelia,' he says, 'and I bettcha I've been in a hospital in it. Go on – name one.'

I'm fed up. 'I don't want to da,' I say.

So he names them himself. I don't really listen. It's a terrible hot August night but my da always lights the fire. I go into the kitchen to make tea and he goes on talking about how many times he's got the last rites.

Shots are fired – four, five, six cracks. A rifle. I go on filling the kettle. Then there's more – rapid, closer together – on the other side of our wall. So I back up against it between the window and the stove. The shootin' stops and I wait a bit longer. Then I drop down and scoot past the window, back out to the patio, which is what my ma insists on calling it. She's never had a room with so many windows. When she first saw it, she said, 'I can have nice things too.' And then, 'It's called a patio.' She didn't know what to do with all the windows so she covered them up. 'Could be dangerous,' she said.

My da isn't there. At first I think he's gone up to her. He's always saying to us, 'Get down! Keep away from that window! Don't turn on the light!' – and what does he do? At the first shots he's out the front door, right into the street, to see what's going on. Then he spots some neighbours and goes over to them at their gate.

At the second burst of shots he pushes Mrs Young and that new woman with the funny name who isn't Irish onto the ground behind the Youngs' garden wall. He pushes Mrs Young into the bullet in the dusk and it goes into her back. Mrs

Lollobrigida screams and screams and keeps trying to jump up. My da holds her down behind the wall, not knowing Mrs Young is shot. He thinks he's banged his foot against the wall.

I go out of the patio and there's my ma rushing downstairs with her bed shawl trailing off her shoulders. She keeps saying 'Tommy oh Jesus oh Tommy oh Jesus' over and over again.

She stops near the bottom and stands still, her jaw working and quivering with no sound coming out, her whole face giving little ripples and jumps. I find it hard to look at her. She focuses on me.

'You!' she cries. 'He's over there, you! Your da's over there!' She reaches out to hit me or grab me or lean on me or something, and she misses and stumbles down two stairs.

'Why weren't you talking to him?' she shouts. 'You were supposed to be talking to him – in there! You'd no call to let him go out!' She opens her mouth and takes that breath that can only mean a scream. I step back away from it but then the door opens and the little Young child comes in. She's in her bedclothes and coat, silent and sleepless and she's going to wait in our house while her da goes with her ma in the ambulance to the hospital. My ma sees her, closes her mouth, doesn't scream and gets ready to go in the ambulance too.

The ambulance comes and my da and Mrs Young are put into it. Mrs Lollobrigida, standing in her flipflops, hysterically tells reporters how she pushed both my da and Mrs Young onto the grass and held them there. Then she took charge, she says, and calmed everyone else down. She says it's because she's an auxiliary nurse and knows about these things. They take her statement and print her story along with a picture of her standing in the middle of the street, a serious smile on her face. The neighbours don't like it. They stop talking to her – some for days, some forever. The ambulance drives down to the Mater.

'Yes Amelia,' said my da in the patio twenty minutes earlier, 'I've been in hospital in Barranquilla, in Yemen, in Malta . . .

let's see, there was that Quaker hospital in New England, St Mary's in Altoona, the Colombo General, even that funny sounding one in Archangel, all the way up in Russia! But do you know what?' he said. 'No, what?' I said. 'I've been in all these hospitals,' he said. 'Could've even died in them! But guess what?' 'What?' I said. 'I've never, ever, been in the Mater, that's what!' He looked to see how I was taking it. He waved his arms, excited, like he couldn't believe it himself. 'Imagine!' he cried. 'It's only just down the road! A hospital only just down the road and I've never been in it! Isn't that funny?' 'Yes,' I said and got up to make the tea.

I bring little Angelica Young into the patio and I sit her down at the table in front of the fire and I give her cheese on toast and tea. She eats dumbly, looking at the flames, not even thinking to take off her coat in the sweltering heat and me not thinking to ask her. Our Josie comes down out of bed and, yawning and rubbing her eyes, sits with her little friend and watches the flames too.

Then I forget them and think about my friend, Bernie, Angelica's big sister. Bernie Young's in the Mater at this very moment with anorexia. Caught with her anorexia. It used to be bulimia and in between it being bulimia and anorexia, it used to be a mixture of the two. She weighs more than four and a half stone now and she's due out tomorrow. There's a big cake sitting on their kitchen windowsill. I saw Mrs Young today in the Spar buying the ingredients. I was buying 7 lbs of Glauber's salt. She smiled at me in the queue.

'Our Bernadette's coming home on Monday,' she said and puts this big bag of brown sugar and a packet of currants on the counter. I looked at them.

'She's better now,' said Mrs Young. 'I'm making our Bernie a cake, a cake. Our Bernie's coming home, she's coming home.'

Shouldn't make her a cake, I thought. She won't eat it. Then I said goodbye and turned away to go.

I get up and go and stand at the door to get a bit of air and watch the Peelers circling things and looking for spent casings and cartridges. Then I see Aunt Dolours and Aunt Sadie coming up through the dark to our house. Their arms are folded across their chests and they have fierce awful looks on their faces. The Brits let them through the cordon and they come in and ask what's going on. They get angry because I can't get to the point. I don't know how to get to the point. I don't know really, what the point is.

'Do you want strangled?' they shout at me and push me a bit, the two of them. So I say something about m'da maybe being shot and about Mrs Young maybe being shot but that I'm not sure, can't remember, and why don't they go away and leave me alone. They do leave me alone then, and sit down in their bedclothes and coats beside our Josie and little Angelica, beside the fire, looking at the flames, and they wait too.

Next day I go into work. During the morning break everyone comes around my table as usual. Deborah's reading an English tabloid.

'Oh look,' she says. 'There was a shooting last night over your way Amelia.'

Isobel rustles Page Three in disgust.

'My tits are better than her tits. Look everybody. Don't youse think her tits are rubbish?' She pulls a face and pushes the paper round for everyone to see. Deborah squints at the newsprint in her paper. She won't get glasses.

'There was a woman and a man shot but the woman died in the ambulance.'

Trudy is gazing at wedding dresses in magazines and tapping her front tooth with a long red fingernail. 'Mmmmm,' she says, her big thick curls falling round her face. Poor Hester's knitting another aran and trendy Karen's pulling faces behind her back.

'And fancy that,' says Deborah. 'This man who was shot even has the same surname as you Amelia.'

171

'Oh yes,' I say, swallowing my creamy coffee. 'That's because that's my da.' And there is silence.

After the break, the news reaches the ears of my supervisor and then my supervisor's supervisor who rings her boss, in the separate Stormont building, and he tells her to tell me that I can go home – must go home in fact. They call me to the top of the room.

'Amelia. We've just heard.' They both stand on the other side of the desk and look quickly at me, then even quicker away.

'Heard what?' I say. I think of health reports, relief work, whatever they want.

'Why! About your father, Amelia. The shooting, dreadful, awful. We're so sorry.'

'What about?'

I don't understand. They look as if they don't understand either. They look shocked and surprised, puzzled – suspicious even. I think I must be looking exactly the same way.

'Oh,' I say, when I finally get what they're talking about. They seem relieved, that somehow, now, we're on the same wavelength.

'Is he in Intensive Care?' they ask. I don't know what they mean again. The words making up the questions slip away and I can't get the hang of them at all.

'What hospital's he in?' they say. They just won't leave it alone. I don't answer. I'm getting angry.

'You can go home,' they say, kindly maybe.

'Why?' I say. Now I *am* angry.

They look at me again, like maybe I'm troublesome. Then they look at one another. I just keep on looking back at them. Then we all look away and down, at the in- and out-trays on the supervisor's desk between us. The typing has stopped behind me. I don't like that.

'I think it would be best Amelia,' they say. 'Take a few days off.'

I'm embarrassed.

'We'll pay you of course,' says my supervisor's supervisor hurriedly. I'm even more embarrassed.

'I'll stay here,' I say and think back to my half-typed report – someone with gastroenteritis, an inflamed gut. Will they get their benefit? It seems I have to know.

'I'm getting back to work,' I say, stepping away from the desk, putting them in their place.

'Oh Amelia, please!' says one. 'Go home. Have a rest.' Fuck off I think. 'Be with your family,' says the other. 'Visit your father. Come back Friday, Monday, even the following week.' She smiles, face bright. I don't smile. She turns to her companion. Spreads her hands. Raised eyebrows. What can we do? I'm trying my best here. She isn't helping much is she? By the way, the eyebrows go on, my boy got his 'A's. What did yours get? We're so proud. Do you know he could walk and talk before he was born? Filtered coffee. Marks and Spencer. The Classics oh, and Shakespeare.

I've read Shakespeare, I think. *Titus Andronicus*. What's the big deal?

She turns back to me. 'How soon after do you Catholics . . . er . . . I mean . . . you bury your dead quick, don't you? Would it be your neighbour's today?' Looks at watch to see if funeral's today. She looks back up. She looks pleading. 'You can't stay here Amelia. You have to go. Go.'

I turn and catch people's heads turning away – Shirley with her comfortable furry slippers on her painful bunioned feet, Carol with her dead sister who crashed drunk into a lamppost, Belinda with her Reserve RUC boyfriend, sweet Deborah with her kindness and her terror of fat thighs, Cushendall Karen with her secret Republican sympathies and poor Hester who looks old when she isn't, and who types and knits, and types and knits, and won't ever speak to anyone.

I get the bus into town, dander about, buy a few sweets in

Woolworths, a cup of tea in Littlewoods, and then I see Vincent in the grounds of St Anne's. A big black bird's flapping about his feet near the pigeons but he's just staring ahead at nothing. I'm right up at him, at his face, which has a line of stitches across it, before he even sees me.

'Come and drink with me Vincent,' I say.

He looks at me properly.

'Oh it's you Amelia,' he says. 'I can't. I have to sell these guns.'

'You can do that later,' I say. 'Come on.'

'But I'm on tablets.'

'Have an orange juice.'

'But I don't want an orange juice.'

'Well take a friggin' drink then.'

I take hold of him with his imaginary guns for imaginary deals with imaginary gunmen and I take him into Kelly's as fast as I can.

'I suppose I could just have an orange juice with maybe a wee sort of vodka in it,' says Vincent.

'Yeah,' I say. 'Have that.'

So he has three vodkas, two pints of Tennent's with a snake-bite chaser then takes out his bottle of schizoid stuff.

Later on, when the light's just going, I bung him into an Ardoyne taxi to be got home. I don't want to go home so I take another taxi up the Falls, call on some others and carry on drinking.

Sinners and Souls, 1982

Fergal spied Amelia by the bar in Terry McDermott's. It was a small club and it was Saturday night and it was crowded. He called over to her above the music. She looked up and waved back. They were both at the beginning of getting drunk.

He went over and said a few words, and then they laughed and Amelia said a few words back. Then, when they both got their drinks, Amelia said, 'See ye again then Fergal' and Fergal said, 'Yeah, see ye again then' too. He went back to where he was sittin', with Gabriel, Mario and Ta. He handed out the alcohol, sat back down round the small table and drank on. At the end of the night the other three said they were goin' to a house to play cards and after that, to bring some girls in, and did Fergal want to come along too? Fergal said no, he didn't, that he'd go on home, that he'd go on home alone and that he'd see them again sometime.

Fergal lived in Ardoyne so first of all he got a Falls Road taxi into town. Then he walked round to Smithfield, only to find he was already too late. The Ardoyne taxis were sporadic but as a rule, nothing much happened after two o'clock. It was already a quarter to three in the morning and nobody else was waiting so that was Fergal's cue to head on home. He did this and it didn't occur to him, as it wouldn't to lots of other similar people in Belfast, to go round and get a normal taxi in Great Victoria Street instead. He began the two-mile walk by himself and he took, it goes without saying, the Catholic Cliftonville route.

First though, he had to go along Millfield, across the bottom of dodgy Peters Hill, then towards Unity Flats and Clifton Street. The town was dead. Clifton Street was dead. Carlisle Circus was always dead. He reached the religious fork at the Antrim Road and, of course, the Antrim Road was dead too. At the Clifton Street graveyard he got a move on. He was going at a fair crackin' pace anyway because Frances, who'd made him angry, had come back into his head all over again. Two nights ago she'd linked arms with Skelly, who was smirking at Fergal and acting superior, and together they'd joined forces and 'It's over Fergal,' she had said. 'Ye have to face it Fergal,' she went on, rubbing the salt and pepper in. 'Eugene and me are just a different sort of people. We're just a different sort of people, a different sort of class.' And then, ten minutes later they were laughing from the bar and he knew, oh he knew, it was about him.

It was lucky for Fergal he paused in this tormenting thought just when he did for, in the next second, as he passed the Home For The Blind on the Cliftonville Road, he looked up and noticed a red Ford Cortina easing itself out of mixed Manor Street. It noticed him, paused, then turned away, sneaked up and across into Orient Gardens and disappeared completely from his view. As he walked, quicker now, by the Poor Clares nunnery with its high wall all the way around, he began to imagine, without really believing it, that that car was weaving its way, down a bit, and right a bit, and left a bit, in and out of those dark side streets until it reached the Antrim Road and, when it reached the Antrim Road, it was going to glide back round to the Cliftonville again. This time though, it would be behind him. It struck Fergal that this fantasy was so strong, so vivid and so full of urgency that he decided the least he could do was turn round to see. He did, and there, not thirty yards behind, was the red Ford Cortina. It was sitting in the dark, facing his way, its engine purring and its inside full of fellas.

'It'll be a black taxi or a red Ford Cortina,' somebody or other had said and this was incredible for a red Ford Cortina was exactly what it was. Even the men in it seemed familiar, right down to the big fat one, taking up most of the room in the back. The driver had on a pair of big glasses, Fergal could make out, and 'The driver had on a pair of big glasses,' he remembered hearing from the ones who'd got away. Fergal was standing still while these thoughts were running through him, and the men in the car, in their turn, were still just sitting, looking out at him. This went on for a few more seconds, then the engine revved up, Fergal caught himself on and, with his old 'kneecapped' calf-wound, tried as best as he could to run away.

He got past the nuns' home, knowing it would be hopeless to bang on their gate to get help from them and he headed straight up by the billboarded grounds where the old Big House used to be. The car screeched to a halt very close behind him and this pause, to allow some of them to jump out and grab hold of him, gave Fergal the extra seconds he needed to burst round the corner of Catholic Rosapenna and throw himself under a big milk truck.

They ran round too. Having had him so close, he knew they couldn't now, just like that, let him get away. At the very least, he reckoned, they'd have to try to shoot him. That was his first thought. His second thought was of how he'd been stupid. He'd somehow, and without thinking, crawled inch by inch, until he was lying between the four front tyres of Eddie Breen's massive truck, used ostensibly for delivering harmless pints of milk. Too late he realised that when they looked under – and they would, for the lorry was the biggest thing in the universe – he would be trapped and at a mercy everybody in Northern Ireland knew just didn't exist. He sucked in a pile of air and before he could use it and get it out again, his throat closed over and he couldn't exhale.

The front of the red car pulled up adjacent to his calf, its engine still running, muffled voices coming from within. Then the car door opened and another man got out to join the others already out there. Fergal heard the sole of his boot scrape the road and smelt the cigarette he was holding in his hand. There were more footsteps approaching, belonging to the men who had been chasing him, followed by whispering, low cursing and a quick conference being held. He saw the lighted cigarette being thrown down near him, and he heard them, all bar the driver, going to look for him everywhere. They whacked the hedges, shoved apart bushes, cracked twigs and opened garden gates. He truly couldn't believe they really didn't know and he closed his eyes, wondering why he was still alive when he couldn't feel his body and wasn't sure even whether he was breathing or not.

No doors opened. No one normal came out to stop this from happening but in the end nothing happened and Fergal became another one who'd managed to get away. The murderers got fed up and climbed back into their red Ford Cortina and went to scour the dark streets to try to find somebody else. If they hurried, they reckoned, they'd be able to cut up Rosapenna, turn back down the Crumlin, get to Carlisle Circus and then to St Patrick's where, with any luck, they'd catch one of them blessin' themselves before dayfall. Also, they further reasoned, if they didn't find a man, it would be all right to take a woman, for it was a quarter past three in the night and they had to get started on someone, now didn't they?

The car drove off and Fergal stayed where he was, the ground beneath his belly, the lorry at his back, his life somehow yet working, all his blood intact in his veins. He couldn't get his arm up though, in order to see what the time was, because he had withdrawn to his centre. His periphery had gone away.

At the end of the night Bossy was going off with Dessie, Mario and Seb were going to a house, Bernie was maybe going off with Marcellus, she wasn't sure, but would Amelia hang round while she made up her mind? No, said Amelia, she would not. She was fed up being doddled about and was heading on home alone. Bye bye Bernie, she said, bye bye. She left the club at twenty past two and got a Falls Road taxi down the town. She got off before Castle Street. The town was dead. King Street was dead. There was no one else going her way. As usual, she was too late for the Ardoyne taxis, so cutting across Millfield and dodgy Peters Hill, she began the two-mile walk, taking, it goes without saying, the Catholic Cliftonville route.

As she walked along, she decided not to think of boys anymore then immediately she thought about Cahal and then she thought about Romano and then she thought about Gabriel and then she thought about Cahal again. Cahal had rubbed her sore stomach in bed and said 'Why don't you eat Amelia? And why don't we do it? Why don't you eat Amelia? Why don't you eat?' But now he was gone to America more than he wasn't and she was still here – for all her saying she was going – she was still here, in Belfast, without him. Of course Romano was Romano was Romano – in jail. Why'd he have to get mixed up with guns for? Gabriel was still around and very much available but when Gabriel kissed, he tried to get his hands everywhere. The ones who couldn't wait to get their hands everywhere, were usually terrible bad kissers. Amelia liked good kissers. So what should she do? She started to ponder this unanswerable boy problem but, catching a movement, she paused in her thoughts and looked straight up ahead.

She had passed Catholic Unity Flats, which stretched from the corner of the Protestant Shankill, and she was now heading up Clifton Street to the religious fork just above. From Carlisle Circus she could head left up the Crumlin but of course, given her persuasion, she would do no such thing at all. She was just thinking that she was wrong, that she hadn't seen anything fleeting up above her, when a shadow crossed over from the babyclothes shop thirty yards on. When the shadow came close, she saw who it was.

'Danny!' she shouted.

'Amelia!' he shouted back. Their voices echoed. They were standing just outside the derelict Protestant churches with all their broken windows and their half-missing walls. Nearby was the Orange Hall, fortified all round, with King Billy, holding his broken sword, sitting on his rearing horse, on top of it. Both Amelia and Danny were drunk.

'Where were you tonight?' said Amelia.

'Where were you?' said Danny.

'Where're ye goin'?' said Amelia.

Danny opened hazel eyes. 'Amelia,' he said. 'Kiss me.'

Amelia got annoyed and was about to say catch yourself on, when she changed her mind and moved closer and kissed him. She put her arms round his neck and he put his arms round her waist and they kissed and kissed, and kissed even more. It was a remarkable kiss Amelia was thinking, and she was just about to be very pleased with it when something occurred to her and she frowned and pushed Danny off.

'Hol' on a minute,' she said. 'Aren't you married now Danny? Didn't you marry somebody once?'

'Oh,' said Danny. He looked sad and hung his head. Then he lifted it. He was smiling. They kissed again. Then Amelia pushed him off for the second time. 'That's enough,' she said.

'Catch yourself on.' But more than that, she said goodbye. 'Goodbye Danny,' she said. 'Goodbye.' And off she went, into the Antrim Road, past the Clifton Street graveyard, up the Cliftonville, past the Home For The Blind, the poor Poor Clares, the row of billboards in front of the wasteground where the big old black house used to be, then into Rosapenna, past the milk lorry, through the Bone, up to the Bally streets, over the Brickfield then round to Ardoyne and her nice cosy bed.

Danny Megahey, happy, cheerful, in very, very good humour, turned away from Amelia and headed downtown. He was going the other way, down into Donegall Street, past St Patrick's Chapel, planning to be home in his house in the Markets in no time. But he wasn't. After hardly going any distance, a red car pulled up out of nowhere, and in an unexpected twist of events, Danny was taken, very much against his will, into the heart of the Shankill, where he met his protracted, grisly and truly awful end. His ordeal began at a quarter to four in the morning.

Going on for six-thirty, wee Eddie Breen came along to get his lorry set up and ready. He had a jaunty wee step because he was a jaunty wee man. Of course it was Sunday so he wasn't delivering milk, though lots of other days he wasn't delivering milk either. He reached his lorry, unlocked the door and was about to get in and get going, when an intuition made him halt. He reached for his gun. The moment the back of Fergal McLaverty's head appeared out from under the front of his vehicle, was the same moment Eddie Breen leaned over and stuck his pistol to it. Fergal twisted round and stared up at Eddie in the morning's summer light, and more especially at what he could see of the weapon in Eddie's hand. He managed to slip his own hands out in a gesture of surrender but didn't say a word or try to move a muscle until the milkman, with a wave of his gun, silently told him to get a move on.

Fergal tried to reconnect himself from the dissociated states his body and mind had got themselves into and Eddie, glancing up and down and around at every second, told him to hurry up, not to be as bloody slow as all that. Fergal tried his best. When the last of him was almost out from under the lorry and standing, the milkman got a grip and slammed him against the driver's door. Rapidly he searched Fergal, but found no weapon on him. All the same, what was he doing under the lorry? He pushed the gun deep into the younger man's side.

'What's going on?' said Eddie. 'Why're you under my lorry?'

'Nothin',' said Fergal, trying to swallow, breathe and talk at the same time. 'No reason.' He coughed. He would have liked Eddie to have been nice to him. But Eddie wasn't being nice to him. His jauntiness had evaporated. He was fed up checking under his lorry every single effin' time.

'Don't frig with me,' he said. Then his eyes narrowed as he looked closer at Fergal. 'Hol' on a minute. Don't I know you? Didn't I have you kneecapped one time?'

'Wasn't me,' lied Fergal. He shook his head. 'It was m'brother, m'older brother.'

'I'll ask ye one last time,' said Eddie. 'What were you doin' under my truck?'

He dug the gun in deeper and stuck his face right up against Fergal. It reached all the way up to Fergal's broad chest.

'I was just . . . just hidin'.'

It was the milkman who was mainly holding Fergal. He let go and Fergal slumped without the support. He stayed leaning against the door, quiet, trying, once more, to get his breath back. Eddie put his gun away and got down onto the ground.

'Listen—' he looked up before crawling under the lorry. 'Don't you be movin'. If I see you movin', I'll get up and I'll take m'gun out and I'll shoot ye from where I am. Understand?'

Fergal nodded. He stayed leaning where he was while wee Eddie got down to see if there was another carbomb. It didn't take long and when he got back up, he was wiping his hands in a cheerful, relaxed way. His short fuse was long again, he felt everything was once again wonderful. He looked at Fergal, surprised, as if seeing him for the first time.

'Okay, so,' he said, rubbing his hands. 'See ye again then big fella. I guess ye can go.' He pushed Fergal off his lorry. 'But hey,' he had an afterthought. 'D'ye see next time . . .' Fergal looked back. Eddie looked stern. 'Next time, do yerself a favour. Hide yerself somewhere else.'

That night Fergal went to the Shamrock in Ardoyne and spied his friends at a table near the bar. He went over and joined them and between big gulps of Tennent's, tried to tell what he could about the night before. It was a red Ford Cortina, he said and he said this a few times. It was full of them, he said. Driver had glasses, big fat guy in the back.

Most of the others weren't listening and the ones who were heard something that came out so different, that in the end they thought it was a funny story about that madman, Eddie Breen. Fergal himself began to wonder if maybe that's all the level it was on. He laughed as well. Eventually, Amelia, who realised, or at least for a moment realised, what it was he was going on about, said she'd walked home, she'd gone that way too. Nothing had happened to her though, she said. She hadn't met a sinner. She hadn't met a soul. She'd forgotten about Danny Megahey. They'd all heard and forgotten about Danny Megahey. Already, he was not remembered. Already, he was gone.

So on the whole it could be said that Fergal was sort of listened to, but when the band started up, life moved on and any attention that was left was only for the music and only for the drinking. This, of course, was just as it should be.

At the end of the night the club's steel security doors slammed shut and the crowd began to separate on the Brickfield. Sharon went off with Dessie, Amelia went off with Gabriel and Bernie said she might go with Mario but would the others hold on while she made up her mind? Fergal said okay he'd wait, but Ta and Frankie said no, they were going to head on to other things. One was going to a house in old Ardoyne. The other wanted home and into his bed.

'See ye again then,' shouted Fergal as Ta walked away on his short journey towards the New Lodge. Ta waved goodbye without turning round. He turned the corner and he'd be taking, no doubt, the short walk over the Bone, then down Rosapenna, across to the Cliftonville and along the Catholic bit of the Antrim Road. It was an hour and a half after midnight. All was silent. All was dark. Ta put his hands in his pockets and began to sing quietly as he went along.

The Present Conflict, 1983

Amelia began to wonder if there was more to life than drinking clubs, hanging about the areas and going out with boys. She decided there was. It was time to get an 'O' level. So one sunny spring evening, she tidied herself up, left the house and walked down the town to the Tech. Two hours later, feeling happy, feeling like a real adventurous person, and with a whole bunch of leaflets in her arms, she left the last of the three adult educational establishments she'd been visiting and headed round to the front of the City Hall where Janto Pierce was meeting her for a date.

As she walked, she glanced over the leaflets and was surprised to find that all the things she used to hate at school – which was everything – seemed much more appealing now that she didn't have to do them. She could do a language, she thought, French. She could do English. Two Englishes. One for reading, one for writing. How funny, she thought. She laughed. She could find out more about that fella Shakespeare, find out about that other fella Thomas Hardy, find out about yer woman Jane Austen and about all those others who were dead but who had once written things she'd here and there heard tell of. As well as that, she could do History, Geography, Politics, Philosophy, Science, Psychology and Sums. Along the lines of singing and dancing, were Singing and Dancing, Harmony and Music, Anatomy and Physiology and Using Her Voice. She could paint and draw and throw things in pottery and sketch and act and look after trees. In small print were courses listed for the future like Personality Development, Cultural Diversity, Community Education and Sexual Gender Politics. Amelia had no idea what any of that meant but whatever it was, it felt great for it was going to be taking place just a few miles down the road from her. Feeling a buzz, she went on walking, and carried on read-ing, until a car at the City Hall gave a sharp, penetrating and very annoyed beep.

She looked up. It was Janto's Cortina and it was huffin' and puffin' and having a fit. Janto, in a similar state, was huffin' and puffin' inside it. The clock above Robinsons & Cleavers said twenty minutes past eight. She wasn't late, so what was the beeping about? She tucked the leaflets into her jacket pocket, picked up her pace and went over to the Cortina to see.

Now Janto Pierce was not somebody she knew very well and to tell the truth, not somebody most people would want to know at all. Amelia though, was one of those unfortunates who had to learn everything from experience. She couldn't take a single thing as read. She'd seen this gorgeous creature about the bars and the clubs, for example, and decided to let the look of him deceive her. He was tall, strong, well-boned, crop-haired, giant fists, big body, a handsome, unruly, bit of a bully, beast and for some reason, her head transformed this data into sensitive, kind, gentle, considerate, attentive, tolerant and liking to put others at their ease. She knew, of course, that he hung around with Mad Brink McCaughey and all that gang but that, she thought, was no reason to judge him. Her friend Bossy Mossy, who knew everything about everybody, said oh yes it was, but she ignored Bossy and, with warnings and dangers not meaning warnings and dangers to Amelia, it made sense that when he asked her out at the end of last Sunday, well of course she'd said yes and had looked forward to the date ever since.

And now she was on it. She opened the passenger door, climbed in and pulled it closed after her. Janto was glaring ahead and saying nothing.

'What's wrong?' she said.

He started the engine with a thick-veined fist.

'Seems to me like ye didn't wanna meet.' His voice growled and snapped.

Oh dear, she thought. 'What d'ye mean?' she said.

'Ach, I'm not stupid you know!' He yanked the car out where the more careful driver would have eased. 'I seen ye! The way you were danderin' along there like ye owned the place, readin' them things in your hands and lookin' at the clock. I saw you look at the clock so don't try to deny it!'

'I'm not trying to deny it!' cried Amelia. 'Why would I deny it? I looked because you beeped. Why'd you beep? You'd no call to beep.'

He stepped on the accelerator. A lone woman crossing the road at Wellington Place had to jump out of the way. He ignored her and so did Amelia.

'Look listen, Janto,' Amelia thought she'd lighten the mood for this wasn't a good way to be starting off for them. Besides, she was excited about her discoveries at the college and wanted to share them with another. She forgot, of course, that on some occasions, in some places, with some people, it was best to keep your excitement to yourself. 'I was just round at the college,' she babbled, missing another warning, which was Janto's stampy scowl, getting stampier and scowlier by the minute. 'This here,' she drew out a leaflet and tried to show it to him, 'is from the Humanities Department.' She said 'Humanities Department' as if she knew what it meant and as if she'd said it more than once in her life.

'College!' The car veered. 'Humanities Department!' Amelia felt pleased she'd made an impression, bizarrely not recognising the type of impression that it was. She was about to carry on with 'adult education', 'GCE', 'extra-mural' and 'textbook' when Janto cried,

'What are *you* going to college for? Sure ye're a girl!'

He swung the car round Carlisle Circus and Amelia banged her shoulder against the side door. Instinctively, she noted it was unlocked and also, instinctively, checked the position of the doorhandle. Best to know these things, she thought. The car righted itself on the Antrim Road and she too straightened up in her seat. She didn't put on her seatbelt either for it was best to be on the safe side at all times.

'Stupid females,' Janto was saying. 'I mean like I mean – they're totally startin' to think they're somethin'.' He tooted at some pigeons, perhaps female, sitting on the wall of the Clifton Street graveyard. They ignored him and went on sitting. He muttered 'bastards' at them and then 'fuckin' bastards' at a British Army patrol that was passing and then 'fuckin' SS bastards' as an RUC Land Rover also drove by. Finally he cast an enraged, wordless glare at a big green bush that had spread itself out, just to the side and a bit up in front of them. It appeared to be an innocent bush, doing absolutely nothing, but this here was Belfast so you could never be sure. Some bushes were indeed real and just grew and obeyed nature. Others were military intelligence – and took pictures. It was hard to see what this particular bush was up to, for the car was going fast and besides, when it came down to it, who gave a damn about those things anyway?

It was at this point Amelia realised she had a frozen smile on her face. Apart from the 'you'd no call to beep' bit earlier, when she'd felt her own temper rising, she'd mostly been placating with 'There there, coo coo. You're great, you're marvellous, you're the grand one and only. You're gorgeous. You're exotic. Am I glad I met you'. It was only now, five whole minutes into listening to him, that she noticed this achy smile and when she tried to remove it, her jaw caught and clicked with the effort. By this time, Janto was going on about women who got in strangers' cars, or the cars of people they'd only just met. Those sorts of women were stupid, he said, but then, as all women were stupid, they were just stupider than the normal stupid kind.

'It's like Blacks,' he went on, yelling now – as if she was deaf but that that was no excuse not to hear him. 'Take Blacks. Take that Bell Curve thing. Blacks are less intelligent than Whites and of course, you'd be more intelligent than a Black man because at least you're—'

He stopped. Something unexpected struck at his system of certainties and he reeled in his seat and his car wobbled and had a sneeze. Although he had never thought of this before, when it came down to it, could Amelia, being a woman, ever be more intelligent than a man? The real question of course was, would it be better to be a man even if you had to be Black, or would it be better to be female with frailties, feelings, feebleness, fragility and no brains – but at least with a skin that was White? Janto had to pull over to examine his regimentally structured hierarchical belief system and decide on an answer that would fit into it.

His way of pulling over was to fly up the cribbie and crash through a wooden fence and put the brake on. Amelia tried to get her breath, check her limbs and pat her hair down again. While doing so, she noticed a bush shaking and trembling some little distance on. It was quivering and twitching and very, very nervous and this may have been natural given it had nearly been run over, but on the other hand, had a bush actually been growing there earlier, when she'd been on her way down the town? So while Janto was engrossed, frowning, biting his lip and crying, 'Black man!' 'No! White woman!' 'No! Wait a sec! Black man!' 'No! No! Give me a minute! White woman!' and so on, Amelia tried to recall whether it was MI5, MI6 or indeed, a completely different secret organisation that dealt with intelligence work in Northern Ireland these days. Eventually she gave up for she just couldn't remember and for goodness sake, it wasn't as if it was an interesting thing anyway.

In the end, for Janto couldn't abide ambiguity, ambivalence, abstraction, paradox or any sort of in-between mussed-up stuff, he decided to opt for being Black and managing as best he could, rather than be a woman, no matter how White the colour. This decision, although he knew it would be for the best, didn't at all make him happy. This was because as a Black man, all them White boys he knew – even the dozy deadhead ones – would end up being more intelligent and superior than himself. Poor Janto's mind couldn't deal with this demotion and so it decided the only way to feel better, would be to take all his pent-up, convoluted, entangled emotions, and dump them – for after all, it was her fault – onto Amelia. He was just about to do this when he was distracted by catching sight of Provie Joe's eating establishment down the road. His face immediately looked strained. Here was another problem his system hadn't yet come to terms with. Life was just one unfair thing after another.

For yes, Provie Joe's establishment, as everybody knew, was a thriving wee Chinese chip shop down the Antrim Road. It had gotten its nickname because Mr Ho had become very complaisant a lot of years back and had started paying the Provisionals a great whack of money. This was so he could carry on his business without any hitches, they said, which was a bit peculiar as he'd been carrying it on without any hitches anyway. All the same, he was a sane fellow and made his payments with great amiability and never missed a week and was very popular with all young people because of the nice, thick, cheap chips he made. This meant that in spite of the protection money pay-out, which was heavy, a bit of a mental strain and something that would go on forever, Mr Ho still made a good income which kept himself, his family and his roaring business intact. Alive, would be another way of putting it.

One day though, a while back, as Janto was eating Mr Ho's thick chips, smothered in brown sauce, tomato sauce, curry, chutney, vinegar, pickled eggs, peas, salt and pepper, it occurred to him that this wasn't at all fair or to his liking. He, Janto, didn't have his own chip shop. He, Janto, had to work hard at labouring, taxi-driving, window-cleaning, bar work and other high-risk, back-breaking, low-paid types of jobs – and look: what did he have to show for it? He had been born and bred in the country. He was a true good Irishman, whereas the likes of Provie Joe there, were nothing but only Chinese. Janto's mind had assimilated this discriminatory attack against him and ever since, whenever he saw Provie Joe, or indeed, the likes of him – which included T V images of Asians, Sub-Continentals, Arabs, Jews, Red Indians (which he refused to call Native Americans), Eskimos, Aborigines, anybody in the least bit dusky oh, and of course, the English – he became livid and speechless and apoplectic and he spat. Like now.

'Chinks!' he spluttered, the words hitting the side window, Amelia's side window. 'Look at them! Just who do they think they are!'

He continued to rave and let loose spittle while his mind, which liked to tie things up and have everything sorted into nice little bundles, knew it would now have to deal with computations of a different kind. These new mental columns would involve working out the cerebral differences between Black males and Chinese males or whether it would be better to be a Chinese man or a Black man given the degrees of variations in their intellects, meaning, of course, their colours.

Amelia, meanwhile, wiping her cheek and wiping it again, began to wonder what she should do. It was starting to dawn on her that the Jantos of this world might be better off staying in the imagination, where at least they could be kept under control, or made different in some way that would be pleasing to her. Although she was as yet incapable of making any connection as to why she might have been drawn to this angry boy-person in the first place, she did know one thing and that was that she'd had enough. This was a first for Amelia and she was just beginning to think that it might be better to go on home and maybe read through her leaflets and pick a subject to do, when she looked through the windscreen and saw the bush part its leaves and a quarter-inch of a metal object poke through.

'I mean like I mean,' Janto was going on, 'it's not that I've anything against people. Don't get me wrong – everybody's entitled to their life.'

'Janto,' said Amelia, interrupting him, 'can we get out of here? I think we should get out of here.' Amelia could now see something else. There was a black tube further down the bush which looked like it had been trained on Provie Joe's establishment but now, given Janto's car was in the way, it was trained exactly upon them. The little metal thing higher up that she had seen earlier, had positioned itself also. Both things were now looking their way.

Janto was oblivious. He was jabbering on, his points mad or at the very least incoherent and he only stopped when a disembodied English voice said, 'Christ! Will you shut up! And move that fuck-een car!'

Silence. The car rocked. Janto recovered first.

'Who's that?' he cried. 'It's that bastard bush! It's those bloody Brit soldiers! Well,' he started the engine, 'when I run it over, we'll soon see who's the bush in the big picture then!'

'Janto,' said Amelia, putting a warning hand on his arm. 'I

don't think you should do that. Don't do that Janto. Those bushes on the end have got guns in their twigs.'

It occurred to Amelia at this point, and forcefully, that Janto was a bit like her father. And what if, went her mind, just like her father, he decided to behave exactly like him? In that case, she worried, they would both be in big trouble. In that case, she bit her lip, they would both be about to come to the end of their lives. This was the first time Amelia had made a follow-through connection – that something or someone, once familiar in her past, can make a comeback again and again in her present. Luckily though, Janto wasn't as mad as her father, so when one of the bushes began to take pictures of them, all Janto did was curse, rev up his bad-tempered engine, and reverse with a lot of squealing tyres back out onto the road. From there, he drove towards the Cliftonville, and even stopped at the lights, which was amazing, but only because he was distracted, not at all because they'd turned red.

Amelia meanwhile tried to act like everything was normal, which is exactly what you're supposed to do when everything is anything but. Without looking at Janto, she leaned over and picked up a cassette which had fallen out of the glove compartment. It was a tape of fairy-tale folk songs with Janto's name scrawled across the front. On the cover was a wispy fair maiden, looking frail and feeble and delicate and lonely, as well as powerless and beautiful and, of course, on her own. The songs were by men. The first was called 'When I Was A Trusting And Virile Young Man', the second, 'Don't Go Up The Glens After Midnight', the third, 'La Belle Dame Something Or Other', set to music by some songster who had 'borrowed' the words from a poem. And so on, went all the songs, along the lines of 'Danger! Danger!' 'Watch Out For Females!', 'Never Trust A Grown Woman With Bows In Her Hair!'. Amelia blinked as she read this and then, sensing something about to happen, she looked up as Janto's fist slammed over to her face.

He snapped it to a halt, a millimetre from contact. She dropped the tape, let out a cry and banged her head back on the cardoor rim.

'See,' he said through clenched teeth. He was leaning over, his fist prodding against her cheekbone. He was staring at her, or at somebody, with naked hatred in his eyes.

'See,' he said. He spoke softly. 'See, Amelia Lovett. It's just that easy. Don't you ever tell me what to do in front of the enemy again.'

The lights changed and he dropped his hand to the gearstick. They turned up the Cliftonville and Janto spoke again. It would be simple to kill a woman, he said. Just lift her up, dash her down, smash her to pieces on flagstones, pull her arms and legs off, then leave her lying and walk away after cracking her skull apart.

Amelia jumped out as they slowed at the next lights. She fell onto the cribbie, rolled, skidded, scuttered along on her belly and eventually stopped when she banged herself off a far wall. She ended up a lot of yards along the footpath, still alive, with her body a bit shaky, everything not smashed but with her face now in a hedge.

'Fuck's sake!' said the hedge. It was tired. It was exasperated. 'Will ye get out of the way, wee girl. I can't see through yer head you know.'

Amelia obliged. She leapt up, not at all caring that a Provie shrubbery from Ardoyne, possibly liaising with another Provie shrubbery opposite, was spying on a tree that was partners with the bush, that same bush that was spying on Provie Joe's down the road. What did that matter? Amelia had more important things on her mind.

For example, it wasn't that she *wanted* to be afraid or miserable on dates, it was just that she was addicted to being so. And it was odd, she noticed, that whenever boys found her attractive, they either ignored her, insulted her or tried to get whatever it was they found attractive about her, rapidly, oh very rapidly, to change. 'I love the way you walk,' they often said for example. 'Hop in Amelia, I'll give you a lift.' Tonight had been the first time with the fist though. Last time too, she decided.

So she was gathering her scattered leaflets and vowing to keep away from mad people, when Janto jumped out of the car bewildered and, from the look of him, about to start to cry.

'Amelia!' he blubbered. 'What happened? Did something happen? Whad'ye jump out of m'car for?'

Amelia ignored him and in answer to her coldness, he fell to his knees and did cry. Tears rolled down his cheeks. They were cannonballs, and like cannonballs, they exploded with big bangs all over the concrete. Cars tooted and cursed as they swerved to avoid hitting him. Oh hit him, hit him, thought Amelia, but damn it, they did not. She turned away quickly, before he could get his first wail out. He got his first wail out. The whole road shook from the shock.

'Ameeliaaa!' he yelled, now on all fours before her, beating the road and bawling his eyes out. How embarrassing, she thought. I hope people don't think he's with me. 'Ameeliaa!' he wailed, not giving a damn about what people thought. 'I neeed yooo! Commmme baaack! Don't leeeve mmeee! Don't go!' He beat the concrete till it was hurting and he exploded more and more tears from out the inside of him. Amelia glanced back and saw they were heavy-volume, massive ones. She turned away quickly again and collided with Mrs Begley. Mrs Begley was a neighbour, on her way out of the Poor Clares convent door.

'Oops!' said the woman. 'Well, hello love it's a great night isn't it, sun still around at this time too. What's that big scratch on your face?'

Amelia touched it. There wasn't any blood but the skin felt ripped, sticky, and torn.

'Hello Mrs Begley!' shouted over Janto before Amelia could

get a chance to get a word in at all. He had, as quickly as he had started, stopped wailing. He was back in his car, and doing three miles per hour alongside them. He seemed cheerful again. How peculiar, thought Amelia. Boys certainly consisted of some very strange stuff.

'Why hello Gervais Joseph son what about your ma?' asked Mrs Begley.

'She's fine Mrs Begley but she wants to give ye the aquarium back because the fish all died. D'ye want a lift?'

Puffing and panting, Mrs Begley got herself into the passenger seat, telling Janto what a nice young lad he'd always, always been. The car sank with her weight. 'I've just bin visitin' those poor auld nuns . . .' she said, 'bringing them a drop of butter, white as anything, skin and bone, skin and bone, skin and bone they are.'

Janto, happy again for he had an extremely short memory, moved off, singing to himself that he was a single girl all alone in a great big world. Mrs Begley, beside him, sang something completely different from her old Forties ballroom repertoire. Every so often they turned and smiled at each other. Amelia, holding her leaflets, stood still and watched as the car disappeared up the road. Before she could move, or get a handle on the situation, Tommy McGivern crashed into her as he ran round the corner of Rosapenna Drive.

'Amelia!' he cried. 'What happened to your face? Did he do it?'

Amelia stared.

'Who?' she cried. 'Janto Pierce?'

'What?' said Tommy. 'No! The flasher! There's a flasher in the area. A menace in a silver Ford.'

'He flashed our Veronica,' he went on. 'Kerbed along beside her. Stopped the car, opened it up, she looked over and there was his dick!'

'We got him trapped,' shouted Fergal, who also came round

the corner. Both of them were excited. 'He's in the area and he can't get away. We'll get him, he can't escape. Bap, Colm and them'ins are blocking off the Oldpark, the Dallisons and the McGarritys are covering the Bone. The others—'

The others ran up.

'Amelia! Have you been flashed too? What way'd he go?'

'He went that way,' cried Amelia. 'Only it isn't the flasher. It's Janto Pierce. He's mad — but not normal mad — really mad . . .'

The others wouldn't listen. They weren't interested in Janto Pierce. He was a wrecker and a tearer, a bully, a nutcase, who hung around with Mad Brink McCaughey and so would be dead soon anyway. Surely Amelia must know that? They looked at her. She realised she could hardly say she didn't. So why was she walking into it? They looked at her again. She couldn't answer that either. They tutted and thought this just typical of a girl.

'Did he have his dick out?' they asked. 'No but—' she started to say. They stopped listening. No dick out, no case to answer. They turned away. Full stop. The flasher now – that was another matter. He was perverted. They got their attention at once back to him.

'Maybe it's a Protestant and he's sneaked through the barricades.'

'An Orangie! An Orangie!' all of them cried.

'Or maybe a soldier, in plain clothes, driving round the area.'

'A Brit! A Brit!' all of them cried.

Bap's wee brother pushed his way through. He had sticky-out ears and a voice that was breaking and was waving his arms all over the place. He doubled over to get a breath. The others jumped up and down.

'What is it Weebap?' they cried. 'Is it the flasher? The menace in the area? The dick? C'mon, hurry up! You've got to tell us before it's too late.'

'It's not the flasher!' squeaked Weebap. He waved his arms. 'Never mind the flasher!' he croaked. 'It's Alex Higgins! He's playing snooker right this minute up in the Star!'

There was a silence. Holy awe and precious frankincense fell over the whole of Rosapenna – but only for a second for then uproar broke out. The boys fought in the narrow street to get by each other, to get into their houses, to grab up their cue sticks and get up to the Star.

'What about the flasher?' cried Amelia. Nobody bothered answering her.

'The menace in the area?' she shouted. They were all running away.

'Your Veronica, Tommy? Tommy!'

Tommy hesitated. He looked put out. The others were disappearing fast, the dust of the street flying from their feet. Cries of 'Hurricane . . . Hurricane . . . Wait for me, oh Hurricane . . . Get out of m'way, will ye!' Tommy, cornered by Amelia, looked at the ground. He shuffled his feet. He shrugged.

'Ach well, you know what it's like Amelia,' he said. 'Probably got away by now.' He himself sidled towards the corner, which brought his body a few inches closer to his idol and to the Star. 'There's no point . . .' He trailed off, he shook his head, took a few more disguised steps – and was gone.

Amelia was alone and disgusted. She kicked an empty Coke tin after them then, seeing a Mars Bar wrapper lying in the gutter, wondered what there could be in the fridge.

She went home and opened it. Two things stood out – the bottom layer of Milk Tray her Aunt Dolours had left for later and the remains of a roast chicken sitting on a cold greasy plate.

Standing with the fridge door open and the cold air biting, Amelia bit into the chocolates while tearing off the slippy chickenskin. She threw this papery high-calorific cover away, far away from her, then sank her teeth deep into the meat. With the carcass still up at her face, she looked over the top of it and saw a string of raw sausages sitting on another plate. Reaching for these also, she squeezed the beef out of its skin and ate the raw and the cooked together.

Then, with more chocolates going down, she ate at the pilchards, munched on the potatobread and carried the milk to the toilet. She drank it off. She swallowed her saliva, breathed deeply to get ready, stuck and twiddled her fingers down her throat and then pulled them out again.

It was no good. She'd never been a great vomiter. Should've drunk the milk first, she thought. Oh well, she sighed, never mind. She'd do an extra day of not eating, as well as taking some laxatives. She got her beloved Senacot out of her stiletto in the wardrobe right away. She counted them into her palm. Twenty-nine, thirty, thirty-one, thirty-two. She shook the container, three stuck at the bottom, thirty-three, thirty-four, thirty-five. No more. Have to do, she thought. She went to the watertap. She drank them down as fast as possible, losing touch with them, as she did with everything, as soon as they went below her neckline.

She took off her make-up, put TCP on her scratches and got into bed for there was nothing else she wanted to do. It was getting dark and the house was empty. She covered her bones with the blankets and closed her eyes and tried to sleep. Thoughts started up. She recognised them immediately. '. . . as if ye owned the place' – 'not that great you know' – 'not that important . . .' – '. . . ugly big breasts if you eat too much . . .' – '. . . men don't like skinny women.'

She got up, put on the lamp and got herself a glass of water. She wished there was some alcohol, but there wasn't a drop in the house. She climbed back into bed again and reached for her leaflets. Taking her time, she read through them carefully, then read through them again, thinking hard.

Finally she picked something, a subject she could start with, and if she liked that, she told herself, she could try a few more.

She lifted her pen and the application form and burping gently, and frequently, wrote her name then her preferred choice at the top of the page.

Incoming, 1986

Marseillaise Jupp didn't know what to do about her husband. She'd only popped in for a couple of gins after all. And now look – because of the bomb, the roads were blocked, the shops were shut and she hadn't yet got the dinner. It wasn't as if it was her fault of course, but that's not how Percival, her husband, would see it. She looked at the cordon and she frowned. She watched the RUC and she frowned. She walked a few wobbly steps and she frowned. Then she stopped, pulled on her ring finger, and tried to think.

'Marionetta!' shouted someone, a woman someone. 'Hey Marionetta!' this female someone shouted, even louder, again.

The crowd, evacuating from the arcade, turned to look at Marseillaise for the tall, blonde woman waiting on the corner with the six blond children and the double-sized pram was definitely, quite definitely, shouting and waving at her.

Marseillaise glanced about, relieved that no one in her life now was nearby to witness that dreadful name from so long ago. She turned with great emotional difficulty and nodded across to her old school acquaintance. If only it wasn't Bronagh McCabe, she thought.

'It's me! Bronagh McCabe!' cried Bronagh McCabe. She swerved the pram round, her long straight hair swishing across the back of her. She surged directly, and as if on target, through the crowd.

Most of Marseillaise stood transfixed. Only her shoulders rose as the pram torpedoed its way towards her. She cried out, thinking it was going to hit her, but it didn't. It scrunched to a halt a millimetre, perhaps two millimetres, from her shins. The blond children immediately tumbled out and began to explore. The remaining child, strapped in, threw his plastic bottle to the pavement. It 'pinged' and 'pinged' and 'pinged' as it bounced along. Then it stopped. Marseillaise stood blinking, looking at it. Bronagh put her brake on, reached over and picked it up.

'Here ye go, Baby Wolfe Tone, ye wee rabbit.'

Baby Wolfe Tone, for that was the toddler's name, took the bottle off his mother and immediately threw it, with more 'pings', straight out onto the pavement once more. Bronagh, patience itself, retrieved it once more. Baby Wolfe Tone threw it once more. By the fourth time, Marseillaise, still standing, silent, spellbound, believed she, herself, must be going mad.

'That's enough now Baby Wolfe,' said Bronagh. 'D'ye hear me? Enough.'

The infant had heard. He held onto his bottle although it was clear from the look on his face he really, really, really, wanted to throw it. His mother caressed his head. 'Good boy,' she said and turned to Marseillaise.

'What about ye Marionetta?' Bronagh seemed to be laughing. She seemed to be laughing at Marseillaise. That's how it looked to Marseillaise anyhow. Marseillaise didn't like it, not one little bit. 'Don't you recognise me then?' said the unmistakeable, the unstoppable, Bronagh McCabe.

Marseillaise looked at her. Although convinced that Bronagh McCabe must have turned into the dirty-ankled, Provie hussy everybody thought she would, there was something in that lovebitten throat, the long legs, the way she took up all that room, that was just a bit much to have to put up with. And she didn't have dirty ankles either. Marseillaise had looked.

'It's nice to see you Bronagh,' she managed to say.

Bronagh threw her head back and laughed. Marseillaise remembered that laugh – how teachers used to scream when they heard it. And Bronagh McCabe laughed at anything – burnt cakes in cookery, plants falling out windows, cockroaches, bruises, bodies. Marseillaise never laughed like that. Her life would not have allowed it.

As Bronagh took a step forward, Marseillaise unwittingly stepped back, but her way was blocked by the police cordon behind her and the blond children playing in a semicircle in front. One of them was trying handstands against a shop window, another was digging dirt on the road with a lollipop stick. These were two of Bronagh's triplets and her third triplet was nearby, rolling up a piece of barbed wire to take home. Meanwhile, the twin brothers were struggling with a breeze-block on the side of the road.

Marseillaise smiled with tremendous effort. 'I really need to get back,' she said. 'Have to go. Can't stay. Could slip up one of those side streets . . .'

'Can't,' said Bronagh, taking the barbed wire from Henry-Joy, who was accidentally ripping his clothes with it. 'Can't go that way. The bomb's up there.'

With one hand she took hold of Marseillaise Jupp in a grip that was absolutely astonishing, while tenderly wiping the nose of Baby Wolfe Tone with the other.

'Perhaps it's just a scare . . .' began Marseillaise.

'Nope,' said Bronagh. 'It's a bomb.'

She steered Marseillaise Jupp away from the heavy police and army presence and down towards Castle Street and then she laughed again. Marseillaise looked round but couldn't find anything funny. Baby Wolfe Tone's bottle 'pinged' once more. Marseillaise jumped and ran a shaking hand across her brow. Perhaps if she approached the RUC and said who her husband was, surely they would arrange to give her access, make a big effort to let her through. She could nip into Marks and Sparks, buy that walnut and cashew sauce thing she was always pretending to Percy she'd made for him. Perhaps the RUC would even make someone come and serve her, and then afterwards – why not? – give her a lift home. Oh, if only she hadn't gone for those gins first.

'How about a wee drink?' said Bronagh, stepping right in front of her.

Marseillaise felt an impulse, a healthy impulse believe it or not, to get away from Bronagh McCabe, and to do it immediately, before it was too late. But she didn't. It was the mention of the drink that had stayed her. Perhaps another wee drink would do no harm, she thought. Perhaps it might even help the situation. Silently, she did as Bronagh instructed, and even preceded her old acquaintance and the six blond children into the Question Mark bar.

Within no time, Marseillaise, Bronagh and the little McCabes were settled round an alcove table, the only alcove table in the bar, placed down at the back away from everybody else. Already it was covered in five glasses of Coca-Cola, most of them empty or spilt, six empty Tayto crisp packets, broken peanuts, a big gin and tonic for Marseillaise and a half-glass of shandy for Bronagh. The barman reluctantly brought over Baby Wolfe Tone's milkbottle, now full of lemonade. Bronagh gave it to him and he threw it onto the carpet. She retrieved it and gave it again. He threw it again. She gave it again. He threw it again. She gave it again – only this time with a gentle quiet warning.

He stopped throwing it right away. His mother patted him, then stretched back on the velvety seat, sighed and looked about her. She seemed very, very contented. Marseillaise crossed her legs and picked her gin up.

'So tell me Marionetta—' began Bronagh.

'Please Bronagh,' said Marseillaise in a low voice as she drained her fourth double drink of that day. 'My name isn't Marionetta anymore. My husband made me change it before we got married.' She whispered even lower, 'He told me what it meant you see.' Bronagh looked amused.

'Did you know what it meant?' asked Marseillaise, placing the empty glass on the table and realising with a stab there wasn't another to pick up.

'I had a rough idea,' said Bronagh. She looked round for the barman. 'Hey mate, another for my chum here. Be quick, d'us a favour and bring it over now.'

'So what's your name now then?' she asked, turning back to Marseillaise.

'Marseillaise.'

Bronagh looked at her.

'It's French,' explained Marseillaise and she looked happy for a moment, but only for a moment. 'My husband didn't like that either though,' she went on. 'Said I was doing it deliberate. Doing what I said? But he wouldn't answer. Just walked out and slammed the door.'

Her eyes began to water, she slumped a little in her seat. Bronagh took a sip of shandy.

'Well, it could be worse Marionetta,' she said. 'You could be called "God Save the Queen" or . . .' she eyed her erstwhile friend. 'In your situation, even "The Soldier's Song" would be a bit dodgy now.' Marseillaise looked blank.

'Soldiers Are We . . .' began the children.

'Not now kids, not here kids,' said their mother without looking round at them.

They stopped instantly and drifted off to burst all the empty crisp packets they could find. Bronagh held the pram for Baby Wolfe Tone to climb out. He ran over joyfully, to be with his brothers, falling down every third step of the way.

'They can't locate that bomb,' said a new man at the bar. 'It could be anywhere in the complex. Turn up the news and give us a Tennent's there.'

'I suppose I should try and get going,' said Marseillaise before her gaze fell on the nice new gin sitting waiting in front. 'Well . . .' she hesitated. 'After this one.' She picked up the glass. 'I have to make a special dinner you see Bronagh – forequarter beef cuts, he said to get, with Creole something and potato something and then that other thing for dessert.' She rubbed the glass against her forehead. She muttered, 'Shops shut. Not *my* fault. I didn't plant it!'

''Course ye didn't!' cried Bronagh. 'A bomb's a bomb.'

'It is, but Bronagh, that's not the point. It's my husband. He gets angry. He invites his friends over every Saturday. He especially gets angry on Saturdays. And his friends you see, well, they're just like him. They're from . . .' She looked askance at her companion, '. . . the office.' Bronagh nodded.

'He says I show him up. Sure everybody forgets to buy stuff.' Bronagh tut-tutted. She lifted her glass too, but held it in her hand.

'What's his name?'

'Per . . .' began Marseillaise.

'Pear?' Bronagh raised an eyebrow.

'I mean Pierce. His name's Pierce – Jupp – I mean Ju – I mean Je – Ja . . .'

Bronagh waited.

'Murphy. Pierce Murphy.'

Marseillaise gave a big sigh. She was fed up with Percival's rules about not giving him away. Anyone would think she couldn't be trusted. Why, even after her own mother's funeral, he'd ranted for days because she'd taken the car into the Bone. More tears gathered on the red rims of her eyes. He took that job too seriously, she thought. More seriously – the auld blue-moulded bastard – than he'd ever taken her.

'What's he do then, this Pierce Murphy?' asked Bronagh.

'Salesman.' The word was automatic. See. She knew how to be careful. She knew how to do as she'd been told.

'I thought he must be,' said Bronagh. 'Rumour was you married a salesman.'

She reached over and lifted Marseillaise's handbag. Marseillaise was sure she wasn't seeing this happening because she herself was too busy reaching over to lift up her gin. The bar door burst open.

'Everybody out!' said a loud RUC man coming through it. 'The cordon's being extended. Leave your drinks and get!'

Everybody reached for their glasses. The policeman frowned.

'It's *ve-ry* sad,' said Marseillaise. 'Marriage is a holy sa-cra . . . sa-cra . . .' She paused, furrowed her brows then took a slurpy drink again. Bronagh glanced once at the policeman, then continued checking through Marseillaise's bag. She turned two envelopes and memorised the name and east Belfast address on both. Marseillaise began to nod to herself. She had been following some fast train of thought which had completely run away from her. She caught the tail end only and sighed it out loud.

'My marriage is over!'

She sighed again.

Bronagh said nothing. She was feeling around the lining of the bag.

'I mean it,' went on Marseillaise. 'When he says "your end of town" in that tone of voice of his, guess what he's really sayin'? Go on – guess! Don't bother. I'll tell ye. He's sayin'

"I wish to God you were dead." That's what he's sayin'. He hates me. There's no bones about it! The man wants me dead.'

Bronagh finished with the bag and looked up at her companion.

'I'll lift all of youse if youse don't get out!' The policeman's voice grew more booming. He thumped the bar. People gulped their drinks as if they were going to be their last ones. Then they ordered some more in case they were going to be their last ones instead.

'And another thing . . .' Marseillaise whined on. Oh, her heart was leaden, everything was cruel and how much she suffered in this world. Nobody ever saw her point of view or cared what happened to *her*.

Moments later Bronagh closed the bag and calmly placed it back on the seat between them. Marseillaise choked back a sob.

'What have I got to live for?'

Bronagh reached for her glass.

'How about a nice big fat claim?'

She spoke quietly and slowly and as if what she was saying wasn't really anything. She also sat facing outward, not looking at her companion now at all. Marseillaise blinked and two single teardrops, dangling from each eye, fell like lead upon the table.

'He'd have to die first,' she said. 'In the line of duty I mean, or at least, I suppose in the line of duty. Don't know much about these things. Do you?' She too sat back and both women gazed forward.

'For Christ's sake!' cried the policeman. 'Who owns these kids?'

He whirled round and round as the little McCabes clambered and whooped and rolled about him, but when Baby Wolfe got tired, the man watched as the child toddled back to his ma. He looked intensely at this woman who was sitting in the alcove at the back of the bar-room. She was a blonde in her mid-twenties and as he watched her, he was sure he'd seen this person before.

Bronagh rocked the yawning child as he cuddled into her chest.

'Your husband's friends,' she said, still looking out, looking now straight at the policeman, 'tell me about them. Are they salesmen too?'

'Yes.' Marseillaise's voice had rose.

'How many? Keep your voice down.'

'Four – five, including Percival.'

'Rank?'

'Two Detective Inspectors and three Detective Sergeants. Sometimes, though rarely, a County Inspector drops by.'

'Every Saturday?'

'Yes.'

'Time?'

'Between seven and seven-thirty, till late.'

'What's late?'

'Two, three in the morning.'

'Shouldn't they be using the social club along with all the other salesmen?'

'Percival says it's full of fifth-rate dregs and cretins and bores.'

There was a silence. Baby Wolfe's eyes began to close. Still watching the policeman, who was still watching her, Bronagh said,

'Tell me about your house, Marionetta.'

Marseillaise brightened. While speaking, now enthusiastically, of the imitation, imitation lava kitchen worktops, actually purchased and shipped all the way from London, the imitation, imitation Aubusson in the conservatory, the imitation, imitation Denton chandelier, the imitation, imitation Jacquet-Tavan chair and an actual, genuine, single imitation Ros Grindling bed, she managed to slip in a specific outline of the building, its entrances, exits, blindspots, pathways and proximity to the road and other properties. Bronagh listened and nodded every time Marseillaise drew breath.

'The dining room, where we have the soirees, is, of course, at the back, to the left of the kitchen door, or right of the front door depending on which entrance is used.' Marseillaise drained the last of her gin and licked her lower lip.

'Sounds lovely,' said Bronagh. 'I'm hugely impressed.' She got to her feet, called to her children and began to tuck the sleeping infant into the pram.

'Bronagh Immaculata McCabe.' The RUC man strode over. 'Conspiring to cause explosions – 1979, wasn't it? Underage shooting – 1975, wasn't it? Grievous bodily harm – 1978, wasn't it? Let's see, what else is there I might have left out?'

Bronagh straightened up from the pram and beamed.

'Ach,' she said. 'I was just a wee girl. Didn't know what I was doin' then. I know what I'm doin' now.'

The man looked at the children. He grunted,

'It would slap it into ye if that bomb got the likes of them. Save me the trouble of havin' to shoot them later on.' He tapped his foot against the wheel of the pram, waking Baby Wolfe Tone, who rubbed his eyes and looked over at it.

Bronagh stood comfortable by the pram and held the police-man's stare.

'Hmm,' she said. 'Very interesting officer. But you see, you might not be around later. You could be going about your business when – bang! – all of a sudden you'll not be able to do anything because oh dear, what d'ye know?, you'll be dead.'

The man's fingers twitched over his gunbelt. Bronagh saw the movement. She laughed. To her, indeed, everything *was* funny. Still laughing, she threw a chunk of her hair from her shoulder and across her back.

'I could take you in right now,' said the man.

'What for?' she said. 'I've been with my friend here all day.'

They both turned towards Marseillaise, who was dreamily watching Bronagh's lips moving. She had begun to move her own, experimenting, giving little soft gasps, trying to imitate the sensuality of Bronagh as she watched her say whatever it was she was saying to that policeman. She, herself, could be warm and easygoing too, she thought. She could also, she was sure, laugh in a devilmaycare way. She tried. It wasn't successful. She tried throwing a chunk of her hair off her shoulder. That wasn't successful either. She didn't have a chunk of hair to throw. Meanwhile Bronagh and the policeman went on staring at her then, involuntarily, they glanced at each other. The little McCabes began to snigger. Bronagh recovered first.

'It's her poor husband,' she explained. 'It's very, very serious. He hasn't much longer to live, you see.'

The policeman nodded. All the same, he turned back to question this unknown drunk. He hesitated though, on seeing her giant gin teardrops. They were big and fat and shiny and about to slide and plop down. Before he could escape and save himself, she reached over and gripped him by the jacket.

'Oh officer! I really really really really—'

'Get off!' He swiped at her hand. Marseillaise slumped back on the seat and her face broke up. The teardrops coursed through her make-up, down her front, and the man rushed to get to safety, nearer to his colleagues, by the door. Bronagh laughed again.

'Ach, you're a geg Marionetta,' she said. 'But listen, I can't stand here splittin' my sides all day. I have things to do.' She leaned in close. 'Remember what we talked about but. If I was you, I'd start going out Saturdays. Nighttimes. Start next week. A wee hobby or something. Know what I mean?'

Marseillaise didn't look at her. Then, as Bronagh turned the pram to leave, the bomb in the side street exploded. The RUC men rushed, radios bristling, out of the door.

'Bye Marionetta,' called Bronagh. 'Remember now – Bingo or something.'

Marseillaise licked her dry lower lip.

'I like opera,' was all she said, before stumbling up to the bar to get just one more.

Battles, 1987

I met Jean at an AA meeting. It was my first. It was Jean's first too. 'Hello,' she said. 'Hello,' I said. We smiled and sat together. After the meeting Jean turned to me and smiled again. 'How about a café and a chat and a coffee?' she said. 'Great,' I said. So we went and had a coffee and a chat in a café. Then I suggested, 'Another cup of coffee Jean?' and Jean suggested, 'Another cup of coffee Amelia?' and after a bit of polite questioning back and forth, the thought struck us simultaneously – But oh! Why not go and have a drink instead? We looked at each other amazed, shrugged, then headed to the bar next door. Bars were always next door. The waiter set down the doubles. 'Yeah that's great thanks,' we said. 'Here's the money. Listen, bring that same order over every twenty minutes.'

We had a lot in common, Jean and I, mostly wine, but gin and vodka and Jameson's too. Sometimes at the end of a night we'd want food – though this was rare. So we'd buy a good Chablis or Châteauneuf-du-Pape then go downmarket to a Bring Your Own Battle. The waitress would get these big eyes and say, 'Did you pay that for a battle of wine? For one battle of wine? The pizzas are cheaper!' 'Of course they are,' we'd answer. Usually during the meal one of us would have to nip next door for another battle – of anything. Off-licences were always next door.

Jean lived with Kelly. Kelly was gorgeous but hardly ever conscious. One morning when I was staying over, which I did a lot, he got up late with his usual hangover to go to work. After he'd banged his way out the front door, Jean and I also got up and stumbled bleary-eyed into the living room. We squinted at each other across the settee.

'How about a cup of tea?' I managed to say. 'Or we could have a coffee?' said Jean, holding her sore head. 'Glass of water?' I said, holding mine. 'Hot, with lemon,' she added. 'Good for us,' one of us mumbled. Neither of us moved. Then I said, 'Any drink left from last night?' Jean shook her head. 'Kelly must have drunk it all,' she said. 'He could've left a drop for God's sake,' I said. 'I know,' she said. 'He could've.' We sat a bit longer.

'What time's the off-licence—'

'Eleven.'

We looked at the clock. It wasn't working. It was cracked down the middle and there was someone's dried blood on it. Naked, Jean crawled over to look for her watch among underwear and empties and that auld pile of manky durex that had been lying, years maybe, by the window, opposite the door. I frowned and wondered about my pocketwatch, my dead da's old pocketwatch, that had been left me. Where had I left it? I didn't know. Jean picked up hers. 'Two minutes to,' she said. We began seriously to move our limbs. I noticed big bruises on mine.

We were next door as soon as he drew the bolt. 'Well now,' we sighed, and looked at the wine. The fine wine. Jean liked Claret. I could take it when there was nothing else but I preferred white. It was Jean's turn.

'You pick Jean,' I said, generously. 'Thanks,' she said, smiling, and lifted her favourite. We went back next door and drank it. 'That's better,' we said. 'How about another?'

'You choose this time,' said kind Jean when we got back
next door. I lifted a Graves and a Pouilly-Fuissé and frowned
over the decision. 'Difficult,' said Jean, sucking in her breath.
'Oh God difficult. Distinctly dry dry or distinctly fruity dry? I
know, let's have both.' I was impressed. 'Can we afford it?' I
said. 'I have my rent money,' she said. 'Me too,' I said. We
laughed and went next door. We drank them. 'How about a
spot of breakfast?' said Jean, wiping her mouth and setting down
the battle. 'Or how about another battle?' I said. 'Listen Jean,
how about this for an idea? We go there now, get it, bring it
here, set it down, eat toast – then drink it?'

'Wow!' said Jean looking for her coat then realising she still
had it on, still naked underneath. 'But Amelia,' she said, stopping and looking worried. 'Maybe we should buy another two
battles.' I saw her logic straightaway. 'How about gin as well?'
I said. 'With lemon?' she suggested. 'Vitamin C,' I said. 'Slice
it up and throw it in.' 'Icecubes too?' she asked. 'No time,' I
answered. We went next door.

Kelly came home at the end of the day. It was winter and
it was dark. It had been dark anyway for we'd forgot to open
the curtains, to open the windows, to let in the air, again. He'd
sobered up and was in a bad mood. Jean and I were very happy.
He set down his toolkit in the hall and scowled into the living
room. We meant to say hello but we forgot. 'Got the sack,'
he said. We laughed. 'It isn't funny,' he said. We laughed
louder. He went on into the kitchen and began to bang things
about. We went on drinking and laughing at all the things that
were funny in the world.

'So how'd ye get back last night?' said Jean all of a sudden.
'Was I out?' I said. 'Did we have this conversation before?' she
said. 'Don't remember,' I said. 'Who was that woman you left
with?' she said. 'Did you say woman?' I said. Jean didn't answer.
'Did you say woman?' I said again, louder. 'I think it was a
woman,' she said. 'Was it a woman?' 'I don't know,' I said.

'I'm asking you!' 'You're asking me!' she said. 'You should know!' We both took a drink.

'Maybe it was a man,' she said, now unsure. 'It could've been a man. Maybe that big one – you know, with the busted face?' I looked at her. She nodded. 'Yeah, that's right,' she said, 'in the bar.' I frowned. 'How'd I get back last night?' I said. She didn't answer. She wasn't even listening. 'How'd I get back?' I shouted. 'How should I know!' she shouted. 'Ye could've answered me!' I shouted. 'Why should I?' she shouted. 'Who gives a damn about you!' 'Well who gives a damn about you!' We finished our drinks in silence. Jean turned her back, reached for her battle and poured herself another. So I turned my back, reached for my battle and poured one for me. Jean was beginning to slur, I noticed. And she got drunk very quick these days. 'D'ye know something?' said Jean. 'You're beginning to slur Amelia. And I notice you can't hold your drink the way you used to.'

Kelly burst in. We had been hoping he was making a nice lasagne out there but he wasn't. We were wrong. 'It's a bloody mess in that kitchen!' he said. 'There's dirt everywhere. Youse have done nothing but drink and burn toast ever since I can remember.' He looked around and threw his arms up. 'And look at the state of in here!' We looked. It seemed all right to us. 'We'll tidy up,' we said, anyway. I leaned over one side of the settee and pushed some rubbish lying about into the dark corners. Jean leaned over the other side and picked up a dusty LP from the carpet. She wiped it on something and looked for somewhere else to put it. There wasn't anywhere, so she dropped it back down to where it had been. Kelly, watching her, slumped into the armchair, which was unusual, so early, for him.

'It's always the same with youse two,' he said. 'Youse never consider anybody else – it's all about whether youse have enough to see youse through the night. And then after that,

it's all about "Yes, but do we have enough for tomorrow?"'
He shifted about in the chair in a tetchy way. 'Youse never
think of me,' he said. 'I always have to get me own and drink
it on me own or else with Pedro and Brodski.' Jean and I didn't
know who Pedro and Brodski were, but all the same, we looked
at each other and we were ashamed.

'There baby, there,' said Jean, staggering over and falling on
top of him. She was in his lap. She kissed his cheek. 'We're so
sorry.' She kissed his mouth. 'Did you have a bad day?'

'Got the sack,' he said. 'No!' she said. 'That's terrible!' She
kissed him again, slower this time, tongue in, one hand pushing through his hair, the other going down to his lower
buttons. Closing his eyes, he began to moan and kiss her back,
lifting a hand to her breast. 'Here,' I said, putting a big gin into
it.

'Tell ye what darlin',' said Jean, struggling to her feet. 'You
sit here and drink and I'll go next door and get us more.' She
pointed to her purse and I threw it over to her, along with
m'own. After all, we had tomorrow to think about.

'How was work?' I said when she was gone. 'Got the sack,'
said Kelly. 'Oh shame shame,' I said. 'What a shock you must
feel awful how'd that happen?'

'I don't think I'm the father of that kid,' he said. 'What kid?'
I said. Then I remembered. 'Oh that – of course ye are Kelly.
Jean wouldn't do that to you.' Kelly looked doubtful. So did
I. I poured us another. 'I can get a test done you know,' he
said. 'Find out for sure.' He frowned. 'At least, I'm sure I could
get a test done. Couldn't I get a test . . . ?'

'Here,' I said. I gave him the glass. He took it. We drank.
'What happened to your job then Amelia?' he said. 'Don't
know,' I said. 'Can't remember.'

Jean came back. She set down more gin plus tins for Kelly.
Jean and I don't drink tins, unless there's nothing else. Smiling,
and now in a great mood, we all settled down and Kelly put

on Steely Dan. After a bit it began to stick. It sounded okay. We left it.

'So how'd ye get back last night?' said Jean to me as she set down her empty glass and reached for the battle. 'Was I out?' I said, draining mine and handing it to her. She poured. 'Did we have this conversation before?' she said. I took the filled glass. I looked at it. 'Don't remember,' I said. We drank deep.

War Spasms, 1988

'You know when you've had really great sex,' began Bronagh, latching onto Amelia just as soon as Amelia came through Bronagh's back door. Bronagh hadn't much time and she had to get this over with. She was never so glad to see Amelia in all her life. She continued, '. . . really great sex Amelia, and you just want to laugh and laugh and—'

'What are you talking about Bronagh?' interrupted Amelia. She was frowning and she was drunk. But she wasn't drunk on alcohol. Amelia Lovett hadn't drunk alcohol in one year, one month and one day. She was drunk on phantom alcohol and it was late afternoon and she didn't like it, it was sunny and she didn't like it, her stomach pains were hurting more than ever and she didn't like it and she didn't like either, that string of words Bronagh'd just said. What was that string Bronagh'd just said? Already she couldn't remember. She tried weakly to push Bronagh, who was climbing on top of her, off from on top of her. She tried to push her harder and she said,

'Stop draggin' on m'arm Bronagh. Get off m'leg. What are you draggin' on m'arm for?'

Bronagh caught herself on and straightened herself up,

surprised at having lost it so frantically. This was unusual. Normally Bronagh McCabe wasn't frantic about anything but today was one of those days when she had to get what she wanted and she had to get it fast. But she controlled herself. She made an effort and she controlled herself. She knew there was no point in frightening people prematurely, better to wait until she'd no choice, and they, themselves, no chance to get away. So she let go of Amelia's arm and she let go of Amelia's leg and she told herself to slow down and to take it easy. She'd set the scene, make Amelia comfortable and when Amelia was comfortable, which in Bronagh's eyes meant 'more drunk', she'd make her move, get what she wanted and move on.

She stood back therefore to let Amelia in and Amelia came in, of her own free will, of her own accord, and Bronagh closed the big door behind her. She locked the door too, got a bottle of gin and a bottle of orange from out of the wall cupboard and set both, with a big glass, before her old schoolfriend. Wasn't it amazing, she thought, she almost laughed, in fact she did laugh, how alcohol worked on everybody? Alcohol was a Godsend. It did the trick every single time. Still smiling, she turned back to the sink to get on with the peeling of the potatoes, acting for all the world like she'd no ulterior plan in mind. It wasn't an ulterior plan anyway, not really, not really. It was just another chore, another task, to be gotten out of the way.

Amelia meanwhile, came into the kitchen. She sat down at Bronagh's table and poured herself a big drink. That's to say, she poured herself an orange juice, which was a bit of hope, a ray of light, in the muck and darkness of what her life now was and, looking at the gin as she drank on the orange, she knew that after a year and a month and a day of not having had any, she'd enough wherewithal to know she didn't want to go back on that other stuff now. Unfortunately for Amelia though, as far as her physical and mental state went, she could have been drinking poteen mixed with poteen. It didn't matter what she drank, for everything made her drunk. Nobody had warned her at the start of giving up, that this was going to happen to her, that when she got off alcohol, she still wouldn't be sober until she stopped being a dry drunk. No wonder she was acting peculiar.

And she was acting peculiar, but mainly because she'd gone round to Bronagh's. She hadn't seen Bronagh in five or six years. She hadn't lived in Ardoyne either in five years, and had only come there especially to check out a rumour, something she'd been hearing about her brother that might or might not be true. It would have been better though, if Amelia hadn't bothered, if she'd kept well away from Bronagh, for everybody knows a Bronagh. They're a laugh and a geg, the life and soul of every party, but they tend to have a whole other side to them you just don't want to know. But Amelia, in her confusion, told herself she had to go round to Bronagh's. She had to check out this rumour, for Bronagh, given her connections, would know if it were true. But now, feeling floaty, feeling in pain, feeling ghost-alcohol-ridden, Amelia couldn't, for the life of her, remember what she'd come round for. Sitting at the kitchen table, fiddling with her orange juice, she tried to get a grip on her thoughts, staring at, without seeing, the other things that were on this table too. There were other things on the table, besides the orange juice and the alcohol. Amelia couldn't see them. She was agitated and her stomach pains every day were getting the better of her. They had gotten sharper too, much sharper, since she'd come through Bronagh's doorway. But as Amelia Lovett always had stomach pains and never did anything about them, they hardly counted as an ailment, or a warning, anymore.

So Bronagh, housewifely, innocently, peeling the potatoes, thought she was getting Amelia drunk and this was a good thing. She didn't notice Amelia's mood and this would be in accordance with Bronagh, for Bronagh was not the sort of person ever for noticing people's moods. In fact, she was not the sort of person even for noticing people, which was the exact reason she was so good always at killing them. And killing them, talk of the Devil, was what she had arranged to do that evening. Her plan, roughly speaking, was first to get the dinner on. While the dinner was cooking, she'd have her way with Amelia and after having Amelia, she'd quickly feed the kids. Then she'd get them to their granny's, meet up with the others, and go and do what she had to, and afterwards, she'd stay overnight in the safe house. Next day, when it was quieter, she'd pick up the kids and come home again, everything being normal and isn't it great, she thought, how life slots itself into place. She was referring, of course, to the arrival of Amelia. Bronagh's husband, you see, had rang earlier to say he wouldn't make it home. His work was going to delay him, he said. He wouldn't be able to help Bronagh. This had sent Bronagh hyper. It had thrown her into a spin.

The build-up to committing murder, as anyone will tell you, takes its toll on a person and Bronagh was no exception to that. Luckily for her though, her unconscious had created an antidote. It was absolutely foolproof and had worked every time so far. All she had to do before killing people, was get some obsessive-compulsive human contact, and the obsessive-compulsive drug of choice for Bronagh was dominating and very fast sex. That's fast sex. Not slow sex. Slow sex came after. Bronagh knew her psychology. Bronagh knew what worked best for her. Speedy sex worked best, and her darling husband always supplied it, but her darling husband wasn't going to be around to service her this time. As regards her children, being the best of mothers – she'd told herself a thousand times – why, she'd cut her own clit off before she'd make use of any of them. But something had to be done, for time was running out, and quickly. And then a miracle happened, which was Amelia Lovett, walking up to her door.

Am I glad to see you Amelia, she thought, reaching for the carrots. 'I won't be a minute,' she said, scrape scrape scrape scrape splash. She threw the carrots half-peeled, nicked and bloody, into the pot that was waiting on them. Oh fuck the carrots, she thought, dropping the rest to the floor. The kids can have chips, her brain computed, the kids can have beans and pasties, the kids can have whatever they wanted when they got to Granny McCabe's later on.

'Bronagh,' said Amelia, holding her stomach for it was hurting her. 'I've just remembered what it is I've come back to Ardoyne to see you for. Has our Mick been shot as a tout?'

The kitchen door was pushed open and Baby Wolfe Tone, Bronagh's youngest, waddled in.

'Wah,' he said, his dummytit falling out of him. 'Ah doh wah!' he added and reached up towards the white slab. The white slab, by the way, was a package and whatever it was, it weighed five pounds exactly. It was wrapped in thin plastic and had been delivered, along with Bronagh's messages, by the Na Fianna boy who worked at the Co-op up the road. He worked part-time at this Co-op, full-time at Fianna na h'Eireann, and was the only boy allowed, ever, to deliver Bronagh's shopping for her. The white slab was on the table beside the thinnest of the screwdrivers, the little boxes, the lighter fuel, the fusewire and insulating tape. Bronagh pushed everything out of Baby Wolfe's little handreach, and opened a big chequered dishcloth. Swishing it into the air, she let it fall over the lot.

'Ah doh wah!' cried Baby Wolfe, now annoyed and very, very frowny. His tongue protruding with effort, he stretched up on all toes once more.

'Aye, son. Aye,' said Bronagh, pushing the stuff back further. 'Good boy, off ye go. Here.' She turned him round, handed him a Mars Bar and guided him by the back of the neck out of the kitchen door. She closed it after him, when he was on the other side, in the living room, with his brothers once more. She turned towards Amelia and, in a split second, carried on from where she'd left off.

Amelia didn't see it coming, didn't stop it coming, didn't know how to stop it coming, didn't admit, in fact, what it really was. There was something childlike about Amelia, but not endearingly childlike; frighteningly childlike. Amelia was no child you see. Amelia was an adult. Bronagh, bending, sliding, moved her leg up and over, sat astride Amelia and kissed her, full on the mouth. As she did so, her fingers ran up and down Amelia's torso. Spiders they were, in and out of Amelia's ribcage. Freezing, stiffening, they'd stop, then off, up and down, again they'd go. Amelia felt the spiders and she didn't like spiders, but she did nothing to stop them. Amelia was in blank mode. Amelia was at a funeral. She knew how to behave at funerals. She'd been to funerals, oh, many times before.

'Yep,' said Bronagh, sitting back when she'd finished the first bit. 'That sure was something. Did you think that was something too?'

'What?' said Amelia. Bronagh's voice sounded miles off.

'What?' said Amelia again, looking at the floor.

Bronagh was surprised and again, this was unusual. Normally Bronagh McCabe wasn't surprised by anything at all. In one sense, this was her greatest asset. In another, perhaps her greatest liability. She looked at Amelia, whom she was still sitting on top of, and whadyeknow, she smiled. Amelia Lovett had surely changed. What she had to do, she thought, might not now be so difficult. She might not have to be so persuasive. This could all be a lot easier than at first she would have thought. Because she couldn't help it, she kissed Amelia again and this time stuck her tongue in. She also took hold of her old schoolchum's dead hand. She positioned the fingers of it inside her own knickers and silently guided Amelia to do the right thing. When the fingers got the message, she let go and began to ease herself up and down a bit. She leaned on Amelia's shoulders to do this, gentle and easy, up and down, up and down, she began to go. That was to start with, only to start with. The slowness didn't last long for remember, this was fast sex, not slow sex. Slow sex came after. Slow sex came last of all.

At first when it restarted, Amelia still did nothing. She didn't push away, she didn't give herself up. Then she did give herself up. She closed her eyes and she submitted, her fingers slipping and circling, the right way, just as Bronagh had instructed them to do. Bronagh's tongue then demanded, pushing itself in further, taking over and expanding to the back of Amelia's throat. When it got there, Amelia swallowed, holding it, keeping it. Bronagh pushed hard against Amelia's breasts for Bronagh had liked Amelia doing that. If Amelia was thinking anything, which she wasn't, for her mind was no longer functioning, it was that none of this mattered, it wasn't as if she was abandoning herself. Bronagh wasn't some desperate groping male person and she herself was just going through motions. It wasn't as if it was going to last long. It wasn't as if it wouldn't ever stop. If Bronagh was thinking anything, which she wasn't, for she was far, far, too busy, she was thinking sex with a woman didn't count as sex at all. It was just a laugh, a geg, the big joke of this party. It didn't mean she was being unfaithful. It didn't mean she was a bad wife.

'Fuck it in, will ye!' she hissed, all jarred up, and yanking her tongue up and out to be verbal and violent about it. 'Fuck it in Amelia, oh fast, oh fast, come on, do as you're told!'

'What's this mammy?' said Kevin-Barry, suddenly there, standing beside them, reaching his hand over and under the big chequered dishcloth.

'It's a tiny wee box,' said Bronagh, getting off Amelia and straightening herself up. She took the box off her son for it was already in his hands.

'Skedaddle,' she said. 'Get out of here Kevin-B.'

'What's in it mammy?' said Kevin-B, reaching out to take it back again.

'What are yous'ins doin' mammy?' said Henry-Joy coming in now also. 'Are youse fightin' mammy? Are youse kissin'? Are youse going to the toilet? What are yous'ins doin'? Tell us. We want to know.'

'Never you mind,' she said and to Kevin-Barry she said, 'Never you mind either' and she pushed his hand away as he grappled to get the box back. By this time all the other children had tumbled into the kitchen also. They consisted of twins, triplets and the toddler, Baby Wolfe Tone. Bronagh had six kids, kids being the name for what she called them. They were doomed, by a legacy, by Ireland, by England, by prehistory, by everything that had gone before them, always and forever to be one, four and six years old.

'Wolfe Tone has a Mars Bar mammy,' they said, except Wolfe Tone, whose mouth was stuffed up with it. He was getting it down quick for if he didn't, he knew he wouldn't have it very long.

'We didn't know there were Mars Bars mammy,' went on the children. 'How many Mars Bars are there? Where are these Mars Bars? Can we have Mars Bars too?'

'Skedaddle I said. Get out of here kids,' said Bronagh, placing her hand on Amelia's shoulder, though it was obvious from the look of it, that drunk woman wasn't going anywhere.

The kids skedaddled for they knew when their ma meant it and they knew when their ma didn't mean it and they knew what would happen if she meant it and they didn't do as they were told. They went back to the living room to find something else to play with and they started by stealing what was left of Wolfe Tone's messy Mars Bar. Bronagh shouted 'Shut the door' after them and they did this and she turned back once more to Amelia. Amelia was staring dumbly at the tiny box in Bronagh

McCabe's hand. Bronagh dropped it to the table, beside all that other stuff, and she leaned over and got hold of Amelia and pulled her to her feet.

'Leave your mouth open,' she said. 'That's right. Leave your mouth open. That's good. That's it. Leave your mouth open. Did you like that? I liked that. I bet you liked that too.'

After finishing the next bit, she kissed Amelia round the neck and on the throat and on the breastbone. 'You did like that,' she said. 'Come on,' she fiddled with Amelia's tee-shirt. 'You'll like it even better when we go in next door.' She tweaked her hand about inside Amelia's bra, and pinched a hold of one of Amelia's nipples, and led her into the room she was talking about, next door.

It was the triplets' room and it was next door and it was a boxroom, a bedroom, a cupboardroom, a downstairs room. It was off to the side of the kitchen, at the back, near the kitchen door. It didn't have any windows. It didn't have much furniture. The only furniture that fitted into it was the triplets' double bed. The bedclothes were all rumpled, everything pushed to the bottom, for every night in their sleeps, the triplets would kick and kick and kick themselves awake. Also on the bed, near the bottom, lay three old teddybears. One had an arm missing, the other an eye missing, the third had stuffing spilling out from everywhere. An Action Man in fatigues, his plastic rifle at the ready, was peeping over at the two women from a single shelf that ran the length of the wall. A nightlight was switched on and it was on the floor beside the doorway. It was squashed against the bedlegs, its lampshade knocked to the side. The tiny door of this room could only be opened outwards and when it was opened, it had no choice but to give directly onto the bed. Bronagh opened it now and she dropped Amelia down into the shadows. Then she climbed in on top of her and shut the triplets' door.

Ages and ages, a whole five, ten, fifteen minutes later, their ma still hadn't come out and the children didn't know what to do. After a hurried, whispered conference outside their cup-board-bedroom-boxroom, the worried brothers decided it was time one of them went in to see. They couldn't send Baby Wolfe, for he didn't know any words yet, so they sent Patrick-P, the next youngest, instructing him to act natural and pretend he was going in for something else. They opened the cupboard door and they threw him in and closed it and he couldn't stop them and he fell onto the bed and 'Mammy' he began. She was sitting up, on top, back to front, her eyes yellow, and she lifted her gaze and yelled and the sound was a fathomless, wordless roar. Her face looked not like his mammy's but like a contorted face from one of his kicking, kicking-awake night-mares, and not inches from himself were monster adult thighs and a giant hairy underbum. Those legs, his mammy's, were twisting, twining, spidering the head of that drunk person. That drunk person, apart from her head, was nowhere else to be seen at all. Her body was missing, maybe under the blankets or maybe not under the blankets, maybe under his mammy, doing invisible things, with his mammy having convulsions and ordering it to do more. He fell back and pushed his way out of the cupboard, glad it wasn't locked and slamming it after him. He had no words to explain to his brothers as they clam-oured round to hear what had been going on. He hated them for making him go in there and when they tried to get him to talk about it, he pushed them off and ran away to be by himself. He ran back to the safety of the cartoons and the canned laughter in the living room and, frightening them with his panic, his brothers ran after him to be in there too.

Sideroom sex successfully completed, all tiny wee war worries taken care of, Bronagh glanced at her watch and 'God, is that the time?' Luxuriously though, just for a moment, she yawned and stretched some more. She was human again, contented, all buttery and honey and slippy slidy lovely. She wriggled her toes and slid one of her hands under the pillowslip. It came into contact with jellybabies, loads and loads of jellybabies. The heads of these jellybabies were the only bits that were left. Her fingers closed around them. She scooped a heap out.

'James-C, bless him,' she laughed. 'He's a soft-hearted wee eejit. He thinks he hasn't killed them as long as he doesn't eat the heads.' She laughed again and threw a handful of heads into her mouth. She ate them, chewed on them, put her own head back on the pillow and sucked and swallowed them. Then she was ready, swinging herself, no nonsense, up and out of that bed. She grabbed her clothes from the blankets as she did so, shouting for her kids to hurry and get a move on. She shut the tiny cupboard door and, just like that, she was gone.

Amelia woke up. It was an hour and a bit later. The nightlight was still on, the rest of the house silent and dark. She had the same spasms she always had on awakening. They particularly hurt after deep druglike sleeps. She sat up and felt funny and saw her knickers and bra were in disarray on her. She'd been having dreams, she remembered, dreams about alcohol. It had tasted lovely in the dream, it had tasted lovely going down inside her. She remembered the gin bottle out on the table – and why not take it with her? Nobody would care that it was gone.

Something came around Amelia's legs then, slid quickly round her ankles and 'What's that!' she cried, jumping and snapping her legs apart. There was nothing there. And there was no one there. Amelia was addressing nobody. The house was empty. There was nobody in the house to address. She felt movement near the bottom of the bed. She looked at the footboard, she peered and oh my God, she thought, what was that thing lying there? She kept looking and a chunk of meat began to crawl its way across. It was raw, bright red, glistening and crawling over the teddybears. After that, it crawled over the jelly heads, coming closer and closer to her thigh. When it touched her thigh, she kicked and kicked and kicked herself awake again. She jumped to her feet, onto the mattress, and tried to clutch at the smooth wall behind. She was afraid to turn round, but she turned round and the piece of meat was gone again. The ripped-up teddybears and the jelly heads were lying in bits, unbloodied, as before.

She grabbed up her clothes and yanked them on anyways, swiped her ankle boots from the bottom of the bed and pulled at the cupboard door. It wouldn't open and she panicked and she pulled on it even harder and then she realised it wasn't a trap and pushed and fell out onto the kitchen floor.

Still on the floor, she crammed her feet into her boots and then started to grow calmer. The bad dreams were going. The bad dreams were nothing at all. She looked up and saw the gin bottle. It was still there, sitting waiting, and she decided that yes, she would take it with her when she went out Bronagh's back door. There was no point in getting off alcohol. What was the point in getting off alcohol? Everybody drank alcohol. Didn't they? In the end?

As she reached for the bottle, stretching her hand out to take it, a shadow passed through her forearm and disappeared into the wall. Her arm still stretched out, because she had become frozen and was unable to move it, she then did move it, and moved herself, as something slid behind her, out of the cup-boardroom door. She grabbed up her jacket, rushed out the back way, running from that house and all the unholy things it stood for. She left the bottle on the table. She didn't want it any longer. There was nothing else on the table. All the other stuff had gone.

Waked, 1989

Amelia bought a ticket for the late boat to Liverpool. Five times in her life she'd done this already and five times at the last moment she'd chickened out. This time, she told herself, she had to go. If she stayed any longer, she'd kill herself. Her plan therefore, was to get the boat out at seven that evening, arrive in Liverpool and then make her way down to London after that. When she got to London, she'd get another plan.

She got up early and went and bought her ticket. She put it in her pocket and came out of the office to go home. It was ten o'clock. She had nine hours to kill before sailing and nine pounds to her name in her purse. To stop herself from spending it, for she needed it all for London, she decided to go home, stay home, have tea and wait there. She'd eat something from whatever was left, pack something from whatever she had, and be ready and at the docks by half past six that night. It never occurred to Amelia to tell anybody she was leaving, and if it had occurred to her, she wouldn't have told anybody anyway.

She walked back to her rented flat in Botanic near the university which was on the other side of Belfast from Ardoyne. It was a different sort of area, in that it was a safer sort of area, or had the illusion of safety at least, if nothing else. She looked up as she reached it. A boy was standing on her doorstep. He seemed about nine. It turned out, when she spoke to him, that he was her second cousin from her mother's side of the family. Neither of them had seen the other before.

His name was Johnny Lavery, she discovered, and he'd come the whole way across town on his own because his Granny Lavery, Amelia's aunt, had sent him. This was because she, Amelia, hadn't got a phone. Nobody else would come, he said, and there was no other way to get the news to her. The news was that her sister Lizzie was dead. She'd killed herself, he said, two days ago, and had been found in the old family house by her friends, the Mary-Marys. She'd been in her bedroom, with her chin propped on the blanket, the rest of her body against the bed but on the floor. Her legs were at twisty angles underneath her – Johnny Lavery spoke faster and faster – and he ended by saying Lizzie's face was facing the window and that her eyes had been closed.

He went on to explain that it was all on account of the massive overdose she'd been saving up for. He said she'd been getting stuff off the doctor for depression for years and years and years. She'd bought stripfoils too, he added, loads and loads of stripfoils, and had taken everything altogether when she'd got home on Sunday night. It was deliberate, Johnny said the doctor said, because there was so much evidence to say so, but everybody else said the doctor was mad. It was an accident, they said. Lizzie had been happy. She'd never have meant to kill herself like that. The Marys found her yesterday, Johnny jumped around in his telling, and at first they'd run out the door screaming. Then they'd gone back in and covered up Lizzie's bottom half. The police, when they came, were very angry about the blanket. The Marys had touched a dead body and the Marys weren't allowed to do that, they said. The Marys barely paid attention but when they did pay attention, it was to shout at the police and to say they'd do it again if they had to, and that if the police didn't like it, then the police could go and fuck themselves.

Amelia brought Johnny Lavery in and offered him tea and biscuits. He said he didn't want tea and biscuits, didn't she have any drink then, to offer him instead? She said no, she didn't have any drink, that she no longer drank alcohol and that wasn't he too young anyway to be starting that mug's game? He told her to stop preaching at him, that he couldn't stand people preaching at him, especially if they were a loser, a drunkard, an auld alcoholic themselves. Amelia could see he'd been drinking already. She felt like crying. She didn't know how to deal with this nine-year-old drunken person and this was in spite, or maybe because of, having often been a nine-year-old drunken person herself.

Johnny went off then, without the tea and biscuits, taking the busfare and some extra which she knew he'd save for drink. She didn't know whether to thank him for coming to tell her the news about her sister, or to crack and bang his head open for being cheeky to her like that. In the end she did neither and nineteen years older than him or not meant nothing. She watched him swagger out, feeling herself useless and afraid. On his way already, she could see, this Johnny Lavery cousin from nowhere, bad-tempered, wanting drink, in need, and underfed. Johnny turned back on the doorstep and cut in on her thoughts to shout that if she fancied saying goodbye to her sister, she'd find her in her coffin in her sister-in-law's house. The Lifting would be at seven, he shouted, the funeral at ten the next morning. He banged the door after him and then he was gone.

Amelia stood in the darkened hallway and looked at this communal door in silence, then she turned round and went back to her flat up the stairs. She started to pack for leaving, but realised she was putting in peculiar things, like stripfoils full of painkillers, a jar of ink, an empty glass. She stopped doing this for it was stupid and she left the holdall where it was lying and pulled out her smaller backpack. She'd use that one instead. She put in a thick jumper for the nighttimes, a bar of soap in case she wanted to wash herself, a towel, a toothbrush and rolled up her sleeping bag. She attached that too, to the backpack, and put her money, that she still had, minus a pound that she'd given to Johnny, into her inner pocket. Her glasses that she needed were sitting on her nose. Her boat ticket was on top of the dresser. She lifted this and slipped it down the side of her backpack. That was her ready. She was all set to go.

She didn't go though. She sat down on the floor and in the morning, in the silence, in the summertime, she felt the air from a breeze coming in around the loose panes. As it surrounded her, she breathed it up her nose. Then she breathed it out and, with her eyes closed, she waited. She wanted to know what to do about Lizzie. She knew she had to do something about Lizzie. But she didn't want to go over, ever again, to Ardoyne. And not just Ardoyne. Apart from going for the boat later, she didn't want to go anywhere in Belfast anymore. She mustn't miss the boat, she knew. If she missed the boat this time, it would be one practice-run too many. If that happened, she knew she'd never get the nerve up to try to leave again.

In the end, she decided to go and see Lizzie. She'd go and see her, but she wouldn't stay for very long. She stood up, took the keys and, for the last time, looked around the place she'd been living in. Loose ends needed tidying but she couldn't be bothered with any of those. She'd do nothing about the electricity, nor return the library books she'd once borrowed. She'd leave them on the table. The landlord, too, would know soon enough. She lifted her jacket, put on her backpack, left the flat and pushed the keys through the letterbox. She walked into town, then out of town, heading towards the Antrim Road.

Amelia hated Ardoyne. She'd always hated Ardoyne and was scared now to set foot in it. She feared that people, now not knowing her, would come, hostile, out of their doors. 'Who's she?' they'd say. 'Does anybody know that woman?'

'Is she a Catholic?'

'A Protestant?'

'Has anybody seen her here before?'

Six years was a long time to be gone in some little areas. People might follow her, she thought – she looked behind, but Amelia was being paranoid. Nobody followed her. Nobody gave a damn and, as this sank in, she made her way with more ease to her sister-in-law's door. It was Mena's house now, not Mick's house, no longer Amelia's brother's house, everybody now accepting that Mick, wherever he was, was never again going to show. The blind was down and a thick black bow was tied to the letterbox. Amelia went up the path, paused, then rapped on the door.

It was opened by Josie, Amelia's younger sister, who looked at Amelia. Amelia looked back at her. She'd never known Josie. Josie excelled in concealing herself. Like an awful lot of people, she made herself very hard to know. Amelia was going to speak to her, say a few words, like 'Hello Josie' or something, but before she could think of anything, Josie turned and left her at the door. She left the door hanging also, and disappeared into the living room. It was a gloomy room, a dark room. Amelia stepped over the threshold and into the gloom too.

The first thing that hit her was the strong smell of alcohol. People had been drinking alcohol for a long time in that room. Amelia hadn't taken a drink in two years and three months and counting. She still needed to count and told herself there was nothing wrong with that. She looked around. There were a lot of people. She nodded to a few. Fewer nodded back at her. She nodded to no one else and made her way to the coffin. It was by the far wall.

Before she could reach it though, a woman grabbed a hold of a loose strap of her backpack. It was her mother's sister, her

Aunt Sadie, Johnny Lavery's granny, the one who'd sent the word across. She was so drunk she couldn't stand up.

'Is that you Lizzie – I mean Josie – I mean Amelia? Isn't it shockin'? Who would have thought Lizzie would have done it for real this time?'

Amelia looked at her. Aunt Sadie was nodding. Amelia held on tight to the other strap of her backpack – her backpack, that had her money, her ticket, especially her ticket, inside. Sadie was talking now, and as if it was common knowledge, about Lizzie's threats of, and attempts at, suicide and about the enforced hospitalisations after the last two times. Amelia glanced at the others. She'd never known Lizzie'd talked of suicide, threatened suicide, attempted suicide. She'd never known there had been enforced hospitalisations. She'd never known there had been two last times. The Marys, fidgeting in the corner, came over.

'We didn't know Amelia,' they said. 'It wasn't our fault. How were we to know she really meant it this time.' They glared at Sadie as if they'd been accused. They had been accused. They went on,

'We weren't inclined to take the others seriously. We thought she was just messin', carryin' on. We didn't think she really meant it this time.'

This made sense to them. Somehow, if someone talked, and always, of one day killing themselves, it could only mean they had no intentions of ever doing so. It was just a protection, they said. A comfort, a final way out, for a mind to hold onto. 'You know what it's like, Amelia,' they urged, 'in bloody shitty life.' Amelia tried to get more information. She couldn't get more information. At least not directly. Direct questions made the Marys clam up. As far as she could gather, Lizzie had been saving anti-depressants. 'The way you do like,' explained Bea-Mary. 'You save them up and you save them up.'

'Until you've got hundreds, loads of them,' said Sharon-Mary. 'Until you count one day and you've got more, oh much more, than enough.'

'You hide them in your underwear drawer,' said Grainne-Mary. 'Or in your bottom drawer,' said Theresa-Mary and Mary-Ann-Kate said, 'For years and years you count and save them up.'

'It doesn't mean you're going to take them,' said Ann-Mary. She gave a little laugh. She was sad. So were the others. 'It doesn't mean you're going to kill yourself.'

'Lizzie killed herself,' said Aunt Sadie. 'Lizzie took the lot.'

'And then the stripfoils,' Sadie added. 'Did you know she was spending her whole dole on stripfoils, Amelia? Paracetamols, aspirins, everything?' The Marys looked at Sadie. 'Old woman,' they said, 'shut the fuck up.'

Amelia turned and went again towards the coffin. She stepped round a pile of children, playing, half-naked, with their toys, on the floor. She reached the coffin and looked in.

The first thing she noticed was that Lizzie didn't look like herself. She only looked like herself from her dark eyebrows up. The rest of her looked older, yellower, clammy, not-Lizzie. Her face was puffy, there were post-mortem marks about her neck and throat. The second thing Amelia noticed was that Lizzie's hands weren't joined at the breastbone. Dead Catholics always had hands joined at the breastbone. Wasn't that the way dead Catholics were supposed to be? It surprised Amelia immensely, that such a thought as this should occur to her. What did it matter to her how dead Catholics were supposed to be? But for some reason it had occurred to her and she obsessed over why Lizzie's weren't joined in the middle. She leaned over and slid one of her own hands down the inside of the coffin to see. She touched her sister's and it was clenched, a stony fist, just as it had been in her life always. Amelia was sad that her sister was to be buried in that way. She put her own hand round the fist and held it and a shadow fell across the coffin. The shadow didn't move. Amelia looked round and then she stood up.

'Shock,' said Mena. 'You're in pain and grief and it's all been too awful for you. Complete mystery, we all loved her, so happy, she didn't mean it. Mustn't have happened. Perhaps it hasn't happened. Perhaps everything's just as it's always been before.'

She spoke in such a dead, automatic, zombielike manner that Amelia got the shivers and stepped back to take a look at her. What's that about? she thought and, what's *that* about? she thought further, for Mena was scrawny and pleated with no fat at all now upon her. Amelia wouldn't know what it was about because it was about drugs. Not the food and drink type. Amelia knew about the food and drink type. These were the others, the ones Amelia had no understanding of. So little did she understand them, she didn't even know the nicknames for them. But Mena was on them, and they were intravenous, and they were supplied to her by Jat. Jat was an old friend of Amelia's family and he was in the room also. He was standing beside Amelia now. He'd come over to say hello.

'Hello Amelia,' he said. 'Sorry about the death of your brother, I mean sister.' He corrected himself easy and handed her a drink. She declined it and stepped back but the coffin was behind her. He stepped forward and offered her the drink once more. He pushed the glass against her chest, her breast, and it was a double vodka, with a little coke lost somewhere inside it. She could smell the vodka. She took it, and held it, then set it on the windowledge.

She didn't like Jat. He had thick, slick, plasticky features. Everything about him was greedy and his greedy eyes were appraising her now. She wondered what he was doing there, for Mick and he had fallen out years ago. He'd never liked Lizzie either, for she and the Marys had put him in hospital once. He seemed comfortable though, she noticed, as if this was his house. Was this his house? Did he live here with Mena and the children now? She looked at Jat and Mena. She looked at Jat and Josie. She looked at Jat and her fifteen-year-old niece Orla, and then she had a shock. Orla looked back. She was like her mother, like a zombie, all druggy, all droopy. Is this grief? Amelia wondered. Why are they dopey and floaty to look at? Orla took a hold of Jat's belt, in the manner of someone who might just start opening it, and Jat put his arm around her and pulled her close into himself. Amelia hoped it wasn't what it seemed. But she had no energy, no energy except for getting out of there. She'd prefer, at the very least though, that it was her sister-in-law and Jat.

A priest came in, along with a lot of other neighbours. Amelia didn't like him. He was loud and unspiritual and gabbled his prayers in a big mad rush. He said hello, hello, terrible, isn't it, then gabbled the first part of the Hail Mary. Everybody, before he'd finished, gabbled the response. Nobody was listening to anything. The Our Fathers were hardly begun when that was it, they were over. It was the end of the race, 'Amen Amen,' he shouted. He came to a full stop. He blessed himself, blessed Lizzie, blessed them all, threw his hands about, up and down and across and it was 'Goodbye,' he said, and then he was gone. 'Bye Father,' said the neighbours, closing the door after him. Amelia felt shaken and didn't respond. She wanted to say one, slow, silent prayer, if she knew how, for her Lizzie. Everybody else went back to their alcohol.

'Who're you?' asked some new people. 'What are ye doin' here? Where d'ye come from? What have ye got that rucksack on ye for?'

'She's leavin' the country I bet,' said Josie. Josie was smirking. She was angry. Very angry. 'Isn't that right Amelia? Isn't that always what you've got yer rucksack on ye for?'

'I'm goin' to Liverpool,' said Amelia. Josie laughed.

'In your dreams,' she said. 'You'll still be here after the rest
of us have long gone.'

'I'll be in London tomorrow.'

'You just said you'd be in Liverpool. No matter. You'll be
here. You'll be nowhere. You're always sayin' you're goin' and
then you never go.'

Amelia had a flash, a premonition, perhaps just angry wishful
thinking, of coming back for this other sister's funeral sometime.
She looked at Josie – superfit, superhealthy, but that was on
the outside. On the inside, Amelia knew, it was rage, always
rage, that carried Josie along. How long could rage do that?
she wondered.

'What's that about Liverpool?' said Aunt Sadie. 'Ye can't be
goin' to Liverpool? How can you go to Liverpool with yer
sister just dead like that?'

'Ye're stayin' for the Liftin' I hope?' said a neighbour. 'Ye're
goin' to the chapel surely?' said a neighbour. 'The funeral?' said
a neighbour. 'In the name of God, wee girl, how cold is it
possible to become!'

'Lizzie, I mean Josie, I mean Amelia,' said Aunt Sadie.
'Where's your mass card? Did ye not bring a mass card? Here's
our mass cards, our last words to Lizzie. You don't mean to
say you've no last words for her yerself?'

Amelia said nothing and, instead, went over to read some
last words. Immediately she wished she hadn't. 'Peace at last
Lizzie. Better off out of it. Life's a fuck. Be glad you're gone.'

A child came over and tugged at Amelia's backpack. Amelia
looked down and saw it was a girl. She was small, nine or ten,
and she was smiling, her eyes bright, and she looked like Mick,
Amelia realised. Strangely though – and how could this be
possible? – although she looked like Mick, she also looked like
Jat. She was pressing something, a tee shirt, into Amelia's hands.

'Smell!' she ordered. 'It's your Lizzie. It smells of your Lizzie.
Smell!' Amelia got down on her hunkers and did as she was

told. She smelled a corner of the tee shirt and the child was right. It did smell of Lizzie, that nice, but rare, Lizzie-in-repose smell. The girl lifted the other corner and they sank their noses in together. 'I liked Lizzie,' said the child. Amelia said, 'I liked Lizzie too.' And she had. Lizzie, in good humour, used to give her lively lectures. Lizzie, a year older, had boasted to Amelia about life. She helped Amelia with her first bra, helped Amelia with her periods, had laughed and said, 'Don't be stupid Amelia – I can see where you're coming from – but it's girls who have diddies, and boys who have the balls.'

The child told her to keep the tee shirt and to put it into her rucksack. Amelia did so and thanked her, thinking what a nice thing that wee girl seemed to be. God help her though, she thought. What'll happen to her in her life? She looked, and the girl saw the look, and smiled, and opened her arms wide. Amelia froze.

'My name's Dawn,' said Dawn but Amelia said nothing. She stayed frozen. She didn't know how to hug children. She didn't know how to be with children. Dawn seemed undeterred and put her arms about Amelia, to hug her instead. Then she tried to sit on Amelia's knee and Amelia was unnerved and stood up, pushing her off it. Dawn took Amelia's hand, then let go, for it was dead. She smiled once more though, then trotted away into the kitchen. She closed the door and Amelia thought, Am I related to that child? She looked around. Am I related to any of these children? There were loads of them, making a racket, pushing and pulling, fighting over toys. Amelia looked at the toys, then she looked again, harder. Amongst the jacks and the cards, the dolls and the crocheted rabbits, was a mound of fat rubber bullets. She gave a cry at recognising her old Treasure Trove.

'Gimme them!' she shouted, startled and hardly knowing what she was doing. She leaned over. 'Those things are dangerous. Those things are not toys.'

No Bones

She grabbed them from the children, who were equally startled and couldn't believe this was happening. An adult had butted in and was trying to steal their toys. Amelia, ignoring them, grabbed up the seven bullets, which weren't many, thirty having gone missing, thirty down the years, having been lost and mislaid. She began to stuff the seven that she had, one by one, into her backpack. Devastated, robbed, the children began to wail. A little boy tore his clothes off and howled for his mamma to do something. Mena said, in a flat, doll-talk-string voice,

'Let the kids have them Amelia. For God's sake grow up. What use are they to you now?'

'Mena,' said Amelia. 'Can't you see that's not the point?' Mena couldn't see. Neither could the others. Josie began to laugh.

'So what are you gonna do with them, Oh Miss Wise One, Oh Miss Goodie Goodie, Oh Miss Know It All, Oh Miss—'

'Shut up!' said Amelia and Josie did shut up. This was surprising. And to everyone. Amelia wasn't known as a person who threw her weight around and Josie had never, except with her parents, allowed anyone in the world to tell her to shut up.

Josie had a point though, and Amelia could see it. She'd no idea what to do with the bullets – her taking them had been spontaneous, her getting rid of them another thing. What should she do? Should she saw them in pieces, she wondered, chop them and burn them or hide them bit by bit in different rubbish bins? Should she give them to some authority? But what authority should she give them to? Sinn Fein? she asked herself. No, she answered. She wouldn't give them to Sinn Fein. The Royal Ulster Constabulary? No. Out of the question. She'd give them to Sinn Fein first. How about the British Army then? And *why* would she give them to the British Army? What was wrong with her then? Couldn't she remember it was the

British Army who had fired them in the first place? She went on thinking about possible institutions and possible solutions, without having the least bit of faith in any that she came up with. Josie, furious, pointed at her and laughed.

'Thinking hard?' she said. 'I see yer lips moving. Decided? Goin' to throw them, then, are ye, into the Irish Sea?'

Amelia looked at her. The others laughed at the joke, the great joke, except the children for they, like Amelia, had taken it seriously. They bawled louder and ran to their mammas, their grandmammas, all the grown-ups. The little boy who had torn his clothes off picked up his toy half-a-brick – which happened to be a real half-a-brick – and threw it at Amelia and it hit her backpack. She turned round and lifted it and squashed it inside also. That'll help, she thought, if she decided to weigh them down. She'd throw the bag too, with the other stuff. What did she need a bag for? She pulled out Lizzie's tee shirt and tied it around a strap for now. The boy shrieked louder, for he hadn't killed this monster adult. Mena picked him up and hushed him and told him there were plenty more bricks to be had. Plenty more bullets too, thought Amelia, but that's okay, she told herself. She didn't have to be responsible for everything. She could be responsible for the little bit she had.

Now it was time. She put on her backpack. The children hurried over, sobbing, to say goodbye.

'We hate you, we hate you, we hope you die. We hope you fall in the water. We hope you bump your head off the boat. We hope sharks come up and eat you. We hope the waves are high. We hope thunder and lightning runs through your body. We hope you drown when you're very nearly saved. We hope—'

Amelia got out and closed the door. She exhaled deeply. Leaning against the funeral bow, she then breathed in slowly, just as deep, again. She felt dizzy with the way feelings went. How did anybody ever survive feelings? Did anybody ever survive them? No wonder, she thought, so many didn't bother having them to try. After a few seconds, during which she did, in fact, survive all her feelings, Amelia looked up and saw a small woman click open Mena's front gate. She came up the path towards Amelia, but before she reached her, the door opened and Dawn came running out and skipped down the path.

'Mammy!' she cried and threw her arms round this woman's legs.

Her mother disentangled her and smiled and took her child's hand. Without looking at Amelia, she turned to go.

'Mary!' cried Amelia, for she recognised who it was in front of her. 'Mary Dolan?' she shouted. 'It is you, Mary, isn't it?'

'Amelia,' said Mary, turning back and speaking to her. She nodded and then, once more, began to lead her daughter away. Amelia hesitated then clicked her backpack at the waist and started after.

People were watching now, from their windows, from their doorsteps and Amelia noticed they didn't look friendly. 'Who's she?' a few looked at her and said. Mary paid no attention to these women and paid no attention to Amelia either, but she did walk slower and soon Amelia had caught her up. They went together, not talking, to the very edge of the area. 'Mary?' Amelia tried again.

'Goodbye Amelia,' said Mary. Without looking at Amelia, she turned back to Ardoyne and walked away.

'Goodbye Amelia,' said Dawn, still smiling and looking back at her. 'I know your name's Amelia.' She waved and waited for Amelia to wave too. Amelia forgot to wave. 'Mary?' she said, distracted, but this time Mary said nothing. She kept Dawn's hand, and Dawn, still looking like Jat McDaide and like Mickey Lovett also, waved one last time and then mother and daughter were gone. Amelia stood on the edge, looking and hoping for Mary to reappear and to talk to her, but when she heard the bus coming, she stopped looking, turned away and rushed over the road and got on.

Triggers, 1991

Amelia went to Camden Town to have a breakdown. She didn't know she was going to have a breakdown. She thought she was going to buy some tins of beans. Amelia hated tins of beans. They reminded her of her father. What she really wanted was a big box of Special K. A part of her said she couldn't have Special K though, because beans were on discount, at nineteen pee per tin. Special K, on the other hand, was a frilly, expensive waste at any time, so it was best not to have what she wanted and to take instead what she could never, ever, stand. 'I know you don't like them,' this deprived, depressed part of her reasoned. 'That means you'll eat less, they'll last longer, you won't starve, which would be the case if you bought and ate the Special K and then had nothing left for the rest of the week.'

Amelia didn't like starving anymore for she could no longer get high on the consequences. So she let herself be persuaded by Deprived Depressed's sound reasoning and turned away from the boxes of cereal and sludged wearily over to the tins of beans. They were piled high in pyramids, tins on top of tins, white labels, blue writing, nineteen pee stickers on all of them and hateful things they were, she thought and oh God, they sure were hateful. Why can't I have what I want? she wondered and that, had she but known it, was the big question of Amelia Lovett's life.

So there she was, in one of those dowdy, dingy, angst-ridden, 'what's the point in living' supermarkets, popular with poor people who didn't have any money, and also with rich people who did, but thought that they shouldn't have. Her plan for the day had been to go out, get her giro cashed, pay a bill, get her food, get back home, close her door and be safe again for another bit of her life. She was on the food bit and after that came the retreat bit and then the closing the front door bit and then, thank goodness, she could stay in for another while.

So she had the beans in her arms and was on her way to pay for them when something came over her and she stopped and turned around. She crossed back over the aisle, returned the beans to Discount, went to Non-Discount and grabbed up the Special K. Deprived Depressed gasped when it saw what she was up to and tried to dissuade her, with words like 'Stop!' and 'Who do you think you are!' This brought her to her senses and she put the cereal back where she'd found it and went again to Discount for the beans for the second time.

'That's right dear,' soothed Depdep, who nearly had had a heart attack. 'Take a few extra, why don't you? They're only nineteen pee this week.'

'Nothing's possible,' said Amelia, doing exactly as Depdep instructed her and she was talking out loud, something she'd started doing more and more of late.

'Nothing's possible,' she said again, but before she reached the till, and in what looked like action replay, the same impulse came over her and she did another turnaround. She rushed back to Non-Discount, shoved the beans anywhere, grabbed up the Special K and stuck it under her arm. Deprived Depressed again got in front of her and demanded she stop being so outrageous but as this other, rebellious part of her kept resisting, this picking and putting went on five more times. Eventually the security guard, for there was one to guard the bean tins, got suspicious and came over to see what was going on. Of course he wasn't going to know what was going on for he hadn't been trained in breakdowns, particularly on how to notice the little things that triggered the bigger things off. All he could see, most likely, was a woman talking to herself and stealing her messages, or else messing the store's stock about, and as a deterrent he placed himself prominently, eye-catchingly, in front of her.

At first Amelia didn't notice anyone prominent and eye-catching, so intent was she on having this fight with herself. When she did notice, she immediately became embarrassed and hoped that, whatever else she'd been doing, she hadn't again been talking out loud. The security guard moved two steps closer and she clocked this with her left eye and was convinced it was because she had a Family Size box of Special K under her arm. She felt ashamed and guilty and was sure he was feeling angry because she was being greedy in buying Family Size all for herself. 'After all,' said Depdep, 'he can see you're giving no thought to the dead people. What about the dead people? Those killed, those murdered? What choice did they ever have?' So, to appease the guard, appease the dead, appease Deprived Depressed and all the gods who might just get jealous of her, Amelia put back the box of cereal and lifted the beans for the last time. Knowing they'd last forever, and knowing how much this would kill her, she trudged to the cashdesk with big tears in her eyes.

She handed over the money, got her change, put it into her purse and her shopping into a carrier, making sure the guard noticed that she'd been good and bought exactly what she'd rather not have. This would show she wasn't a bad person, she thought, that she wasn't being callous about the dead people, but it was all for nothing, for the guard stood and watched anyhow. After she left the shop, she looked in through the window and there he was, still staring, arms folded, and what a bastard, she thought, for hadn't she paid for what she now had?

She stopped then on the pavement for 'He didn't own it' she told herself. He couldn't make her move off it, and if he called the RUC, she'd say, 'Look, don't you believe him. He's a liar. I didn't buy that cereal. I bought the tins of beans.' She'd show them the beans and then he'd be in big trouble, for after she'd been vindicated, she'd make the RUC go in and find out what big fat food his greediness consisted of.

She jumped as a police siren or an ambulance or a fire engine sounded behind her. A police car speeded past and went racing up the road. Looking away from it, she realised she'd been talking out loud again, for people were looking back, as they too went up the road. Most people didn't look though, for this here was London and mad people were everywhere. Best to pay no attention in London. Best just to move on. It was frightening to Amelia when she caught herself out-louding. In retrospect, she'd noticed too, it was always about bad things. People who talked to themselves, she'd always believed, were lost, disturbed, anxious sorts of people. She'd never imagined she'd be a lost, anxious, disturbed person herself. Well, she'd been wrong, she thought and 'I was wrong' she said out loud and, this time, some people stopped and glanced around at her. She saw them and caught a grip and Best to get on home, she thought.

She was about to start walking, but a man, already walking and, it seemed, in some action-packed daydream, bumped, bang, right into her and only noticed after he'd knocked her down. He picked her up and said, 'Sorry . . . er, sorry. Are these your bean tins?'

'No,' said Amelia. 'Yes,' said Deprived Depressed, taking

them back off the man. When he let her go, Amelia noticed
he wiped his hands down himself. He wiped his hands down
his jacket and I'm not dirty, she thought. 'I'm not dirty,' she
thought, only this time she only thought she thought. 'My
clothes may be dirty,' she shouted, 'but what you don't know
is that that's all deliberate. Inside's my body, and my body's *my*
body. My body's very clean.' From the look on the man's face
as he kept on backing away from her, Amelia realised she'd
said something she shouldn't have out loud. The man kept on
backing, quickly, nervous, then he moved away completely,
and after that, he only looked back a few more times. To make
sure I'm not following him, she thought. 'He's afraid I'm gonna
follow him,' she said. She began to follow him, to ask what
the hell made him think she'd want to go following him for
anyhow?

Then she stopped. Right away in fact, for the crowd had
almost caught her. It was getting fatter. People kept appearing
and adding themselves onto it. The pitiless sun, she noticed,
was also coming out. She moved back to the shop window in
order to get away from it, to get away from everything. She
took hold of the shop grille and just in time too. A man and
a woman, speaking Belfast, walked by.

'. . . walkin' in front of me backwards,' said the man, who
was pointing his finger out in front of him as if it were a gun.
'He was pointin' it at me,' said this man and he stressed it to
the woman. 'Pointin' it at me, dressed in his skull and cross-
bones, pointin' it at me, as if it was a gun. "Trick or Treat"
he shouted and when I gave him nothin', guess what he done?
He took an egg out, so he did, and he threw . . .'

They laughed and were gone and the crowd went on
moving, seething, unstoppable, dragging everyone along. It
occurred to Amelia that although she couldn't go into it, she
could inch her way along the side of it. She could get herself
home, to safety, even if it was a bit slower, that way. She'd

hold on to the buildings, she told herself. She'd use the ridges of the brickwork. She'd go slow but she'd go steady. She'd get there in the end. In spite of this though, she stayed where she was, her back against the window, watching the mass of people as she held onto the grille.

Trying to concentrate on her predicament, for it kept moving in and out of focus, she looked up and realised she had another problem now on her mind. She was having dual realities again, right here in front of her. As well as being in Camden Town in London, she was also on Belfast's Crumlin Road. Dual realities weren't new, of course. She'd been having dual realities for a while already. And she'd learned that, as long as she didn't panic, ten times out of ten, Belfast always went away. So now, all she had to do was edge herself along the sides of the buildings, London buildings, not Belfast buildings, and to try not to panic, to try and keep her plan in mind and head in the direction of home. Ten times out of ten also, home was always where it should be and, although she knew all this in theory, still she wouldn't move from the grille. This time it was another phenomenon. Something else was starting to bother her. It turned out to be Roberta McKeown who, at that moment, was walking by.

Roberta shouldn't have been walking by and Amelia had no business to be seeing her, for Roberta'd been blown up by a carbomb in 1975. 'That can't be Roberta,' said Amelia, knowing it for a fact because she remembered that she'd forgotten, deliberately, to go to Roberta's funeral. After all, just how many funerals was one expected to attend?

'I'm daft,' she said and some people started to laugh at her. Hearing the laughter, Roberta turned and Amelia tried to back away. Roberta wasn't laughing and then Amelia smiled. Why, it wasn't Roberta. She laughed herself. She was relieved. She could see it was only a schoolgirl. A different sort of schoolgirl from Roberta. And then Roberta, who wasn't Roberta, simply turned and walked away. She went on by and Amelia watched her go and then saw Bronagh McCabe coming from the opposite direction. 'I don't like the way this is going,' said Amelia as Bronagh, too, walked on by. Bronagh, a woman, and a woman still living, probably happy ever after in Belfast, didn't look at her, but her old basket from her schooldays was hanging from her arm. Amelia looked away from the people. She didn't want to see any strange phenomena. 'This can't be a breakdown,' she said. 'I thought I left all that behind.' She went on to hope that if she was having a breakdown, then she wouldn't have to have it in awful Camden, unable to realise that, when having a breakdown, there was nowhere so awful to have it, as the place one happened to be.

She looked about, still trying to get a handle on her situation. If a breakdown were imminent, she'd much prefer to have it indoors. But looking up the High Street, all she could see were forks everywhere – left forks, right forks, middle forks and side roads. She couldn't get clear, nor respond to somebody who was speaking to her, so intent was she in trying to slot her religious geography into place. The somebody who was speaking to her, turned out to be two somebodies, an old man and an old woman. 'What dear?' they said. They came close. They had been watching this girl with the plastic carrier talking to herself on the pavement and thought it terrible that these things should go on.

'Are you lost?' they said, coming even closer, too close for Amelia, and they shouted for they guessed that in her disturbed mental state, this girl might need her decibels very high. 'Are you from the alcoholic shelter?' shouted the old man. 'Are you from the Ardoyne shelter?' shouted the old woman – or at least that's what Amelia thought she shouted and she grew worried by this outright question as to what religion she was made of. As for the alcoholism, well, what was wrong with them? Couldn't they see they were completely mistaken? She opened her mouth. She'd give them the facts and put them straight about the alcohol.

So she tried to explain, quietly, patiently, absolutely in confidence, that she was cured, so they were wrong about the alcoholism but right about her being lost. She didn't refer to their question about her religion, hoping they might realise they were being rude and undiplomatic. Best for her too, given she no longer knew her forks, to be cautious and let the whole matter drop. In clearer fractions of time, she told them, she knew she was losing it badly, and that those fractions of time, daily, clearly, were slipping further and further apart. Only in her bedsit, she said firmly, could she feel she was on top of things. Only in her bedsit was she sure she could keep it all at bay.

'I might be having a breakdown,' she said, 'but I'm not sure. I'm not feeling connected. I feel as if, really, I'm standing over there.'

She indicated with her chin, for she wouldn't let go of the window grille to point out the spot to them. Some people looked. Some people laughed. Amelia realised she'd again said all of that out loud. She'd only meant to say the first part, whatever that first part had been, for already she could no longer remember. Why was her mind going funny? Why was everything becoming forgot?

It was a small crowd that had gathered, a semicircle round her. But it was growing and it was the sort of crowd, the sort of thing, this getting attention, bad attention, or even good attention, that Amelia couldn't stand. The old man and the old woman were still there. They weren't laughing. They weren't smiling. They were perplexed and the man reached down for something lying at Amelia's feet. Her bean tins in their bag were swinging against her bones. She was shaking. Her purse and her keys dropped and she turned round to the grille, and faced away from them all.

253

'What's she doing?' cried a man, coming out from his 'every-thing must go' shop. 'What's she selling?' he cried. 'She can't sell it here.' His shop was next to the 'let's kill ourselves' super-market and he had left off booming on his microphone to come out and check his display stock was still there. He checked it and it was there but still he looked suspicious. He wasn't at all satisfied. What was the crowd around her for?

This is interesting, thought Amelia, for, as one part of her continued to panic, another part of her clinically recorded the fact. 'Isn't this interesting?' she said. 'But why is this interesting? And why does it feel as if I really am over there?'

'What's she's saying? What's the cow doing?' The micro-phone man again, disbelieving, checked his fireworks, his sparklers, his party poppers, his bargain handcuffs, his men's handkerchiefs, his women's underwear, all his funny Halloween hats. 'What's she up to? What's she playing at? Has somebody called the police? Somebody's got to do something. She can't stand around here selling something or selling nothing like that!'

'What's wrong dear?' said the old woman. 'Where do you come from?' The old man straightened up. He had picked up her shopping list. It said 'Beans' followed by 'Beans', the handwriting big and angry. Her purse and keys which had fallen, had been picked up by somebody else and were gone. She was wary of telling the couple, of telling anybody, where it was she came from. She didn't know their persuasion, their inclination. What if she got it wrong? Long lines of sweat slid down the back of her. She was warm, she was cold, the next thing she wanted water. She wanted water and she wanted into her bedsit but every time she looked up, she was confronted by Protestant and Catholic roads.

'. . . don't know Alf,' said the woman. 'She's not saying any-thing. Very white and look – her lips are turning blue.'

'Can you tell me,' said Amelia, taking a chance and trying

to be tactful, 'does that road lead up to the Shankill or does it, by any chance, lead into the Bone?'

'What dear?' said the woman.

'Are you from the alcoholic shelter?' said the man.

'What's wrong?' said some horrible voice at the back of her too. 'Why's she standing like that?' it went on. 'Yes, why is she?' said some others. Amelia was standing peculiar, her arms and legs spread out very wide. She was holding onto the grille, the way men do, the way men did, over and over, being searched, by soldiers, in her childhood. The bean tins in their plastic carrier slipped down her upstretched arm. Children began to laugh.

Amelia panicked when she heard them. The sound of children was like the sound of terrorists. She hadn't known there were children and she knew that this was the time, if ever there was one, to run. Her brain and her nervous system, her heart, couldn't cope with children. They were the ones who became the adults and she slipped into powerless frightened childhood every time. Still she couldn't move, except to push her fingers into the metal grille tighter, staring at the bright blood so as to think of nothing else. The children were wearing Halloween masks. She could see this in the reflection of the window. Halloween was over, days, weeks, months, minutes before. She peeked round to double-check this, and they giggled, unsure, disbelieving of her fear of them. They didn't have on Halloween masks. 'Oh,' she thought. She said, 'So who had on the masks? How did I get that wrong?'

'I don't understand,' said a tiny, red-cut shaven man. 'Why *is* she standing there? What is it anyway, we're supposed to be looking at?' Others nodded and one of the children kicked an empty tin to the wall beside her. He's going to kick it at me, kick it at me, she thought, her panic rising even more. But he didn't. He kicked it to the side and she thought maybe it wasn't deliberate, but the tin clattered and then she caught sight of another child reaching into his bag. Amelia saw the reflection of this movement and thought this would be the end of her. This was what war was, she knew, this putting hands into bags. She could never get away, and that was what war was also. So how could she fall to her knees? How could she surrender? How could she trust what would happen to her when she knew what would happen to her could only be much worse? Instead, she held on, and she held on tight and she looked into the supermarket. She locked eyes with the guard. He'd been staring out all this time.

In his brown and green uniform, and from his brown and white eyes, in his brown dark smooth face, he did nothing except stand, four feet away, behind the mesh and behind the glass and look straight out at her. His face said nothing. His features gave nothing away. He must really hate her, she decided, and he was going to come out and push her, to hurt her, to try and move her on. These were Amelia's thoughts and she saw him turn round and go over to the wall telephone. He lifted the receiver, tapped in three digits, without hurrying, and looked out at her again. He continued to look as he spoke into the receiver. He didn't gesticulate. He didn't need to. So that was it, she thought. He was going to get her arrested. People grew silent around her. She saw him ring off.

They stayed silent and they parted, for here he was, coming now in his uniform. They waited expectantly as he made his way through the crowd. She held the grille tighter for she knew he was coming out to shove her, and when she'd fallen, then what wouldn't they do?

Now he was behind her, this security guard. She could sense him. She could smell him. Why hadn't she run earlier when she had at least something of a chance? He leaned in towards her. She heard him open his mouth. She closed her eyes. Now it was all too late.

'I've got some help,' he said. 'Tell me. Can you hear me?

Is there someone you want me to call for you? Can you hear
me? What can I do for you? Is there anyone you want me to
call?'

The window grille rattled. The beans banged as they fell out
from the bottom of their plastic carrier. She would have fallen
too, only her fingers were stuck in the holes. He put his hands
upon her back and he held her up against it. He wouldn't pull
her hands out. He told the children to gather the tins up. They
did as they were told, and the old man and the old woman,
they too, stood beside him. They were sentinels. Amelia, in
London, or in Belfast, did nothing. She kept her eyes closed.

No Bones, 1991–1992

Amelia went up the Glens in the dead of night. She had just reached the white slabs of the old famine graveyard, when something made her stop and turn around. Roberta McKeown was standing on the edge of the cliff.

'Bert!' she cried. 'Roberta McKeown! Is that you?'

Amelia didn't seem to find it strange that her friend from so long ago was standing 400ft up on a precipice, beyond the fence that warned of land giving way. Even more, she didn't seem to notice that Roberta was still a teenager, dressed in her school uniform, when in fact, she should have been thirty, the same age as Amelia herself.

'Oh, I got lost,' whined the schoolgirl. 'I'm lost. This isn't Belfast. I don't know this place.'

Amelia remembered the voice but was puzzled as to how she could have so long forgotten it. Roberta stirred first. She sighed, heaved her squat little shoulders, heaved them again, turned to Amelia, linked arms with Amelia and it was then Amelia noticed she was on the edge of the cliff too. They looked over. It was a heavy drop, a deep, sleepy drop, easy, so easy, to let go, just fall over, and disappear. Out in front though, it was different. Crashing and banging were coming from out there. It was the wind. It threw itself onto the rocks, whipped itself into caves, howled around inside them, then screamed its way out again. Water trickled down from somewhere behind them and in the woods, animals cried and killed each other in the night. It was dark. Roberta though, seemed to be shining.

Like Roberta, Amelia didn't know this place or why it was she had come to be standing there. She turned to say so to her friend but instead of just the two of them, there were now others, half-present, half-not-present, inching their way out of the darkness towards her. Amelia felt they were familiar and not at all welcome so, in order to get away, she stepped back without hesitation and fell off the edge of the cliff.

She stopped falling and without opening her eyes, felt someone move her about in the bed. So she was in a bed, she thought, and someone was moving her about in it. Someone else was putting something into her arm. She didn't know who these people were and she didn't care either. She kept her eyes shut. There were murmuring voices and one came close and said, 'Amelia?' but Amelia didn't want to respond. She didn't. The blanket was put over, and again she found herself back in the night, up the Glens, beside Roberta, standing on the edge of that cliff.

'Now why'd ye do that for?' said Roberta, her hands on her hips, getting herself ready, as she used to, for fights. 'Something on your conscience Amelia Lovett? Something you're not facing up to? Something, for example, you don't want to be reminded of?' In answer, Amelia again looked over. Nothing wrong, she told herself, with taking one's life if one had to. It might be the ultimate act of self-loathing, but couldn't it also be the ultimate act of honouring oneself? Roberta came closer. She linked arms with Amelia and held her.

'D'ye know something?' she said, and now in a casual voice,

as if they were not standing exactly where they were – on a dangerous spot, in the middle of nowhere, thinking of suicide, thinking of death. Roberta's manner had changed. She was no longer argumentative. 'I was just going to get ready for Toby's tonight,' she said. 'I love discos. Discos are great. Are you gonna call on me or am I gonna call on you?'

Amelia tried to pull away for she had started to shake at that question. Roberta kept holding her and was now pointing out, into the night, in front of her. In the middle of the air, in the middle of nothing, stood a kitchen chair with a pair of Bay City Roller trousers draped over it. Under the seat were two Size Three Monkey Boots, shined up and ready for dancing. Amelia remembered Monkey Boots. 1975 she'd had a pair. Black blazer, gold buttons, Bay City Rollers, Monkey Boots, eyeshadow, kohl pencil, discos. She'd loved discos too.

'Come on Amelia,' said Roberta. 'Answer me. Are you gonna call on me, or am I gonna call on you?' The words were a throwaway and that should have been a warning, for who ever heard of a casual person living in Northern Ireland who honestly turned out to be one? Nobody, that's who. But because of the hospital drugs and because she was very, very sleepy, Amelia's brain wasn't working the way it used to do.

'You call on me Bert,' she said, easily, carelessly, indifferently – in fact, in just the same way she'd said it one afternoon coming home from school in 1975. 'You call on me Bert,' she said. 'Then we'll call on Bernie, and then—'

Roberta whipped her arm away. 'I didn't call but, did I!' Her face was fiery, her voice all sudden and sharp.

'Youse went dancin' without me! Youse heard and forgot in less than a second and then youse went out dancin' without me!' She turned away.

Amelia felt herself disintegrating. She knew with a certainty that whatever it was Roberta McKeown was talking about, forgetting it and going dancing was the exact thing she and the others must have needed to have done. She didn't know how to say this though.

'Oh Roberta,' she cried. 'We couldn't, we had to, it wasn't, you were, you see you were . . .'

'Well!' said Roberta, turning back and taking hold of her again. 'What was I Amelia? You may as well say it. There's no bones about it now.'

Amelia backed off. She looked over the long drop and decided the best thing to do was again to fall over it. She'd try to move her legs, she'd try to get herself over, and she'd take Roberta McKeown with her, if Roberta McKeown wouldn't let her go.

'Ah, you're awake,' said a voice in a face that wasn't Roberta's. The face was looking down. The voice was English. It was a woman's. It said,

'Would you like to stay here awhile Amelia? I think you should stay here awhile. Here, this'll help the shaking.' She bent over and Amelia smelt her perfume or maybe it was her soap. Again Roberta was there, standing behind this doctor, right in the hospital, huffing her shoulders.

'You can't get away Amelia Boyd Lovett. You have to go on. And you won't get rid of me you know, unless *I* decide to go.' Then she was gone.

Amelia wasn't expecting that. It startled her and it frightened her and back up that Glen, alone, she would have liked to have called to Roberta, but her friend had taken the light with her and Amelia was afraid to call in the dark on her own. After a bit, she felt her way back from the cliff, pulling her dirty, baggy jumper closer about her. She'd go down and look for some people, she decided. Some people who might, if she let them, help her, and suggest to her things that could be done. She made her way round trees, stumbled among rocks, jumped over a culvert, climbed the fence that led back to the rest of the world and walked towards dwellings she knew were down below.

This time either a very young woman, made up to look a very old one, or else a very old one who wasn't accepting of her age, was sitting on the edge of Amelia's bed. She was thin, her bones were sticking out of her and they were held in place by a uniform. It was a big and shapeless uniform as far as Amelia could make out, but Amelia couldn't see at present very well at all. She was having double vision, triple vision, zigzag vision, polka dot vision, things missing out of corners of eyes vision and a stye that had come out because of all the disrupted sleep she had had. This person, as far as Amelia could make out, was picking tiny bits of skin off all parts of her face, examining them closely, then eating them. She looked up from doing this when she saw Amelia was awake.

'You lived in a thatched cottage I suppose?' she said, as if it was her turn in an ongoing conversation. She too was English, but not the same English person as before. 'I once knew somebody from Ireland called Mary. Do you know her?' She sighed and leaned over and took and ate a chocolate from the box belonging to the unconscious person next door. 'Oh!' She gave a big angry sigh. 'I wish I hadn't ate that chocolate. That chocolate you just saw me eat. I wish I hadn't ate it. I wish I was thin. I wish I was under five stone. People under five stone must be very very happy.' She got up then, and sauntered off as some fierce woman, twenty times her size, appeared and told this stick person to get up and get on with her work. The big woman had a giant red nose and a big purple face. Amelia realised they were both nurses and that they didn't like each other all that much. The young girl – she was young, Amelia now knew – had gone off, probably to have a lie-down someplace else. The older one began to thump and thud Amelia's bed.

This was called fixing the bedclothes, and Amelia tried to

say something, to ask this woman what had happened to her. and why she was here and for how long. But the woman didn't notice for Amelia wasn't saying anything and soon this person, without once having looked at her patient, finished plumping and straightening and straightened herself and went off. As it was warm in the bed, and as nobody was wanting her to get out of it, Amelia thought she might as well stay. She closed her eyes once more.

'. . . no bones about it . . .' said the wind or something else in it. It chased her down the hill and it shoved and pushed her along. It pushed her along and it pushed her along quickly, down a coast, through a footpassage, through a hill, up the path of a house in a village and there it left her. At the door of this house, she could see Roberta McKeown waiting. Bernadette Young was also standing there.

'Well hello Amelia!' cried Bernie. She was smiling. She was friendly. Bernie'd always been friendly. 'Long time no see!' Then she frowned. 'But Amelia, what are *you* doin' here?'

This time Amelia was ready. She knew trick questions were best answered with no clarity. 'Let's see,' she said and 'Oh' and 'Ah' and 'Ummm', and 'What are you doin'?' she threw right back. Bernie grinned and leaned in close to tell her.

Standing in her nightclothes, her overcoat, her furry slippers, her rollers in her hair to help the new perm settle, she was looking as young and as skinny as when Amelia had last seen her – though quite when that had been, Amelia didn't want to know.

'Can you keep a secret?' she said, breathing faster, coming closer. Amelia groaned and moved back for she remembered she'd heard this secret before. Bernie had told it in the school toilets after the school dinners sometime in April, 1974.

Stick Nurse was back. It felt like immediately, but it wasn't because it was dark and Amelia could see stars in the sky through the hospital glass. Again Stick was on the edge of her bed. Amelia could see she was very young, very sickly, very starving, very killing-herself. Did Amelia, Amelia wondered, ever look as ninth-tenths dead as that? This was the first time Amelia had pondered such a big question and it was as close as she'd ever come to getting a true image of herself.

'I eat cardamom seeds to fill me up,' said Stick. 'Stops me eating other things. You can suck them forever, they don't have any calories and they're good for bad breath after you vomit. It's a secret but I can tell you because you can't hear, you're not awake properly, you can't talk, you won't remember, you're not really well, and in case you don't know it, you're in a mental hospital, you know.'

'As I was saying,' said Bernie who went on to tell Amelia her new invention, as if for the first time, and in exactly the same way she had told it that day in 1974. She was full of joy at her discovery and she wanted to share it with Amelia. She'd always been a generous person, everyone at her funeral had recalled. She described how it was possible to eat and throw up, and eat and throw up, in a happy endless cycle. 'There's no bones about it,' she'd laughed. 'It's as simple as ahh bee see. The only thing to remember,' her face went serious, 'is to calculate the arithmetic. If you don't calculate the arithmetic Amelia, then you'll get fat for sure. But don't worry,' her face was all smiles again. 'The sums are extremely simple. Addition something in, subtract the same thing out. Go on. Try it. If you keep to the rules, you just can't go wrong.'

Amelia had tried it and hadn't liked it for the sums had made no sense to her. The whole point about food was not to go eating it at all.

Stick dug her fingers into the chocolate box and popped another Brazil Crunch into her mouth. It was down her neck in no time. 'Oh, I'm bloated and tortured,' she said, holding her baggy uniform out and away from her. 'I hate clothes touching me after I'm full.' She lowered her voice so that Amelia could hardly hear her. This meant she was about to say something that was top secret and classified. 'Dieting's really difficult you know.' She looked at Amelia. She pulled down the blankets and she looked at Amelia. She didn't look friendly. 'You wouldn't know though, would you?' She threw the blankets back. 'You're a skinny rake.'

'Hurry up!' barked Roberta. 'I want in!' She was standing by Amelia's side, her arms folded, her eyes mean, dirty looks flashing like riflefire from her face. Amelia fumbled with a key that was in her hand and let her in. At once, Roberta began to mutter, 'I knew it! Not a thing! Not a single thing!' She was opening kitchen cupboards, drawers and doors, or doors, drawers and cupboards were opening by themselves in front of her. It took Amelia a while to realise this was happening and that utensils and dishes were getting strewn all over. They made no sound as they fell to the floor. By the time Amelia did notice, she was alone in the kitchen and doors and cupboards were creaking open upstairs. Amelia frowned. What was Roberta thinking of, to behave like this in what appeared, after all, to be Amelia's own house?

She started up after her old friend to give her a good talking to, but stopped when something in her mind jarred and fell into place. It was a memory and remembering it, Amelia lifted her head and stared up the staircase at Roberta McKeown above her, and Roberta McKeown, the schoolgirl, stopped what she was doing and hung over the bannisters and stared back down at her.

'About time too,' said Roberta after a silence. Amelia leaned against the wall and made no reply. She simply went on looking at Roberta, or at least, at what she could see of Roberta, for after the bomb, there wasn't that much left of her old friend at all.

'You could at least have kept a photo,' said the ghost.

'Never had a photo,' said Amelia.

Neither of them said anything more.

Over the next lot of days, the house was quietly wrecked. Roberta continued to search for memories of herself, while Amelia kept out of the way, unable to give her any. As well as the schoolgirl's bad-tempered mutters, Amelia also began to hear other sighs and despairs coming from other corners of the house. She knew, as one would, that these were going to turn out to be more dead people, so she told herself she'd have to be gone before they all started to show.

The following morning, while dead Roberta had her head stuck in a box of old newspapers, grabbing them up and shouting 'Is this about me?' and while dead Bernie was engrossed in advanced top secret food mathematics next door, Amelia sneaked out the back, taking not a stitch with her. She slunk down the yard, in just the clothes she was slinking in, and she slunk lower by the railing, until she was far clear of the house. Then she skirted round the corner, flew across the bridge opposite, and hopped onto an empty Ulsterbus that was just that moment pulling out.

Giggling at how simple it had been, she shrank down on the back seat and chuckled. Safe, she thought, oh safe, safe, safe, forevermore. She opened the windows of the bus after a bit and breathed in the air and breathed out the air and kept on doing this the rest of the journey into Belfast. She watched the curves and the bends and the sheer cliffdrops and was even starting to think she was enjoying herself. It was only when the bus screeched to a halt at the top of the Cliftonville Road in Belfast that she hopped off and realised it had been driverless.

'Hiya Amelia!' cried Roberta. 'Well well. Are you calling on me or am I calling on you?'

The bus was gone and Amelia was at one side of a zebra

crossing, with her dead friend stepping off the footpath at the other. The teenager now had her Bay City Rollers on her legs, her shined up Monkey Boots on her feet and overdone clumpy make-up on her perpetually cross face. Putting two and two together, Amelia guessed her friend had about thirty-five seconds left to live, and although not wanting it to be 1975 all over again, she knew that this time, if she could get herself to Toby's and start dancing before the explosion, then she couldn't be accused by Roberta of hearing first and going dancing after. That would cancel out the first time and make everything all right again. She could forget about Roberta, for after all, Roberta was no more. So, ignoring her friend, and ignoring the strange car parked further down in the area, she hurried away to Toby's which, by her reckoning, should be somewhere round the corner and further up the road.

There was a 'crump' and Amelia woke to find yet another woman sitting looking at her. This one too was on the edge of her bed. What was going on? Amelia was beginning to wonder why she was putting up with it. She was sure she'd be very cross if these women were all men. This one was a sort of man, although something about her said that she shouldn't have been. She had dark eyes, dark eyebrows, a long nose, a long swan neck and a pageboy cut of thick, shining black straight hair. She had thin frail man's hands, slim nervous man's feet and a tall graceful bony man's body – except that it wasn't. Her breasts were tiny, low, loose, not breasts at all really, and visible through her nightgown. She was stroking this short pink neg-ligée with the backs of four of her fingers, one leg poised high over the other, making circles with her right ankle round and round. Her toenails were pearl, her skin was pearl and her pearl cheekbones went up to the ceiling. She was arresting and Amelia, on God knows how many grams of valium a day or not, was arrested.

'Hi,' Amelia heard this person say. 'I'm Jewels. I've got no uterus, fallopian tubes or upper vaginal area. My testes are hidden inside me. It's all because of Chromosome Twenty-Three. They're my Undescendeds. They are called my Unde-scendeds. But enough of me. Tell me about yourself. Have you, for instance, been eating my chocolates? You may as well tell the truth. It's the best thing in the end.'

Amelia shook her head and croaked a feeble 'No.'

'Mmmm,' said Jewels, then, 'I'm sorry, but I don't believe you.' Then, after another moment, 'I'm a voluntary patient – are you?'

'Don't know,' said Amelia.

'Probably not,' said Jewels. 'Did you try to kill yourself?'

'Can't remember,' said Amelia.

'Did you try to kill somebody else?'

'Don't think so.'

'Did you have a psychotic episode?'

'What's one of them?'

'You speak extremely slowly,' said Jewels, 'and you hardly lift your tongue from the floor of your mouth as you do so. There is an accent. Your English is distorted. Is it the medication? What have they put you on?'

'You're scaring me,' said Amelia. 'You're a scary sort of person.' She closed her eyes for, generally speaking, she discovered that whenever she got in too complex, all she had to do was close her eyes and she'd at once fall asleep and be gone. Amelia didn't know where her body had learnt this clever trick of escaping, but it certainly was a handy one for living. She felt the vibrations change in the ward and knew it was because Big Purple had arrived.

'Jewels baby,' Amelia heard her say. 'Not yet. She's not awake.'

'She is awake. She says she didn't consume them but somebody did and I shall track down the culprit sooner or later. Tallulah, don't savage my Harvey Nichols. I asked you before not to do that. It's a Therese Reiser. It's pink. It's delicate. It's precious. It's me. Don't savage me.'

As she drifted back to Belfast, Amelia thought she liked this person Jewels and hoped she might meet her again some day.

'What way ye headin'?' said Danny Megahey, coming out from the Catholic side of the Deerpark Road. He fell into step beside her and of course, he made her jump. Not with the sight of the damage his body was in – because that, it goes without saying, she wasn't taking any note of. She'd jumped because he'd taken her unawares. 'That's how I was took,' he said. She jumped again. That was low, she thought. That was mean. That was dirty. She would never have expected mean, low and dirty from the likes of Danny Megahey, oh no.

'Go away!' she said. 'I don't remember you, Danny. I don't remember anything and anyway, I'm not in Ireland. That's all over. You have to get on with your life.'

'What life's that Amelia?' said Danny and that was the nastiest thing he'd ever said, the sort of lowdown, sarcastic remark she'd expect from the likes of Roberta.

'What life's that Amelia?' said Roberta, coming up behind her, even though Amelia had heard her being blown up not that long ago.

'What life? What life?' said a few other dead people. Amelia thought the best thing to do was run away at once.

'London!' she cried, taking off and away from them. 'I'm in London!' she shouted, trying to get free from them all.

'You are comical, Amelia,' said Jewels. 'Stop pushing. Every day you ask where you are and every day we tell you and every day you forget again. Then you insist at the top of your voice that you're in London when no one's contradicting and it's obvious you're the only one who thinks it's not true.'

Amelia looked around. It was true. She wasn't at the top of the Cliftonville. Other patients were concurring with Jewels and, yet again, she supposed they were all about her bed. But no, this time everybody was on chairs in the middle of a big room. There were lots of chairs, some benches, people on them – men and women. They were Black and White, Asian, Oriental – maybe even Protestant and Catholic. There were big groups and small groups, groups of one or two only and then some individuals. The individuals were huddled. They were rocking by themselves. Amelia was sitting in a big crowd, and it was of women, and she was worried because although she recognised some of them, she didn't recognise all of them, and she didn't remember, ever, being in this room before.

They laughed and told her not to worry, that she was in this dayroom every morning. They said she always sat in the same chair, facing the window, by that long table that led up to the door. She looked. It was a long table, and it ran the length of the room. The window was a Lego window, a plastic window, pretty, neat and tidy. It was unbreakable. She remembered now someone had once told her that. 'Ghosts, you know Amelia,' he'd said, 'couldn't come through that window.' She knew that that had been meant as a joke. There were white plastic flowers in pink, blue and yellow vases and there were shelves holding Agatha Christies, Len Deightons, John Grishams and Mills and Boons. There was just one door that led in and the same door that led out again. It had a little calculator code and at that moment it was propped open with a red fire extinguisher. People kept knocking into it, and then into the edge of the door as they shuffled in and out of it. Amelia looked away and turned her attention back to those she was sitting with. Two of the Black women, Charlene and Phyllida – she remembered them – were starting to fight again. They were always fighting, she remembered that also. This time Phyllida was the one to begin first.

'Your ancestors sold our ancestors!' she cried.

Charlene laughed although she, too, was very angry. She boomed,

'At least we know who our ancestors were!'

They were in two factions and these factions at that moment were nodding and egging them on. They jeered and cheered and the White people in the group pretended nothing was happening. Amelia was perplexed. She wondered how to get a handle on this new situation. In Ireland, she knew, it was all about Green and Orange. In England, she had thought till now, it was all about Black and White. So what was this Black and Black thing?

'We know our villages!' Charlene shouted louder. 'We know our locations! We have tradition, culture, we can point to exact spots!'

'Backward!' taunted Phyllida, and her supporters taunted with her. 'Tight-assed traditionalists! Stuck in patriarchal pasts!'

'I don't understand,' said Amelia. 'Why're youse fightin'? Don't youse all come then, from the same place?'

There was silence. Did the White girl really say that? The other Whites, as one, turned their heads away. Charlene pounced first.

'Amelia whatever your name is, and wherever it is you come from – don't you realise that that's a racist remark?'

Amelia hadn't realised and wondered if she were to say so, would that be a racist remark too? Oh dear, she thought. So now she was a racist. Oh well, she thought further. Never mind. As long as she didn't tell anybody, as long as she asked no further questions, as long as she kept her mouth shut, no one would be any the wiser, no one would ever know.

'I suppose you'll be saying next,' said Phyllida, 'that we're exotic little ethnic creatures.' They all laughed, but not for very long. Amelia was still confused but more than that, she was frightened. She decided to get away, so she fell asleep at once. Immediately she was back in safe Belfast.

She was on Alliance Avenue and had just reached the old Morelli house, when she saw she was holding three plastic bags of shopping from a Co-op that had been bombed out of existence years and years ago. She dropped them for they were meaningless and silly and tins of beans rolled out and rolled along the road.

'But don't you remember *anything*?' said Jewels as the doctor moved away and Amelia was this time sitting on the edge of Jewels' bed. It was nighttime again. Day and night blended easily here, the way Belfast and London also seemed to do these days. Amelia held her knees and rocked herself on the mattress. She didn't know how she'd be able, ever, to get herself out of this place. How could she? She wouldn't be sure of the country, she wouldn't be sure of the decade, she wouldn't be sure if the people she was talking to were even alive or dead.

'I remember tins of beans,' she said. 'Ah,' said Jewels. 'That'll be it. You were stealing them. You were stealing them and got caught, and that was the catalyst. I steal things. Kleptomania it's called. Can't help it. It's all on account of my kleptomania, they say. It's top secret but I can tell you. It's not really the kleptomania though. It's the bulimia. Hell no, it's not that either. It's because of Pearl. Pearl Winter. She's my lover. She went away.'

Amelia was surprised.

'You mean you're not in here because of your Undescendeds?'

Jewels was offended.

'You really are the limit Amelia. And *why* would I be here because of my Undescendeds? How many people do you know have both sexual anatomies?' None, thought Amelia. 'Exactly,' said Jewels, reading her mind.

'But I thought——' began Amelia. 'Wrong,' said Jewels.

'Fighting to keep my natural anatomical ambiguity was my very greatest achievement. What was your greatest achievement Amelia?' Amelia thought. 'I got off alcohol.' Then, after a moment, 'And I don't do food the way I did before.'

'Not enough,' said Jewels. 'I hate to say this Amelia, but the others are right in what they say about you. You're narrow-minded and insular and you suffer from a lack of information. You must have had some very sheltered upbringing, that's very plain to see.' Then she softened. 'I'm only telling you this for your own good,' she said. 'Don't you want to know then, Amelia, about the world and about people?'

Not really, thought Amelia. What she knew about the world and about people hadn't done her any favours. What she knew about the world and about people so far had put her in this place. She didn't say this though, in case she got it wrong again. All she said was, 'I'm sorry. Come on, Jewels. Don't stay angry. Let's be friends.'

'It's because of your sleeping,' said Charlene. They were now sitting in the dayroom again. 'We know being mentally ill means you've got to alternate between being an insomniac and falling asleep a lot, but all the same Amelia, we think you take the second part far too far.'

The others nodded. 'If you're not careful Amelia,' they said, 'you'll end up like Grace there.' They turned to look at Grace, who was sleeping in the bed across the way in their ward. Grace slept in the next bed to Amelia, on the other side of her from Jewels, and Amelia had not, in all the time she'd been there, seen Grace open her eyes or say hello even once.

'At first she'd wake up and talk to us,' said Sally. 'But more and more she kept drifting off and not coming back for ages. Since the last time she went, she hasn't come back at all.'

'You'd best be careful,' said Jewels. Regina said, 'Yes, you'd best. You sleep an awful lot, Amelia, you know.'

273

'I'm just tired,' said Amelia. Now she was annoyed. They were exacting, going on at her, as if they themselves weren't in a mental hospital. Didn't they know then, everybody needed to have something in their lives?

'Doctor wants you prepared,' said someone. Amelia woke and turned her head with difficulty. They were speaking to Grace, asleep, in the next bed. They were four strangers, nurses and orderlies, and they were looking grim and unfriendly. Some patients sidled up to watch. Immediately, they were chased away.

'This is probably her last chance,' said Stick, looking on. She was filing her stump-bitten fingernails on the edge of Amelia's bed, swinging her stick legs, stick-stick, stick-stick, in and out, in and out. She was happy. She was on a diet. It was Christmastime. That meant lots of parties. She was going to be ready, and thin, for every single one of them.

'Grace Meek!' said a nurse sternly. 'I know you can hear me! I'm going to take some blood. Johnny, pull the screens across.'

The other nurses also shouted at Grace and shouted at Stick to stop being so lazy and to come and help them, but although they were shouting, neither Grace nor Stick would respond. Amelia grew frightened. What did they mean, the doctor wanted her prepared? What were they going to do? What was going on? She looked to see if Jewels would help her, but Jewels was still not talking to her. Jewels was very cross. She was angry at Amelia for not knowing the difference between a pseudo-hermaphrodite and a plain hermaphrodite and had accused her, furthermore, of stealing her chocolates on the sly. Stick couldn't have helped either, for Stick couldn't have helped anybody. At five stone and going under, she was heading for disaster herself. So Amelia pushed off the blankets. She sat up. She was feeling black-out and dizzy, but she got herself out of the bed, and tried to get herself to the door.

A movement up the overgrown path to the side of Amelia

made her turn and forget all about Grace and the ward. She looked towards the old Morelli house where two of the three brothers were beckoning her. Lizzie was by the bay window. No, she thought. Surely Lizzie can't be dead. Somebody would have told her. Wouldn't somebody have told her? Oh! She remembered. That's right. Somebody had.

'Look! She's getting away!' cried a voice.

'She can't get away,' cried another. Amelia looked back but a thick cloud had descended upon them all. 'Guess who's dead?' said someone.

'I'm making our Bernie a cake, a cake,' said another. 'Our Bernie's coming home, she's coming home.'

'We lost him,' said a cheerful brave voice. 'But guess what? We just pretended he never existed. The pain went away. Bang! Just like that. *You* should try it.'

'Guess who's dead!' said the first voice again.

'We thought we'd be safe, under the table, behind the cushions, behind the chairs.'

'. . . and she even pretended that her brother – you know – the one you and me knows is *really* dead – had been popping in and out for cups of tea the whole time!' – 'No!' – 'Yes! Aren't people funny! And that's not all . . .'

'Those scavenger flies are a giveaway.'

'Guess who's dead!'

'It's me!' cried Amelia. 'Oh, it's me! It's me that's dead, isn't it?'

'It's that Lovett woman,' said Stick. 'She's lying there raving. The doctor cut her medication but it's my opinion she should've increased it even more.'

It was nighttime. Again Amelia awoke and sat up quick in her bed. She felt worried. The pipe radiators were roasting hot, the nurses were busy and she could see in the darklight that others were awake and that something was very wrong. They were looking up towards Amelia, but no, they were looking past Amelia. Amelia, feeling shivery, turned to look too.

Grace's bed was gone. Grace was gone. She had been wheeled away, the space now bone empty. Someone let out a piercing wail. It was Sally, and it was a long wail, on a long note, down the other end of the hospital ward. Amelia couldn't stand it, and she couldn't stand either the rocking of the person in the bed on the other side of her. It was Jewels and what Amelia couldn't stand, was her friend no longer being the fearless one. Sally keened on, got out of bed and began rolling, and this set off other huge-heap crying, from everywhere, throughout the ward. A nurse called for more help and that's when Amelia got up to leave. It was time to go. She couldn't stay here, she now knew, anymore.

It was strange though, in this hospital, because sometimes she couldn't lift her head off the pillow and other times, like now, she'd be shuffling, shuffling along. It was daytime again, and here she was, urgently, determinedly, trying to pass all the other shufflers. They, too, were taking ages as they hurried along. Looking up, she saw steel dishes ahead of her and was sure she'd give a wide berth to them, but as always, she didn't and walked, smack, bang, into them every time. They fell over with a great clatter and she stopped, scared, sure the Grace-stealers would come down and shout at her, sure they'd take a hold of her and make her go back in the bed. But they came down as always, and they bent over and they picked up everything. She stood and watched and then they went away, leaving her on her own as before. When they were gone, she shuffled faster, but again, before she could reach the exit, she grew sleepy, closed her eyes and leaned against the wall. She waited. She always waited. Someone would come sometime. They'd come down eventually and help her get back to her ward.

This time was different. She stumbled out of the thick cloud and all the voices were still following her. She was outside the small block of flats where her Aunt Dolours used to live. She threw herself at the communal door and it fell open and she fell through it. She shut it. She locked it. And just in time too. They rushed to the glass and silently, they stared in at her. They were her friends, her neighbours, some people from the area. Roberta was in front. All of them were dead.

Amelia backed away, telling herself none of this mattered, that it wasn't happening, that in a moment or two she'd be back again on the ward. But she wasn't. They kept on staring, so she kept on backing, moving towards the stairwell, not knowing something was already in the stairwell, tapping upon the tiles in the shadows, and waiting just for her.

It scuttled over before she got a look at it, fastened onto her calf and pulled her down and into place. Disoriented, seeing in broken vision, Amelia turned, or was turned and, as its pincers squeezed around her, she realised what it was doing and screamed until it made her stop. It made her stop by getting a feeder down inside her, fast and slick and that was familiar, somehow that was familiar. Try as she might, she couldn't scream then anymore. A second went in also, both spindly, tapered, both strong in their positions and, still conscious, she clawed and scrabbled to get both out again. It had the face of her brother and he was eating her calf muscle and he ate it, making neat little slapping laps. He sucked methodically and he kept his eyes closed and when he'd finished with her calf, he moved on to her thigh muscle. Two voices were heard in the corner. They were vying to dominate.

'Me!' cried one. 'No, me!' cried the other. They were in the shadows and it was her dead parents, arguing, as they'd always done, over which of them was going to die first. Help! Amelia tried to shout, but no sound came out of her. Help! she tried again. It was her mother's turn to speak.

'It'll be me!' she said. 'No me!' said her da.

'You're selfish Tommy,' said her ma. 'I'm not going to die second. How can you expect me to die second when you know I love you so much?'

'You're the selfish one Riah,' said her da. 'How can you say you love me! If it's true you really loved me, then you'd save me the pain of losing you, by letting me die first!'

Ma! Amelia cried in her head. Da! she cried also. She began to cry really. Mick was going to go on until he'd eaten her all up.

'So it'll be me!' cried her ma. 'No me!' cried her da. 'No, me!' cried her ma. Help me, went Amelia. Mick chewed on.

He had eaten the flesh of her thigh and was now crunching into her thighbone. His underbelly was cold and his legs squeezed and released as he made his way along. She began to grow sleepy but kept telling herself not to do this, that she mustn't drift away while this thing was going on. She dragged herself, with him attached, towards the concrete stairs where her parents were impassioning. They were impassioning so intently, they couldn't see their daughter wanting by.

'The only thing I could be accused of,' said her da, 'was of loving you more than I should have.'

'The only thing I could be accused of,' said her ma, 'was of loving you even more than that.'

Amelia clawed by them. She grappled for a hold of the long poker lying on the first stair. It was the same poker, she remembered, that had been used in her family for hitting people whenever they got too close. Mick was too close. He was going fast and had finished off her thighbone and was moving to her groinbones. She lifted the poker, holding the shaft aloft. She brought it down and into him, and into him, and into him, but it was useless. He was unstoppable. She dropped it and it clattered into the corner of the hall.

'I love you,' said her ma. 'You're the only one for me.'

'I love you,' said her da. 'You're the only one for me.' They kissed and made up as Amelia reached the middle stair. On it was a box marked AMELIA BOYD LOVETT'S TREASURE TROVE. She knocked it out of the way. Rubber bullets, fat and muted, tumbled out and down the stairs. She ignored them and dragged herself to the top step, Mick's body knocking against her and blocking her sight by now.

'Kiss kiss kiss. You're the only one for me,' they said. 'No, kiss kiss kiss,' they contradicted themselves. 'You're the only one for me.' Amelia felt for his revolver as he felt for what he wanted. She pulled the trigger. Her brother disappeared.

Her parents stopped their lovemaking and were now standing, looking up at her. Once again, as always, they got it completely wrong.

'Don't do it Amelia,' they said. 'We're your parents. You have to obey us. You can't shoot your brother. Go and shoot somebody else.'

Amelia shot them and then she shot everybody who started up the stairs after her, and pretty soon she was shooting at anything at all. When the gun was empty she went on click-clicking, then she stopped clicking, and threw the thing to the floor.

She pulled herself across the landing to her Aunt Dolours' flat. On the door was a notice saying AUNT DOLOURS IS DEAD NOW, but the door was unlocked. Amelia got herself in and banged it shut. She looked around.

The room was bright and airy and this was a surprise. The nightmare must be over. She got herself to her feet. She could feel her legs once more. They weren't bloody or painful and so she became happy. She could live here, she thought. She danced to celebrate and hugged and sang herself into the next room. There, her smile dropped a little at the difference in what she saw.

Why no, she decided. This was a nice room also – smaller, cracked windows, cold, with something unpleasant in the atmosphere. But she cheered up. She could live here too, she decided, and she tried to dance once more. Her bitten leg wouldn't let her though. It was septic and her groin was hurting. She hummed instead. A sad tune. Repetitive. A tearing, searing sore.

There were whisperings. She heard them immediately. She stuck her fingers in her ears to try to make them stop. They were outside, planning what they were going to do to her. Looking down, near the ground, she spied a tiny door. She pulled it open. Inside was black. She squeezed in and pulled it shut. And now, as long as she didn't think about her feelings, about her family, about sex or about Ireland, she could live here happily, holding her breath, forevermore. She settled down to do this, but the voice of her sister spoke over her intentions. 'Amelia,' Lizzie said. 'Ye're nothin' but a wee dope.'

She looked around. It was crowded. They were all in here with her, including her parents and her brother and all the others she had forgotten. Lizzie said, 'Ye've got to get it into your head Amelia. We can't do it all y'know. We didn't come back to get you. You came back to get us.'

She opened her eyes and was again on the ward. It was bright. Jewels was shaking her.

'Amelia,' she cried. 'You really scared us this time.'

Amelia yawned and leaned against Jewels and said she thought she was beginning to see what they were talking about. Having those sleeps was important to start with, but perhaps they weren't the answer in the end. Jewels helped her with her juice for she still couldn't drink without jerking. Then Jewels said, 'How about a murder mystery, goddesses? Lie back and I'll read to you all.'

So she read them an Agatha Christie, with three murders, not one murder, and Amelia found, this time, she could concentrate on what was going on. She enjoyed this fiction, they all enjoyed it, and Jewels said she very much enjoyed reading to them, and did Amelia want to have a go at reading aloud to them as well? The others nodded, and said yes, that it was time Amelia took her turn and Amelia laughed and said okay, but they'd have to wait till she could see right and the words stopped jumping around. They laughed too and said they'd put her down for Friday. Then, setting the book aside, they went off in a crowd to have their evening tea.

Safe House, 1992

It was a late afternoon in January when Amelia went to see about the room. She arrived outside the four-storey house in north London, depleted, exhausted, and again checked the address in her hand. This was where Jewels lived, where Jewels' lover had lived and where Jewels' landlady was yet again looking for someone new. Amelia hoped it might be her. She needed a room quick.

She leaned over and tried to open the gate but it didn't want to let her. Eventually it did, because it realised she wasn't giving up either. She then walked up the broken path to the door. The door was steel and it was shut and it had no windows and it had no letterbox but there was a peephole in the centre and a pushbell at the side. The curtains on the upstairs windows were closed and made of a heavy grey material and the curtains on the downstairs were nailed shut and made of wood. Amelia didn't like what she was seeing so far, but told herself beggars couldn't be choosers, that she wanted to get out of the hostel, that she wanted some privacy and that she needed a room quick.

She pushed the bell and it shrieked. Pulling her finger off it, she hoped both she and it wouldn't have to go through that again. They didn't. Stealthy footsteps sounded pitter-patter, pitter-patter, pit-pit-pit and, after a few moments, during which Amelia knew she was being spied on through the peephole, long bolts were drawn, locks unlocked, chains dismantled, shorter bolts slotted back and finally the massive steel door swung out – just a bit and not a bit more. It gave one long, painful moan as it did so and it was this sound, rather than the mass of steel swinging out towards her, that really made Amelia jump out of the way.

A moment later she peered around and saw a woman standing on the threshold. She was small, just like Amelia, anaemic, just like Amelia, in her thirties, just like Amelia, but whereas Amelia looked on the alert and ready to duck if she had to, this woman looked on the alert and ready to attack even if things were happy ever after. She had a baseball bat in one hand and what looked like a gun – oh no, I hope not, I really hope not, thought Amelia – in the other.

'Ah,' said the woman, snapping the bat out of the way and putting the gun in its holster. 'You must be Amelia. Jewels left me a description. Lucky for you, you fit it. I'm Helena. Come on in.' She glanced up and down the empty street then, 'Hurry!' she cried. 'There's no time to lose. I need to bolt and bar and lock and secure the door quick.'

Amelia jumped or was pulled over the threshold, and the landlady's hand then waited for the door to swing back shut. It did and she barred it up, slid the bolts, locked the locks, hung the chains and Amelia, standing in the hallway, smelt the fetid air and the damp in the walls and the growths underfoot in the darkness.

'You must think this time-consuming and a bit gothic,' came Helena's voice, 'but really, you wouldn't believe the precautions needed in London these days. Dreadful people. Awful people. Mad people. You wouldn't believe. Monsters.

Marauders. Murderers. You wouldn't believe, you wouldn't believe, you . . .' – she snaked her arm out along the wall to a lightswitch and Amelia, feeling it coming across the air towards her, shivered and moved out of the way. She banged her shin on a sandbag.

'Careful of sandbags!' came Helena's voice. 'Come on. Let's go. Urgent. Urgent. It's on a timer, move!'

She pressed the lightswitch, which seemed to make no difference except for the notion that if it had been possible for the hall to get any darker, then it did. Helena then ushered and pulled Amelia as fast as she could down the hallway towards an invisible back staircase somewhere at the end. This hall, although Amelia couldn't see it, was narrow as a coffin, piled with boxes, papers, files, folders, briefcases, tea-chests and more sandbags. The whole passage was cluttered with an amazing amount of non-collectables and Amelia tripped and fell over all of them on the way. When eventually they reached the second staircase, going down, the timer went off, leaving them in a somewhat lesser darkness, which wasn't all that helpful for it was still total gloom.

'Careful,' hissed Helena, pushing Amelia down the stairs and she had a surprising amount of power in her, Amelia noticed, given her rampant fragility and her tiny totey size.

'You'll get used to this,' she went on. 'There are fourteen steps and if you count them, you should never have any problems negotiating the darkness and finding your way around. But careful. Potential drop coming up.'

Drop? thought Amelia, realising in time that her hand, which kept wanting to touch something solid, kept touching nothing at all. She clung to the wall of the poky thin house and fumbled, mentally counting 'One two three' quickly to herself, with Helena counting 'One two three, keep going, keep going' out loud behind. Amelia, almost always prepared to be paranoid, hysterical and completely on-the-edge on any occasion, realised too late she'd forgotten to be those things this time. It seemed that this time, she could be walking into anything and that this time, it seemed most likely that she was. So it came as a relief that, when she got off the last stair, turned a corner and went through a doorway, she wasn't in a Do-It-Yourself graveyard but in a brightly lit, cheerful, warm, big room.

It was the kitchen and after the clutter of the floor above, Amelia could have been forgiven for expecting some filthy minging pigging bog, piled high with sprouting dead things and fat rats having naps in dirty dishcloths. But it wasn't. The place was clean. The overhead light was on and it was covered by a cosy, homey lightshade with two further sane, well-adjusted lamps throwing domesticity and jolliness all around. A sharp lemon smell was everywhere. A gleaming fridge, gleaming cooker, gleaming dishwasher, gleaming lots of things sparkled over at Amelia while a television gave out safe, workaday babbles from a sideboard. A pine table with its leaves opened, was covered by a chequered tablecloth, with Helena's house-hold stuff spread out on top. These were fusewire, insulating tape, an assortment of screwdrivers, EverReady batteries, clothespegs with their jaws prised open and candles with very long wicks. Apart from this pile of DIY equipment, which gave Amelia an unpleasant déjà vu feeling, the only other disturbing thing in the whole of the kitchen was the double-sized window covered completely by hardwood. Thick planks were held in place by tight rows of nails, two thousand of them, Amelia would have reckoned. A Royalty Moments calendar hung from the centre of this woodwindow and twelve small Zen, Good Heart, Good Cheer, Prosperity and Peace plants were arranged in a row alongside it. All of them were dead.

Safety back in her bunker, Helena now seemed to change. She set aside the baseball bat, took the gun – which still looked like a gun as far as Amelia could see, although she kept waiting for it to change into something else – out of its holster and set both it and the holster in the wok and put the lid on. She became softer, breathed easier, was more relaxed, seemed a gentle little nice person. Amelia knew different. Amelia had come across these sorts of people before. An extreme personality in one room, a completely different extreme personality in another. It did no good in the long run, she now realised, blocking people's less favourable bits out of her consciousness. She always paid dearly for that in the end.

Helena gathered her wires and candles and batteries and so forth and locked them, using five padlocks, in a cupboard off to the side. While doing this, she explained in a gentle, soft, non-threatening tone that Jewels was not there, that Jewels was out looking for Pearl again, but that Jewels would be back a bit later on. They were all alone, she smiled. Just the two of them together. So why not shoot the breeze, get to know each other, talk about tenancy details, check out the spare room and who knows, come to a decision in no time? First of all, how about a nice cup of tea?

The first thing Amelia thought was that Helena was going to put poison in it, then immediately she told herself she had to stop thinking things like that every time she met someone new. So she said yes, that tea would be lovely and while Helena got busy, Amelia went over and sat on a chair. There were four chairs in the kitchen and they looked comfy, with cushions on their seats, cushions at their backs and with nice cosy armrests on every one of them. It turned out though that they weren't comfy. They were lumpy and bumpy and on lifting the cushion of the one she was trying to sit on, Amelia discovered a hatchet and a bowie knife underneath. Not wanting to be impolite, she didn't lift either of these objects, but put the cushion back and tried to perch on top. Both she and the landlady, she realised, were keeping an eye on each other. If, for example, she moved a finger for absolutely any reason, Helena spun round to see what it had moved for. If Helena trotted behind

Amelia, say, to pick up the teapot, Amelia turned casually to make sure it was the teapot and not something more sinister she was reaching out for.

'We have a few basic rules,' said Helena, setting down the tea-tray. She offered Amelia a biscuit. 'Just a few basic rules, Amelia, to help everything along.'

That seemed fair. Amelia now knew basic rules were important. At the hostel she'd learnt they stopped people killing each other over bathsoap. So she nodded and said, 'Oh yes?' and took and held the biscuit. She didn't eat it of course and Helena, not noticing, or cleverly pretending not to notice, that her guest might be thinking that she might be trying to poison her, set a cup of tea in front of Amelia as well. She smiled again. Amelia smiled back, and noted the teapot – a khaki-like affair, strangely in the shape of a turret gun – sitting with its barrel pointing her way. Helena too sat down on a lumpy bumpy and, not in the least discomposed by the tomahawk underneath it, drew twelve sheets of foolscap from out of the air.

'Ahem, ahem,' she coughed, though too softly and gently and kindly and peacefully to be followed by anything brash like exclamation marks. 'Basic Rule Number One,' she read, 'which I'm sure you must be aware of . . .' She looked over at Amelia. Amelia looked back. She had no idea what Basic Rule Number One might be. 'It's the one about men,' said Helena. 'And it goes without saying. Basic Rule Number Two . . .'

Amelia knew really, she ought to stop Helena right there and get her back to that Rule Number One. She had a suspicion it was the 'They're not us, we don't like them, we don't have anything to do with them, we don't let them in' rule she'd heard tell existed in some quarters. This was not a rule Amelia herself wanted to adhere to. Just out of a psychiatric ward or not, difficulties with men or not, she'd never been that far gone. It wasn't even that she particularly wanted one. Depressed and even more depressed, with further depressions on the way, there was no question she'd be venturing into that area. Still, she thought, wiping her brow with the biscuit, pointless trying to get well if she was going to spend all her time in another person's mad world. She must make her own decisions and not accept those coming from someone even crazier than herself.

Helena, adjusting her soldier's helmet to make it more comfortable, was now running through what she called 'the usual routines'. These were routines for washing, cleaning, food, phonecalls, pots, pans and so on. The household put great stress on rotas, Helena said, and they were very peculiar rotas, Amelia noticed. They were for reveille, for nightwatch, for inbe-tweenwatch, for bugle-calling, for kit inspection, for code-breaking and for survival techniques. Amelia felt a rising anxiety as she listened to all these basics and wondered if she was having some sort of hearing episode.

Finally Helena pushed back her chair and decided it was time to show Amelia the room. They were outside it four timer switches later with Helena jangling large keys on a large keyring in her tiny hand. She selected one, stuck it into the first lock, then another into the second lock, then another and another and another after that. Six locks and keys later, the door opened and Amelia took a breath and looked in.

It was a sad room but not a negative room and it had good points and one of them was the door itself. Although the locks were disturbing, they were both a good and a bad thing, for at least she would have privacy if she were to move in here. She stepped inside and saw an old ripped-up armchair. It had a high back and a low seat and was positioned behind the door. Another good point, thought Amelia, looking at it. And the two windows opposite were good points too. She could repo-sition the chair and put it in front of those windows. Outside was a plane-tree and, apart from Christmas trees and redwood trees, London plane-trees were the only trees Amelia knew the sight of. Good, she thought. She'd sit in that chair and she'd look at that tree. Maybe one day she'd get energy and learn how to put curtains up.

'I've taken the curtains down,' said Helena. 'It's not safe in London. Deedee's putting boards up at the weekend.'

Amelia slumped on the bed and Helena handed her the Basics. They were relentless and unwholesome and very much like mental illness, so Amelia didn't read them. She dropped them and they scattered all over the floor. She leaned back instead against the headboard for she was starting to feel sleepy. This was the last of her medication which was once more kicking in. It was a fierce little medication. It came and went, obeying no clock or no person, and did exactly what it wanted whenever it felt like it. If Amelia tried to speak while it was expressing itself, her words came out drunken, her vowels and consonants thick and awry. Her brain would slow down, her arms and legs even more so, and she was glad she'd told the doctor she didn't want to take it anymore. Lying on the bed – and yet having the sensation of floating a little above it – she yawned and closed her eyes, finding it easier to listen to Helena that way.

The landlady was marching about the room, indicating drawers, pointing out a wardrobe, waving to the armchair, explaining what further pieces of furniture in the room were called. She described a wooden door, then she described a doorhandle and said it was called a doorhandle and that it was made of wood. It could be made of other things, she added, but that wasn't the point of doorhandles, but that with screws, and sometimes without screws, they could be attached to these things, doors. This was a door. She pointed it out again. And then she showed the locks and then she turned on a little TV. This was to demonstrate that she wasn't a bastard and had gone to the trouble of providing one, but then she said nobody in that household ever watched their TV.

'We latch the gate on going out,' she said, 'we collect the post from the pathway, we ring three times before entering, we change the password once a week. We don't open the door to unexpecteds, we don't open the door to men anytime, wehavemeetings-in-progressinterminably, weputournames, wedon'tlike, wedon'tallow, we ra-ta-ta-ta-tat!' She sighed, contented, looked over at Amelia, then squealed when she saw her Basic Rules on the floor.

'What's going on?' she cried. 'Why are you sleeping? For what reason is your mouth going funny like that?'

I'm sorry, Amelia tried to say, I don't normally do this, I'm just tired and tipping over, I'll get up at once. But she didn't, because she couldn't, and her words came out as 'wa-ril-wiel-am-if-jude-ka-la'. Then she added, 'I slink it's count the med-cinnn Im annn.' That was enough. Her tongue lay down. It needed a little nap now. Amelia again closed her eyes, knowing it wouldn't be for long. She knew the side-effects of the medicine only lasted a short while. Helena, unfortunately, did not have that insight.

'Medicine?' she reeled. 'Did you say the word "medicine"? Are you sick?' She had a thought – one of her great horror ones – 'Are you *mentally* sick? You're not one of those peculiar people Jewels sometimes brings home?'

She was gripping the ends of her cardigan which meant she was thinking that if Jewels' friend were on medicine, especially mental medicine, mightn't she be dangerous and try to pull the place apart? That would be most dreadful but no, she thought further, that wouldn't be the most dreadful. What would be the most dreadful would be if she had mental health problems *and* were on the dole. These were the thoughts running through Helena so she asked Amelia outright if she were on state benefits or if she had a job. Amelia nodded, shook her head and tried to say 'Sickness' but it came out as 'Cluckness'. It sufficed. Helena got the point.

While the landlady gave a strangled cry, stepped back and struggled with the thought that it wasn't often you found yourself in the presence of a mad person, Amelia, who of course, thought the opposite – that it wasn't often, in fact, you found you were not – couldn't help now thinking of her mother. Her mother must be turning in her grave, she thought, her *early* grave, to see what a disappointing daughter her Amelia had become. Mariah Lovett would never have stood for this nonsense, would never have put up with Helena. She would have told Helena where to put her Basic Rules, her wooden windows, her fifty detonators under the floorboards, and would have insisted on personally putting them up there for her. Amelia, however, had never been of her mother's calibre and for a long time had thought that this was a great lack. That was before. This was now. Now she could see her mother's way of doing things was just one way of doing things, and that she, Amelia Lovett, didn't have to do things that way. She didn't have to have the last word. She didn't have to annihilate in order not to be annihilated. It would be all right, she could now tell herself, not to have to be her ma.

'You can't stay!' Helena was shouting, peering over from the far corner. 'You're drifting off! We're afraid we can't have you. There aren't any vacancies. Go and look for someplace else.' Amelia couldn't answer, for her words weren't ready to come out yet. Helena took it personally, which was understandable, given it was, after all, this woman's own house.

'The truth of the matter is . . . !' boomed a loud Belfast man suddenly. He was on the TV beside them and both women jumped at the sound of his voice. The happy burbles of afternoon television broadcasting were over and now it was time for the horror stories of the day. Two Northern Ireland community leaders were having a fight. It was called a debate and, furious, each leader let the other start but then couldn't believe the big lies the other was telling and would burst in with 'Liar! The real truth of the matter is . . .'

'Liar!' cried the first. 'The truth of the matter is . . .'

'Liar yourself!' cried the second. 'The truth of the matter is . . .'

'Janus-faced bastard,' cried the first. 'The truth of the matter is . . .'

'Up yours, arsehole. The truth of the matter is . . .'

'The truth of the matter . . .'

'Oh, who cares!' cried Helena, striding over and zapping them. 'Silly people.' She turned away. 'Let them have their little war.' She was determined again for she had remembered all her stashed-away weapons. They were hidden about the house for just such an emergency as this. She walked back to Amelia.

'This is your last chance,' she said. 'You can't say I haven't warned you. The truth of the matter is, we don't take disturbed violent Scottish people into this house.'

The front doorbell sounded three times in warning and then the big door opened and someone came in downstairs.

'Ah, that'll be Jewels,' said Helena. 'Thank God. She can get you out of here. I'm sorry, but you're mad. I'm afraid you just won't do.' She walked off then, calling to Jewels to come upstairs and clean up something, and thanking her for her interest, but in future, not to bother, she'd find her prospective tenants herself.

Jewels climbed the stairs and came into the top bedroom and Amelia opened her eyes and was glad to see her friend. She put out her hand from her drowsy druggy spaced-out state, but instead of pulling her up, Jewels flopped down beside her. They lay like that, saying nothing, for a while. Then Jewels said,

'Let's get downstairs and wake up properly. It's not good for our psyches, Amelia, to be lying about like this.' Amelia didn't answer. 'If we're going to get better and get out into the world again—' went on Jewels – 'No no!' cried Amelia, burying her head in her arms – '—then we're going to have to restore our energy. We mustn't fall depleted at every single setback.'

So there they lay, depleted, another while, just a little while, but then they did get up and struggled down a flight of stairs. When they got to Jewels' room, they went in and flopped down on her bed, just for another bit, just for another while.

'Do you want a leather jacket?' said Jewels, sometime, maybe an hour or so later. 'I stole a leather jacket today. Do you want it Amelia?' She waved her hand feebly, towards the corner, where it lay. It was brand new and it was lying on top of all the other brand new leather jackets Jewels had a habit of stealing. Kleptomanicking she called it, and she had been doing it ever since the time leather jackets first began. She stole them as a distraction whilst looking for Pearl, her lover. A bit like having a coffee break, or a pastime one might say.

'No thanks,' said Amelia, who always said no thanks on these occasions. She was starting to wake up a bit, the medication taking itself off. 'Listen Jewels,' she said. She sat up. 'I didn't get the room but you know, I don't want it. If I moved in here, I'd be back in hospital in no time.'

'Yes, I suppose you would,' said Jewels. She was still sleepy, her eyes closed, her head heavy and sunken into the soft pillow. Like a sculpture, thought Amelia, that's depressed and got the flu. She looked around the room. It was big and dark, crimson, with a tiny gloomy lamp in a lopsided squashed corner – another unpleasant déjà vu feeling hit Amelia when she saw that. She looked away from the lamp and cast her gaze towards the windows, but the windows in this room were all boarded up too. Amelia sighed. What had happened to Helena, she wondered, to make her so afraid in her life? How many times had she been attacked, and was her house really so under seige? Jewels too, Amelia looked at her friend again. Rich as fuck, she thought, could live absolutely anywhere. Yet why live anywhere, Jewels would tell her, when she could stay forever in her lost lover's old world? Amelia lay down once more.

'All this "we" business,' sighed Jewels, with her eyes still closed. 'It's really just her you know. She tries to rope everybody else in, but everybody else just gets exasperated, packs up and goes away. Except me. I stay. Because of Pearl. But I tune out. I close the door and can't hear her—'

'But Jewels,' said Amelia. 'The door's closed now and listen, she's plain as day.'

This was true. Helena had gone back down, to urgent, top secret business in the bunker. They could hear her shouting, issuing instructions, barking commands, giving directives.

'Is anybody with her?' asked Amelia. 'No,' said Jewels. 'She raves all on her own.'

Amelia woke again to find Jewels up and with her coat on. She was going out once more to look for her Pearl. First, she'd made them both tea. Amelia threw the blanket off, which her friend had placed over her. She herself wanted to get back before the next drug phase came on. The room was colder but the tea tasted lovely and Jewels gave her some biscuits to have with it. Amelia accepted them, the vestiges of anorexia no longer stopping her.

They went downstairs and the front door opened just as they got to it. It was DeeDee, the rebel, who on principle never rang three times. She flung the door to the side and strode, unbullied, into the hallway. Helena, her antennae out, rushed up from Mission Control downstairs. The steel door hung open and the light from a streetlamp fell in on top of them. Thank God for streetlamps, thought Amelia. Both she and Jewels stepped out onto the path.

Behind them, and in her edgy, just about to fly off the handle voice, Helena laid into DeeDee on the question of the Heterosexual Woman. Amelia was surprised, and on two counts too. One was that heterosexual women weren't allowed in this household and two, DeeDee was a heterosexual woman. That wasn't so much a surprise as an absolute astonishment, given DeeDee had been winning Miss Diesel Dyke in Brixton for the last six years. Well well, thought Amelia. Who would have thought it? Learn something always. Then Jewels leaned over and tried to put her right. Amelia, on the whole not fast as lightning in these sexuality matters, hadn't caught on that the Heterosexual Woman wasn't DeeDee but somebody else. The point was, some bad tenant had been heard bringing in the Heterosexual Woman, and had been comforting her and patting her and making her tea. This bad tenant had tried to calm the HW, while the HW had blurted and whined on about having had her heart broken by – of all things – nothing so mediocre as a big bloody man.

'And it was you!' screamed Helena, pointing her finger at DeeDee. 'Fuck off I'll do what I like!' shouted DeeDee, adding, 'Bees and sees and effs if I won't!'

'Not in this house!' shouted back the landlady. 'You know the rules. You broke them. You brought in a heterosex—' – 'Oh that's right, I forgot,' whispered Jewels. 'I told her you weren't heterosexual.' – 'That's all right,' whispered back Amelia. 'Maybe I'm not, although I sure hope I am. I've enough troubles to be gett—' – 'She's my sister!' cried DeeDee. 'Can't I bring in my own sister!' 'No!' shouted Helena. 'Not if she's a hetero you can't!'

'By the way,' Amelia lowered her whisper, 'have you told her yet about your Undescendeds?'

'No' whispered Jewels. 'I could be wrong but I don't think it's the right time for it. I'll delay it a bit longer and then pick a good day.'

So, all in all, Amelia thought it was a good sign she was leaving, a good sign Helena didn't want her, a good sign she was still homeless, a good sign she didn't want the sad room. Feeling lighter, she left, to spend another night in the 'cut your throat, gimme that sheet' hostel. Jewels walked with her as far as the lamppost.

'Goodbye Jewels,' she said. 'I hope we'll both be well soon.'

'Goodbye Amelia,' Jewels said. 'I hope we will be too.'

They hugged. Then Jewels stepped back and turned away and went in the opposite direction, off again to look for her long-lost pearl. Amelia walked towards the hostel, and all things considered, now she was out of that madness, she felt safe and sound at last. She'd tell her keyworker the place she'd gone to see today hadn't been suitable. Tomorrow, she decided, she'd go look for someplace else.

A Peace Process, 1994

They were watching something on the TV about a possible ceasefire when out of the blue, Amelia made an outrageous suggestion. It was so outrageous they all turned round to look at her.

'What do you mean?' they yapped. 'A day out? Why? What's wrong with staying here?' They frowned, their mouths fell open and they went on staring, hoping Amelia wasn't saying what it sounded very much like she was. Their old friend had gotten a bit strange these days.

Amelia set down her 'Ciao, Bonjour, Hello' teamug and pulled herself up in her armchair, Bossy and Mario's armchair that is, Bossy and Mario's teamug that is, too. Bossy and Mario were now married, which was astonishing, given there had never been any sign of this happening all the time they'd been babies and growing up together. Amelia was over visiting from London and was sitting with them, and with Fergal, Vincent and Sebastian in Bossy and Mario's living room. It was a neat little house, in the Bone, on the Oldpark, and it was teatime. The Oldpark Road itself was very popular, but only with joy-riders joyriding all over it, and with toddlers breaking things up on the sides of the road. Often, these things were the sides of the road themselves. Amelia, looking a lot better than she'd looked in a long time, in fact ever, recklessly continued to throw out ideas and suggestions without seeming to think once about the consequences.

'I mean just that,' she said, looking round, a big smile on her face which must have been an accident, nothing like it ever having happened on Amelia Lovett's face before. 'A day out,' she said. 'We can go sightseein', go to the beach, the hills, stroll about, not worry, take fresh air, buy sticks of rocks, have tea in teashops, those sorts of things, relaxing sorts of things, all sorts of things. Why don't we?'

Unbelievable. Inconceivable. And what exactly did she mean by 'not worry'? They backed off, for Amelia was different. And she'd been in hospital in England, they'd heard. Not just an ordinary hospital either. A mental sort of hospital. Like Vincent. They looked at Vincent. He was busy nibbling his nails and watching the ceasefire. They turned back to Amelia. They exchanged looks. Their famous frowns got deeper, their mouths got opener, their armrests got gripped tighter, not a single one of them was easy and relaxed. Naturally, they went on the defensive.

'Is this some sort of joke Amelia? Are you makin' fun? If this is a trick—'

'No joke,' said Amelia. 'It's called a daytrip. People do it all the time. And not just in England. People do it in Ireland, too.'

'What people?' they demanded, knowing full well she wouldn't be able to name a single one.

And she couldn't. Everybody she'd ever known, who lived here, had never once, just like herself when she'd lived here, thought to take themselves off for the day. And why would they? Wasn't it bad enough trying to exist in your own house, trying to do a weekend in your very own surroundings, without going off and looking for trouble someplace else? Amelia should have known better, their looks said. Amelia should have stuck to her roots. Amelia shouldn't have gone to live in England, ending up in hospital, anyway.

'Besides,' said Bossy, her body giving a big, demonstrative shiver. 'It'll be freezin'. We'll catch the flu, then pneumonia, then tuberculosis, and then we'll die.'

'It's August,' said Amelia. 'It's roastin' hot.'

'How would we get there?' asked Mario.

'Train,' said Amelia.

'It's bin blown up,' said Fergal. 'Or maybe it hasn't. But it will be. Or the track. One or the other. So there's no point. We can't go. We have to stay here.'

'We could hire a car,' said Vincent and this was unexpected. 'Amelia could drive,' he said. This was unexpected too. The others looked at him, pondering, their eyebrows now rising. In spite of themselves – absolutely in spite of themselves – they were starting to consider what it might feel like, tentatively, to say yes. Perhaps Amelia could drive, their eyebrows now said. Perhaps they could sit and be driven. They could go to this place, wherever it was, have this thing, this daytrip, then come back and be themselves again at the end. It wasn't as if they'd lose anything. It wasn't as if their lives would be transformed by one, single, extraneous outing. It wasn't as if their long-established, insular identities which they relied upon so heavily, could be ravaged and taken away from them just like that. So yes, they decided, a daytrip was within reason, just so long as they could come back and be miserable later on.

'We could give it a go,' went on Vincent. 'If it doesn't work, we don't have to do it again. I think we might like a daytrip. How about tomorrow? I'll bring my wife.'

Ignoring the wife bit, because, of course, Vincent was raving, Amelia immediately tried to downplay this hiring of the car. For yes, in the way that life and people are – which is contrary or miraculous depending on how you look at it – she was now the one starting to say the whole thing was a bad idea. This was because she didn't want to do the driving. For her, driving hadn't happened in a very long time. It was true, she was the only one with the valid licence. The others had either never had one (Bossy, Vincent and Mario), or had had one that was only imaginary (Vincent), or had had one that was real but which was lost through drunkenness and then later on, was lost again through the flare-up of an old kneecapping wound (Fergal). Sebastian, funnily enough, did have a licence, which he kept hidden, top secret, and in a safety deposit box. This was so that the Provisionals wouldn't find out he had one and come round and commandeer his vehicle. He didn't have a vehicle but he was thinking of what might happen if he ever got round to getting himself one. Seb lived in 'what could have happened', 'what should have happened', and 'what might happen' land, and hardly ever appeared in his present at all. Amelia's licence, as everybody knew, was spotless, saintly, upstanding and moral and this was because she'd hardly driven a car since passing her driving test thirteen years before. The idea now of driving, had gone into the 'impossible things' section of her brain. Also in 'impossible things' were 'hanging up curtains', 'organising a pleasant livelihood', 'mortgages', 'pensions', and 'not always being afraid'.

Bringing herself back from the impossibles, Amelia saw the others nodding and looking more animated, jabbering on now about the daytrip and how it sounded a sparky idea. She tried to dissuade them. First, she said there weren't any places to go to, and then she said that there were so many places to go to, that choosing one would be impossible, so why didn't they all just stay here? They ignored her. She didn't get a chance either to protest any further for they took a vote and she lost five to one and was left wondering if she'd crash the car on the way out, on the way back, or if she'd be allowed to do five miles per hour on the motorway at all.

Next day was bright and sunny, which was just the way picture books from primary school always said Days Out were supposed to be. More than that, the weather forecast, which none of them thought to listen to – degrees centigrade and degrees Fahrenheit and that other thing, Celsius, being alien and incomprehensible to their natures – nevertheless promised more brightness and sunniness later on. At least in most places. There were five of them to start with, for Vincent hadn't arrived yet, and this went up to six, then back down to five and then up to seven before the car had even left the side of the road. First, Amelia and Fergal went off to get it.

Amelia would have described it as a red car, not too small, not too big, with normal sorts of wheels and normal sorts of windows. It had four doors, a boot, an engine, a roof, seats and a steering wheel. That was why she took Fergal. Fergal dealt with her request for help first by feeling superior, second by insisting he'd only help if he was allowed the roomy passenger seat all the way there and all the way back and third, by criticising every single thing his friend Amelia did. Amelia let him do this because she now knew that what another human being did was totally out of her control, and because she could only cope with one important thing at a time. At that point, it had to be the driving.

When they arrived back with the car, the others jumped in immediately. Then they jumped out for that first jump had only been a practice one. They jumped in again, and then out again and then in again and shouted, 'Come on, youse two, let's get this thing over with.' But before Fergal and Amelia, who had gotten out of the car, could get in again, Bossy, Mario and Sebastian had jumped out for the third time. While doing all the jumping, they continually pushed and shoved each other, settling one way, settling another, then rejumping to do it again. Sebastian was fat, but also soft, so he became a cushion, which was seen as justified by the other two, given he was taking up so much room in the back. He was in the middle, with Bossy and Mario squeezed in on either side of him, and then there was a further squeeze when one of Joe McLean's girlfriends happened to chance along. She was the blonde one, the slim one, the one who lived down the New Lodge, and she came dandering round the corner swinging her furry handbag. She asked what was going on and when told that it was technically called a daytrip, she said it was an idea mindblowing in its total originality and would it be all right if she came along too? The others said yes, even though there wasn't any room for her and this was because, although nobody actually knew this person, it was commonly held that Joe McLean's girlfriends were warm, inclusive, friendly sorts of people to whom it would be very hard-hearted ever to say no. So she squeezed in beside the other three, meaning she was on top of them and it was then Sebastian changed his mind and decided to squeeze back out.

Now this had nothing to do with the arrival of one of the girlfriends, for everybody was always in favourable agreement about them. No, this was entirely to do with Sebastian, although it could be argued by nit-picking mental health workers that 'entirely' was not at all the right word. In spite of everyone's courage in deciding on the daytrip, there was still a strong unacknowledged panic floating about in the air. It was Sebastian who expressed this panic the most succinctly, the 'presenting problem' he might even be called. Whatever the technical term for such a piece of shared psychology acted out by this one member of the team, the facts of his behaviour were evident and undeniable, for Seb trampled and scrambled and got hysterical over the back seat's ankles, crying, 'No! I can't take it! Let me back out!'

What he couldn't take was the fear of the unknown and the letting go of an identity that had gone on far too long. To expect poor Sebastian, the most nervy of the lot of them, to contemplate a daytrip, and then follow up his contemplation by actually setting out and going on it, was a damn cheek and inconsideration on somebody else's part. That somebody else, the others decided, was Amelia Boyd Lovett, who'd come over from England with her mad, pat, silly ideas.

'Now look what you've done!' cried Bossy. 'You've upset poor Sebastian. I don't know if this is a good idea at all.'

'Is this a good idea?' asked Mario, looking round, appealing to the others. 'I don't know if it's a good idea either. Maybe we should stop now, get out, go back in, close the big door, turn on the TV and in another six or seven hours, we can watch *Barrymore*.'

'But we haven't gone anywhere!' cried Fergal. 'How can we stop when we haven't got started? Come on Sebbie, pull yourself together. Stop that blubberin' and squeeze yourself back in.'

'Can't!' gasped Sebastian. 'It'll kill me! It'll kill me!' and Amelia jumped out to pat him on the back. Not being terribly tactile, she didn't know what else in the way of comfort she could offer, and Seb just went on fretting and sweating and swooning over the bonnet, his wee eyes watering up at the demands being put on his life.

'It's all right Seb,' said Amelia – pat pat on the big shoulder now. 'It's only a wee drive' – pat pat. 'We'll have a nice time and come back and it'll be over, you'll see' – pat pat. 'Just give it a try' – pat. 'Just once' – pat. 'You might even like it' – pat pat. Joe McLean's girlfriend clucked sympathetically and got out of the car to offer some comfort too. She went round the other side of Sebastian and 'There there,' she hushed, leaning over the bonnet. 'Coo coo,' she smiled. Bossy got out to do some cooing too. She took over the cooing while the girlfriend went on to purring and she purr-purred while Amelia pat-patted and Bossy coo-cooed until Sebastian, hardly believing all this was happening to him, pushed through the lot of them and managed to break free. He ran, he bolted, he booted down and round the corner, disappearing into Ardilea Street and busting through his front door. The inner door was heard to be slammed, the springs of his settee were heard to be sprung, before any of the others could blink, do anything, or suggest taking another vote.

'Hurry up!' shouted Fergal, banging on the car roof. 'We can't wait for Sebbie. It's too late for Sebbie. Sebbie's made his choice. We can do nothing for poor auld Sebbie now.' He shouted further that they had themselves to think about, that they had to carry on, for they needed time for this thing called a daytrip. Days Out, he dimly remembered from those picture books, always started in the region of somewhere like nine o'clock. It was already coming up to eleven, so everyone jumped in, closed the doors and got ready to set off again. It didn't look like Vincent was coming either, so Amelia turned over the engine and took the handbrake off. Biting her lower lip, she began to ease the car out gently, saying a prayer that fate, or to be truthful, she herself, wouldn't knock over anybody while out driving that day. 'Or any day,' she added, covering all eventualities, just in case God was feeling contrary, and was refusing to take unspoken requests as read. She was finishing with 'Thanks a lot God, you won't regret it', when the others cried, 'Halt! Stop talking to yourself Amelia! Here comes Vincent, and look – he's brought his wife along!' Amelia slammed on the brake in amazement.

It wasn't just that Vincent was married, and to a real person, not a figment, some mysterious killer assassin from his own imagination, let's say. It wasn't even that she was Japanese. For she was. What really told Amelia things were certainly changing round here, was that here was a flesh and blood woman, an Oriental, an unusual, a non-Bonian, non-Ardoynian, dandering about the area, without people coming out their doors and demanding what religion she was of. She was tiny, delicate, holding onto Vincent, and staring adoringly up into her husband's grey eyes. Nobody explained to Amelia who this person was or where it was she'd come from, or how long she'd been married to Vincent and Amelia wondered if any of them really knew themselves. She went on staring and, it must be said, rudely, until Vincent and his wife reached the car door. When they did, they opened it and clambered in on top of the others and of course there weren't any introductions for introductions were things that only happened on the TV.

Turning back to the steering wheel, Amelia started off for the second time, the amazement she was feeling about Vincent and his wife pushing all fear of driving initially from her mind. She drove easily out of the Bone therefore, and didn't knock over a single hedge or a bent-over old person or some intense, engrossed child playing with his or her hammer on the side of the road.

So there they were, on their way, driving along, with their plan, if it could be called a plan, which was to go somewhere a bit different and do something a bit nice. They had made no preparation, had no information, no destination, no clue whatsoever as to what was supposed to be going on. Although they'd all given up alcohol, because, excepting Vincent's wife who had never been one, they were all reformed alcoholics, it didn't occur to any of them, now they weren't bringing liquor, to bring anything else along. There were no sandwiches therefore, no fruit, no sweeties, no fingerfood, no biscuits, no lemonade, no cake, and worst of all, no tea. There were no maps, no compasses, no extra clothes, no flashlights, no tour guides, no road directions, no storybooks for a light read. They brought nothing except themselves, full of fear and trepidation, feelings which only grew stronger the more they left the Bone behind. Only Amelia, who was more used to being out of the area, didn't mind the leaving. What she minded though, was the actual driving out.

She didn't know motorways for example, or rather, in theory she did know them, but not how to get on them and not how to get off. Maps were another language, signposts a conspiracy. All official-looking things made her nervous and afraid. She told the others she was sticking to A roads and if that got difficult, she'd go onto B roads and if that got difficult, she'd work her way through the alphabet and after that, they'd have to walk. She confused the Highway Code with the Green Cross Code, her Twelve Times Tables and the Ten Commandments and she didn't hope for encouragement from any of the others which was just as well, for given the state of the others, encouragement was the last thing she certainly would have got.

Fergal in particular was very good at blaming, indeed he was an excellent blamer, and he started off doing this as soon as the car left the side of the road. He disguised his criticisms, especially from himself, as 'being helpful', 'being rational', 'making constructive observations on Amelia's reality', 'offering fair and objective comment', without coming to the realisation he hadn't once been asked.

'Where d'you get your licence?' he said after harping on at her for twenty minutes about going slow for twenty minutes. 'Admit it Amelia. Isn't this terror of yours on account of you now being mad?'

Without waiting for an answer, without wanting an answer, for Fergal was God in the sky and had all the answers already, he launched into a list of faults and failings – though not of his own of course. He did a moral inventory on Amelia and the crunch of it seemed to be that she was a timid driver because she'd had a nervous breakdown and that she'd had a nervous breakdown because she wasn't him. 'Look at me,' he said. 'I'm fine, I'm cured, I got off alcohol and I didn't have a nervous breakdown. I'm completely all sorted. There's nothing wrong with me.'

The sooner he has his breakdown, thought Amelia, the better. She didn't say this though, for she knew Fergal wouldn't have got it. Instead she said he was an irritating, frustrating, mustard sort of guy. Since he'd gotten off drink for example, she said, he'd gotten flabby and slabby, which he hadn't, he was deeply physically unattractive, which he wasn't, he had a closed mind, which he had, and a big mouth, which he had, and that she was in charge of the car and could throw him out of it if she felt like it. This was debatable or, in other words, not true. Fergal laughed and said those words of hers were exact examples of her madness and he continued to take her inventory, now and again throwing critical, 'fair and objective' comments back at the others too.

In the back, after low-grade mumbling and high-grade pushing and telling the back of Fergal's head where it could go and jerk off – the others, finally, after a whole half-hour, had just about had enough. 'Is it over?' they said. 'Are we there yet?' they said. 'Can we go now?', 'What's gonna happen to us if we can't ever get back?'

They looked around, not happy, at the fields and the fields and the lanes and the lanes which the car, as if in an anxiety attack, just kept on driving by, and at those aggressive yellow things, gorse bushes, which kept popping up everywhere. All of them – the daytrippers that is, not the gorse bushes, although maybe the gorse bushes also – were sulky, refusing to calm down, or make the slightest effort even to try and enjoy themselves. The car speeded by summer greens, dark greens, emerald greens and other greens and the daytrippers looked at these shades and couldn't help it – they simply were not impressed. So what? they thought. The countryside wasn't interesting. It was bleak, hostile and full of paranoid, anti-social things, and they kept on complaining about it because they couldn't stop.

They felt claustrophobic, agoraphobic, xenophobic and just plain phobic. 'Stop!' they'd shout. 'No, it's okay. Go on for another bit. That's enough! Turn round. Isn't it time we called a halt?'

At first Amelia stopped and started every time they told her to but eventually she didn't because the engine was getting wrecked. She was frowny, her shoulders were up, and she sat far, far forward in the driving seat. She clutched the wheel, her hands raw nerves, her mind fielding off every one of their attacks. In the midst of all this bickering, she was getting a headache from having to check mirrors, check dashboard, check windows, re-check mirrors and was nervous when cars appeared behind her, nervous when they appeared in front of her and nervous when they appeared anywhere at all. She decided to turn off onto a B road in order to get away from them. She did this and a bunch of cars did exactly the same thing too. So she turned onto a B minus road and then a track and then a dribble, which became a toy path and then a squiggle, eventually dying away on the edge of a cliff. They had come to the end of the country. There was nowhere further to go on it. Amelia decided this was a good time to put the brake on.

They looked around, uneasy. There was nothing – no cars, no people, just them, nothing further, except those gorse bushes which seemed to be following them everywhere.

'Is this it now?' cried the back of the car. 'Have we arrived? Are we enjoying ourselves?'

'No,' said Amelia. 'We're lost. We haven't got there yet.'

They continued to look about them. Everything was big and empty. Most of all, it was lonely. Joe McLean's girlfriend tried to cheer them up. 'Perhaps this is somewhere nice,' she said. 'Perhaps it's the Giant's Causeway – that famous place with the funny stone arrangements I once heard of as a child.' But there weren't any funny stones, only the edge of the cliff and snarling yellow gorse bushes. Nothing else was near them, for miles and miles around. Mario said, 'That was a good guess and you're a very nice person, but I'm afraid Amelia's got us lost. We're in the Glens of Antrim in the Mountains of Mourne for sure.' Fergal said Mario was a spacer for the Glens of Antrim weren't in the Mountains of Mourne. 'Nor vice versa,' he said. 'We're in the Irish Republic. The car was going down that way.'

'No it wasn't,' said Bossy. 'It was going up, towards Scotland.'

'Your arse it was,' said Fergal. The girlfriend covered her ears. 'Oh now, let's not fight,' she said. Amelia said nothing. She pulled down the handmirror for she wanted to check a tension spot. She'd felt a tiny bump growing there, just under the skin earlier on. Because of the stress, she thought, and she looked in the mirror but when she saw her reflection, she got a big shock. There wasn't one spot. There were three spots, and three spots equalled a clusterbatch. She was stunned at getting a clusterbatch. And so quickly! Who would have thought being ordinary could cost a person so much?

They stopped bickering eventually, but only temporarily, because they had to get out of the car to stretch their legs and walk about. They took some breaths also, which even they noticed seemed to have a good effect upon them. So, breathing deep, they decided not to panic but to think things out over a nice cup of tea. They went to the car to get this tea and it was then they experienced the horror of not having packed any. They reeled and spun and tottered to the edge of the cliff. Amelia stopped tottering when she got there for she recognised this cliff immediately. 'Imagine that!' she cried. 'I dreamt of this cliff when I was—' She stopped herself again. She didn't say anything more, like 'when I was in hospital' or that she'd met dead Roberta McKeown on the top of it, or that she'd thrown herself over it, once or twice, to make it all stop.

The others weren't listening. They had dashed back to the car after finishing their own tottering. They had to find a café immediately and get themselves some tea. They were so eager to do this, they didn't fight over who was sitting where this time, and Amelia got in too and backed away from the cliff. Soon they were out once more, on a proper road, and it led to Ballycastle. They'd all heard of Ballycastle, with its seaside, teashops, the famous Lammas Fair and the sweet toffee called 'Yellow Man'. 'Teashops,' they kept muttering, although Vincent's wife, who was called Kayo, said, 'Hair Head and White Head. They are big stones that are also near that town.'

'Big stones,' she explained further, though the others were thinking of teabags, 'named for two plincess who long ago were blutally murdered and slown over cliffs into sea.' 'Hmmm,' said the others, hearing something about murder and mayhem. 'That's very interesting. When we've had our tea, why don't we have our daytrip there?'

So they drove into Ballycastle, parked, and although there were many cafés, they saw the sea and, hypnotised, ran towards it instead. Vincent shouted, 'Look, a boat! It's leaving! Come on! Let's jump on it!' And they did, without thinking to check its destination or whether they were allowed to or not. It turned out they were though, for it was the small passenger boat, on its way over to Rathlin Island, and the two boatmen, apart from muttering, '. . . not dressed right', '. . . should have brought coats' and 'There might be a storm later' – meaning 'The boat might not be going back' – didn't say anything else during the whole journey across.

'La-sa-lin Island,' mused Kayo, settling with the others along the front edge of the boat. She looked over the water. 'I've heard of that place.' The others looked at her. How come she knew so much about Ireland? 'I'm nurse,' she said, as if that explained the fact. 'Is La-sa-lin not place, my dear husband,' she turned to Vincent, 'of many, many murders?' Vincent said probably but the others had turned away. They didn't listen to what she was saying for their enthusiasm had returned and they didn't want it to go away again. They were back on track for this innovation called a daytrip.

It was a small vessel and there were only themselves and the two boatmen going over on it. The boatmen kept exchanging glances and the Belfastians noticed this undercurrent and felt uneasy and annoyed. They didn't want to start doubting. They didn't want to feel suspicious. They didn't want any secret exchanges which none of them could understand.

So, in spite of their hopes and the temporary lift of their spirits, they found it hard to let go of the familiar dread and their depressions came back and enveloped them once more. As soon as this happened, they remembered they'd wanted tea and that they'd forgotten to get some while they were in Bally-castle and they started worrying about what would happen if they still couldn't get any when they got to the other side. They looked to the other side, to Rathlin, to the land which was getting closer. There were cliffs and more cliffs. They seemed to go the whole way round. Amelia recognised them again, for again, they were the same cliffs she'd met dead Roberta McKeown on. She hoped this wasn't a bad omen, some legacy following them everywhere. She didn't say this to the others, for she didn't want to make them uneasy, but the others were already uneasy. They needed no prompting from her. Although the sky was blue and the sun was piercing, it was chilly on the water and all of them were shivering by the time they got to the other side.

They got off the boat and they looked back and saw the water even choppier. It would be very nasty, they thought, ever to have to swim in that. None of the daytrippers could swim. Learning might have meant drowning. So they had decided, years ago, to stick to things like getting drunk instead. The bright sky had gone also and grey clouds were now swirling. The seven were unsettled although the boatmen didn't seem to care. They paid their money to these men and forgot to check what time the boat went back, if it went back, or what they could do on a raw place such as this. They hurried away in one direction, which to them was as good as another, trying, at random, to find shelter from the rain.

They were on a street, a sort of street, and they ran quickly along it, holding their hands up as if to keep themselves dry. They ignored the green hedges and the fields and the trees and all the other things of nature, for these were the exact objects they could never understand. It became clear to them quickly, that there was no café, no shop, no restaurant, no pinball machine, not even an awning to stand under from the rain. They spied an elderly passerby and went over to speak to her. 'Where can we go?' they wanted to ask. The woman shuddered before they could say anything and she glared as if they'd insulted her. She pulled away and, after watching in confusion, they stopped someone else.

'Excuse me,' said Vincent. The man was big and burly and covered in equipment, nets and pokes and bags of stuff.

'We're hungry,' said Vincent. 'But understand please, we don't want any alcohol. We don't drink alcohol, not any of us, anymore.' The others rolled their eyes. 'Is there somewhere we can get tea?' asked Fergal before Vincent could launch into the conditions of their births and how all their first days at school had been. There was a pause, a big pause, while the man looked them up and down. The daytrippers looked back. They grew more uncomfortable. They didn't like the way he was looking. What had they done wrong now?

'So!' said the man, and they knew from the one syllable that they'd made a mistake in stopping him. 'So!' said the man again. 'Do *youse* think *youse're* tough coming over to our land?'

They were startled but could say nothing. The waves looked high behind him. He looked scarier than the waves. About fifty, he was, with big red bursting-out cheeks, a giant solid belly and a smile that was nasty, an unpleasant arrangement, stuck on his face.

He laughed, and it seemed at nothing, or at something invisible that he thought was funny, and then he stopped and frowned. The others moved away.

'Where are *youse* goin'?' he boomed, in his imitated Belfast accent. He didn't like this moving away. He moved forward to get close again. He stood in front of them. Then, without giving any warning and in spite of his giant size and bulkiness, he leaned over and nimbly slipped something into the breast pocket of Vincent's wife's pinafore dress. She squealed and tipped it out again, and leapt closer to the others. They surrounded her. The man doubled up, pointing, stamping his feet on the ground.

It had been a bit of rubbish, a sodden, torn, damp, scrunched-up piece of rubbish, like a paper, or a hankie, something incomprehensible like that. Some joke, thought the others and although all the time on this daytrip, they'd been expecting bad things to happen to them, it still shocked and upset them, now that a bad thing actually had.

'Auld nut,' said Fergal. 'Come on everybody. That man mustn't get out much. That man must get out even less than any of us.'

They backed away from him and the man took this as a victory. They knew he would take it as a victory. They didn't completely care. They did a bit though. Tit-for-tat actions had always been their upbringing. Two lives for one life, that was the rule of their land. They walked away and left him, maybe because they were scared, maybe because they didn't want to enter his mad world. So there he was, in his triumph, dancing up and down on the ground.

'Bit disturbed like, wasn't he?' observed Vincent. He had put his arm around Kayo. 'I know, let's go and see what's at the top of this road.'

They went to see, looking back now and then, to make sure the madman wasn't following them. He wasn't. He was still pointing at the rubbish, and then pointing up at them.

'What have you done to upset poor Ambrose?'

They had bumped into another person. She had appeared out of nowhere. There was nothing but hills and cliffs as far as the others could see behind her. She was about sixty and was wearing a scarf that was tied tight about her neck and throat. The daytrippers didn't answer. They were jumpy and they hadn't, at least from their perspective, done anything to upset 'poor' Ambrose. But from his perspective, or from this woman's perspective, who were they to know?

'Miss Cissadaye Farrell,' said the woman and the others thought, for some reason, she was giving her name to them. She wasn't. She was offering assistance. 'House Number Three,' she said. 'Further down the road.'

They looked at her, wary, but she gave no other explanation. She pointed back down behind them, to a row of houses, beyond the spot they'd just come from. Ambrose was gone and when they turned back, so had this woman also.

'What was that about?' asked Fergal. 'Where did she disappear to? And where did she come from?'

'I want to go home,' said Joe McLean's girlfriend, taking her foot out of a lump of dogshite, or sheepshite or deershite or horseshite or cowshite or prehistoric monstershite – in this place, it was hard to know. 'I'll see when the boat's leaving,' she said and off she went, leaving the rest huddling, unsure what to do next.

'Are we goin' to this Cissadaye woman or not?' asked Bossy.

'Do youse think it'll be worse if we stay here or go there?'

'I think we should go,' said Vincent. 'We're cold and hungry and need some cheering up.'

They hesitated then agreed, for the rain was getting heavier. They tossed coins as to who would do the talking when they reached the Cissadaye door.

By the time they did reach it, they were drenched and the breeze, which had stopped being a breeze to become a cold wind, was a cold wind no longer. It was a gale and it was pulling their thin clothes and they felt despair when they looked and saw no 'Meals', 'Snacks' or 'Dinner' sign upon the lawn. There was a fire lit though. They could see it from the chimney. This gave them the hope they needed to go on.

They stepped over the gate, which was footery and low and so was probably meant to have been stepped over, and after doing this, they went up the doll's path to the closed black front door. They knocked the brass knocker. They waited. They knocked the knocker again. A woman came and opened it. They hoped like mad she wasn't Cissadaye Farrell for she poked a pointy face out that looked anything but kind. Amelia showed her spotty one back and the woman, startled, retreated and looked affronted. But after a moment her white bony face came round the doorframe once more.

'I heard what you done to Ambrose Gray,' she said. They stared. This was incredible and Amelia, the designated speaker, was speechless. None of the others could say anything either. Cissadaye went on,

'Don't think you can get away with that here. We know your sort from Belfast.'

'Don't do food!' she then snapped, before Amelia, who had thought of some words, could manage to get them out of her. 'I make snacks and meals,' she contradicted herself. 'But I'm not making any for you. What would you be wanting exactly?'

'Tea, sandwiches,' they said. They shrugged. They were

confused by this woman, confused, dismayed, angry, about everything. The sun was coming out. What the hell was going on? Cissadaye's jaw fell.

'Oh no no no no no. I'm not opening up for sandwiches. Sandwiches! What sort of person do you take me for?'

They didn't say, although they were sorely tempted, for they were trying not to use obscene expressions anymore. Cissadaye shook her head. She pointed at Kayo. 'What's she? Who are you? What sort of sandwiches? What reason is it really, you've come to our island for?'

'Cheese,' suggested Amelia, answering one of the questions, thrown by all the others. The woman was outraged and went in and slammed her door. They stared at it, unable to fathom anything, unable to think either, of another course of action. Their mutual depression got deeper and, 'Come on,' said Fergal, for the blizzard, which had been raging just after the hurricane but before the sun had come out, had come back, and was driving the last bit of the feeble sun away. It drove them down the path also, where they stepped over the tiny gate and Best to get away, they said, before Cissadaye reached for her rifle and decided to take potshots at them all.

'What're we gonna do now?' said Mario. 'I thought that was our salvation. If things don't get better, I'm gonna be wanting some alcohol.'

'Us too,' said the others. 'We should never have gone on this daytrip.'

'Seb was very wise,' said Vincent.

'No he wasn't!' snapped Amelia.

'Yes he was!' snapped the rest of them at her. They thought of wise old Seb for a moment, safe at home, or maybe not safe, but at least at home, with everything predictable. They thought they'd light little devotion candles to him – if they ever got back again, that was.

They said nothing more for a bit and went further down the

road and then stopped again in another huddle. Glumly, they watched some activity going on in front. A bird with a yellow beak had flown down from a bush and secured a fat worm to feast on. A cat, keeping the bird under surveillance, positioned itself under another bush to pounce. While it was getting ready, on its back, a millepede was crawling. So intent was the cat on watching the bird, it didn't notice at first what this millepede was up to. Eventually it did and, looking annoyed, took a swipe at the tiny creature, then pounced at the bird and, at the same time as the millepede fell into a ditch, the worm was abandoned, the cat fell onto nothing, the bird made a getaway and everything ended up just as before.

'I can't believe we're huddled here, watching this,' said Fergal. 'Imagine having to be engrossed in a cat, a bird and a worm!' They began again to blame Amelia and they couldn't see the funny side. Maybe there was no funny side, being stuck on a cold island with nothing familiar about them at all.

Before Amelia could answer, or try to answer, for really, she had no answer to give them, the girlfriend, called Audrey, came rushing back happy from the boat.

'Good news, good news!' she cried and Kayo saw her coming.

'The boat is going to be leabing?' she asked.

'Yes!' Audrey reached them. 'But not for another two hours.'

They all looked at their watches and were tempted to push them on a bit. But there was no point in doing that, so they didn't. Audrey again began to speak. She said there was further good news, without any bad news added onto it, and that was that she'd spied a corner shop down the road.

They went in, cautiously, and saw a bunch of elderly women. These women were huddled in the corner, standing still, looking back at them. Cissadaye was to the fore and she hadn't aged a second, so great was her need to get to the shop first. Clutching her shopping bag with cold white bony fingers which matched the cold white bony face, she had already primed the others as to the sort of mainland people they were now dealing with. They had tortured poor Ambrose, she whispered. They had wanted cheese sandwiches. They had ganged up in a huddle and, for the fun of it, had kicked her gate in. The daytrippers sidled round this muttering, for it was a shop, and they'd come in to buy things. The women, still watching these trouble-makers, sidled round also. After all, their looks said, it was their island's shop.

Eventually something had to give and it was the daytrippers who shifted their stares in order to see what was available. The first thing they noticed was that the woman behind the counter was smiling over at them. This was unexpected, and naturally, they were suspicious. Should they smile back? Was it some sort of trap?

'Many things of nature to see on Rathlin,' said the shop-keeper. She was wrapping up their juice and their bread and their biscuits and talking over the drone of Cissadaye. 'Are you birdwatchers or walkers – oh! You're neither.' She smiled, taking in the unbirdwatcher, unwalker, bedraggled state of them all.

They left, thanking this woman, but still aware of the others' silent stares going after them. They were relieved when they got outside and could close the shop door. The rain had ceased, again as abruptly as it had started and, as they wanted a sit-down, they went up the hill to see what there was. They passed a church and a chapel and headed on out, past both, westwards, then they cut off this switchback road and went over to one of the cliffs. They sat down, divided their food out and tried to eat it. But this was impossible. In order to relax, they needed to fight first.

'Stop sucking your teeth,' said Bossy to Fergal, who was eating a custard cream sandwich. 'Stop biting your nails,' said Fergal to Amelia and also to Audrey, the girlfriend, who was just about to start biting hers. 'Get your feet off my husband,' said Kayo, even though nobody had their feet on Vincent. He had fallen asleep and Kayo had gotten cross, in advance, just in case. Amelia said to Mario, 'Stop saying "What?" Mario, every time somebody opens their mouth to speak to you.' – 'What?' said Mario. 'Bust those spots Amelia,' said Fergal. 'They've gone on far too long.' – 'You do something about your highly critical attitude then,' said Amelia. 'Yeah, do that,' said the girlfriend who, miserable on this daytrip, had decided on no more Miss Nice Girl. 'Well, you stop clicking the catch on that furry handbag,' said Fergal. 'It's very irritating and it shows you're nothing but a nervous wreck.' – 'Oh,' said Bossy. 'She's a nervous wreck? And I suppose you think you're not one?'

The bickering went on, nobody could stop. They split into factions and after they did this, one faction, consisting of Amelia, Bossy and Audrey, got up and walked a little distance and sat down with their food on another edge of the same cliff.

Both groups ate their dry bread, their custard creams and drank their bottles of orangeade in silence, pointedly ignoring the other group, which would damn well serve it right. The cliff they were sitting on was called the Cliff of the Screaming, but none of the daytrippers knew this. What they also didn't know, was that on this cliff, as on every cliff on Rathlin, at sometime or other in its history, people had been butchered and murdered and then thrown over it. This, they didn't know, but what they did know was that there was something familiar about sitting, nervy, on the edge of such a borderline. They had felt the cliff's pull and had gravitated naturally towards it. It afforded a relief and a release that made perfect emotional sense to them. Ah, that's better, they thought, sitting down. At last. Something feels safe. Something feels like home.

So there they were, eating their food and calming down because they were perched 400ft up on an edge in a strong wind with their legs dangling over, having a break from this difficult thing called a daytrip. They were breathing big breaths and starting to feel better, when, hearing a commotion behind them, they looked over to the road and saw Ambrose Gray coming up.

He was striding, swinging his arms, fists at the end of them, his bags and nets no longer holding him back. Both factions stood up quickly and moved together from each side of the screaming cliff.

'Mine!' cried Ambrose. He was very, very furious. 'My cliff! My cliff! Go away. Go back to Ireland. Nobody invited you here. Go and find your own!'

'I bet this isn't really a tourist island, is it?' said Fergal and 'No,' said Kayo. 'I should have said. It is not leally tourist island at all.'

Just under their skins, they had been expecting, indeed, they had been waiting, for Ambrose Gray to show up again. They knew he would – for how could he have not? And now, here he was, raging, standing there, in his very own big person. The thing was, they weren't sure whether they had to fight with him or not.

They could walk away again, they supposed. But then, what if he again came after? They could throw him over the cliff, they supposed. But call them failures; in spite of their upbringing, they weren't really the sort of people for throwing other people over cliffs. They could have the thought of doing so, they supposed. Hatred and revenge thoughts were also within their upbringing. But hold on – the next thought occurred. What if Ambrose, himself, tried to throw *them* over the cliff? They moved away from the cliff. That seemed far and away the best thing to do in the circumstances. They hoped Ambrose would be satisfied and call it a day. Ambrose wasn't satisfied. He came after once more.

'See!' said Bossy. 'It's just not enough that we can recognise he's mad and try our best to get away from him. People like him, they always come after. Safety doesn't exist. What are we gonna do now?'

'It's an attitude of mind,' said Amelia. 'I must admit, I don't exactly have it. But I'm sure it's an attitude of mind and maybe it can be got from somewhere, somehow, further down the line.'

'But what are we gonna do now, Amelia?' said Mario. 'Can't you be a bit more helpful.' All the while they were talking, they were moving further inland. They kept looking behind them and there was Ambrose, somehow aggrieved, somehow infringed upon, somehow vengeful, and relentlessly coming after. Eventually though, he stopped, for something dawned on him at last.

'I won! I won!' he shouted, dancing up and down for the second time since they'd met him, and 'Oh! We lost! We lost!' they cried, then, 'Hold on – he's mad, he's mad. C'mon. Let's get down to the boat.'

So they got down to the boat and they embarked and they left sad, often-massacred little Rathlin. But what if they hadn't? This was the question all of them now asked. What if they'd hadn't been able to leave? Or what if they hadn't wanted to leave? What if Rathlin Island had also been their homeland? How could they have lived there and yet constantly not be on the defensive, with people like Ambrose Gray always turning up? It was a difficult, scary question and as yet, none of the daytrippers had an answer to it. But it was brave of them to ask it, and they sat close together, and didn't bicker, not once, all the way back to the land.